EDEN'S REVENGE

An Eden Paradox Novel

Barry Kirwan

EDEN'S REVENGE

for my sister Janice

Contents

PROLOGUE

1563 AD, the Himalayan Kingdom

No birds ever approached the Fortress of Alessia. This was the first thing Esma noticed when she arrived after her long trek into the barren Tibetan foothills. The second was the architectural precision of the gothic castle, its steep black ramparts, towers and twisting spires rising skywards, as if uprooted from the earth by the stars themselves. Its cruel beauty went beyond anything she'd ever seen. Although it was over four hundred years old, Alessia's Fortress looked as if it had been built yesterday.

Archers' slits in its three tall towers stared out over the surrounding land, unblinking eyes daring anyone below to step onto the path to its iron gates. The guide had left a mile earlier, unwilling to proceed further, and in the end had begged her to return with him to the safety of his village. But Esma turned her back on him, as she did on the rest of humanity, and continued alone.

A savage wind scoured her sheepskin coat, leather face-mask and gloves as she walked with a measured gait under anvil-shaped clouds threatening winter's first snowfall. Atop the towers, red and gold pennants displaying bloodied eagle's claws whipped and crackled, the emblazoned talons seeming to grasp at the air. Prayer wheels, adapted from naïve Buddhist ideology to worship another entity, one altogether more sublime and not of this world, whistled like banshees across the bleak countryside.

Esma had left her family for good this time, after one beating too many, and had not told her bitter mother or sickly brother where she was going. They would not understand, and she no longer cared. For two years Esma had secretly followed the Order of Alessia as an acolyte-in- waiting, after being noticed by a wandering monk visiting her home city, Padua. He made a speech in the central plaza, addressing anyone who would listen, and asked what they all saw when they raised their eyes to the night sky. Most in the lingering crowd talked of God and his marvels. Esma waited till the throng dispersed and approached him on her own; she had often looked up, craving an alternative to the misery she and others endured.

"Our star, the sun, has worlds around it," she said. "I believe, and I pray, that other worlds are up there too, better ones." She glanced around to ensure no one else was listening. "With a God less tolerant of human depravity."

Within a year she had a job working with a scribe, learning to copy and translate theological documents; a cover for her induction into the Alessian Order. Esma had to endure two more years at home, but each time her father's hand raised above her, she knew that revenge would come, and never once cried out in voice or with tears, which only angered him further. On the night she left, Esma slit his throat with a razor-sharp knife clutched in trembling hands, where he lay snoring, drunk, in the kitchen. Only then did the tears come, as she watched the life bleed out of his bloated, twitching body. She knew that her mother, despite being regularly beaten herself, would never forgive this act, but after Esma had finally stopped shaking, she left a note for her mother and brother that simply said, "My parting gift."

On her way to the mountains, she passed through a village where the very same wandering monk who had first inspired her three years earlier had been arrested for heresy. As an outsider sheltering against the winter at a local inn, she was questioned by men in scarlet cloaks, witch-finders. Seeing his battered, tortured body chained in the market place, scorched eye sockets in his listless head, and beholding the faces and shrieking accusations of the local villagers filled with rage and bloodlust, fear seized Esma. When dragged before the monk, she vehemently denied knowing him, adding her voice to those crying out for him to be burned at the stake.

Once released, she fled the village. Huddled in her coat on the hillside that evening, she watched the smoke rise from the pyre, occasionally catching the shrill screams of the monk's voice that had so entranced her in Padua, and the jeering of the crowd. Afterwards, Esma wandered for five days and nights, not eating, punishing herself for being so weak, vowing it would never happen again. On the months-long journey, she studied hard, always dwelling on the words of Alessia, promising a better life than Esma had known.

Now she would finally meet the High Priestess herself, or at least glimpse her. As she strode against the wind, up the winding cobbled pathway and endless granite steps, she spied something from the corner of her eye – a blue-black beast, its carapace shining like that of a beetle. It had a strangely shaped head, not quite a rectangle, more like the silhouette of a half-open book. But this creature was the height of two men, and moved so fast it was gone almost before her mind could paint its picture. Esma had heard the rumours. So, it was true, they were here. She quickened her pace.

When the great gate opened, uncreaking and seemingly of its own accord, three men in full-length grey robes faced her, their hands hidden in long sleeves, eyes intense, uncompromising. While the tallest asked questions concerning the Order's scripture, which Esma had to answer without reflection or error, the other two walked and stood close behind her. After what felt like half an hour of relentless examination, she faltered, unsure of the answer, and rather than give a wrong one, bowed her head. She heard a blade slipping from its sheath behind her. The man in front paused, his deep blue eyes scrutinizing her. "And what if you are called upon to kill those of your own flesh, Esma, your family?"

She raised her head high as she slowly pulled out the curved knife from her coat pocket, showing him the dried blood on its blade. "I already have."

The man before her gave the barest of smiles. "I am Brother Tilgar. Welcome, Esma, to the abode of Alessia."

Life in the fortress was hard, its rules strict and unforgiving, but Esma endured it, doing whatever was asked no matter how menial, without question or complaint. Tilgar was stern with her in front of others, gentler when it was just the two of them, as he instructed her in the Order's ways and in her chosen specialism, the study of written scripture. With his quiet but sharp mind and constant attention to detail, and his patience with her, he became the father figure she had never known.

When she had a spare moment she would approach the narrow windows where the wind howled, and stare out, hoping to catch sight of the beast, but to no avail. Esma told no one what she had seen; in the Order, it was dangerous to know more than one should. She did however catch rare glimpses of Alessia, easily recognised by her mane of flowing red locks as she swept across the inner courtyard from the base of one stone tower to another.

Early one morning, Esma had to fetch a bucket of water for her master, Tilgar, for his morning ablutions. Ice with a dusting of snow covered the surface of the deep well, and she had to lean down precariously and hack at it with her knife, chopping hard. The ice suddenly cracked, and her foot slipped and she lost her balance, tipping forward, arms flailing as she tried to grab onto anything to save her from an icy death. A firm hand seized her ankle and hauled her back from the brink, another yanking her back out of the well's embrace by the shoulder, turning her around with deft ease and power. Esma landed on the frosted ground, panting, by Alessia's feet. Aghast at

4

her mistake, she got to her knees in front of the High Priestess of the Order, though she maintained eye contact: in the Order, deference was never blind. "I am sorry for my foolishness, Your Eminence."

Alessia at first said nothing, the hint of a smile playing across her lips. Her jade eyes fixed on Esma, the smile evaporating. "Once is a mistake, twice is a fault." Alessia turned and continued in her whirlwind fashion towards the principal tower where the Order's Council met regularly. Esma watched Alessia go, feeling as if she had just been touched by an Angel of God.

Esma had never been interested in boys, or in the sinful pleasures of the flesh, but she was still young, and that night she found herself unable to sleep, and with a gnawing sense of disgust, she exorcised the bad thoughts in the only way she knew. But it was different this time. Instead of trying to conjure up enthusiasm in her mind's eye for the handsome young groom other girls fantasized about, Esma imagined Alessia's beatific face, her slim but strong hands caressing her. In her ecstasy Esma cried out in the female dormitory. But in the morning her shame at this profane, animalistic activity bubbled to the surface like acid on skin. She had been disrespectful to Alessia, and Esma vowed never again to demean herself or another by proxy. She threw all her energy into her work.

Months passed, and Esma progressed in her duties – she could write well, and Tilgar had been teaching her a challenging new script, one with serifs, barbs and jagged points, an aggressive rune alphabet that looked sharp enough to draw blood. But she didn't just copy, and learning more, Esma began to translate, occasionally finding herself staring at these words and their unfolding concepts like none she had ever heard, even inside the Order. Her ability to fathom meaning behind the alien language didn't go unnoticed by Tilgar. Esma did not know if this was good or bad news.

One night Tilgar woke her quietly – she had been summoned to a room at the top of the second tower, where the elite lived. Once there, Tilgar ushered her inside and then left, closing the heavy oak door behind him. A flaxen-haired knight in chain-mail armour sat upright in a high-backed wooden chair. Silburn: she had seen him occasionally in the fortress, often with Alessia. He was second-in-command. Silburn rose.

"Come," he said, walking out to the balcony where flurries of snowflakes swirled, in no rush to reach the ground. She stood a little behind him but he gestured for her to stand at the edge, a knee-high stone wall separating them from a sheer drop into darkness. Silburn's hand went to the small of Esma's back. She stiffened. One small shove and she would depart this world.

"Look up, girl, and tell me what you see."

Esma's heart raced. "Stars," she said, the word barely escaping her lips, her mind trying to ignore the hand that could end her life so easily. A snowflake entered her left eye, ice cold, making her blink rapidly. She was not dressed for outside, and the chill air bit through her woollen dress. She ignored it, tried to focus, unsure what was required of her, or which answer would spare her life. But the Order was not about closing minds; that was why she had joined. She remembered Alessia saving her from a messy, futile death in the well, and cleared her throat. "Stars," she said again. "But they do not circle us, for we are not the centre of the universe."

The hand remained firm, a judge deciding her fate. "Continue." Silburn's voice was as unfeeling as the stone wall at her sandaled feet.

Esma tried not to shiver. "Somewhere out there is another life, another way, more than us." She paused, then decided to say it. "I saw one. When I first arrived. Barely a glimpse. But what I saw... impressed me. Such grace and power." She waited, then continued. "I know they are not gods, yet it seems to me – from what I have read – that they are closer to God than we." She dared to glance across to see Silburn's reaction, but his face was as unmoving as the granite walls. Her own face turned downwards, to the oblivion below.

"Have you told anyone else?"

"No," she said, a shiver breaking through despite her best efforts. "Not even Tilgar?"

She had hinted several times, asked Tilgar questions that might have given away what she had seen, but Esma didn't want to get her master into trouble; he had been kind to her. She shook her head. Esma knew that words held deadly power in the Order, especially secrets. Sometimes acolytes disappeared, and no one asked questions afterwards. The line between savant and heretic was of a hair's breadth.

"Esma, would you die for the Order?"

The words echoed in her head, like the eddies of snow before her, making her feel giddy. "Yes," she said, swallowing, guessing she had over-stepped the mark. For the first time in months she visualised her mother, sneering, saying that Esma had always had too much to say, had never accepted her place, and would now pay the price. She would end her life gashed open on the rocks below, leaving carrion birds and insects to pick her bones dry. Esma thought of her sickly brother, Arnault, surely by now taken by the plague ravaging the land. At least he would be sad for her fate. So be it, she and her sibling would comfort each other in whatever came after.

Silburn's face turned to her. "Then *will* you die for the Order, Esma?" He removed his hand from the small of her back.

Esma found her hands shaking, her lips quivering. She stared into Silburn's eyes, but they were pitiless, they had probably seen and dispatched such death that there was no mercy remaining in his soul. Bracing herself, she squeezed her lips together, clenched her fists against the biting pain of cold in her fingers. She lifted one foot on top of the low wall, then pushed up and stood atop the slippery, uneven stone. Her mind, awash with fears and inner cries, suddenly cleared, as if she had broken through its surface ice to clear water underneath. The shaking stopped, and she felt at peace. She wanted to say some last words, and then it came to her, the only two things she cared about. "I do this for Alessia, and for the truth that cannot yet be known or spoken." Eyes wide open, she sucked in a deep breath, leaned forward and took a step.

Silburn's large hands snatched the waist-band of her dress and held her in place, Esma's right foot stretched out over the abyss. "You will indeed die for the Order one day, Esma, but not this night."

Meeting his eyes, she stepped back down cautiously, the shaking returning with a vengeance, her breathing ragged. A single tear escaped. She brushed it away as if it was snow, and in her mind's eye her mother was silent for once, while her brother beamed.

To her surprise, Tilgar joined them on the balcony, wearing a look somewhere between shocked admiration and pride as he wrapped a blanket around her trembling frame.

Silburn patted her on the back. "Go with him. From now on you are no longer an acolyte, you are *Sister* Esma. You will have new chambers, and new duties. Oh, and Tilgar, I know it is late, but give her some ale to warm her, or else she will not sleep."

Esma found she needed Tilgar's arm to steady herself as she walked to the door.

Alessia chaired the Council meeting, the atmosphere around the heavy oak table tensing with her news. "The last Q'Roth surgeon will depart shortly. We will be on our own now, for exactly five hundred years."

Silburn banged his fist on the table, rattling his chain mail. "Our enemies, the Sentinels, are hunting us down, and our number diminishes every month. Without our Masters' aid our ability to quicken new members in the Order will be severely limited."

Sister Esma recalled her own 'quickening' three months ago, the day after that fateful night on Silburn's balcony. She had been transformed, her muscles and tendons made stronger and tougher. Several organs had been changed or even replaced, notably the heart, kidneys, and liver, extending her life expectancy by centuries. But it was her mind that she noticed reborn; faster, able to grasp ideas formerly occluded, though she knew it would take another fifty years for the treatment to raise her intellect to Level Five.

Her transformation had also been a chance to see the noble Q'Roth in action as they performed surgery on her; they were indeed God-like, tremendously powerful yet elegant creatures, with scientific and medical marvels beyond her wildest imaginings. And such discipline and harmony – they never bickered or suffered the endemic pettiness and rivalry afflicting mankind.

She snapped herself out of her reverie, back to the grave matter of the day – the last Q'Roth were departing, going into hibernation, leaving the Order to take care of things until their return. But Silburn was right; it could not have come at a worse time. Those damned Sentinels, the only people who knew of the Order's existence, were hunting them down, one by one. They were not as advanced as the Alicians, but were just as determined, and had been given instruction by a visitor not of this world, warning them of the latent threat to its populace. She had witnessed the torture of one of these infidels, captured and dragged to the fortress. He had been resilient, but Tilgar, draped in a butcher's full apron and armed with a dazzling array of metal implements, spent days and nights working relentlessly on the man who screamed and squirmed, extracting valuable information before the end, when the whimpering wretch's heart gave out.

The Sentinels had been given a formidable weapon, a device hidden somewhere in one of their strongholds, to locate those touched by the Q'Roth surgeons; something to do with the blood. The Sentinels used their influence with the Church of Rome, and the paranoia of the great witch hunt gripping Europe, to prosecute their silent war. When someone of the Order was suspected and arrested, a Sentinel masquerading as a witch-finder would prick their thumb with a special dagger to see if they bled – witches would not bleed, they told the crowds. Esma did not yet understand how, but the knife would detect the hint of Q'Roth blood and stem the flow, after which the man or woman would be dragged away in chains and burned at the stake. Those of the Order who used their new- found strength to try to escape only confirmed and enflamed the local people's convictions of witchery in their midst, and were hunted down and slain like dogs. The Sentinels preyed upon the wild, ignorant fears of ordinary men and women to amplify their power base. And they were winning.

Silburn continued. "If the Q'Roth gave us some of their weapons, or left just a handful of warriors, or one of their flying machines, we could destroy our enemies."

No other Council Member spoke, all awaiting Alessia's reply. "They have done this many times before, Silburn, as you know well, on a number of worlds. This is their way, and we do not question their methods. The automaton they have left behind will still be able to quicken those we judge worthy, but only at a rate of ten per year. We must be careful, bide our time and use stealth until the Q'Roth return. Remember that it is us, Silburn, whom they have chosen. We must determine a way to prevail, or else we are not worthy of their patronage."

But Silburn's grim face remained set. "The Sentinels, backed by the soldiers of the Church of Rome, outnumber us ten to one. They use the witch hunt as a pretence, or any other excuse, to track us down and kill us. We have lost two hundred members of the Order this year alone, a third of our entire force! We cannot keep taking such losses. Soon they will trace us here." He sat back, folding his silver-coated arms. "What is your grand plan, Alessia, now that our Masters are all but gone? I am sure we would all like to hear it."

All eyes fell on Alessia. She stood, leaned across the table on splayed fingers, russet locks tumbling over her shoulders, and glared at Silburn. "I sense you have a proposal, great warrior that you are."

Others shrank away from the table, knowing how quick to anger both of them were, but Silburn leaned back, the fire gone from his voice. "I have a strategy, but it requires great sacrifice."

Alessia righted herself. "I am listening."

Silburn spoke in an unusually quiet tone. He stared down at the gnarled table in front of him, for once not meeting Alessia's eyes. "The only way to make them relax their efforts is to make them think they have won. They believe that if they cut off the head of the snake, the snake will die."

There were gasps in the chamber. Esma glanced from Silburn to Alessia. Surely she would not even consider it!

Alessia glared, then spread her arms wide, addressing everyone, but keeping her eyes fixed on Silburn. "Get out, all of you, now! Leave us!"

Esma fled along with the rest, but waited in the snow-bound arches under the meeting room. An hour later, when all the others had departed to the relative warmth of their rooms, Silburn walked out, head proud in his armour, and tramped across the courtyard's fresh snow. Esma waited, but no one else stirred. For once the wind had stopped, leaving the prayer-wheels idle and silent. The castle's pennants hung as if in mourning of what was to come. Quietly, Esma climbed back up the steps, wondering what she would find.

Alessia sat alone at the great oak table, studying a wooden chessboard with carved pieces, the black queen lying down. Alessia looked up. "Ah, the gifted translator. Remind me your name, girl."

Esma bowed deeply, and told her, adding her honorific, as was appropriate.

"Do you know this game, Sister Esma?" Esma nodded. "A little, your Eminence."

Alessia gazed out the window into the far-off, approaching snowstorm. "What have you gleaned from their writing?"

Esma thought carefully. She had been pondering the most recent document day and night. "That the heavens and time are curved. And this means that although the stars are very far away, our Masters can arrive in an instant."

Alessia turned back, giving her a searching look. "Bravo, Sister Esma." She smiled, and picked up a pawn from the board, weighing it in her hands. "People think a pawn will always be a pawn, because they think the game is flat, in two dimensions. But it is also curved by time." She nudged the fallen queen with a finger.

"A queen cannot become a pawn. Her destiny is set. She is strong yet entrenched by her own power. But a pawn…" Alessia pursed her lips, deliberating. "Sit," she said.

Esma obliged, sitting next to Alessia, the chessboard in front of them.

"Few truly understand that which you so easily grasp, Sister Esma." She played her fingers across the king, bishops and rooks next to her fallen queen. "You see, all of these may fail, or may fall to the Sentinels. I need a pawn to stay in the background, to wait, just in case."

Esma stared at the pawn in Alessia's hand. "Your Eminence, I –" "Five centuries hence, if your wits keep you alive that long, you will see our Masters again, and they will feed on the life energy of ordinary men, and take us to the stars, to a better future. Mankind is fatally flawed, and will be forgotten. Only we and our progeny will reach our true potential." Her eyes gleamed momentarily. "We will travel to the very stars themselves! You understand this, don't you Sister Esma?"

Esma nodded.

"Take this," Alessia said, handing her the wooden queen. "Remember this day, but tell no one of it." With that, she stood, carried the rest of the wooden set to the window, flung the pieces into the snowdrift outside, and stormed out.

Six months later, a long and bloody battle ensued. Alessia was slain by the Sentinels, alongside fifty of her acolytes who defended her until the last. Alessia and her most trusted had attacked the Sentinel stronghold that held their locator device, and finally destroyed it, but during her escape she had been overwhelmed by hundreds of Sentinels.

Sister Esma arrived the next day with Tilgar and a handful of others to retrieve their leader's body from the battlefield, only to find it almost unrecognisable apart from strands of red hair. Esma spent hours gathering Alessia's hacked-apart remains and assembled them into the semblance of a corpse. She wept openly during the cremation, and vowed vengeance, swearing never to forget nor forgive.

Alessia's sacrifice had of course been a gambit, one that worked. The Sentinels grew complacent and soft, believing they had won. But the Q'Roth-enhanced upgrades, Alessia's chosen, lay low with Silburn, barely ageing, and never forgetting. They emerged a hundred years later with a savage pogrom against the Sentinels' descendants, rooting out their hidden cells from the Russian Steppes all the way to the shores of Ireland, slaughtering nine tenths of their number in a single week of synchronized fury. Assassinations of key vassals in the Vatican in the same week forever broke the support of the Church of Rome. These and subsequent brutal murders were masked by a more virulent, genetically- concocted version of the plague still ravaging Europe, forever tipping the war's balance in the Order's favour, though enough escaped to be a constant, if greatly diminished, menace.

Silburn was slain in one of the final raids on a Sentinel stronghold in Tibet, though those who found his body said he looked serene. Esma was not surprised – a king might sacrifice his queen, but will never be the same without her.

In the spring of 1693, when the Order had shifted its headquarters to the New World to escape the lingering political influence of Rome, Tilgar was arrested as part of the trumped-up Salem witch trials in colonial Massachusetts, while he and Esma were recruiting for the Order. Esma had been in a distant village when Tilgar had been cornered by two Sentinels masquerading as witch-finders, backed up by a dozen local soldiers. Esma arrived just in time to be present in the seething throng gathered to watch him hang. Ordinary people yelled obscenities, threw rubbish at his limping, tortured and battered frame. His left arm was missing, a cut so clean just below the shoulder it could only have come from one of the fabled Sentinel nano-swords.

Tilgar had been one of the best of their new breed she had ever known. He held his head high despite his injuries and time on the rack. He raised his remaining hand, and the crowd briefly grew quiet to hear and then spit on his last words. "Your time will come," was all he said, looking over them, catching her eye at the end. The crowd, including men, women, children, young and old, screamed "Witch! Hang him! Torture him some more! He still has another arm, cut it off!" and other profanities she tried to close her ears to. One young man looked so much like her long-dead brother, Arnault, that Esma caught her breath. With spittle on his lips and an ugly snarl, he hurled abuse at Tilgar, as she knew Arnault would have done, and inside her the last vestige of her umbilical cord with humanity snapped.

Hot tears streamed down her cheeks as she regarded Tilgar's brave face for the last time. He could have taken half a dozen of the guards on the stage with him, but now more than ever the Order needed to snuff out the last public embers of this war, and so he accepted his fate. Her eyes met his, and she nodded the unspoken vow to avenge him. As his body twisted and turned at the end of a crude rope, bloating his face purple, she could barely breathe, long fingernails inside her fists digging so deep they drew blood. Esma wanted to kill all those cheering, stinking peasants with her bare hands, not only the two Sentinels masquerading as witch-finders, who she dispatched the following summer.

That year was the turning point for her, when she saw how the Q'Roth classification of ordinary people as Level Three – galactic weeds that would never be fit for Grid Society, instead ripe for culling – was right and just. Humanity's future was a dead end. Ordinary men would wage war and kill and violate each other for all eternity. More likely, men would annihilate all life once they developed the type of weapons she had read about in Q'Roth scripture, weapons that could raise the heat of the sun on Earth itself. No, the only possible future lay with the brothers and sisters of the Order of Alessia, later to be called Alicians, augmented by their Q'Roth patrons. Alicians were neither fractious nor small-minded, and worked together tirelessly toward a common goal – their salvation at the hands of the Q'Roth, deliverance from this flawed world to a new one, and a better way of life. Helping the Q'Roth to cull humanity would only bring forward mankind's inevitable demise.

As time passed, the balance of evidence against humanity accrued in her mind. By the nineteenth century, the Order's numbers had swelled, and they had a stronger foothold, subtly influencing many political decisions. The Alicians fomented wars to keep mankind off-balance and divided in collective mind and spirit. However, individuals began to appear amongst the normal population, showing great intellect. This had always been a concern – that humanity was beginning to produce Level Four specimens – Leonardo, Galileo and others had until that time been statistical outliers. Now, a clear trend emerged of new men and women with genius potential, and the Alicians set about finding them, detecting them through universities and learned societies. Some were recruited, but most were unreceptive to Alician ideology and became the unfortunate victims of accidents or strange illnesses. A few inevitably slipped through the net, Darwin one of the most dangerous.

Esma and others in the High Council realised mankind was nearing its evolutionary 'cusp', when it could actually advance on its own from its dismal Level Three status. The surviving and greatly weakened Sentinels grasped it too, and tried to find and protect such individuals. If another visitor from the faraway galactic society she now knew as the Grid were to come and re-evaluate the human race, and found evidence of the rising frequency of such individuals, the planned and Grid-approved Q'Roth cull would be questioned, postponed, perhaps even cancelled.

That was when Esma and other Council members came up with the strategy of world wars as a way of killing off large sections of young people. What better way to demonstrate the prospects of humanity, than peoples' willingness to slaughter each other in their millions without question. It was so easy to incite fascism and hate, fanning the flames of man's pathetic innate barbarism. Those few lone voices arguing against the atrocities and insanity of war were drowned out in an orgy of bloodletting. Esma, as other Alicians, relished the arrival of each new update of casualty statistics, almost unbelieving how well the wars went. At one point, Sister Esma and other Alicians actually had to rein in the world's leaders to prevent mankind's total annihilation. After all, the Alicians had to hold up their end of the bargain, ensuring that the newly hatched Q'Roth, upon their return, could harvest humanity.

Once, Esma and a group of Alicians visited the aftermath of a First World War battlefield, thousands of bodies lying in poppy fields, some of the soldiers not yet dead from fatal wounds. One man called out to her, in agony, lying in a growing pool of his own blood. She stood above him, listening to his lamentable supplications, while she recalled the bravery of Tilgar and Alessia. Her lip curled in disgust. "You deserve to die," she said, "all of you." Esma placed the heel of her boot on his skull, and applied her weight until his inferior brain squeezed out onto the blood-soaked grass. This single act calmed her, but only momentarily. She would need many more deaths, billions, to quench her hatred: every last human. One thing she and Darwin had agreed upon years earlier was that evolution leads to complete eradication of mal-adapted species; irrevocable de-selection. There are no half-measures in nature, and no sentimentality. A new, superior breed displaces and eradicates an inferior one. That was the way of things.

Many years later, while reading Einstein's brilliant, if imperfect and ultimately flawed understanding of relativity, Esma realised something else about the curved nature of time. The Alician perspective, granted by their newfound longevity, was so different from normal men and women with their short lifespans. As centuries passed, she watched nations fight bloody wars – often catalysed by the Alicians to keep humanity off- balance – then generations later, become allies, friends even. Despite losing their loved ones and sons and daughters in battle, eventually they wanted their grandchildren to find peace. But those touched by the Q'Roth did not age appreciably, did not forget, and so never forgave. The faces of Alessia, Silburn, Tilgar and dozens of other fallen comrades called out to her every day, demanding retribution. And she would deliver it.

By the twenty-first century humanity was where the Q'Roth needed them to be, hopelessly divided by politics and religion, and on their knees after a third world war that had finally made humanity averse to nuclear weapons and nanotechnology, the only two defences against the Q'Roth.

Esma had risen slowly and stealthily through the ranks. When new Q'Roth hatchlings stirred on Eden in 2063, right on schedule, she had taken Alessia's place. But she never accepted any honorific other than 'Sister'; that is what Alessia had called her, and she wanted nothing more.

2081: Savange, Alician Homeworld

Sister Esma sat on the Bridge of the Crucible Class battleship as it undocked from Savange's orbital tether. Twice she had come close to completely eradicating humanity. Two had stood in her way: Blake – a rook – and Micah, a pawn, but like her, one who had grown into something more. This time there would be no mistake. She would wipe the board clean once and for all, as soon as Quarantine came down around Esperia, their pathetic excuse for a world. Never mind the war raging across half the galaxy. As the plague had helped mask their revenge on the Sentinels centuries earlier, so the galactic invasion led by Qorall would hide her intended actions. Worlds fell every day. Who would miss another one? Her hand dipped into a recess in her cloak and clasped a small wooden figure whose edges had grown smooth. Soon, Alessia, soon.

EDEN'S ALIENS & ARTIFACTS

Alicians – neo-human race genetically altered by the Q'Roth to increase intelligence, resilience and longevity. Alicians are named after *Alessia*, their founder, who brokered a deal with the Q'Roth in 1053 AD to prepare humanity for culling, and to eradicate Earth-based nuclear and nano-based weaponry, in exchange for genetic advancement and patronage. Alicians are Level Five, and are led by *Sister Esma. Louise* is an Alician renegade imbued with too much Q'Roth DNA.

Dark Worms – leviathan-like creatures that live in the space between galaxies, feeding off both dark and normal energy sources. They are almost impossible to kill. Normally they are kept outside by the Galactic Barrier, which was breached by *Qorall*'s forces.

Esperia – formerly Ourshiwann – the spider planet serving as mankind's home after the fall of Earth and Eden, with only two major cities: human-occupied Esperantia, and spider-occupied Shimsha.

Finchikta – Level Nine bird-like creatures who administrate judicial affairs for the Tla Beth, e.g. during the trial of humanity in 2063.

Genners – following the trial of humanity, prosecuted by the Alicians and the Q'Roth, mankind was quarantined on Esperia for its own protection and all children genetically upgraded to Level Four (with Level Five potential) by the Ossyrians. 'Genners' surpass their parents intellectually by the age of twelve.

Grid – ring-shaped ultra-rapid transport hub that runs around the inner rim of the galaxy, for ease of commerce. **Grid Society**: established by the Kalarash ten million years ago, based on a scale of levels of intelligence running from one to nineteen, with Kalarash at the top. Mankind was initially graded Level Three.

Hohash – intelligent artifacts resembling upright oval mirrors, designed by the Kalarash, known as 'omnipaths' due to their powerful perception, communication and recording abilities. Their true function is unknown.

Kalarash – Level Nineteen beings believed to have left our galaxy. Only seven remain in the universe. Little is known about them. They are called 'the Progenitors' by many Grid species, as the Kalarash fostered civilisation in the galaxy, based on a strictly hierarchical intelligence-ranking system.

Mannekhi – human-looking alien race except for their all-black eyes. Level Five. They sided with Qorall in the ongoing galactic war, due to millennia of oppression under Grid rule.

Nganks – full name Ngankfushtora – squid-like Level Twelve cosmetic surgeons whose services are usually reserved for higher-level species.

Ossyrians – dog-like Level Eight medical race, charged as humanity's custodians after the trial, their eighteen-year long stay on Esperia led by *Chahat-Me*.

Qorall [kwo-rahl] – ancient enemy of the Kalarash, and invader of the galaxy.

Q'Roth [kyu-roth] – Level Six nomadic warrior race who culled Earth as part of the maturation process for its hatchlings, in a deal with the Alicians. Currently engaged as soldiers trying to stop the progress of *Qorall*'s forces across the galaxy. The Q'Roth are formal Patrons of the Alicians.

Rangers – Level Fifteen taciturn reptilian creatures working for the Tla Beth. Ranger *Shatrall* crash-landed in Tibet in the early part of the twelfth century and realized the Q'Roth had targeted humanity for culling. He was unsure the Level Three assessment of humanity was correct, and so unofficially warned a local warrior tribe who became the Alicians' principal adversary, the Sentinels.

Resident – internal alien-designed symbiote implanted in *Micah*'s head prior to the Trial of humanity, which acts as a semi-intelligent Level Five translator, with various additional survival-oriented functions.

Savange – new home planet of the Alicians, ruled by *Sister Esma*.

Scintarelli – Level Twelve legendary master shipbuilders, whose shipyards dwell in gas giants. Their star-ship designs include the *Starpiercer* and the *Scythe*.

Sclarese [skla-ray-zee] Nova Stormers – Level Nine semi-intelligent stealth missiles based on energy amplification technology, aimed at turning stars nova. Built by the Sclarese.

Sentinels – blood enemies of the Alicians, involved in a silent war over a period of nine centuries. Last remaining Sentinel alive is *Ramires*. Sentinels were famous for their nano-swords, able to slice through a Q'Roth warrior's armoured flesh.

Shrell – Level Nine matriarchal ray-like creatures who live in deep space, guardians and 'gardeners' of the space-environment, invisible to most other species. As well as protecting and 'fixing' spatial tears, they can also 'poison' space. They work for the *Tla Beth*.

Spiders – Level Four race harvested by the Q'Roth one thousand years prior to the culling on Earth. Homeworld called Ourshiwann, renamed Esperia. Visually-oriented race, otherwise deaf and mute. Now live in *Shimsha*, near *Esperantia*, humanity's last city.

Steaders – the 'non-genned' human population on Esperia, so called because of the preponderance of farms and homesteads surrounding Esperantia.

Tla Beth – Level Seventeen energy creatures, rulers of the Grid in the absence of the Kalarash. Homeworld location unknown.

Transpar – *Blake*'s pilot *Zack* was transformed by the Tla Beth into a glass-like transparent living witness, unable to lie, and devoid (mostly) of his original personality, as part of the judicial procedure during the trial of mankind. *Zack*'s wife *Sonja* decided to keep the Transpar rather than let it be returned to the Tla Beth after the trial and be destroyed. The Transpar's longevity and capabilities are unknown.

Wagramanians – Level Seven forest-dwelling tripeds famed for art, but also employed by the Tla Beth as shock troops during times of interstellar war.

ABBREVIATED GALACTIC HISTORICAL TIMELINE

Ossyrian School Notes for Genners

TIME (past)	EVENT
2 billion years	War between Kalarash – highest Level beings known in Universe – and Qorall, in Jannahi Galaxy. Qorall believed dead. Galaxy destroyed. Seven Kalarash travel to Silverback Galaxy (human name: "Milky Way").
Unknown	Various civilisations rise and fall. Five Kalarash leave Galaxy.
>2 million years	Grid Society established under Kalarash guidance. Grid is a transport hub traversing a third of the galaxy. Grid Society strongly hierarchical based on Levels of intelligence. Kalarash are Level 19. [Humanity is Level 3].
2 million years	Kalarash disappear. Level 17 Tla Beth left in charge, supported by Level 15 Rangers (reptilian).
50000 years	Anxorian (Level Sixteen) Rebellion threatens Grid. Tla Beth genetically alter Grid species 195 [Q'Roth] to become galactic foot-soldiers. Rebellion quashed. Anxorian species extinguished.
40000 years	Ossyrian (Level 8) race patronised by Tla Beth, become Medical race for the galaxy.
30000 years	Last sighting of a Hohash – Kalarash intelligent artefacts known as 'omnipaths'.
Every 1000 years	Q'Roth newborns must seek out 'nourishment' by culling species Level 4 or below.
~1000 years	Q'Roth cull spider race on Ourshiwann (renamed Esperia)
~1000 years	Q'Roth scouts land on Earth. Broker a deal with Alician sect in exchange for upgrading Alicians to Level 5 and promised sponsorship by Q'Roth
~900 years	Ranger Shattrall crash-lands on Earth. Realises humanity targeted for culling. Warns local Tibetan tribe who become Sentinels. Sentinels engage in silent war with Alicians.
~500 years	Q'Roth terraform Eden and plant egg nests.
40 years	Nanoplague on Earth. 50 million dead. Nannite technology

	banned. Plague instigated by Alicians, as harmful to Q'Roth.
30 years	Third World War on Earth. Environment sent into irrecoverable global warming. Alicians gain power through religious sect known as Fundies.
20 years	Eden discovered. Blake and crew arrive and find Q'Roth eggs hatching, and Hohash artefact. Micah uncovers Alician plot on Earth. Battle ensues. Earth destroyed, refugees flee to Esperia. Alicians escape.
19 years	Alician known as Louise attacks Esperia. Humanity prevails.
19 years	Qorall and his forces attack, breaking through galactic barrier.
18 years	Micah and crew enter Grid. After murder of Q'Roth ambassador, humanity placed on trial by Tla Beth. Humanity acquitted but placed in protective Quarantine for one generation. All children to be genetically upgraded by Ossyrians.
18 years	Kalarash presence detected on Esperia along with spider egg nests. Kalarash ship disappears with three humans onboard (Jen, Dimitri and Rashid). Believed to have left galaxy, reason unknown.
Today	The Tla Beth, aided by the Q'Roth and other races, have lost half the galaxy to Qorall. Eldest human 'genned' child is eighteen.
In one week	Quarantine will come down. Ossyrians scheduled to leave. Humanity will have to fend for itself.

PETRA'S NOTES

1.   The last Kalarash (apparently) was hiding on Esperia, and left just before Quarantine, along with three people: Jennifer, Dimitri and Rashid. Why was it here? Maybe they'll come back.

2.   The Ossyrians have been kind to us, especially my godmother, Chahat-Me.

3.   Micah is just about holding things together between Steaders and Genners on Esperia. Tensions will spike as Quarantine down-date approaches. Good luck, Uncle.

4.   Blake is now a recluse, lives in Shimsha with the spiders. No one goes there, except Micah, though not in a long while. Zack's Transpar sometimes goes to see Blake.

5.   Mom1 (Kat) disappeared two years ago, after she went looking in caves where the Kalarash ship was last seen. Someone abducted her, but who, and why? Mom2 (Antonia) devastated. Buries herself in work for the Council.

6.   Father (Pierre – never met him) disappeared with a Ranger known as Ukrull just before Quarantine. He's never coming back.

7.   Gabriel, beautiful as ever, still intent on revenge against the Alicians as soon as Quarantine comes down. Micah is trying to keep him in check, but that won't work for much longer.

8.   We've become farmers. People don't want to face the prospect of another war or battle, hoping instead that the Alicians and Q'Roth have lost interest. But Gabriel and his Youngbloods might be right: the old enemies may be waiting just outside Quarantine, in which case we'd better be prepared.

9.   Being Level Four isn't all it's cracked up to be. We've gained a lot, but we may have lost something along the way; most Steaders certainly think so. No turning back now, though.

10.   We are defenceless and blind, unknowing of what is out there. The Quarantine has been an eighteen-year stay of execution. If only there was someone out there, an ally who gave a damn about us, especially with the ongoing Galactic War. We are on our own, perhaps about to be written out of history. But we'll go down fighting, as long as we get the chance.

PART ONE – QUARANTINE

CHAPTER 1 - DUEL

Micah stood on Hazzard's Ridge surveying Esperantia, the last human city, wondering if it would still exist in a week's time. He glanced upwards to the clear blue sky where the invisible quarantine barrier hung, protecting them these past eighteen years from alien invaders. One more week and the barrier would come down. Then they would see if anyone was out there waiting for them.

Esperantia's zinc-coated buildings gleamed in the late afternoon sun, laid out like the eight points of a compass star. As his eyes swept across the city he'd helped build, his vision stalled on the blood orange blister at the southern perimeter – the dome – where the duel awaited him. People were already gathering. Micah's resident, an alien gift lodged in the software of his mind, dating back to his brief time travelling in the Grid, reminded him of the hour, flashing a subtle countdown in his left eye's visual field. It was getting late, but Micah was in no hurry to arrive, especially given how he intended to try and win the match.

He gazed beyond the outlying farms – a patchwork quilt of corn, rapeseed and astrasa – to the Ossyrian crystal pyramid, three kilometers away at the far end of the valley. The three-hundred-metre-tall vessel glistened, reflecting tangerine rays as Esperia's sun dipped towards the Acarian Mountains. The giant space ship housed humanity's guardians, a hundred and fifteen Ossyrians, who rarely ventured outside these days. Micah could barely imagine how it had been for the upright, dog-like aliens, enduring all these years as mankind's caretakers, trapped with them in the quarantine placed around the planet. Still, under Ossyrian husbandry, crops had prospered and humanity's surviving ranks had doubled to twenty thousand and, thanks to Ossyrian medical wizadry, mankind was disease-free for the first time in its history.

Yet Esperantia was a divided community, and Micah had been instrumental in that social division. Facing annihilation, he'd negotiated protection for mankind in exchange for an agreement that all future human children would undergo genetic manipulation, to advance them from what the ruling pan-galactic alien Grid Society called LevelThree, to Level Four, a kind of basic entry point to avoid future culling. It had seemed a good idea at the time, in fact the only non-terminal solution on the table.

The resulting Genner children, the eldest just eighteen, had been incredibly resourceful with the basic materials available on Esperia, whether in agriculture, developing more efficient crop strains and irrigation methods, or energy, creating new solar cell systems that boosted lighting and heating for the entire city. Even if parents couldn't always relate to their kids, they were proud of them. But it had been a high price to pay. One father had summed it up neatly a month ago at a Council meeting, addressing Micah, who was, after all, President.

"They're unemotional... cold. No other word for it, though few parents will say it aloud. I... I watch my son, but I can't reach him. He's way smarter than me, has been since he was twelve." The man paced before Micah and other Council members, who could offer little solace. He continued, wringing his hands. "And what have we created? Our old enemies, our 'cousins' the Alicians, were genned to Level Five by the Q'Roth, and they damned near exterminated us. You, Micah, you and Blake, you fought so hard to save us so that humanity would survive. But now we're doing the same thing to ourselves. Don't you see?"

Micah did see. If he could turn back time...

His train of thought was interrupted by the sound of the young Genners' polyphonous chant carried along the breeze, their adolescent voices sharp and clear. He paused to watch their procession along the main street leading to the dome. Most ungenned people – all, if they were honest – could not really appreciate the mathematical music. But many of the parents trooped behind, trying to follow a rhythmic melody that Micah knew was too fractal for ungenned tastes. His resident supplied subtle harmonics and he heard how clever it was, brilliant by normal human standards, but also how clinical, lacking emotional resonance. *That about sums it up.*

Zooming in, courtesy of his other secret 'gift', a bunch of overactive nannites his former friend Pierre had injected him with just before Quarantine, he picked out tall and wiry Gabriel, his opponent in the upcoming duel. Next to him, Sandy oozed pride for her son. Micah hadn't seen her for two years. Squatting, he hefted a large stone in his hands, to keep his balance. Down below, Ramires came up to Gabriel and Sandy, and Sandy kissed her partner full on the lips. The stone snapped in Micah's palms with a loud crack. A line of blood appeared on his right palm, fizzed grey, and withdrew, healing in seconds, courtesy of the nannites. His resident began to intrude, telling him to get going. Micah ignored it, and spoke to the wind. "Pierre, wherever the hell you are out there, couldn't you have given me something more useful?"

But Pierre *had* left him something far more precious. Micah tried to pick his adopted niece, Pierre's daughter Petra, out of the crowd, but couldn't find her. Micah had never married, though he'd had offers he largely attributed to his being President; he'd never had children, and now figured it was too late. But he cherished Petra as if she were his own daughter. He kept his fondness for her hidden, though; in the past, every time he'd let his feelings for someone be known, it had always backfired, and he couldn't stand to lose anyone else.

His mind returned to the end of Quarantine, the Alician/Q'Roth potential threat, and the Genner issue. Genners were faster, stronger, more intelligent, able to truly multi-task, and adept with languages and art. Most of them weren't children anymore, and like all adolescents they wanted to be treated as equals. But while most Genners were pacifist in outlook, and some even apologetic for their enhanced abilities, the Youngbloods were a breed apart. They held a strong lust for vengeance against the Alicians who had almost eradicated humanity.

Micah never quite understood why the Youngbloods were more angry with mankind's mortal enemy than their parents were, who after all had suffered near-annihilation first-hand. He wished the psychologist Carlson was still around to try and explain it. Eight years ago, Petra, who wasn't tattooed but nevertheless spent all her time hanging out with this warrior caste, told Micah he must ask Gabriel himself. Instead, a year later, he'd asked Ramires, the last Sentinel, and the Youngbloods' trainer in the arts of war. Ramires had been indignant...

"Don't you want the Alicians dead, too, Micah? Sister Esma? Louise? Seven billion people slaughtered, their voices silenced forever. Don't you feel them waiting, watching, demanding justice? Do you sleep well, Micah, knowing the Alicians and the Q'Roth are still out there, probably plotting out demise?"

Micah didn't sleep well. But he'd argued with Ramires, pressing him as to why the Genners should take up the cause so fervently. Then Sandy came out. He'd not seen her in ages, and the sight of her stilled him in an instant. She spoke with that same cutting edge he'd once loved to hear. Hell, he still did, but she belonged to Ramires now.

"It's not so hard to grasp, Micah. Genners may be less emotional, but they're not blind. They see the sacrifice their parents made, the one to which you bound us all."

Ramires' eyes widened. "Darling, that's not fair. Even our son, Gabriel – "

Sandy's eyes remained fixed on Micah, ignoring her husband. "They think relativistically, Micah, long term, causes stretching backwards, effects rushing forwards; one of the gifts you handed them. The way they see it, the Alicians *have* exterminated humanity, because in fifty years' time, even if they do nothing, all that will be left will be Genners. Our children –" her voice quavered "– my son Gabriel, and others like him, wish to avenge us, their parents, while we still breathe. You have denied us all so much already, do you deny them that right as well?" She turned and headed back inside Ramires' cottage, not waiting for an answer.

"I'm sorry, Micah, she's upset, she doesn't –"

"She does, Ramires, and we both know it. And she's right."

Ramires seized Micah's shoulders. "If you hadn't agreed with the Tla Beth ruling, we wouldn't even be standing here today, and Gabriel would never have been born."

Micah felt hollow, as if his innards had been sucked out, as if he might collapse, like walls of empty skin. Only Sandy could do this to him. He stared towards the cottage, then tore his eyesight back to Ramires, and collected himself. "But she's wrong about the other part. I won't deny the Youngbloods that right. When the time comes..." An idea struck him. "We have to train them, Ramires."

Ramires shrugged. "I do train them, you know that. I teach them Sentinel fighting arts every day."

"No, more than that." The idea took flight in his head. "Battle simulations, space warfare..."

That was how the annual duel had started. But still the Youngbloods weren't ready. Micah knew that these would-be avengers would rush off at the first opportunity to attack the Alicians, and get themselves killed. The Ossyrians hadn't managed to breed hubris out of the children's DNA; which brought him back to the impending contest, and the last lesson he could give Gabriel, one that might save the boy's life. A light breeze whispering up the mountain told him evening was approaching. Micah already knew he was cutting it fine; it started in ten minutes.

He turned and squinted westwards towards the adjacent valley where Shimsha lay, humanity's refuge for its first two years on Ourshiwann – renamed Esperia – before the spiders who'd lain dormant for a millennium hatched and reclaimed their home. The spiders hadn't been violent about it, just moved back as inexorably as a tide. No one wanted to stick around after the first night of their return, and besides, Esperantia had been ready, just. Now the alabaster spider city, with its trapezoidal buildings like upside-down cake moulds, and its ivory minarets, bustled with metre-high, four-legged spiders. Micah could just make out a few spiders in the city, milling about, going about their business, whatever that was. Their black, furry, headless bodies were circumscribed by a jagged band that fluoresced rainbow hues. It was how they communicated, and since the band was three-sixty degrees, any spider within sight could see what any other spider was 'saying'. Blake, the only human allowed to live in Shimsha, and the only one they trusted, had pointed out that the spiders never lied, never deceived each other. How could they? Micah wondered if humanity would have been better off with such a mode of communication, especially since he was about to perpetrate a lie.

Shimsha glimmered, its light display twinkling in the approaching dusk. Micah wondered what the spiders would do if war came, whether they would fight this time. He doubted it.

His resident pressed, initiating a nagging buzz inside his skull, and so Micah got up, dusted off his trousers, and headed down the slope towards the dome.

As Micah neared a side entrance, he spied one of Esperantia's staunch citizens, Albert Schwartz, gaunt and stiff as if walking to attention, but still strong for a sixty year old. Albert cut directly across Micah's path, blocking his route. This wasn't Micah's first encounter with Albert, and as usual, he guessed it wasn't going to be pleasant. Micah's resident pressed.

"Good day, Mr. President," Albert said.

"Mr. Schwartz. Can I help you? I'm running a little late."

"You don't have children, do you, Mr. President?"

It was a rhetorical question, as they both knew, but Micah shook his head anyway, sensing what was coming.

Albert's lips squeezed together, almost white. Then he spat it out, while staring at the distant blue mountains. "Do you know what it's like to have your own daughter look at you as if..." He squeezed his eyes shut, opened them again. "As if," he continued, "you're some kind of dumb animal to be pitied?" He glanced up at Micah, his face flushed.

Micah shook his head again, then spoke quietly. "No, Mr. Schwarz, I do not."

Albert swallowed. "That's not the end of it. After pity, which usually comes when they're aged about ten, well, by twelve they lose respect."

"Mr. Schwartz, I'm sure –"

"You hold your tongue, Mr. President. You hear me out!"

Micah nodded. This had happened before. It could be any of a hundred parents in Albert's place, standing there, trembling with bottled- up frustration verging on desperation.

"Their eyes go cold, indifferent. Crushes our hearts! My wife's..." His voice cracked. He closed his eyes again.

Micah took a risk, and spoke. "Your daughter Virginia is probably the brightest of all the Genners, maybe even more so than Gabriel. She's solved more technical and engineering problems on Esperia than I can remember. I can't pretend to know how you and your wife feel, but... I'm not blind to it, Mr. Schwartz, and I wish with all my heart I could change it. But you should be proud of her." He lowered his voice. "God knows, I am."

Albert stood, chest heaving, head bowed. He gave Micah a sideways glance. "You know why you keep getting re-elected?"

Micah smiled. "If I did, I would do something about it."

"It's because you're the only one who can win these damned duels."

Micah raised an eyebrow.

Albert walked up to Micah and grabbed him by the arm, with a surprisingly strong grip. "You go in there, and you win, Mr President, because it's one of the few things that enables us normal folk, us *Steaders* as our children call us, to retain some dignity." Albert let go, as if realising how hard he held Micah, then sagged, the anger drained out of him, making him seem older, more fragile.

Micah touched him gently on the shoulder. "I'll do my best, Sir, for all of us, Steaders and Genners alike."

Micah noticed his resident had given up warning him how late he was. He broke into a run.

The arena was brim-full of people in tan clothes with brightly coloured scarves and hats to stave off the chill autumn breeze outside. Murmurings subsided as he headed straight for the central stage, shaped like an old- style boxing ring. Two high-backed wooden chairs faced each other; one was empty, Colonel Vasquez standing bolt upright behind it, with his shock of white hair and eagle-sharp eyes. Gabriel waited in the other, fingers loosely curled around the ends of the arm-rests, calm, confident, his blond hair reaching square shoulders, a mauve maze tattooed around his left eye and temple. He had a presence – with Gabriel sitting in it, the chair became a throne.

Just below the stage, on the far side of the 'ring', fifteen other Youngbloods sat, headsets in place, already immersed in the simulation. Above the ring a darkened cylindrical holoscreen glittered with stars, awaiting game activation.

Micah overheard a Genner somewhere in the front rows of the audience, speaking in Hremsta, the fast-click dialect that only Genners – and Micah via his resident – understood: "Twenty seconds before you forfeit the match, Mr. Asshole President."

Micah shrugged it off, leapt up to the stage and dropped into the seat facing Gabriel. He nodded to Vasquez. "Ready."

Vasquez planted the headset on Micah, clicked the 'trodes into active mode, then leaned forward towards Micah's ear. "Are you sure you don't want any human backup this time?"

Micah shook his head. This time he preferred to have simulated human generals and fighter pilots, because he'd need them to obey tough orders without hesitation. He met Gabriel's almost black eyes head on, resisting the urge to look at Sandy, sitting in the front row just behind her son. He and Gabriel both raised their right hands, the crowd hushing. The rule was, the first one to blink had to start the game. Within thirty seconds, the crowd began stamping their feet to a slow drumbeat rhythm, gradually getting faster. Still Micah held Gabriel's eyes. Whistles flew forth from the crowd, cheering, shouting. Genners chanted Gabriel's name, all the time his face not showing the tiniest crack of emotion. Micah knew he could win this part of the game courtesy of his nannites, but instead he tilted his head back, raised his hand a little higher to a cheer from the crowd, let a smile spread across his face, nodded slightly to Gabriel, and slammed his hand down on the start button.

Micah found himself on the bridge of an Axion Class Battlestar, orbiting dust-brown Esperia with its Spartan patches of malachite – the great lakes – overflows from the planet's underground oceans. A small patch of light indicated Esperantia and Shimsha. Micah winced – they looked so fragile from up here, such easy targets.

His data-screens told him he had six Blaze Class Destroyers, a hundred single-man Reapers, and four thousand remote Shuriken drones at his disposal. *Defence*, he gathered. Which meant Gabriel would be leading a simulated attack on Esperia. Micah eschewed the standard strategy of arranging his resources in a defence grid around the planet and moon; Gabriel was far too smart. In such a tactical battle, with Gabriel's heightened reflexes, Micah would lose.

"Long range," he instructed the bridge comp, then studied the unfolding hologram. Nothing. No sign of Gabriel and his genetically advanced crew. He knew people back in the dome could see avatars of him on the battle-bridge, Gabriel on his ship, wherever it was, and the general situation on a star-field map, along with a digital score of the number of remaining ships on both sides. Custom was for each opponent to talk through his thoughts, but Micah didn't feel like talking today, and the taciturn Gabriel habitually flouted that particular tradition.

Micah had anguished for months over what he was about to do, had almost decided against it. He despised any form of cheating. But he knew that politically – a word he grew to hate more with each year of his Presidency – he could not afford to lose this match; it would destabilize everything just when they were most vulnerable. Besides, the information from the program would only give him an edge, nothing more. Gabriel was still a formidable opponent. Micah instructed his resident to activate the search program he'd installed the night before into the simulation software, using Presidential access codes, and waited.

Within seconds a set of coordinates appeared, and Micah did all the necessary calcs in his head, assisted by his resident. Leaning forward in his command chair, he tapped in a set of commands, then sat back and steepled his fingers, a habit he'd borrowed from Blake. Two of his destroyers peeled off and took up position on the other side of the larger of Esperia's two moons. The other four destroyers blinked bright then vanished into transit, the arrowhead-shaped Reapers and three quarters of the Shuriken – spherical drones spiked with laser turrets – following in their wake. The remaining Shuriken streaked out of Esperia's system. He imagined the consternation in the dome; it appeared he'd left Esperia almost defenceless, and he couldn't know from which direction Gabriel would attack. Except that he did. He stared at the screens, then walked up to the bridge's starmap holo and moved inside it, so that his eyes were close to a particular star, as if inspecting it. Micah knew he was giving the game away. But he'd decided that if he was going to cheat, he was going to be honest about it. He wondered if Petra was out there somewhere, watching, and whether she would hate him for cheating, or, being a Genner, be impressed. Reluctantly he realized that of all the people who would judge his performance tonight, her opinion – and Sandy's – mattered most.

* * *

Petra leaned against the dome's rear wall, hands sunk into dungaree pockets, observing everything from a distance. With her genned eyesight she had no need to be up front, easily able to pick out the stars and the expressions on Micah or Gabriel's closed-eyed faces. She gazed across the seated crowd, all of them bent forward, eager to see the outcome; a lot was riding on this particular game. As for her, she didn't care who won, but she didn't want either of them to lose. She switched back to the holo-screen.

Gabriel's small attack force of sixteen ships arranged themselves into formation, his hundred-metre-long, javelin-shaped Starpiercer in front, encircled by three waves of five single-pilot, delta wing Hawks. The overall effect was of a skeletal bullet. The ships winked out as they entered Transpace on an attack vector towards Esperia that would take a minimum of two jumps.

Inside the dome, chatter subsided as everyone watched Micah's avatar saunter over to where Gabriel's fleet had been moments before. Four Youngbloods rose to their sandaled feet, shouting first in their own language, Hremsta, then in English. But for once the Steaders needed no translation.

"Cheat! He knew Gabriel's location! He should forfeit the match!"

Petra felt the temperature rise in the throng. She studied Micah's simulated face. *He's doing this on purpose.* A crooked smile spread across her lips. "Sneaky, Uncle," she said to no one in particular. Her smile faded. "Mum would have been amused." But she noticed a couple of the Steaders were now on their feet, too, shouting back.

Brandt, one of her fellow Genners near the front row, a Youngblood nicknamed 'Hulk' due to his size, caught her eye. She used the face- code Genners had developed as kids so they could communicate without their Steader parents knowing, to tell Brandt to cool the Genners down.

Brandt gave the barest of nods, then turned back to his friends, clicked a command, and his colleagues silenced themselves in an instant, regaining their seats. The two Steaders who'd got up looked pleased with themselves, and with much fuss regained their seats.

The bridge shot of Micah receded to reveal an open section of space, halfway to Esperia. Gabriel's golden attack fleet burst into the space just as two of Micah's vermillion Blaze destroyers popped out of transit and opened fire. Petra had studied enough of transit hyper-math to know that two ships on a converging vector would both be pushed back into normal space-time by their bow waves nullifying the warp effect, like two waves colliding and cancelling each other out. But what was Micah playing at? In a straight, evenly matched fight, Genners always won against Steaders.

Gabriel's fifteen Hawks dodged the much larger Blaze destroyers' particle beam sweeps, even when Micah's simulated generals used coordinated lattices, but the Hawks couldn't get close enough to fire. Petra figured it was a matter of time before one or two Hawks would be hit. But then Gabriel's Starpiercer shot off at an angle, as if running away. One of the Blazes turned in pursuit, and Petra saw what was coming. "Nice one, Gabe," she uttered under her breath, as his ship spun around and micro-jumped, evading the beams and punching straight through both destroyers' hulls. Every Genner, Youngblood or not, was on their feet yelling and whooping. Through the melee, she regarded Micah again. He hardly followed the battle. *What are you up to, Uncle?*

She sighed and walked forward. Small as she was, the runt in the Genner litter as she called herself to save everyone else the trouble, she made her way nimbly towards the front, a little to the side. She watched Gabriel's beautiful face, calm as marble, blond locks tumbling down to his shoulders. Virginia, Gabriel's tall, tawny-haired girlfriend, glanced in her direction, so Petra switched instead to staring at Sandy, Gabriel's mother, and her partner Ramires. Though Sandy held Ramires' hand throughout, and cheered along as Gabriel's forces outwitted Micah's, Sandy's eyes often flicked towards Micah's inert face. Although Petra was a natural at reading people, she couldn't work out what was going on behind Sandy's eyes.

Gabriel's ship and his Hawks winked out – not bothering to engage Micah's foundering destroyers – for the last transit toward Esperia. She had no clue how Gabriel would face down an Axion Class Battleship with a Starpiercer, but knew he must have a good plan. His Hawks could take out the Reapers, even though they were outnumbered more than six to one.

Petra's gaze again swept over the expectant faces in the dome. Everyone knew what was hanging in the balance. Gabriel wanted to hunt down the Alicians as soon as Quarantine came down. Micah had said for years that they weren't ready, but she'd heard that some of the Council members were wavering as the end of Quarantine approached. If Micah lost this simulation, there would be more defections towards Gabriel's ambitions, represented by Ramires in Council. Colonel Vasquez, the militia commander, would never vote against Micah, but others could be persuaded.

She and her fellow Genners outstripped their human parents on every parameter and desperately sought their own destiny, their freedom. Technically, no parent could force their genned child to do anything, nor win any argument with them. But emotionally – though branded even by their parents as cold fish – the Genners needed the stamp of approval from their elders. Most of all, though few would care to admit it, they needed it from Micah, who had continued to win these matches against the odds each year. She'd tried to tell him the day before when she'd cornered him arriving for a Council meeting by the rear entrance...

"I thought Presidents wanted to be seen, Uncle."

Micah frowned. "I'm late, Petra."

Leaning against the wall, Petra glanced at her antique watch, a present he'd given her on her eighteenth birthday three months ago. "Not quite, actually."

Micah shook his head. "What's on your mind?"

She jerked a thumb towards a poster next to her advertising the duel. "Why do you do this every year?"

He sighed. "Ramires, Vasquez and I developed the simulated battles seven years ago to prepare you Genners for the eventuality of attack, either in Esperia's system or in deep space."

"But why you? Why the President? Why not Vasquez, for example? He's the military leader in the absence of Blake."

"Maybe –"

"I'll tell you what I think, Uncle." She gave him a measured stare. "I think you don't like being President anymore. I don't blame you, no one would. This annual ritual isn't exactly an election, but if you lost, it might get you off the hook eventually, maybe at the next poll."

Micah folded his arms. "Where's this going, Petra, because I really don't have much time."

She pushed off the wall and walked right up to him. "This contest means a lot to us Genners, especially the Youngbloods. You've never lost a match, and none of us know how you've kept it up all these years, especially now we're maturing, reaching our intellectual peak. But Gabriel has to win it fair and square. Don't you dare lose on purpose. None of us would ever forgive you. Especially me." She backed away. "You'd better go, Uncle."

Micah nodded. "Don't worry, Petra. I have zero intention of letting him win."

She hadn't expected Micah to cheat, though. Maybe it was for the Steaders; they needed Micah to win, to remind them they weren't obsolete. The day Gabriel beat Micah would be the beginning of the end for ordinary folk. Added into the mix, the Steaders wanted to hang onto their kids, especially since the Alicians had already robbed them of so much. But as she gazed at her Genner colleagues, her friends, she knew it was time, time for their parents and Micah to let them go. She gazed toward the stage, to the two inert figures, settling on the younger one. *Come on Gabe!*

Petra was just wondering where Micah's drones had gone, when she saw Gabriel's fleet drop out of transit again, approaching something that looked like a mist. *Uh-oh.* Five Genners were on their feet again in loud protest: not only did Micah somehow have Gabriel's flight plan, he was actually tracking Gabriel in Transpace – which wasn't technically possible, even by cheating. But it didn't matter for now: the rule was, once the simulation started, it was played out till the end. She watched as a silver hail of drones raced towards Gabriel's fleet.

But soon the Genners were cheering Gabriel's Hawks on as they raked across the frontline of drones that should have torn them apart. His five lead Hawks pinpointed the laser-armed Shuriken, despite the drones' erratic avoidance manoeuvres, with amazing speed and accuracy, as if the spiked mines were drifting in space. The Hawks doused them with rapid pulse fire, lighting them up like fire-crackers. Hundreds of spheres winked out of existence, the digital scoreboard for Micah's diminishing resources blurring in an effort to keep up. As the five lead Hawks'beam weapons overheated, they peeled back, allowing the next five to push through seamlessly and open fire. Gabriel's Hawks kept up this rotation for a full minute, destroying more than half of Micah's drones. Petra noticed even the hard-liners amongst the Steaders were impressed with their genetically-enhanced offspring. Valiant as the Hawk pilots were, however, the swarm of mines began to close around them like an engulfing antibody. A section of drones within the cloud fell behind Gabriel and suddenly attacked the rear wave of recovering Hawks, obliterating three of them before the middle wave could fend them off.

There's too many, Gabe.

Gabriel's Starpiercer veered away from the swarm, allowing the Hawks to shelter on its leeward side, then his ship whiplashed back into the heart of the drone storm, three Hawks in tight formation at its rear. Petra held her breath, thinking this was a suicide run, but Gabriel unleashed hidden cables anchored to his hull. As his ship began to spin, the cable-ends glowed white-hot, flailing outwards, lacerating the attacking drones, carving a boiling corridor through the drone-cloud's centre. *Anti-matter! Way to go, Gabe!*

* * *

Micah watched Gabriel's flawless performance. But it wasn't enough. Together with Vasquez and Ramires, Micah had devised these annual games with one sole objective: to train Genners, to ready them for battle. But the odds were always stacked against them, because even upgraded to what Grid Society called Level Four, with a potential to develop to Level Five in generations to come, that's how it would always be outside Esperia's small system, out in the Grid. Still, Micah knew he could only hold the Genners back so long. Yet time and again, whilst Gabriel and the others excelled at tactics and strategic planning, they shied away from the tough calls and sacrifices necessary in any field situation. He knew it was because their group was tight-knit and small; Gabriel never wanted to lose anyone. But that was a colossal blind-spot, one an adversary like the Alicians would see and exploit fast.

He turned up the heat.

* * *

Petra heard gasps as Micah's Reapers appeared in stealth-mode, black shadows against the dark tapestry of space, only visible by the occlusion of stars, engaging the nine other Hawks now on the opposite side of the drone cloud. At first the Reapers were no match for the reflexes of the Genner pilots; in less than a minute half the Reapers were cut down without a single Hawk casualty. Petra managed a subdued punch in the air.

Then the dome went eerily quiet as the remaining Reapers did something no one had seen before. If any Reaper got close to a Hawk, it exploded its engines and detonated all its weapons, sending debris in all directions. Because they were dark, it looked as if space was mined, random explosions spattering around the Hawks. Soon five Hawks were damaged enough to slow them down. Petra guessed what was coming. Two Blaze destroyers appeared. Steader cheers competed with Genner expletives as a broiling dogfight erupted before their eyes, particle beams criss-crossing the holo-screen.

That was when she detected a shift in the Shuriken pattern and saw the deeper layer in Micah's plan. She pushed through to the ring, and rushed towards Gabriel's chair, clicking a command to Brandt above the din. He heard it, and blocked Vasquez' attempt to intercept her. Virginia's eyes were steel, but she remained seated. Petra reached Gabriel's side, noticing a single bead of sweat clinging to his temple. She spoke in clipped Hremsta: "Compression wave; jump now; higher goal," then turned to the holoscreen, ignoring Vasquez' glare.

The Shuriken were no longer in a loose cloud formation, but were in concentric circles, cocooning Gabriel's Starpiercer and its attendant three Hawks. The outer sphere of drones flashed blinding white, then the next one followed suit, then the next. It happened so fast, and the light pulses were so intense, that everyone in the auditorium shrouded their eyes momentarily. Two seconds later, darkness flooded back in. Through blotchy vision, Petra searched for Gabriel's ship, but could only see a vast area of carnage and scorched metal.

Brandt pointed at Gabriel's scorecard and cheered. "He escaped!" Petra let out a long breath, and felt Sandy's hand squeeze her arm.

Petra turned back to the holo to watch the remaining Hawks fight the destroyers and Reapers till the end, against impossible odds. When the last of the Hawks was destroyed, all the Genners clicked a single Hremsta word, Petra too, raising her right fist in the air. The Steaders all knew what it was, a word that translated as "Honour in life, honour in death." As the slightly dazed Genner Hawk pilots came out from under their headsets on the other edge of the ring, Vasquez saluted them. A number of other men and women, Steaders no less, stood and followed suit. *That's a first.* She turned back to Virginia, only to meet a cool stare, before Gabriel's girlfriend turned and pushed her way back through the crowd. Petra shrugged, and took Virginia's seat, and gazed straight ahead.

Within seconds, Gabriel's Starpiercer was thrust out of Transpace again by the two Blaze destroyers that had just eradicated most of Gabriel's Hawks. Destroyer jump range was farther than a Starpiercer's, but she still didn't see how Micah was doing this. How had he been able to track ships in transit, since, after the first encounter, Gabriel must have realised Micah had advance information, and would have altered his next transit vector? She wasn't alone; both Steaders and Genners were shouting unorthodox and unrealistic tactics. Then she got it. The first two destroyers must have tagged Gabriel's Starpiercer, probably via coded micro-debris from their hulls clinging to it when Gabriel tore through their hulls. Not for the first time, she wondered how Micah thought like a Genner.

This time Gabriel did not turn to fight, and instead bore onwards into a nearby solar system, unable to pull away from the closing destroyers. The three remaining attendant hawks, knowing they would hold Gabriel back from reaching his maximum speed, bled away from the Starpiercer and headed back towards the lead destroyer. But it was futile – they were incinerated in the beam-fire before they could inflict any damage or even slow down the destroyers. Gabriel aimed straight for the sun. It had been a hot discussion topic with the Ossyrians as to whether the Starpiercer could really live up to its name. Petra twisted around for a moment, noted that the entire audience was on its feet, eyes glued to the chase scene. She joined them.

As Gabriel approached the point of no return, with the destroyers almost in firing range, he wavered to the left, then swung right, accelerating into a hard curve. The destroyers had momentarily adjusted direction to catch Gabriel, and now had to swing back. But they were less manoeuvrable, and laboured hard to make the course correction. All three ships skated along the lick of the sun's corona, and Petra could only imagine the stresses on the hull and engines. Gabriel's ship jettisoned all its cables. The lead destroyer caught several of them, atomizing the front half of the ship and flinging fireballs into the tandem destroyer, tearing off one of its engines, sending it careening down into the sun. Gabriel's ship pulled away, and then jumped back into Transpace.

Unanimous applause broke out, but it sputtered as a quadrant of the star-field shifted, as if there had been a glitch in the holosim. Not everyone had seen it, but as the noise died down, two ugly black scars, rips in the fabric of space, opened up some way out from Esperia's sun. All eyes darted first to Micah's avatar returning to his battle chair on the bridge, then to Gabriel, who, in his last transit, was oblivious to something that had happened ahead of his ship. Petra couldn't warn him this time, not while he was in transit.

Petra realized she had really hoped Gabriel would win this time. The Genners had earned it; deserved it. But Micah obviously had one more trick. She did the hyper-math in her head to predict where Gabriel would drop out of transit. Even before she finished the calcs she'd been able to do since seven years of age, she knew where he would arrive, and glanced towards the two remaining Blaze destroyers on the other side of Esperia's larger moon.

People quietened down as the holo zoomed in for the final showdown. If Micah had miscalculated by even a fraction, Gabriel would have had his target right there in front of him, with only a single battleship to fight. But she knew Micah hadn't faltered, his strategy had been orchestrated with ruthless precision. Petra folded her arms, and stared at her adopted uncle, realizing she didn't know him as well as she thought.

The two destroyers began blasting a focused beam on the moon's surface, interspersed with 'burrower' nuclear torpedoes. Within seconds, rock spewed forth into space. The destroyers came about.

She knew now that Micah had used the remaining drones to explode two black hole mines close to the final transit route, creating a gravimetric shock wave; a ripple, in effect, but one strong enough to divert Gabriel's transit vector by half a million kilometres. As his Starpiercer leapt back into normal space, instead of having the planet before him and Micah's flagship in his sights, he met two destroyers head on, gun ports blazing. As yellow beams lit up space, Gabriel hardly had time to detect the dark avalanche streaming toward him from the moon. Pummelled by the rock, his ship was caught in the destroyers' crossfire. The Starpiercer was sliced in half.

A single, space-suited figure ejected from the disintegrating ship, amidst a collective intake of breath by the audience. Petra held herself, then noticed something blink onto the scoreboard; another Hawk had entered the game. She spotted Virginia sitting in one of the dummy simulation chairs on the other side of the stage. Petra turned back to the screen. Just as the destroyers moved in for the final kill, a single Hawk dropped out of transit for a few seconds, then disappeared again, snatching up the avatar of Gabriel with it. Petra smiled. *Way to go, girl.* She vacated her seat before Gabriel came to, avoided Sandy's searching stare, and headed toward the exit.

✻ ✻ ✻

Micah leant back heavily in his chair. He knew he should feel elation, but his overriding reaction was closer to nausea. He prayed he'd never have to do anything like this for real. But although Gabriel had lost the match, he had made the necessary sacrifices this time.

Micah would have preferred to remain inside the simulation till everyone had gone home, but no sooner had he thought it than he found himself 'back' in the dome.

Some of the Steaders were euphoric, cheering, but many were quiet. Micah gazed across to Gabriel, who was leaning forward, staring at the floor, a frown across his normally smooth brow. A phalanx of Youngbloods jumped onto the stage, placing themselves between Gabriel and Micah, with Brandt at their head. He jabbed a forefinger at Micah, shouting so that all could hear.

"You cheated, Micah, you got the location of our fleet. And black hole mines are illegal – "

"He won." Gabriel hadn't raised his voice, but it cut through Brandt's onslaught nonetheless, and Gabriel's cohorts turned to him, opening up a path between him and Micah. Gabriel stepped into the middle ground, and addressed everyone while staring at Micah. "It doesn't matter how: cheating, use of illegal weapons, whatever. War is war." He turned to the rest of the crowd, the Steaders, and his parents. "Once again we are reminded that we should be proud of what our elders can accomplish. We still have much to learn."

The dome fell silent. Micah couldn't judge the mood at that point: some pride, and maybe some mutual respect, which had been sorely missing in the increasing tension building during recent months. Gabriel turned to leave. Micah saw Sandy glaring at him, a look he knew too well.

"Wait," Micah said, rising to his feet. "Gabriel, everyone, I have three announcements to make." He cleared his throat. He'd rehearsed this over and over, to get the words exactly right, but he mentally binned his memorized speech, and said the first thing that came into his mind. "I cheated." He met the eyes of the Steaders, other councilors, people he'd known and worked with for a generation. "I'd do it again to save this planet. And our enemies would do a lot worse. I rigged the simulation yesterday to deliver me the enemy's position. But a real enemy can use various means to achieve the same end. A surprise attack isn't any guarantee when facing a more advanced enemy. Surprise is a two-way street when it comes to war." *Especially with the Alicians.* He remembered how they'd betrayed humanity, and stayed one step ahead, all the way. He faced Gabriel.

"But it says something when the only way I can beat you is to cheat." Micah tried not to look in Sandy's direction. "So, as President, by the powers vested in me, I now declare formally that you Genners are of age. The oldest of you is eighteen, but we all know that by the age of twelve you surpass us intellectually. I declare that any Genner at least sixteen years old is to be considered a full citizen of Esperia, with full voting rights." Micah could barely hear the end of his sentence in the din that erupted. Some of the Council Members kept quiet – this had of course been discussed at length with them – most of them thought it was time, and agreed to let Micah decide the right moment to announce it. But Micah had two more surprises to unveil.

Gabriel stared back at him, and nodded, a rare smile sculpting his lips. Ramires leapt up into the ring and shook Micah's hand, as he patted Gabriel's shoulder. Micah nodded, risking a glance once more in Sandy's direction, detecting one eyebrow raised slightly higher than the other.

Gabriel raised a hand, and waited for the shouting to die down. He stood close to Micah, his dark eyes glinting. "Mr. President, then I formally request that we be given a ship to hunt down and kill the Alicians who helped slaughter seven billion people."

Micah paused before speaking. "That's for Council to decide. And I hereby nominate you to Council." There were gasps from some of the Steaders; a Genner had never sat in Council. Nominating Gabriel to Council was partly intended as a delaying tactic, aimed at stopping the Youngbloods from stealing one of the space-craft as soon as Quarantine came down. But Micah reckoned Gabriel would work that out pretty fast.

"Seconded," Ramires said.

"Thirded," Vasquez added, sealing the vote.

Micah nodded, and spoke just to Gabriel. "Welcome to democracy, good luck with it."

Gabriel folded his arms "Are you still going to block me in Council?"

Micah turned to the crowd and raised his hands high, and shouted. "Third," he waited for the noise to abate, then spoke quieter, but with a firm tone. "My third announcement is that I'm retiring from the Presidency and the Council, effective immediately." He rushed on.

"Colonel Vasquez and Antonia have agreed to look after things until the next election in three months' time." Without another word, he jumped down off the stage, and made his way through the crowd toward the exit.

By the time he got outside it was dark. Petra sat astride a skimmer, revving the engine. She unhooked an earpiece. "Get aboard, Uncle. I'm of age now, according to you, so you can't send me home, and anyway you promised my mother you'd look after me, which means we have to stick together."

Micah sighed. "And where are you taking me?"

Petra tilted her head. "Didn't you just say we surpass you intellectually at twelve? We're going where you want to go, of course. Shimsha. Spider central."

Micah heard others coming out of the dome. "Okay, but I drive." "Genner eyesight is better than –"

"I can see in the dark."

She cocked her head. "You're serious, aren't you?"

"Move. Your mother – your biological one – would beat me to a pulp if she knew how badly you'd been raised these past couple of years." He swung his leg over the seat in front of Petra, switched off the skimmer's lights, and took off down the valley, his resident automatically supplying him with night vision.

As they left Esperantia, he accelerated into the darkness, so that Petra had to shout above the wind. "We're going to see Blake, aren't we?" Her voice was light; she'd always liked speed, he remembered, having taken her on desert rides more than once.

Micah nodded.

"I heard he still believes Mum's alive," she shouted.

Micah gripped the throttle harder. It wasn't necessarily good news if Kat was still alive, given who had abducted her and a Hohash two years ago, somehow managing to break through a Level Twelve Quarantine barrier. If Kat *was* still breathing somewhere, she sure as hell wouldn't be having a good time of it.

CHAPTER 2 – PRISONER

Beneath a lapis sky skewered by towering redwoods, Kat dodged the pine spears raining down on her. Each one whistled on its fifty-metre descent before puncturing the mossy ground with a dull 'pfft', spattering musky soil into the air around her. *Bastard trees!* She hurdled a root rising from the spongy undergrowth, then ducked as a branch swung down to head height – it would have knocked her out cold. Up ahead a small clearing invited, but she knew better – the shards of pine, dropping like weighted arrows as they tipped off the trees, would get her for sure if she fled into the open. She should have done as she was told and stayed by the lake. Then Tomar wouldn't be dead.

Kat wasn't as fit as she used to be, but adrenaline had kicked in, and she ran fast, keeping close to the broad, gnarled trunks in the forest that was trying to kill her. She imagined snarling faces in the bark's twisted patterns, but she knew the forest wasn't highly intelligent, barely self- aware; just reacting to something which didn't belong in its midst. As she lingered next to an old bough, trying to catch her breath, a vine curled up her leg. She pulled out her knife and rammed it hard into the tree. Kat doubted the forest felt pain, at least not at the level of her small blade, but she needed to make a statement. She yanked her leg out of the coil and worked out her sprint path, squinting through the branches and leaves that surrounded her, trying to cocoon her into a compost grave. A jet engine flared overhead – Louise, her captor these past two years, searching for her – another reason to stay under the canopy.

Kat bolted away from the malevolent fir, buffeted by leaves as the wind swirled through the branches; the trees used it to their advantage, and she had to dive and roll on the mossy ground as a gust drove wooden claws down towards her. Just as her head was lifting from the ground, a patch of violet daisies squirted virulent pollen, catching the left side of her face. Pain seared through her left eyeball. While staggering blind for only a moment, a branch from behind connected with her head likea baseball bat and sent her sprawling.

Thick vines lost no time in trapping her ankles. Struggling onto her knees, she fished for her knife and found its sheath empty, the glimmer of her blade out of reach, sinking into the undergrowth as if it were quicksand. She looked upwards: four massive redwoods loomed overhead, swaying in the gale above, closing around her. She knew what was next. Considering her options, she decided she had none, other than becoming fertilizer, probably the fate of many an alien landing on this inviting, green, and thoroughly deadly planet. Sharp cracks above announced a shower of spears on its way. Kat kept her eyes open. Rather than pointlessly placing her hands over her head, she folded her arms, spat at the ground, then held her breath.

Two boots thudded in front of her. She tried to think of it as good news. The air around her shimmered, just as the wooden javelins pounded like hail on the shield her captor had just erected.

"Pleased to see me?" Louise's voice was deep, sultry, mocking as usual.

"Tomar's dead," Kat replied. That *was* a good thing, given what Louise would have done to him had he survived; Louise wasn't the forgiving type, especially when it came to betrayal.

Louise knelt down, her eyes level with Kat's. "I left the other four Mannekhi at the lakeside."

Kat's grey eyes flared. "They had nothing to do with it. It was only Tomar who –
"

"Your word that you won't try again. Or else they stay here on this planet."

Kat turned her head away. She hadn't cared much for the Mannekhi, human-looking companions but for their all-black eyes – except Tomar – but they wouldn't last a night on this lethal forest planet, and even if they did, they'd starve to death within a week. Louise didn't seem to be paying attention – the Alician-Q'Roth hybrid treated everything as a game, one she wasn't that interested in, except when she might lose. Then she could get unbelievably nasty.

Kat nodded.

"Say it."

Kat looked Louise in the eyes. "I won't try to escape again. You have my word." She waited a second while Louise watched her, like a cobra deciding whether to strike or not. "Okay, Louise, I've had enough countryside for one day. Are we done here?"

Louise smiled. "You are more amusing than the others, I'll give you that." She pulled out a pistol and fired at the vines trapping Kat's legs, releasing her. She held out a hand to help Kat up. "Let's go home, shall we?"

Kat found her legs were numb below the knee, and she had to accept Louise's help to get up. She wanted to spit again, but decided not to push her luck.

Back onboard the long range Q'Roth Marauder, Kat met with the four remaining Mannekhi crew in one of the many jade-coloured walled chambers with no furniture save a table extruded at one end, too high to be of much use for non-Q'Roth passengers. Q'Roth never sat, apparently. The Mannekhi appeared so humanoid, except for their pure-black eyes, that Kat wondered if they were somehow related. Like her, they wore grey one-piece suits, purely functional affairs.

Kat made the first move. "I'm sorry about Tomar, really." She was. It had been his idea – he'd thought they could escape. But nobody except Louise had known the nature of the forest, and he'd been speared in the first five minutes of leaving the lake.

The bald Elder, Tarish, fingered his short white beard. "We thank you for getting us back aboard."

Aramisk, the only female in the Mannekhi group, glared at Kat from beneath a dark mop of hair. She flexed her arm muscles, like a male gorilla. "If this precious bitch hadn't tried to escape... Where were you going to go, anyway? Did you even have a plan? You humans may look like us but I can see why the Q'Roth cull on humanity was sanctioned."

Kat advanced, her nostrils flaring, readying her fists to see just how tough Aramisk's bony cheeks were, how easily her thick lips would split.

Tarish stepped between them, held up his hand. He turned to Aramisk, bowed his head slightly, said "Forgive me, Aramisk," then slapped her right cheek hard.

Kat winced. She'd been stuck with this group for the past nine months, and still found their culture shocking. Mannekhi valued free speech and discipline in equal measure. She wouldn't fancy being brought up as a Mannekhi child. Tomar had been the youngest, a rebel by Mannekhi standards.

Aramisk recovered, bowed, and gave the customary reply. "Thank you, Elder, for reminding me of my place."

Kat tried again for the umpteenth time to reach them, wondering if their blood debt to her, for making sure Louise didn't leave them to die on the forest planet, might incline them to listen this time. The Mannekhi had chosen Qorall's side, and these four – plus Tomar – had been an advance scouting party tracking down the almost mythical Kalarash known as Hellera, last seen in the Ant Nebula. Louise was delivering them to Qorall's generals with a piece of critical information they wouldn't even tell her, which was maybe why she had a cavalier attitude to their survival.

Kat spoke up. "Qorall is using you, you know that don't you? Once he gets his way, he'll cast the Mannekhi aside, assuming there's anything left of the galaxy by the time he's finished."

Tarish nodded heavily, as always. She knew from Tomar that this wasn't just an affectation. Mannekhi looked human, but they were far more advanced. Tomar had explained to her one night how Mannekhi considered premises from all angles, playing them backwards and forwards in time with multiple what-if scenarios; like four-dimensional chess. Humans, by comparison, seemed to be guessing all the time, failing to include vital pieces of information or likely events that didn't fit the view they wanted.

Tomar had made love to her that night. At least in that sphere of activity they hadn't been too different. That was the first and only time, just a few days ago, before Louise had decided to go down to the forest- planet to re-stock certain rare minerals, or maybe just to stretch her legs.

Kat missed Tomar, though they'd barely known each other. He'd been her first real emotional contact in the two years since Louise had taken her prisoner. She focused her mind back on the issue at hand.

Kat appreciated that Tarish was weighing not just the words, but the context, motives and personality of the speaker, and factoring in knowledge about her cultural origins. Mannekhi did not waste words; there was never any banter. Maybe that was their problem, Kat mused; this crew is too damned serious.

"Try to imagine," Tarish began, with a voice that commanded absolute attention, "an alien occupation lasting your entire people's history. Sponsorship is a difficult process. Over millennia, it gets inside your cultural DNA. Growing up knowing that you are not considered good enough for anything but the Grid's menial work. Our earliest artifacts and artistry from fifty thousand years ago show us as subservient to other races. It has shaped our identity."

He approached her, and placed a smooth palm on her shoulder. With any other man, except maybe Blake or Zack, she'd have brushed the hand off immediately, but this Elder – his sincerity and humility were like nothing she'd ever encountered before.

He smiled, the way she imagined a saint might, except for the glimmering all-black eyes. "For the first time in our entire history, we have been given respect by a higher order species. We are on the winning side now. If you were us, would you not take this opportunity?"

Louise entered the chamber, and the four Mannekhi immediately dropped to one knee. Kat folded her arms.

Louise walked up to her. "You should listen to him, Katrina."

"You should listen to yourself, Louise." It was a game they played.

Something ugly flared behind Louise's eyes, and Kat found herself on the floor, her chin smarting. Goddammit, Louise was quick; Kat hadn't even seen the blow coming.

"You are too familiar with me. You will address me by my formal Q'Roth designation as the Mannekhi do. You will address me as Arctura." Louise wandered around the kneeling, heads-bowed group, and paused behind Aramisk. The fingers of her left hand traced the girl's chin, then cupped it in her palm, the other hand on the nape of the girl's sturdy neck.

Kat leapt to her feet. "No... Please, Lou −" She met the part-woman-mostly-Q'Roth's eyes, taking in the steadfast look on Aramisk's face, despite her trembling lower lip.

Kat knelt on one knee. "Please...Arctura."

Louise's fingers traced Aramisk's cheek, stroked her hair, and then let go of her. "You've come a long way today, Katrina. There is hope for you yet. You and I will dine together tonight, there is much to discuss." She stood in front of Tarish, and lifted up her palms. As one, the Mannekhi rose. "Elder," she said, "Your loyalty today has not gone unnoticed." She left the room.

Kat got up, wishing one of the spears had gotten her earlier. She stared at the floor. Two sandaled feet appeared before her. Six toes per foot; the other difference, she remembered.

Aramisk's voice was firm. "Thank you. But you must understand, I wish you had died today. Because of you, Tomar is dead."

She reached out and touched Kat's face; another gesture Kat had noticed, a way of saying, "listen to me", or rather, "I need to ensure you hear my words." But Aramisk's fingers were iron. The others departed while she held Kat's chin. Kat knew that by custom she had to wait until the speaker let go. When the others were gone, Aramisk continued in a lower, less aggressive tone. "You cared for him, didn't you?"

Kat realized the power of this form of exchange. She could not lie, and emotions rose to the surface. Her eyes misted. She said nothing.

"We Mannekhi are neither stupid nor blind. We look for opportunities." She let go of Kat's face. "When the time comes, we will see whose side we choose."

Alone, Kat sat on the cold floor. For the first time in days, she thought about her daughter Petra, wondering how she would look now, two years older. And Antonia, her wife. Kat missed her. But the face she kept coming back to was Micah's. They'd never got on, especially since he'd originally been interested in Antonia. But she'd been counting the days carefully over the past two years, and knew Quarantine would be coming down very soon. Blake was getting on in years and would not leave his beloved spiders. Gabriel would go after Sister Esma and the Alicians − that much bloodlust could not have abated in such a short space of time. Micah, though − he would come looking. Not just for her, but for Louise, because he knew, as Kat did now, that Louise was the larger threat.

But the question arose in her mind, as it had almost every day since her capture, of what Louise wanted with her, and where exactly she was taking her. Not for the first time, she wondered if it was better not to know.

Kat was roused from her slumber as ocean blue light drifted into her room, rippling over the dark walls. She rubbed her eyes. "About time." It had been three weeks. "You know I worry about you spending so much time with that bitch."

The Hohash, an alien artefact she'd first encountered on Eden, was about the same height as she was, its oval mirror-like flow-surface bordered by a golden tube. It hovered within arms' reach of her bedside. Its fluidic surface mimicked Pacific rollers, one of her favourite vistas, reminding her of her surfing days with her older sister.

"What's new?"

The Hohash could not make sounds, but had learned to lip-read human speech. Abruptly its face changed to a star chart, showing the entire galaxy from above. The colour of more than half changed to deep red: Qorall-controlled space. Worse, a finger of scarlet edged towards a yellow-highlighted star, where Esperia, and Kat's loved ones lay, presumably oblivious to approaching Armageddon.

"Zoom in please."

She did a rough count of the stars between the front and Esperia. Six months, at most. "Where are we?" Her heart sank as a blue dot flashed, deep inside Qorall space. "Do you know where Qorall is?" A band of orange appeared. It included many star systems – so the Hohash didn't know exactly where Qorall was.

Kat dreaded asking the next question. She cleared her throat, and found herself closing her eyes as she asked it. "Where is Pierre?" She prayed he would still be out there somewhere, even though he was no longer *her* Pierre, and had advanced to God-alone knew what Level on the Grid scale. She held her breath and opened her eyes. A purple dot, between the front and Esperia. She breathed a sigh of relief. "Do you know what he's up to?" Her Hohash had never answered this question, though Pierre evidently had one on his ship.

To her surprise, she was shown an image inside Pierre and Ukrull's compact ship. She saw the Ranger Ukrull, a big, reptilian alien with disgusting table manners, and a perfectly silver Pierre – her former lover and Petra's father, inadvertently advanced to Level Ten, shedding his emotions along the way. The Hohash was showing her far more than usual, so Kat decided to push her luck. "Petra? Antonia? Micah?"

She half-fell, half-clambered off the bed down onto the hard floor on her knees as a series of images flooded across its face. She gripped the golden edges of the Hohash, her arms trembling, as she saw her daughter, laughing with Micah, and then Antonia, for the first time in two years. Pride surged in her breast: Petra was quite the young woman, Antonia as regal as ever. Was that the first tinge of grey on Micah's hair? She wiped tears away, not wishing to miss a second of it. Abruptly the images ceased. Mustard light flooded into her room, Louise's silhouette framed in the doorway.

"Katrina, I made a deal with the Hohash when I first brought you aboard. It likes you, and I made it clear that if it showed you any images without my permission, I would blind you; you don't need sight for what I have in mind for you."

Kat felt winded; these past two years, she'd thought the Hohash didn't trust her anymore. She turned to face Louise, letting go of the Hohash's rim. "So, why now, Arctura?"

Louise folded her arms – something Kat had never seen her do before.

"I need your cooperation... Kat. If you work with me – I mean really cooperate, then the Hohash is free to show you all the images it can. I will not intervene."

Kat turned back to the Hohash's dulled surface, its familiar oil-on- water swirl of browns. She knew the Hohash had an extremely limited emotional repertoire, being an intelligent device rather than a species. Still, she wondered how it felt about the situation. She guessed she'd never know, so it was her decision alone.

Her chest felt tight, but there was a longing deep in her belly. She felt like she'd been in prison the past two years, ripped from her friends and family, from everything. She'd become a ghost. She didn't want to help Louise, let alone Qorall, and yet... she had needs.

She remembered Tarish's words, and knew that a Mannekhi would weigh all this up in an instant and come to a different conclusion. But Kat wasn't Mannekhi. She traced a finger over the Hohash's mirror surface. Louise had waited all this time, not to break her spirit, but to bend it to her will.

Forgive me, Micah.

She stood up. "What do want me to do, Arctura?"

Kat stayed up all night. Hellera, the last Kalarash in the galaxy. Not myth after all. A Level Nineteen female, one of the so-called Progenitors who had breathed sentient life into the galaxy, the original masters of the Tla Beth, the Grid's current rulers, and sworn enemies of Qorall. Qorall wanted to know where she was. Apparently the Mannekhi had tracked her to the Ant Nebula but she had moved to one of three potential locations – Tarish had finally told Louise earlier that evening. Hellera possessed a Hohash, for sure – the Kalarash had devised them – and Kat could communicate with Hohash...

Hohash were data-plexers – omnipaths – capable of receiving all sorts of signals and processing them, and interfacing with other Hohash, of which there were not many left – a few on Esperia, maybe a few others scattered across the galaxy, and one with Hellera. And Kalaran. That's where she had been when Louise captured her, in Esperia's caves, together with the Hohash, looking for anything left behind by the only other Kalarash, who had left the planet just before Quarantine. Micah had sent her to the caves to look, and Louise had somehow gotten past the barrier.

Kat realized her hands were clenched into fists, her lips squeezed tight, and released them. She'd had so much anger, had spent so much time working on a way to kill Louise. But Louise – Arctura – whatever, was bloody tough, and might look human on the outside, but inside she'd been re-engineered by the Q'Roth more than any other Alician.

She sat back. At least she had something to do. She had been accessing all sorts of war reports from both sides – the Hohash translated everything for her – but nothing yet, not even a mention of Hellera or a Kalarash. She thought of Antonia, of Micah, and her former captain, Blake. What would *you* want me to do?

For Antonia, it would be simple – come home; not so easy. For Blake, kill Louise; ditto. But Micah. He could be devious. Then it came to her. It was as blindingly obvious as it was dangerous: play both sides.

She accessed the Hohash again, interfacing with it via the node in her brain, and began surfing the information streams again, but this time she was looking for something different.

She missed breakfast. She skipped lunch. Aramisk came to check up on her and forced her to break off for ten minutes to drink some water and take a shower. By early evening, Kat found something. Although the Q'Roth had culled humanity, and so were her sworn enemies, they now worked for the Tla beth, and were actually on the 'good side', fighting against Qorall, as were the Alicians, though they seemed to have their own agenda.

She accessed encrypted Q'Roth battle reports – Hohash could decrypt anything, it seemed – and found several obscure references to a human. The Q'Roth were losing most if not all battles against Qorall's forces. She couldn't bring herself to feel sorry for them, even if it meant that Qorall was getting closer to Esperia. But this reference to *Jorann* kept cropping up. Apparently, now a low-ranking general commanding a battleship, this Jorann was once human. After cross-referencing many reports and notes, her mouth dropped open as she realized who Jorann really was, who he used to be.

Kat leapt off the bed and paced in her room. Here was a potential ally, someone who could help Esperia from the outside. But apparently, although he knew he used to be human, Jorann had no recollection of who he used to be, of his real name, and had been re-engineered into a full Q'Roth warrior. Her heart beat fast, nonetheless. Jorann could be the best hope to protect Esperia when Quarantine came down, though apparently he was about to engage one of Qorall's main fleets. But what could she do with the information? She bit into her knuckles.

Louise appeared at Kat's doorway.

"Not now!" Kat shouted, then added, "Sorry, Arctura, but I may have something, a possible lead on Hellera, but I need time to think." *And come up with a good lie.* Louise glared, but left without another word, sealing the door behind her.

Kat went back to the Hohash, grabbing its rim. "Pierre. You have to tell Pierre." No, that won't work, Pierre can't access a Hohash. "Ukrull – the Ranger; show him." Kat closed her eyes and opened her mind, focusing on the Jorann information, his last known location, and a single word – his original name.

She collapsed back on her bed, exhausted. At first there was a sense of elation – she'd done something, and maybe it could make a difference. But her loneliness – something she kept at bay every day – fuelled by fatigue, surfaced and threatened to overwhelm her. She lay thinking of her wife Antonia, longing for her soft touch and tender kisses. For once, she let the emotions out. She pulled the cover up over her shoulders. While the Hohash showed her images of rain falling on the sea, Kat fell asleep on a wet pillow.

CHAPTER 3 – SIDES

If Jorann had still been human he'd have shaken himself. The Q'Roth had been his sworn enemy, that much he remembered; he'd nuked a quarter of a million of the warriors in the last days of the fall of Earth. Then he'd been captured and offered a stark choice – join forces or die. He'd spat at Sister Esma, told her where to go, and she'd obliged him by venting him into space. But she'd downloaded his memories beforehand and taken enough DNA to produce a hybrid clone. She told him later that the Q'Roth leaders usually got what they wanted – in this case his intuitive battle strategies. Initially they'd tested the clone without his memories, but its performance had been rudimentary. So they'd uploaded his personality, and he'd woken, surprised to be alive, and then disgusted at what they'd turned him into – a six-legged, black-carapaced three-metre-tall Q'Roth warrior.

His trapezoidal head had a lipless gash of a mouth that rarely opened, communication achieved instead by stone-like throat muscles that clicked and grated in Q'Roth language whose sound reminded him of rustling leaves and grinding rocks. Instead of eyes he had six vermillion slits, like razor cuts, arranged in two opposing sets sloping diagonally downwards toward the centre of his forehead. Although the slits occasionally oozed blood-like sweat, Q'Roth warriors could not cry. That suited Jorann just fine.

He only wished he could remember his human name.

"Bring the Hunters forward, they go in hot," he signaled the other battleships. There was no reply, no confirmation – Q'Roth war tactics were largely silent, they would only speak if they disagreed. But he knew they also disliked talking to him, let alone taking commands from a hybrid once-human. Yet this was his battle strategy, his call. Pride and prejudice were irrelevant today; if he had miscalculated, they would all be dead very soon.

For seven years he'd refused to cooperate with his Q'Roth captors. But they kept taking him on missions. He witnessed the inexorable slaughter as the invader Qorall slashed and burned his way across the galaxy, and Jorann knew where the remnants of humanity lay – right in Qorall's path. They wouldn't last a second. Four ships full of human cargo had fled the Q'Roth's culling of Earth eighteen years earlier, and without doubt still saw the Q'Roth and their Alician cohorts as their principal enemy. But Jorann had seen many species far more malevolent; he knew how brutal the galaxy could be, and Qorall put even those alien races to shame.

So, here he was, fighting alongside the species who had almost erased mankind. He even had command of a four hundred crew, kilometer-long battleship, sculpted from obsidian Scintarelli tree-metal and shaped like Thor's hammer, dripping with weapons turrets. If he'd wanted to, he could cause it to self-destruct or fire on the other Q'Roth ships and take out as many as possible. He had enough command overrides on the Bridge, and was alone – his lieutenants worked a deck below in Tactical. But futile bravado had never been his style. He'd learned that to survive in this galaxy you had to play the long game.

"Your guest is en route." A voice message from Granch, the senior commander, interrupted his thoughts. The fact that Granch had announced it fleet-wide was significant. Perhaps he finally trusted Jorann, or more likely he wanted all his troops to be focused and follow commands.   In any case, it was good that the 'guest' was en route; Jorann's whole strategy depended on it.

Jorann knew the nine other senior commanders never fully trusted him, despite his strong performance in the last dozen battles. He'd saved most of the fleet from near disaster in the Ossyrian sector less than a week ago, seconds after Qorall fired an anti-matter cluster into its sun, triggering a super-flare, engulfing four defending fleets and two of Jorann's destroyer squadrons unable to jump fast enough. Still, to his colleagues, Jorann was an aberration. One of them had even fired on Jorann's flagship a month earlier during a firefight. Qorall had surprised them all by launching planets through a wormhole at the third largest Q'Roth shipyard, after destabilising their cores to turn them into world-sized grenades. None of them, even the oldest Q'Roth warriors from the Antechratian Campaign five centuries earlier, had ever seen anything like this level of carnage or firepower. The errant commander who'd fired – luckily Jorann had just raised his shields – confessed his misdemeanour and took the honourable way out, piloting a Hunter vessel stacked with atomics deep into enemy space, taking out one of Qorall's supply convoys.

He checked his displays, densely packed with Q'Roth three- dimensional script no normal human could ever hope to fathom. Sixty seconds till they emerged and met the leading edge of Qorall's forces.

Jorann understood the Q'Roth sense of frustration – they were warriors, foot-soldiers of the highest calibre, space dog-fighters extraordinaire. But such skills were useless against Qorall's Inferno Class weaponry. Moreover, Qorall's strategy eluded the galaxy's indigenous species – he did not seem interested in the spoils of war, whether worlds, technologies, or resources, except for swelling the ranks of his armies and navies. Instead, he spread inexorably across the galaxy like a cancer. What perplexed Jorann in particular was that the arrowhead of Qorall's general front had from the start charted a course towards the new homeworld of humanity, Esperia. It didn't make sense: mankind – what was left of it – was as much a threat to Qorall as an ant was to a Q'Roth warrior. And yet through eighteen years, despite brief deviations, Qorall's forces held this course. Perhaps that was one reason the Q'Roth High Guard wanted to keep Jorann alive.

His ex-humanity lowered his standing amongst the commanders' ranks. He had no Q'Roth 'friends', and certainly never any female companionship – which would have been a step too far in any case. Despite being in the largest army in the galaxy, and having four hundred crewmembers on his ship under his command, he often felt completely alone. He'd learned to live with it, channeling his energies into battle tactics and strategies. That was all that kept him going; quite Q'Roth, he realized. But he sensed he had had a vibrant social life before, when human; a wife, friends, camaraderie. But there were so many holes in his memory, locked away somehow, the key being his original name. If only he could remember it. He didn't want to go to his grave as Jorann; he wanted his human name, whatever it was. Surely he deserved that much? But after eighteen years as a Q'Roth, and perhaps even as a military commander back on Earth, he knew that 'deserved' had nothing to do with it. And so he'd prefer his grave, if there ever was one, to be unmarked.

As with all front-line commanders, his nights were numbered. Yet the Q'Roth High Guard grew increasingly desperate – they had lost thirty- three battles in a row, more than eight thousand ships; they couldn't keep taking those kinds of losses. This mission was different. Jorann had outlined a new strategy, enlisting the aid of the mysterious Tla Beth, the very top layer of the Grid hierarchy, who were apparently pure energy creatures whose Homeworld remained a closely-guarded secret. One of them was venturing out from their hyper-dimensional safe haven where they strategized, moving ships and inter-stellar counter-measures on trans-dimensional maps that no species below Level Fifteen understood. The Q'Roth all but worshipped the Tla Beth, and if anything happened to this one... But that was why they'd recruited Jorann into their ranks in the first place, to think outside the sphere. He prayed his gambit would work.

The normally green display in front of him flashed blood red, and the Q'Roth equivalent of adrenaline surged through his arteries. Jorann deplored war and its inevitable carnage, but he nevertheless felt the thrill of battle he'd known so many times before. He'd always been a career soldier, and was never more alive than when his life was on the line, knowing he could be killed at any second. His upper claw hovered above the 'fire' button during the extended jump into Qorall-controlled space.

His fleet re-materialised as planned, the enemy's flotilla dead ahead, and he and nine other commanders unleashed the planet-breakers. Waves of energy whipped like fluorescent barbed wire at the darkly translucent, bubble-shaped shield protecting the enemy's ships. Secondary artillery fired automatically, spewing volleys of energy pulses and strange-matter- tipped missiles, which crashed into the energy barrier like psychedelic hail on glass. He hated using strange-matter weapons. Aside from their precarious nature – they sometimes 'went off' before being fired – they tended to rip the space-time fabric, leaving jagged potholes for any traffic transiting through the affected sector. But as the Q'Roth were in permanent retreat, that hardly mattered, and conventional atomics and anti-matter artillery seemed to have no effect on these shields. In any case, as had happened the last three times he'd encountered this enemy formation, the shield remained intact. The enemy's strategy was simple – they would wait until the Q'Roth forces had expended considerable firepower, then lower the shield and attack. Jorann's gash of a mouth opened a crack and a hiss issued forth.

As planned, five Q'Roth Hunter Class crab-shaped ships broke formation and hurtled toward the sphere. Ten other Q'Roth destroyers vectored particle weapons around the tightly-packed quintet, creating a halo of white plasma fire around them, as they converged toward a single point on the barrier's surface, inflicting the heat of a hundred suns. In eighteen years of warfare, no one had successfully breached one of these shields, and Qorall's army had remained unstoppable, conquering more than half the known galaxy, laying waste to any sector refusing to surrender.

Jorann's claw squeezed hard as the glare of the beams blotted out all the stars. *Now would be good...* On cue, his 'guest' appeared. A small Tla Beth single-occupant ship, iridescent blue and shaped like a gyroscope, popped into existence behind the five Q'Roth Hunters, sucked along in their wake. *Steady...* He'd not been able to 'talk' with the Tla Beth directly, having instead to explain his strategy through several layers of intermediaries. He accepted this state of affairs – after all, he was a mere Q'Roth, Level Six intelligence standard, and the Tla Beth were Level Seventeen. He'd never even seen one up close. He hoped the upward briefings had been effective.

Intel on the holo dashboard contained nothing but bad news: the barrier was holding. Their drenching of the shield with enough energy to rent apart a star was looking increasingly like a suicide dash. If any more Q'Roth ships joined in with their weapons, the radiation backlash would fry their compatriots. Still, he'd seen too many futile deaths.

He signalled, "Break off?" to Granch, but already guessed the answer, which remained unspoken. His suggestion was broadcast to all commanders simultaneously using the mind-plexing system the Tla Beth had granted them, enabling them to communicate and react as one. Humans could never use such augments, it would sound like a deafening cacophony and paralyse them; one of the advantages of being Level Six. He imagined his own standing amongst his commanders had dropped a notch for even suggesting aborting the charge.

Space appeared to ignite as the Hunters pummelled into the shield, vaporizing on impact, cremating their crews. *Fifty.* He always counted the dead; he'd never know their names, but the least he felt he could do was to recognize the sacrifice of those under his command. The explosion would have burned out his retinas if he'd still been human, but instead the six slits on his trapezoidal head oozed a little more vermillion than usual, rendering the scene blood red. He missed human vision, but then his Q'Roth senses allowed him to see what no human eye could have. Amidst the explosive swirl of plasma boiling off into space, the Tla Beth craft launched a missile of unknown origin directly at the glowing area of the barrier wall, which sprouted electric blue fractures, then shattered as the toy-like Tla Beth ship rammed it. Jorann's mouth-gash widened into something approaching a grin. *Fire and ice – smart bastards.*

Jorann wasted no time. His flagship and four other battleships supported by ten destroyers jumped according to a pre-ordered pattern, and punched their way through the fissure. *Finally!* A message from

Granch appeared fleet-wide, a staccato Q'Roth phrase translating as "Kill them all, no prisoners, leave nothing alive."

But as soon as Jorann was inside he knew something was wrong. His battleship stuttered, its engines faltered, losing speed. Black ships shaped like sea urchins approached, but the beam weapons he fired on them dispersed like a lamp in fog; letting loose the planet-breaker would simply backfire on his own ships. It took him a second to recognise what was happening: they weren't in normal space anymore – it looked like so-called 'empty' space, but it had a much higher *density.*

He ignored the storm of comms from other commanders; instinctively he knew what it was – he'd been a nuclear submarine commander back on Earth a lifetime ago, and knew how a craft handled in space, and in water. *They were in a very low density, transparent fluid.* Some of the Grid scientists had conjectured this possibility, how some form of unknown 'liquid space', presumably from Qorall's galaxy, could make the shield more resilient, offering internal pressure, and dampening any energy-based attack on it.

"Torpedoes!" he barked in Largyl 6, the formal Q'Roth command language. His battleship spattered the nearest enemy ship, and he relaxed as he saw hundreds of other Q'Roth-launched intelligent missiles to port and starboard, snaking their way through the invisible medium, homing onto their targets. He recognised the enemy ship design: *Mannekhi, Level Five.* So, they'd joined ranks with Qorall. Not surprising, they'd been treated like dirt by Grid Society for eons. But such defections bled away effort that should have been targeted at the real foe.

The Mannekhi ships returned fire, purple pulses spitting from their spines, unaffected by the fluidic space. He ignored the battering as the energy bursts slammed into his battleship, keeping one sensory slit focused on the damage indicator, dropping slowly from ninety-three per cent. At fifteen per cent his ship would implode. He leaned forward, two of his six slits trying to see what was behind the ranks of Mannekhi vessels. His battle instincts kicked in; he had a bad feeling...

The enemy sea urchin in front of him ignited, a third of its spines flaring before melting. Something nagged at him; a seed of doubt growing fast, but he and the other commanders drove on. This was the first time they were actually progressing; for eighteen years it had been a cycle of defeat, retreat, re-group, attack, defeat. He checked that the other ships outside the sphere had installed a stent to ensure the hole didn't close; he didn't want to be trapped inside a galactic pitcher plant.

His battleship forged through three ranks of Mannekhi ships, decimating dozens. Fifty-three per cent integrity left. That meant casualties. Connection broke with three destroyers whose hulls were less protected. Jorann and his fellow Q'Roth commanders were winning, but the attrition rate was punishing. He sent a coded message up the chain to the Tla Beth: <Leave – we'll take it from here>. He knew how many Q'Roth were vanishing in this battle, but that would pale into insignificance against losing a single Tla Beth.

Amidst the flashes and blossoming flares of space battle – his lieutenants and the automatic systems handling the Mannekhi ships – his old rage unexpectedly surfaced. He recalled watching as the Q'Roth purged a dying Earth of its atmosphere and all its water, all its life. When he'd first emerged as a Q'Roth clone, he'd promised himself one day that he would exact revenge, seizing an opportunity to eradicate a large number of Q'Roth. And here it was. If he turned and opened fire on the other battleships, the Mannekhi would not stop to question, and together they would annihilate the Seventh Fleet. He'd promised himself that he'd never empathize with his blood enemy, the Q'Roth, no matter what. Seven billion people wiped out, he reminded himself.

Five years ago he would have done it without hesitation. But he didn't know himself anymore. What he did know was that against all odds, Blake and Micah and thousands of other humans had survived, safely quarantined on Esperia, the so-called spider planet, protected by a Level Twelve shield and Ossyrian guardians. But the quarantine – always intended as a temporary measure – would come down soon, and Jorann wanted to hold back Qorall as long as possible. If they had any sense, as soon as quarantine ended, mankind's refugees would run like hell to the far end of the galaxy.

And if Jorann somehow met them one day – Micah, Blake and the others – he wouldn't expect them to understand. He'd be quite happy if they dealt out rough justice, court-martialed him for treason as a Q'Roth sympathizer and executed him. That would be more than okay.

A shudder, as a crumbling enemy ship rammed his own ineffectually, jolted him back into the present. The Tla Beth ship was still there, buzzing about like a mosquito, occasionally visible, then moving too fast for even Q'Roth vision to keep up. *What was it doing? Why hadn't it left?* But he knew why: *curiosity.* Like him, it was trying to determine what was lurking in the background. The Mannekhi ships had given up firing at the Tla Beth ship, their sprays of purple pulses failing to touch it.

Jorann's ship nudged through more wrecked sea urchins and dispatched Hunter Class vessels from his bays to clean up the mess – just as well, he'd run out of torpedoes. He ignored the charred corpses drifting around cracked hulls – the Mannekhi were humanoid in shape, the only species he'd seen that resembled humanity. More than once he'd wondered if they were distant cousins. Too bad, they'd chosen the wrong side.

The last row of sea-urchin ships was white instead of black, burning bright, masking whatever was behind. Seven Q'Roth ships remained active inside the shield-bubble; five others including two battleships were now debris. Two destroyers limped back to the stent. Jorann knew that their commanders and crew would have preferred to fight to the death, but the Q'Roth ship-yards were finding it hard to keep up with daily losses, so any ship not obliterated was towed back for re-conditioning.

The tiny Tla Beth ship spun into view ahead of Jorann, and fired a metastaser – a weapon he'd only heard rumours of until now. Orange light bathed one of the sea urchins then leapt across to adjacent ships, spreading outwards to the entire array, latching onto any material with a Mannekhi signature, ignoring Q'Roth ships. The sea urchins shimmered then exploded one by one, opening up a gap in the final defence perimeter.

That was when he saw it. His claws flexed defensively of their own accord. It was darker than anything around it, a slug-shaped hole in space. Except that it writhed. One of the fabled *dark worms.* As he tried to take it in, to see any features, a priority message plexed into his mind: the stent was collapsing. His gun turrets trained on the worm, fifty times the size of his battleship, but he didn't fire – he'd read the reports. One of his fellow commanders lit it up with focused particle beams, but as Jorann had heard before, no sooner had the beams touched the worm's vacuum-hardened flesh, than black tendrils traced their way back to the firing ship – as if they could latch onto light – and yanked the ship towards the worm with alarming speed, enveloping it inside its dark folds.

He now knew why the Mannekhi and the liquid space had been present: to exhaust the Q'Roth's supply of torpedoes. Even so, he wasn't sure they could really have inflicted much damage. These creatures usually inhabited the null-space between galaxies, surviving on dark energy and any vessel foolish enough to attempt such a voyage. Qorall had used the worms in the first battle to breach the galactic barrier, but they'd hardly been seen since, and most in the Alliance had hoped they had returned home. Jorann sent a priority message to those outside the stent, to dispatch one ship immediately back to the High Guard with news of this development.

The worm slithered towards the Tla Beth ship. *Why wasn't the Tla Beth running?* The other commanders were eerily silent. Breaking protocol, he tried contacting the Tla Beth ship directly on the emergency channel, but there was not even a transponder response.

He skimmed through sensor readings and then his mind snagged on one: the worm had emitted a dark energy spike that had been off the scale, directed at the Tla Beth ship. No one knew much about Tla Beth tech or physiology, but Qorall must have somehow gained intel on their weak spots. But then another thought struck him: how had Qorall known a Tla Beth would be present? The idea of a corrupt Q'Roth was impossible. Never mind, he told himself, that would have to wait.

Qorall's tactic was suddenly clear to him: all this slaughter had been a ploy with a single objective: to destroy – or more likely capture – a Tla Beth, the highest level of intelligence in the galaxy. Qorall wanted one, presumably alive, to study. The Tla Beth were the only species of any real threat to him, and Qorall didn't know enough about them, coming from a different galaxy. Jorann understood the importance of military intelligence: if Qorall captured a Tla Beth...

He mindplexed the other commanders, not bothering to apologise for involving the Tla Beth in the first place; that was in the past now, and regret wasn't in the Q'Roth psychological lexicon.

Immediately the two remaining battleships lurched forward to place themselves between the worm and the Tla Beth ship. Jorann received a message <Recover Tla Beth> the commanders appending the Q'Roth equivalent of "Sir". In all Jorann's years serving with them, even when he'd led entire fleets, they'd never used it. He understood why – for the first time they'd penetrated one of Qorall's fleet spheres and had gained valuable intelligence, even if they now risked losing one of their masters. Jorann had an instinct to salute them and their imminent sacrifice, but his Q'Roth anatomy wouldn't do it justice. Nor did he return with "Good luck" – Q'Roth warrior culture scorned such concepts.

Instead he spun his ship into action, plotting a loop-and-catch manoeuvre that would push more 'G's than human physiology could have handled. Using a gravity web he snatched up the inert Tla Beth craft into the main hold. As he raced back toward the collapsing stent, the liquid space increased its density, slowing his ship down. That made him realise something about the sphere – it had intelligence. He wondered if it was alive in some rudimentary way; so much of Qorall's arsenal was organic, compared to this galaxy's focus on techware. Instinct could react faster than intellect. Jorann wanted to think this through but he had other priorities: his ship's integrity was at twenty-five per cent and falling. Two destroyers paved a way before him, attracting mines which hadn't been there on their way in. The two battleships behind him went silent. He gunned all engines and thrusters, ordering his faster Hunter craft to make a dash for the stent. Instead, they turned and charged the worm, trying to slow it down.

Jorann wasn't going to make it. The stent had already buckled. One of the outside commanders informed him the whole sphere was shimmering; it was about to jump, presumably away from the War's front, back deep inside Qorall space. The destroyer to port exploded, and two seconds later the one to starboard peeled off, its drives heavily damaged, drifting backwards to detonate in the worm's pathway. Jorann watched the gargantuan creature ease through the debris field, nudging the exploding destroyer aside like driftwood. Jorann and his surviving crew were alone.

His sensors told him the worm was increasing its speed, gaining on him. He calculated he had twenty seconds before it would make contact and leach the energy from his battleship, including all Q'Roth life, and capture its Tla Beth prize.

Jorann set the self-destruct timer for ten seconds and broadcast a message to Granch and the other commanders outside. "They won't get the Tla Beth. Take the intel we've gained back to the Ch'Hrach staging point. Prepare better next time." He didn't add what he thought: that it had been an honour serving with them, that they were the most impressive, fearless soldiers he'd ever seen. He counted down. At three seconds everything around him turned quicksilver.

A second later he found himself in a cramped metallic compartment gazing through a porthole at a distant luminous sphere. A spark flared briefly inside it, then the bubble itself flashed and was gone, leaving a motley flotilla of healthy and injured Q'Roth ships, which soon jumped out of this space as well, onto their long trip back home.

Jorann tried to turn around, but the area confining him was like a cylindrical coffin. He heard a voice behind him. It took him a moment to realize it was human, though it spoke perfectly accented Q'Roth.

"Sorry for the discomfort, this is really a two-person craft, but we needed to talk."

Jorann thrashed his legs, manoeuvring his body until he could rotate enough to see who the voice belonged to. As he finally managed to turn around, he saw a compact cockpit with two occupants: the first was humanoid, but made entirely of platinum flow-metal. Next to him was one of the mud-coloured reptilian Rangers he'd seen once or twice, two and a half metres from snout to tail, with serious teeth. Some said they served the Tla Beth; others that they had unknown allegiances. The Q'Roth considered them to be anachronistic mavericks the Tla Beth should have weeded out long ago.

Jorann tried to speak human, but of course it came out Q'Roth. "Who are you? Why did you save me? And for that matter, *how* did you save me?"

The platinum man stared a while, then smiled. "We know who you really are, General – well, who you used to be. We were here on reconnaissance back-up for the Tla Beth, when we, er, received a message, and discovered you."

Jorann could not see how any of this was possible. "Is the Tla Beth safe?"

The reptilian Ranger answered in Largyl 6, though it sounded as if he had bricks in his throat. "Tla Beth in hold. Unconscious. Stasis. Second Tla Beth ship on intercept. Will take home."

Jorann gathered that was as much information as he was going to get. "Then we need to return to the Q'Roth High Guard, and –'

The platinum man held up a hand. "The other commanders have all the intel they need. Besides, we have another mission for you, one involving humanity."

Jorann's gash pressed closed. He couldn't accept this was happening. In the first five years after awakening as a Q'Roth he'd plotted, and dreamt of somehow being rescued by humans. But the Q'Roth warriors he'd lived with until now were infinitely more pragmatic, and didn't indulge in wanton optimism. It had been so long. Despite having yearned for human contact all these years, now he found he couldn't face it. "Any humans would kill me on sight if they could."

The platinum man's face rippled for a moment, as if he had momentarily been elsewhere. "Fair point. But maybe I can help you out. Would you like to look human again?"

Jorann stared with all six slits at the humanoid creature, wondering if he was some kind of agent for Qorall, if this was some kind of trick. Maybe the sphere had jumped with him and his crew inside it, and Qorall was using some form of mental simulation to get his guard down. It seemed infinitely more likely than being rescued by a humanesque figure promising to deliver his most heartfelt, and most discarded, desire. Jorann steeled himself. The Q'Roth had trained him for such interrogation. All he had to do to break this charade was ask for a piece of information which the enemy couldn't know, that even he himself didn't know.

"If you know who I am, then tell me my name." There, that would stump him for sure. Only Sister Esma knew, and she'd withheld it even from the Q'Roth. Once they failed to answer this question he would attack, or die trying. He readied muscles in all six of his legs; his claws curled, ready. He would show Qorall what a Q'Roth warrior could do at close quarters.

The man's silver brow creased in a frown, which then morphed into a measured stare. Again, he did something very human – he folded his arms. "You're General Bill Kilaney." His tone grew softer. "She hid that from you all this time, didn't she?"

Jorann heard the name echo inside his memory, at first like a small tinkle, but then it reverberated, resonated, a massive church bell getting louder. His muscles eased off. *Of course.* General William "Bill" Kilaney. Hearing his name was like a cadence, as if a thousand memories, a thousand voices, suddenly snapped into coherence. Instead of an irritating background cacophony, it was an orchestrated choir. How clever Sister Esma had been to extricate that one memory from all the rest, keeping his humanity off-balance, off-key, all these years.

He couldn't speak. He kept intoning his name over and over, terrified he might forget it. Q'Roth physiology wasn't strong on emotions, but his upper claws shook. He clenched them, and closed all six slits for a moment. *Thank you*, he intoned, not sure exactly who or what he was thanking, and in the same moment he paid his last respects to all the Q'Roth who'd perished inside the sphere. 26,012. From this day on, he would count them no more.

The platinum man waited patiently, seeming to understand. "Will you join us, General? We mean to stop Qorall, and to preserve humanity. Blake and Micah are still alive, and they're going to need your help when the quarantine comes down in a week's time. We believe that some of the people there are set to engage in a war with the Alicians and the Q'Roth, which is the last thing any of us needs. Until finding you, I wasn't sure how to prevent this from happening, but as you can imagine, your presence, and your unique perspective, would be invaluable."

Jorann – Kilaney – found he could utter no words. He'd been Blake's mentor for two decades. All the smaller memories flooded back to him – all   of   the detailed ones that ultimately mattered most, the ones that defined him – unlocked by the simple keystone, his name. Everything he'd done, everyone he'd known, who he really was. Amidst the tumble of images, his wife's face emerged, so clear in front of him, lost to cancer four years before the fall of Earth. She seemed to smile, as if happy to see him again. He raised his two shaking, upper claws in front of him, stared at them, saw them as alien, so alien, despite they were his. The shakes passed. He stretched open the claws like fingers, and meshed them into a crude steeple, like he used to do back on Earth.

Purpose crystallised inside him: defeat Qorall, hell yes; but also –   despite   what his rescuer had said – Sister Esma would pay for her crimes.

"General, will you join us in helping humanity?"

Kilaney gazed at the platinum man. He no longer felt like uttering a further word of Q'Roth – he would put that behind him. Instead, he manoeuvred muscles in his armoured thorax, shoulder carapace and neck to approximate a movement he'd not practiced in eighteen years.

He nodded.

CHAPTER 4 – ARSON

Micah and Petra sped through the night along the rarely used dust- track towards Shimsha, Spider Central as Petra called it. But Micah wasn't in search of spiders. One way or another, war was coming either soon after Quarantine came down as Gabriel predicted, or whenever Qorall's forces reached Esperia. Mankind needed the best tactical commander left alive on the planet. But Blake had become a recluse since his wife had passed, staying hidden in Shimsha. Micah hoped to persuade him to come back, rejoin the effort, and fight once again if necessary. Blake was respected by Genners and Steaders alike, and could perhaps heal some divisions.

Petra shouted above the wind as they roared closer to Shimsha. "Do you reckon he'll even talk to us? He's so wrapped up with the spiders. Who knows if he even cares about us anymore?"

Micah knew he should have called on Blake more often. "His wife died, Petra. He needed some peace, and some space. Anyway, I sent a message, so he knows we're coming."

"I wasn't criticizing his motives."

"He's not going to let us down, that's not who he is." Micah prayed he was right about that.

There was a short pause. "I know he was a great commander," began Petra, "by the old standards."

"Look, intellectually he's not at your or Gabriel's level, Petra, he can't be, I know that. But he has a damn sight more experience of fighting a war. We need him."

Petra made a skeptical noise but didn't say anything further.

Micah swerved the skimmer around a tight bend and braked hard, skidding to a halt, Petra slamming into his back. Four spiders barred the entrance to Shimsha.

"Guess we walk the rest of the way," she said, easing herself off the seat.

Micah powered down the engine and dismounted. The vehicle sank to the ground, crunching hard soil underneath. He waited for the spiders to part, but they didn't move. In the moonless night, pale blue light seeped out from the city, casting long shadows towards Micah and Petra, making the spiders' legs appear spindlier than the muscular, single-jointed limbs Micah knew them to be. He'd heard the outlying farmers gossip about how fast they could move, even jump, though he'd never seen them do it. Petra edged forward but he stayed her with his palm. Out of the shadows six more arrived, surrounding them.

Petra backed away from them. "Micah, tell me this is some weird greeting ritual I've not heard about."

His adrenaline kicked in. This wasn't just unusual, it was exceptional. In sixteen years of co-existence since the spiders had hatched, they had never once threatened any human. "Whatever happens, don't run," he whispered, unsure why; the spiders had no hearing, relying completely on visual and olfactory senses. "Get back on – "

Suddenly, a spider was right next to him, its broad, headless body nudging his forearm. It was the first time he'd ever had physical contact with one, and although the body looked black and hairy, he was surprised how soft it felt, like velvet. It pushed him away from the skimmer, just as another two separated him from Petra. That was it. "Blake!" Micah yelled, as he and Petra were herded to the side of the road. One of the spiders' legs curled around Micah's and knocked him onto his back. He heard Petra shout his name, but he was too busy avoiding piston-like legs. His nannites rose to high alert, allowing him to react quicker than would have been possible for a normal human, his hands and feet hardening as he kicked back at the spider's legs.

The night sky flashed brilliant white. Micah flinched, elbows and knees up to protect his head and body, temporarily unable to see, expecting to be trampled at any second. But as the flare diminished and his vision readjusted, he realized the spiders had gone, leaving Micah with nothing more than a few bruises. A lone, gaunt figure stood silhouetted by the city light, two large spiders behind him.

Micah got to his feet and dusted himself off, glancing in Petra's direction. She stood with her fists clenched, but seemed to be okay. She gave him a crooked smile, like Kat, her mother. "I'm okay, Micah, I can move fast, and I play mean." She opened her hands. Black fur drifted to the ground. Micah wondered if the spiders had really meant to hurt them, and if so, why.

They walked over to his former mentor. Micah shook his hand. "Care to explain what just happened?" He expected some sort of apology from Blake, as the spiders' overseer.

"I was delayed getting here, Micah. This shouldn't have happened. They forget how fragile humans are, and they're pretty upset right now. Come with me, you'd best see for yourself." Blake turned without another word and strode into the city.

Petra drew to Micah's side, speaking softly. "We could have been killed, intentionally or not. Remind me, how long have you two been friends?"

Micah stared in Blake's direction. "There has to be a good reason."
"One I'd like to see," she said.

Micah realised it had been a year since he'd last visited Shimsha, and many more since he'd walked its streets at night. Single-storey dwellings with low domes, either rounded-off rhomboids or kidney- shaped affairs, lined the curving pathways, sharp cyan light spilling through broad doors and arched windows. Whereas Esperantia was all Cartesian angles, Shimsha was slow-twisting arcs. It was easy on the eye, calming. Wide plazas opened up every hundred metres or so, but the squat tables, where huddles of spiders would normally be seen conversing via flickering rainbow light exchanges, were empty. Where were they all? A fluorescent glow hung behind a row of longer buildings. As they approached the source, the aurora shimmered. It began to strobe faster. Blake held up a small device and projected a purple beam into the cloud of light. Abruptly, the night flooded back in. Micah sped up, turned the corner and stopped dead.

The plaza was filled with spiders, so many that it was as if there was a four foot high black lake rippling all the way across the square in the night breeze. Blake strode ahead, the spiders parting before him. The lack of light, the sudden absence of spider communication, put Micah on edge. He wished he'd come alone, though it wasn't safe to leave Petra now. The two of them had never been very physical, but he stretched out his hand, half sure she'd ignore him or brush it away. Instead she clasped it, and they walked tall together behind Blake. As they reached the other end of the plaza, and the last spiders moved aside, Petra's hand flinched inside his own.

He stared at the blackened remains of one of the larger domiciles on Shimsha's western edge, near the slope trailing up to Hazzard's Ridge where he'd sat just a few hours ago. Amidst the ruins, four spider carcasses lay upside down, stumps where half their legs had been burned away, their torsos charred husks containing remnants of organs and entrails grilled to charcoal. A smell of sulphur seared his eyes. Petra let go of his hand, looking like she would puke, and confirmed his assessment   a moment later. Without taking his eyes off the scene, he passed her a handkerchief.

Stepping forward, he inspected the smoking, crackling remains of a house that had stood unblemished for more than a millennium, and switched into analysis mode. The burning had blazed brightest at the home's entrance, sealing them in, in a clear attempt to cremate the occupants. The scorch-marks were consistent with the bio-fuel used to power the five jury-rigged tractors shared by Esperantia's farmers. The spiders' fur made them averse to any form of combustion, and there had never been a case of spider domestic violence or inter-spider rivalry. His jaw clenched of its own accord, a cocktail of emotions inside him: sadness and outrage, but also anger at the stupidity of such an act of aggression. He could only imagine how Blake felt. "Any idea who did this?"

Blake's stern features were sharp enough to cut metal. "I sent Zack to find out."

"That maybe wasn't the best..." His sentence wilted under Blake's glare. He turned around. In the dim light from the homes surrounding the plaza, the spiders seemed to loom towards him. He had little idea of their emotional repertoire; the spiders were supposedly pacifist, but he reckoned anger had to be in there somewhere, deep down. Besides, he and Petra had just experienced the first aggressive act towards humans. He turned back to Blake and tried another tack. "Who were they? I mean, why this group – or family." Micah regretted how little he knew of their social structure.

Blake's voice was taut, emotions locked down. "Random hit; soft target on the edge of the city while the annual simulated battle in the dome distracted most people; easy escape over the hill back to Esperantia."

Micah noticed how Blake had slipped back into his military persona so quickly. Another thought intruded. "Why did the other spiders attack us at the perimeter? My lucky timing, or –"

"You're President. In their book you're responsible."

Petra finished wiping her mouth, stood up. "He just resigned, though I guess that won't count for much here."

Micah wondered out loud. "Why now?" But he knew why. Most likely it was one of the Steaders; the Genners were respectful of the spiders, and their aggressive ambitions were entirely focused on the Alicians. A few faces popped into Micah's mind of Steaders who might be stupid enough – or scared enough – to pull a stunt like this.

Blake kicked at a piece of steaming rubble. "Quarantine comes down in less than a week. The Ossyrians pick up their pieces and leave. Genners of age will follow suit, leaving just the Steaders and the spiders, with a new generation about to hatch."

Petra spoke up. "A provocation, an act out of pure fear or bigotry, or both. A first strike, probably intended to stoke itself up into a decisive war, assuming the spiders are pacifists, and if not, proving they are a threat to be defended against. Typical human rhetoric; doesn't help anything."

Micah stared at her a moment, recalling she was a Genner, far smarter than her years. He ran through various options, including trying to persuade the Ossyrians to stay.

An unwelcome thought broke in: Sister Esma... If she knew about this, she would rub her hands with glee, and add it to her mountain of evidence that humanity should be eradicated for the terminally destructive species it was. For a second, as he stared at the corpses in front of him, he could almost agree.

"We have to deal with this quickly, Blake, contain it. And you have to keep the spiders in check."

Blake faced Micah, the afterglow from the embers highlighting the grey strands in Blake's reddish hair, and the pockmarks on his right cheek from Earth's Third World War. Micah knew the Ossyrians had offered more than once to remove those scars.

Blake's voice softened. "Sorry about what happened to you both out there. They were young, upset, two of them were..." He swallowed, seeming to search for the right word. "... related." He nodded to the corpses.

Petra jumped in. "They could have killed Micah, you know, injured him at least." She gave Micah a curious look. "Not sure how he got off so lightly, actually."

Micah ignored the remark. "Blake, tell them we'll find who did this, and deal with them severely."

Blake walked up to the spider closest to them who, to Micah, looked somehow different to the rest – maybe it was the way it stood. Blake raised the hand-held device he'd used earlier, his fingers dancing over its surface. A small holo of flickering hues appeared between him and the spider, then vanished.

The lead spider's band around its circumference lit up, repeating the pattern. Colour cascaded backwards to all the other spiders behind it, fanning outwards to all sides of the plaza, like a rainbow wave. Then it rebounded back to the front, terminating at the lead spider. Micah had just enough time to see that the returning pattern was far more dense, more nuanced, but with a central scarlet diamond that seemed to shake. At last the light-show stopped, the original spider being the last one to go dark. Micah surmised that they'd all just discussed it, and 'voted'. It had taken four seconds.

Blake shook his head. "Not nearly enough, Micah. They want whoever did this delivered here, to them."

"Blake, you know –"

"I know what will happen if you don't."

Micah wished Glenda was still around; she'd softened Blake, moderated him. But although the Ossyrians had saved Blake's wife from cancer and extended her life by a decade, there had been too much damage. Blake had taken her death hard, as had the spiders, since she'd raised many of them, tending night and day to the nursery in their first vulnerable year. Micah had seen spiders at her graveside more than once, standing vigil.

He cleared his throat. "Blake, I came to talk to you about something important."

Blake turned away, crouched down, and laid a hand on one of the husks. "Her name... It can't be pronounced, it was a particular light pattern. She was an artist, taught Glenda how to sky-paint, was with her at the end..."

Micah walked over to Blake, thought about placing a hand on his shoulder, then thought again. The commander had been his mentor, and that relationship could never reverse in Micah's book. "I'll find out who did this, Blake." He turned to Petra. "We're leaving."

They made their way unhindered back to the city's edge, though Micah had the feeling they were watched every step of the way. Neither of them felt like talking until they reached the skimmer.

Petra's shoulders were hunched as she climbed aboard, her lips pursed. Micah waited, not mounting the skimmer. At last she spat it out.

"You Steaders *are* dangerous, Micah. We Genners understand why the Tla Beth executed the judgment they did back at the trial."

He'd thought this over a thousand times. "Do you think we should be condemned to oblivion as a species? Our only heritage Genners and Alicians?"

She folded her arms. "Evolution isn't always kind, Micah. There's no conscience behind it."

He stared at her. "But this wasn't natural selection, Petra, this was a conscious societal act that –"

"No difference. I'm surprised at you, Uncle. Don't you get it? Whether it's like the vids I've seen of lions and gazelle on the plains of the Serengeti, or us and the Q'Roth in the Grid, it's all natural selection."

"There are choices. There's room for empathy."

She shook her head. "Not much. Billions of stars, but not that many planets capable of sustaining all the life in the Grid. It's always been a jungle, always will be." She unfolded her arms. "I don't want to argue with you, and I'm getting cold sitting here, so can we go?"

There was tenderness in her voice. He dropped the argument and mounted the vehicle. She touched his arm.

"What did you come here for, Micah? What were you going to ask him?"

He primed the engine. "War is coming. Soon after the quarantine comes down, we'll be in the thick of it." He thought of his original intent, to persuade Blake to come back. This arson, this murder, had hardly helped that cause.

"Looks like we started early," she said.

He remembered something Louise had said to him a lifetime ago, that men carried war in their heads, wherever they went. For the past eighteen years he'd begun to hope she was wrong, but now even Petra had said as much. Still, he hoped; there was so much good in people if you knew where to find it, and they'd all had such a rough time of things in the past two decades. He gunned the engine and they sped off into the darkness.

"Where are we going now?" He didn't really know.

"Antonia would like to see you," she said.

His first thought had been of Sandy; she'd have ideas, but seeing her was out of the question, and she hadn't talked or listened to him in years. Antonia? She would offer good counsel, but what about Petra's absent mother, Kat, Antonia's wife? It seemed a dangerous idea. Then again, Petra was wiser than her years, or maybe just shrewder. He decided to follow her recommendation. Besides, he needed to drop Petra home. He'd just stop to say hello to Antonia. Just a quick hello. Maybe a cup of coffee, as he was tired.

Petra wrapped her arms around his waist, her head leaning against his back. Micah had never understood how Pierre could have left her behind.

Antonia answered the door, auburn hair piled on top of her head, eyes a weary red.

"Working late?" Micah asked.

She sighed, rolled her eyes. "Sewage reclamation project, mainly. Come in, Micah, I was just making tea."

"Are you sure, it's late, and – "

Petra shoved him in the back, pushing him across the threshold. "You two kids go talk, I'll fix tea."

Micah sat in one of the four wooden chairs in the lounge, while Antonia powered down her pad. He watched the contours of her body move within her shim-dress, the ubiquitous functional material leant them by the Ossyrians. Micah remembered how glamorous she'd been back on Earth, an ambassador's daughter. He caught himself staring as she bent over to put things away, and reminded himself she belonged to Kat, something he'd accepted long ago.

"How's it going? You know, the, er, sewage project." He felt idiotic.

"Well, if we can bring it off, it will help the farmers immensely; after all, it's something we're never short of." She smiled, almond eyes flashing, dimples opening on her cheeks.

Her smile disarmed him; it always had. He wanted to... well, at the least, console her about Kat having been missing now for two years. She caught his look, held it, then sat in the chair opposite him.

Petra arrived with a tray carrying a crudely fashioned metal teapot and three cups. "Still talking shit?"

"Petra, don't start, please." Antonia took the tray and placed it on the squat table.

Petra sat cross-legged on the floor. "I spoke with Chahat-Me yesterday."

Micah sat up. So did Antonia. Petra said nothing more. "Well?" Micah asked.

Petra gave him a look. "Are you sure you're interested? I mean excrement reclamation sounds enthralling."

Micah had been trying to extract the latest news out of the Ossyrian leader for weeks. Petra was close to Chahat-Me, having been the first to be genned by the Ossyrians, followed shortly thereafter by Gabriel. He knew Petra liked Gabriel, and Gabriel liked her too, though not that way. Given his own lingering and unrequited interest in both Antonia and Sandy before either had gotten married, he realized he and his adopted niece had a lot in common.

Petra pouted. "I'll trade. A truth-swap game us Genners play when we're nine, before we grow up. When we're stuck in the playground phase, and we twist the truth, rather than speak it." She shook her head. "Do you have any idea what it's like living with you people, watching the pathetic games you play, hurting each other all the time?"

Micah half-stood to leave, but a glance from Antonia set him down again. Besides, he needed the information. "Okay, what did Chahat-Me say?"

Antonia began pouring the tea.

"First, Micah," Petra said, "we trade truths. Do you love Antonia?" Tea spilled all over the table. "

Petra!" Antonia cursed.

"Why do you do this, Petra?" Micah asked, feeling tired. He stood.

Petra stood too. "Louise has Kat. She's still alive."

Micah's eyes flashed to Antonia, who froze, still holding the teapot. She swallowed, then with a shaking hand, placed it on the table.

Petra pointed to Micah's chair. "Sit please, if you want to hear the rest."

Reluctantly, Micah did as he was told.

"She is taking Kat to Qorall. You know why, don't you Micah?"

He stared at the floor. "Her node. She can communicate with the Hohash."

Antonia stared at Micah. "So what?"

Only he, Blake and Chahat-Me knew about the Kalarash having been on Esperia. They'd agreed to keep it quiet; another reason he had wanted to see Blake. From what little he knew, and what scraps of intel he'd gleaned from Chahat-Me on the historical legends of the Grid, only the Kalarash could stop a force such as Qorall. Maybe it was time everyone else knew, it might give them some hope.

Petra continued. "Chahat-Me said you believed the Kalarash were here once, on this planet, when we first arrived."

Antonia took her cup and leaned back in her chair. "I thought they were pure myth, bedtime-story material for Grid parents to lull their young to sleep. Well, Micah?"

He reached over and picked up his dripping cup, blew across the top of the steaming liquid, then inhaled: lemon and ginger. He shook his head. "One of them was here. It left just before Quarantine."

Antonia's mouth dropped open.

Petra closed on him. "Do you love Sandy, Micah?"

He cast her a look of disdain, but her eyes were defiant, and he felt Antonia's on him too. "Same answer: why do you do this, Petra?"

"Mom said – before she was abducted – you're the saddest man she knows. You love two women you can't have, and do nothing with the half-dozen others interested in you. *Sit back down!*" Her eyes flared. "And you're the closest thing I have to a father, so I'm sick of seeing you miserable."

Micah sipped the tea, cradling the cup in both hands, and closed his eyes.

Petra's voice quavered. "Do you think of me as a daughter? You've never said it."

He leaned forward, head bowed, so she couldn't see his eyes, controlling his breathing. He'd never had children, never been in a relationship long enough. Most kids... he found it difficult to interact with them, though he could smile at them from afar. He wasn't what he considered great 'father material', until Petra had come along. If he'd had a daughter, he'd have wanted her to be just like Petra.

He nodded.

"I need to hear you say it!"

His eyes met hers. She looked vulnerable, and he wanted more than anything to protect her from the savage jungle outside Quarantine. "I think of you as the daughter I never had."

"Thank you." She said it in her small voice, the one he remembered from her second birthday, when he'd brought her a present, a toy horse, something which made no sense on a world without horses, and she'd looked up at him with such intelligence and understanding, and undemanding love, it had taken his breath away.

Petra continued. "I know where Qorall is. Chahat-Me showed me the latest projections from the front line. Where he is doesn't really matter, of course. But I know when he'll be here."

Micah stood. "Okay, Petra, that's enough, we need to know, now. Stop this game!" Antonia joined him, so that they loomed over her like two parents.

Petra rose slowly. "You must stop your games first. Do you have any idea what it's like surpassing your parents intellectually at the age of twelve? Watching the futile games you play, watching you suffer all the time? Listening to you lie to each other and yourselves all the time, every second of every fucking day?"

Antonia advanced on Petra. "That's enough, Petra! You may be way ahead of me intellectually, but your emotional IQ needs a lot of work. Go to your room!"

"Do you love Micah? I mean even a little bit?"

Antonia turned her back on Petra, facing Micah. "She's utterly impossible!"

"Mother, answer me!"

Antonia's eyes rolled, but Micah thought he detected moisture there as she turned away from them both, and spoke to the wall. "What do you want from me, Petra, from us?"

"I want you to go to your room, Mom. You haven't had a lover for two years, Micah more like seven. You're both hurting, it eats away at you, and we're all probably dead in the next week once Quarantine comes down and lets in whoever's waiting for us out there, with Qorall's army just six months behind. That's your answer, by the way, as I already have mine, even if you're both too weak to answer me directly. I'm going to leave for a few hours. I'll be back in the morning. It's your lives." She stormed out.

Micah half-expected to hear the door slam, but it didn't. He stood motionless in the silence which descended.

Antonia broke it, facing him again. "Do you think she's right? Are we such a lost cause?"

Micah frowned. "I'm afraid that one is usually right, even if she's sometimes emotionally immature. But at least she has emotions. I think that's why I put up with her quirky nature. You've done a good job raising her, Antonia. I often wish she was the leader of the Genners, not Gabriel."

Antonia nodded. She stood within arms' reach. "Has there really been no one these past seven years, Micah?"

Micah suddenly felt fragile, like he was made of glass. "I've been... busy, you know, being President and all that. Listen, it's late, I should go. I'm sorry for... Well, I should leave, Antonia."

But he didn't move.

"A goodnight kiss, Micah. Please."

Micah felt the glass crack. "If I kiss you now, Antonia, it won't stop there."

Antonia moved closer to him, took his hands. "I know."

*　*　*

Petra sat cross-legged outside Gabriel's home, underneath his bedroom window. She'd hoped to find him alone, but Virginia was there. The pre-dawn air was chilly. A robin was singing somewhere close by, one of the few birds to have been rescued from the destruction of Earth. Beneath its chirping, she heard Virginia's soft moans, Gabriel's gasps of rapture. She carved the Greek letter Phi into a piece of driftwood with her knife. When she and Gabe had been five years old, she'd cut it into the bark of a tree, told him it was like a 'g' and a 'p' back-to-back, that they were like brother and sister, like Apollo and Artemis, and they would never be apart.

She heard Virginia tell him she loved him, and paused her whittling, straining to hear his reply, but couldn't make it out. The piece of wood was wet. She wanted to kick herself, having just berated Micah and Antonia for not telling each other their feelings, when she herself had never once let Gabriel know how she really felt. Not for the first time she wondered why she was more emotional than other Genners. She'd been the first one to be genned; maybe the Ossyrians hadn't quite got it right. *More advanced, my ass. Hell, I'm even sitting here like a goddammed stalker.* She got up silently and wiped her eyes, and walked towards Carlson Plaza as the first rays of dawn breached the tops of the slate-grey prefab housing units. Ramires was doing some form of martial arts exercise.

"Do those techniques really work?"

He paused from his kata. "Petra, hello." He studied her. "Are you okay?"

She took out her knife and threw it so that it thwacked into the   wall of one of the zinc-coated units. "I'm fine. I could use a workout, though." She took off her jacket, and hung it on her home-made coat- hook. "Apparently you have the best fighting skills left in the human race. Let's see how you fare with a little Genner girl like me, shall we?" Without waiting for a reply, she launched her attack.

CHAPTER 5 – SURGICAL PROCEDURES

Kilaney – formerly Jorann – stared at his hand for the umpteenth time, curling his fingers, watching supple skin stretch and contract over fresh knuckles. He still had difficulty believing it had happened. It had all been so fast, so matter of fact, almost as if being fitted for a new uniform, not changing his body for God's sake. Becoming human again had been something he'd literally dreamt of during his early years as a Q'Roth. He remembered – though it was difficult for him to go back there – how he'd tried to commit suicide more than once in that first awful year. He nearly succeeded, but then the local station commander executed the Q'Roth surgeon supervising Kilaney's 'transition'. Kilaney hadn't wanted any more blood spilled on his account, so he gave up hope and accepted his fate. Yet now, within a couple of days, they'd simply changed him back. He stared at his hands again.

But his new skin felt terribly flimsy after Q'Roth armoured flesh. His arms, however, still had the appearance of corrugated iron, blue-grey from shoulder to wrist, petering out into pinkish hands. *Good enough.* He held his breath as he pulled the sheet off to reveal his legs. A metallic blue sheen glistened over powerful, hairless musculature, tailing off in sturdy feet with five toes, all of them prehensile.

But he was missing a second pair of Q'Roth legs – he could feel the ghost limbs where they should have been attached at hip level. Kilaney closed his eyes. It was done. The DNA transplant, supercharged by Pierre's specialised nannites, would override the Q'Roth signature, given enough time. His brain would remain quadro-spherical, but he could live with that.

He lay back on the pillow, inspecting the stars through windows on the domed roof. The vast hangar containing him and other alien patients was so unusual that at first he thought the eye surgery had gone awry. Swathes of colour – violet, red, teal, and apple, swirled in the air as far as he could see, never mixing. Each layer was grainy, with fine particles that moved like sand beneath a wave, shifting and flowing, occasionally surging from one spot to another. The 'air' around him was a pale blue, had no taste or texture, and he had no idea of its function. The surgeons – squid-shaped creatures, transparent so that he could see all their organs and watch their two hearts twitch – drifted and surfed in the currents. When they had worked on him it had felt like a feather-touch, even when they had peeled back his armoured ribcage as if it were made of silk. He'd expected terrible pain when the anaesthetic wore off, but there was none at all, not even an itch.

One of the squids had gurgled to him in Largyl 6. "Sure want this? Q'Roth physiology beautiful design – human arrangement clumsy."

Kilaney told him it was necessary for political reasons. The surgeon made a strange gulping motion, then got back to work. Afterwards, the squid whispered that he understood, and continued that he had added some refinements to make it more bearable. Kilaney wondered what those might be, but no surgeon had approached him again since the operation, several hours ago.

He guessed the various coloured layers were for different patient species on the hospital ship, run by the Level Twelve Ngankfushtora – he could no longer pronounce it properly with a human tongue – and that the swirling sediment had multiple purposes including bio-containment, regeneration, sterilisation, and monitoring of recovery progress and health parameters.

He'd encountered the Level Eight Ossyrian medical race during his time as Q'Roth, and had been impressed, but the Nganks were something else: massive surgery and rewriting DNA while keeping cognitive faculties and memories intact in a matter of a couple of days – he'd assumed it was impossible. Pierre had told him that the Ossyrians were advanced medically, but fundamentally they were triage doctors, relieving planets beset by new plagues, or assisting wounded in Grid wars. The Nganks, however, were more like cosmetic surgeons, called upon by the higher races, up to Level Fifteen, for specialised work. When Ukrull had first brought him to the hospital ship, Kilaney has asked who tended higher species like the Level Seventeen Tla Beth. As usual, the reptilian Ranger had grunted and refused to answer.

The Nganks' ship had looked impressive from space, a large purple lozenge studded with ghostly translucent struts, stretching outwards to eight luminous jade globes. Pierre had said that when it travelled, the outer spheres emitted a trail of fluorescent waves in their wake. Evidently, Level Twelve species weren't beyond a little panache.

Kilaney fidgeted, scratching idly at non-existent scars. He'd always hated hospitals, and wanted to get to Esperia as soon as possible. While on Ukrull's ship, assisted by Pierre, he'd accessed and interrogated Q'Roth news data-streams, and found that Sister Esma had been loaned a warship for a 'tactical mission' of unspecified intentions. He didn't like the sound of that one bit; the timing couldn't be coincidental.

The teal-coloured channel around him throbbed, as if sensing his antagonism. Cooling rain tinkled down his spine, massaging him, and he realized they had drugged him again. His consciousness winked out.

Kilaney awoke to see something shimmer to the left of his cot. As he propped himself up on his elbows, an avatar of Pierre coalesced out of the ether.

"General, it's good to see you human again. How do you feel?"

"Fine. Where are you? When do we leave?"

"Better, I see. That's good. Can you run?"

Kilaney tried to shake the fuzz out of his head. "Excuse me?"

"Run, General, now, to the left end of the chamber, as fast as you can. This is not a joke or a test."

Kilaney blinked, then rolled off the cot, meaning to break his fall with the mid-legs he no longer possessed, instead slamming hard onto the floor with his knees and hands, feeling sharp stabbing pains. He staggered in the direction Pierre had said, following the avatar, trying to remember how bipeds walked, let alone ran.

"Pierre, mind telling me what the hell –"

"Take a deep breath now, and grab something fixed!"

He'd barely inflated his lungs when space outside lit up, and a thunderclap behind him announced a hull breach. *Hellfire, we're under attack!* Kilaney gripped a metal pole next to an empty bed, but as a sandstorm of swirling colours fled through Pierre's holo-avatar, another alien patient resembling an eight-legged rhino buffeted past him, snapping the rod in two. Kilaney began travelling back towards open space, longing for his Q'Roth claws that could have easily dug into the floor.

The suction stopped with a 'phtum' sound, and he crashed to the floor. Gasping in the scant air left in the room, he turned and saw the snagged rhino's legs flailing. The screaming alien was being slowly sucked through the gash, no doubt being bled dry on the part of its body exposed to hard vacuum.

Kilaney remembered how to run this time, and sprinted to the automatic airlock door, which was trying to close, Pierre's avatar somehow preventing it from doing so. One of the squid surgeons zipped past him, swimming in the violet channel. On instinct he swerved into it too, just as the rhino's scream spiked and was lost in the rush of air vortexing out of the chamber. Kilaney felt like he was running in slow motion, but at least was not being tugged backwards, and his urge to breathe ceased. The squid turned back to glance at him, then swished through the gap into the cylindrical strut. Kilaney made it through three seconds later, suddenly accelerating so fast that he smacked into a wall on the other side, hearing the airlock door clamp into place behind him. He remembered how to sit up against a wall, and his new lungs had no trouble recalling how to pant.

Pierre's platinum avatar lost no time. "Ukrull and I are seventeen long-range transits from your position. We got a lead on Hellera's location while you were being remixed, she's the Kalarash – "

"My memory is fine, Pierre, you told me about her yesterday. Who's attacking, what do I do?"

"Mannekhi raiding party; grab one of the Nganks and don't let go, no matter what happens." Pierre's avatar started fizzing. "Interference. Losing transmission. Good lu– " The avatar vanished.

Kilaney got to his feet. He was at the juncture of two major struts – the   squid had bolted down one of the connecting tubes, but he didn't know which. He charged down the left one.

Midway, he passed rectangular windows, and saw a black sea urchin ship spitting fire at the Ngank lozenge. Normally, Ossyrians or Nganks should have been able to use bio-weapons, eradicating a certain DNA- type within a five million kilometre radius, but if there was one thing Qorall knew about, it was biological warfare, and he'd evidently handed down a few tricks to his Mannekhi foot-soldiers.

Kilaney's conduit lurched, throwing him to the ceiling, enabling him to see a Mannekhi beam slice a clean break through the opposite strut half a kilometre away. The central purple ovoid was criss-crossed with breaches: equipment, patients and no doubt medical staff haemorrhaged from energy-beam incisions. *They're dismembering the ship.*

Artificial gravity failed, and he began to drift away from the ceiling. He managed to kick against it just in time to avoid floating uselessly mid-tube. He drifted to the opposite floor, allowed himself to crouch on it, then kicked off hard. Flying ten metres along the strut, he reached the ceiling again, and shoved his hands against it, effecting an upside-down handspring, making less distance this time, but heading to the floor. As he spun, he saw the Mannekhi ship lance another strut. He kicked off again and reckoned he had just another fifty metres to go. *Six struts left, so if I'm lucky...*

His ears filled with a noise somewhere between a blow-torch and a rocket engine, and he reached ground just in time to grab a conduit as once again air whipped past him. He squinted through the howling rush of air towards the auto-sealing shield door at the end of the strut. No way would he make it. Then he spied the squid surgeon, tentacles flapping, as if trying to swim against the current. As it tumbled towards him, he remembered what Pierre had said. Timing it carefully, just as the Ngank passed over his head, he let go of the conduit and seized the slippery creature's tentacles with both hands.

His fingers and palms burned, then his eyeballs felt like they were aflame, then his whole body. *Don't let go!* Kilaney's eyes scrunched closed against the freezing pull of space, while the bastard squid sent electric shocks through its tentacles till Kilaney tasted blood in his mouth. Still he held on. He knew he had only seconds of consciousness. *Sorry Blake, looks like I'm not going to...*

"Where are we?" Kilaney saw black everywhere except for the luminous squid he still gripped with bleeding hands.

"Let go now. Mannekhi ship. Maintenance shaft."

Kilaney released the Ngank. "You nearly fried me alive back there."

"Saved you. Side effect. Emergency micro-jump."

He studied his palms. The blood was drying. No scars. "Fixed you. Easy. You basic model now."

He knew he was missing some of what the squid was saying, because Largyl 6 included consonants undecipherable by the human hearing system. "Your ship, your comrades?"

The squid's head did a small pirouette. "Ship gone. Comrades?"

"The other surgeons... Wait a Goddam minute, you mean to say you were the only Ngank aboard?"

"Clone projections. Tell you secret. You work out soon, but need know now. Higher Level, less number."

Kilaney thought about it. Pierre said there were only seven Kalarash left in the entire universe, including one who had quit this galaxy, and Hellera, who remained. Q'Roth were Level Six and numbered hundreds of billions, Ossyrians were Level Eight and numbered a few billion, Rangers were Level Fifteen, and were few and far between, maybe a few thousand in the entire galaxy from what he'd heard, and Tla Beth... In all this time he'd never done the math.

"Why?" he asked.

"Think later. Now you take ship."

Kilaney thought he'd heard it wrong, then laughed out loud. "I used to be a general, but I haven't seen my troops in a long time. Why don't you take the ship?"

"Not harm. Ever."

"I thought you used bio-weapons when you had to?" The squid shivered. "Not Ossyrian. Never harm." "Not a great survival philosophy."

One of the tentacles swiped Kilaney's arm, stinging it. "What happened to 'not harm'?"

"You hurt, not harmed. We are old race, ninety million your years. You very young race, know nothing, understand less."

Kilaney bristled. "Still –"

"Survival not everything. Bigger picture."

Kilaney shook his head. This was going nowhere. At least he was still alive. And he had no pain, though by rights he should have. *No pain.* An idea crystallised in his head. "Anaesthetic doesn't do harm, does it?"

The squid didn't answer, but its tentacles braided around each other as if it was crossing them.

Kilaney held out his palms. "Micro-jump. Bridge. Anaesthetise everyone there except me."

The squid didn't move. "You not kill them. Aiding harm, causing harm."

Kilaney grimaced. He'd prefer not to deal with prisoners. "They stay anaesthetised, I'll leave them alone. You have my word."

Two tentacles unfurled into his palms. "This will hurt."

Story of my life.

He tied the last knot around the wrists of the twelfth Mannekhi crewmember on the bridge, then moved over to the comms console. Twice in the past decade he'd boarded a Mannekhi *Spiker*, so he knew his way around. He sent the comms signal, the one Ukrull had shown him.

Pierre's avatar appeared. "Esperia, fast as you can."

Kilaney wasn't much of a man for sentimentalism or congratulations, but he'd expected some surprise that he'd survived and taken the ship. But Pierre continued before he had time to reply.

"General, we've gained some new intel while trying to reach Hellera. We've confirmed that Sister Esma is onboard a Crucible bound for Esperia. Micah and Blake have nothing to match that level of hardware, and frankly neither do the local Ossyrians stationed there. The vessel you're on might stand a chance, if you can surprise her. Can you pilot it alone?"

Kilaney had thought about that. Navigate and operate tactical weapons at the same time? He shook his head. Pierre's avatar looked away from him, and Kilaney heard Ukrull's grating voice.

"Crew still breathe?"

"Yes," Kilaney answered.

"Then listen."

Ukrull told Kilaney something. It made his jaw drop. He stared at the inert crew on the Bridge.

Pierre took up the lead again. "General, there are Shrell en route to Esperia. They will poison space around the planet. You must arrive quickly. We have to jump now. The Ngank can explain about the Shrell." Pierre's eyes grew intense. "You must hold Esperia till the very end, General, whatever the cost. Even if you defeat Sister Esma.

Tell Blake not to leave the spiders. Qorall will come to you. Sorry, we have to jump now."

Kilaney stared at the space where the avatar had been a second ago. It was almost too much to take in, and Pierre had left a lot out. While he chewed it over, he checked weapons status, then set the navigation controls and powered up the engines for the first jump. A low bass rumble vibrated the soles of his feet.

He turned to the Ngank. "So, tell me, who are the Shrell?"

"Space-dwellers, born in outer layer of gas giant." Its tentacles sketched an outline in the air. It flash-filled with colour to produce an image in 3D: *picting*. Kilaney had heard some species could do this, but never actually seen it before. The picture vanished. What Kilaney had seen reminded him of the eagle ray from Earth's tropical oceans, some kind of techware along its wings' edges.

The Ngank's tentacles coiled and twisted around each other. "This bad news. Shrell space-fixers. Patch space after too many high-energy transits bruise subspace. Care about habitat."

Kilaney imagined serene, eco-friendly rays swimming through space. But he'd seen how wars could twist allegiances, particularly those who tried to stay 'neutral'. When a war went global, or in this case galactic, there was no neutral party or territory, everyone took sides sooner or later, out of choice or coercion.

The engines reached mid-pitch. "What did he mean, 'poison space'?"

"Fracture subspace harmonics. Stops transits, creates eddies and vortices."

Kilaney envisioned ships travelling full speed then slamming into a lattice of supercharged exotic particles, like a giant cheese-grater, shredding vessels and occupants, leaving their fragments to drift forever in quickspace. Qorall would send in the worms later to mop everything up. Bad news indeed.

The engines' keening hurt his ears; he wondered how much of a jump they were about to make. He shouted over the rising crescendo.

"Can we stop them?"

The squid's tentacles braided again. "My relief transport arrived. You on own now." The squid teleported, vanishing in front of Kilaney's eyes.

Never harm, it had said, and never abet harm. Kilaney sighed and took the command chair. He doubted he could do anything about the Shrell, except hopefully arrive before them. Sister Esma, though, that was a different matter. But he would need the crew lying unconscious on the floor to help him. That wasn't going to be easy. The engine noise suddenly ceased, as if the ship were holding its breath.

Just as every surface around him turned mercurial, signifying jump initiation, Kilaney smiled, and it felt good on his new face. Despite the odds – his ship was no real match for a Crucible – this was a battle he was looking forward to.

77

* * *

Three hundred Shrell flew in V-formation, their leader Genaspa at the front, setting the pace. They noticed a ship tearing past on a similar vector, ploughing a furrow through the rolling hills of folded Transpace. As one, they flinched at the taut wake-line etched into space-fabric behind its pathway.

<Destroy?> inquired the Second.

<No, Mannekhi vessel, probably escort sent by Qorall> replied Genaspa, the First.

<Repair damage?> inquired the Third.

<Continue> Genaspa replied.

They watched the time-frozen ship race ahead of them on its long trek to Esperia' s system, their own destination, then, as one, increased their speed to match its velocity.

CHAPTER 6 – EYE OF THE STORM

Micah awoke as Esperia's dawn rays stole through the curtains, glancing off Antonia's bare shoulder. She slept on her side, facing away from him. He nuzzled closer, inhaling her scent, nestling his forehead against her hair. Years earlier, a lifetime ago, he'd dreamed of being in bed with her – not just the love-making – of simply being with her, and of them sleeping together. For the first time in months, he felt peaceful, even if he knew it wouldn't last. His fingers traced the curve from her ribs to her hip, then cupped her perfect buttocks one after the other. He moved closer, kissing the back of her neck as he nudged his groin to make contact with her, and he felt himself harden against her soft flesh. She stirred, a hand reaching behind her, finding him. She held him, rubbed him gently between fingers and thumb.

Micah gasped, gnawed at her neck, then coaxed Antonia onto her stomach. She parted her thighs. He stroked the wetness there, her buttocks rising as she moaned softly against his finger.

"Don't be a tease, Micah."

He mounted her, entered her, closed her legs between his, and moved as slowly as he could. Levering up onto his left elbow, his right hand reached around to caress her pert breasts, finding her nipples erect. She made a moaning noise, and both her hands reached behind her, flat against her buttocks, palms upwards, touching him.

His mind reeled, and his body shook. Micah took both her wrists and pinned them to the pillow above her head with his left hand, while his right lifted her chin up so his lips could meet her mouth. She kissed him hard, devouring him. He kept up the same rhythm, thrust deeper, felt her tighten around him, never letting go of the kiss.

They lay entwined, neither of them speaking. Micah basked in the moment, knowing their world was soon to unravel, but savouring every minute that passed. He etched every second of the past ten hours into his memory. Antonia's finger played with the hair on his chest, tugged at it. He kissed her again, urgently, knowing he was in forbidden territory, somebody else's bed. He felt the guilt rise inside him, like a gathering storm in his chest. As he drew back, she read his look.

"Another lifetime," she said, kindness and warmth in her eyes, letting him down gently.

A lyric from an old classic song popped into his head. "You're fuckin' perfect, Antonia."

She glanced away, bit her lip. "Kat used to sing me that song."

He rolled onto his back. She had always belonged to Kat. This night had been an eye in the storm for Antonia, too.

He sat up. "I intend to find her. Bring her back to you."

She stroked his back, then sat up, and kissed his shoulder. "Do you think you can find her?"

"It's top of my agenda, why I resigned."

"To find Louise, or to find Kat?"

He gave her a sideways look, which made her smile. He knew that while Antonia looked demure, she wasn't naïve. "Both, I hope, but I only plan to bring one back alive."

Her eyebrows edged closer. "But if they split up and you have to make a choice?"

He'd thought about it. "Kat," he answered, wondering how he might really react if faced with that particular choice.

"Because she can link to the Hohash?"

He nodded. And because the Hohash can link to the Kalarash, and only they can stop Qorall.

Micah mock-pinched her thigh and got out of bed. "I'll make breakfast."

"Micah?"

He paused, turned around to face her, naked in every way. "Whoever gets you is a lucky woman."

He winked. "Perhaps. Or maybe you just don't often sleep with a guy who hasn't had sex for seven years."

She grinned, and was about to say something else, but he pre-empted her. "Toast or eggs?"

She lay back down, put her hands behind her head. "I like both, Micah."

He laughed and walked into the lounge and froze. A Hohash mirror hovered soundlessly a few centimetres off the floor on the other side of the room. Kat stared through the mirror straight at him.

"Kat!" he said.

Kat's face cocked an eyebrow, and he remembered he was completely nude. But Antonia had heard him utter Kat's name, and dashed into the room, a sheet hastily draped around her. Kat raised the other eyebrow, but Antonia rushed past Micah to the mirror, her sheet falling off as she seized the Hohash's frame and knelt before her lover, her wife. Micah couldn't see either of their faces, but Antonia's shoulders trembled. He moved out of line of sight into the kitchen, retrieving one or two of his garments on the way.

He wondered how timing could be so cruel. Hohash were mute, like the spiders, so no verbal communication was possible except through a third medium, somebody with a node. His guilt went into overdrive, but that was secondary – this could have ramifications. Kat had every right to be angry and could turn away from them. But there was nothing he could do. Even if oral communication were possible it would probably not help. Sometimes words only made it worse.

Antonia called him over. "Micah, I think she wants to say something to you."

Micah didn't see how. But no sooner than he was in line of sight of Kat, his head started to hurt. A searing pain stabbed at him behind his eyeballs, blinding him. He cried out and dropped to his knees, gasping with pain.

"Micah, what's wrong?" Antonia put her arm around his shoulders, but he could see nothing, and the pain bit deeper. His forehead was on the floor, his hands to his temples.

"Kat, stop it, please, you're hurting him!"

Micah groaned, unable to think. His resident, she must be using it. How? He gasped again.

Antonia was shouting. "Kat, stop it now. Please! Hurt me, I'm as much to blame!"

Abruptly the pain shut off, and Micah collapsed onto his back, his hands over his eyes, his breath ragged. After a while, he dared to open them. Antonia knelt next to him, red-eyed, wiping her cheeks, sheet back in place around her. He laid a hand on her thigh. "Are you okay?"

She shook her head. "I'm so sorry, Micah, really. Kat's gone now; she looked sharply at something to her right and then the Hohash just cleared."

Micah tried to get up, but his head started to split. "Not all her fault," he said.

"What do you mean?"

His thoughts were clearing, but he was still catching his breath. "The Hohash accessed my resident."

"What? You still have that thing in your head? I thought the Tla Beth neutralized it during the trial?"

He shrugged, then winced.

"How can a node interface with a resident?"

"I don't know, but it did. Kat was trying to send me a message. The Hohash... it picked up on Kat's anger – pretty natural, really – and amplified it."

Antonia frowned. "Are you just saying that, Micah? Because I'm –"

He squeezed her thigh. "I felt her; she was willing it to stop. Honest."

Antonia bit her lip. "This is all my fault. I don't deserve either of you."

Micah tried getting up again, Antonia helping him. "Listen, Antonia, she's alive. That's what matters." Micah had also felt something else in the 'transmission'; Kat's intense loneliness verging on despair. He'd tried to convey emotions back to her: that she was sorely missed; that last night had been a one-night fling; but he wasn't sure he'd gotten through.

Antonia's face brightened. "She is alive, isn't she? My God, Micah, you've no idea..."

He held her, saying nothing, while her tears rolled down his chest. Then his resident interrupted his thoughts. He had no idea how Kat and the Hohash had done it, given that nodes and residents were completely different technologies, but two verbal messages appeared in his mind's eye. The first said that Kat would somehow find a way to forgive him, but if he did it again she would kill him, adding that she already forgave Antonia, and to tell her so. His relief translated into a tighter hug around Antonia.

The second message said: "General Kilaney is alive. Pierre went to retrieve him. Complicated. With luck he can help you from the outside. Will try to find out more. Have to go. Difficult to communicate. Louise is –". The message ended.

He closed his eyes, relishing Antonia's touch for the last time. *Thanks Kat, we owe you one, and this will never happen again.*

They ate, or at least Antonia did, once she'd calmed down. Kat's first message helped. Micah had black coffee, a rarity grown with haphazard success some three hundred klicks South of Esperantia. He cradled the cup, sipping the steaming bitter ultresso as he stared through the window towards the Acarian mountains. If Kilaney was able to come... He needed to tell Blake, this news would turn things around for sure, since Kilaney had been Blake's commander back on Earth.

"Is Pierre coming back, too?" Antonia asked.

Micah knew why she was asking. "I don't think so. At least the message to me implied Kilaney would be coming back. I think she'd have said if Pierre was, too."

Antonia didn't comment further, blowing across the top of her coffee cup, looking to Micah as if she were miles away, most probably light years.

Micah put down his cup and stood up.

"Blake needs to know about this, Vasquez too," he said.

She rose. "And Petra. And Zack?"

He stared at her. He hadn't thought about involving Zack's Transpar, Blake's former right-hand man. Antonia had a point, since Kilaney had also trained Zack, apparently. But during the Trial Zack had been transformed into a man of glass, completely transparent in every way, unable to lie and therefore the perfect witness for the prosecution. They'd also taken away his personality. His wife Sonja said that every now and again she saw glimpses of the old Zack, but if so, she was the only one. Even Blake believed there was nothing left of the original Zack.

"Maybe," he said. "The Council should be informed, but I'm no longer on Council, so –"

"I'll inform them, Micah." She touched his arm. "I see now why you resigned. You don't want to be second-guessed and compromised by eleven other people."

He nodded, and was about to say goodbye, but she placed a finger across his lips, and shook her head.

In the doorway, as he was about to leave, she spoke again. "You know, Micah, you and Gabriel aren't so different. You want the same thing, and neither of you play by the rules. He's fixated on the threat from Sister Esma, you're more worried about Louise. And Pierre, wherever he is, well, he went off to fight against Qorall." Her face darkened. "Micah, what if all three enemies are coming here?"

Micah stroked his chin. "We can't have that much bad luck, Antonia."

Once he left, foreboding flooded in. What if Antonia was right? He needed to see Blake. But then he also needed to see the Ossyrians. They alone had sensors reaching outside the quarantine barrier, and they alone could call for reinforcements. They might be pacifists, but they were Level Eight, two notches higher than the Q'Roth and three above the Alicians.

He headed into the centre of town, wondering how he was going to set up a meeting with them. For the past nine months as the end of Quarantine approached, excepting a couple of medical emergencies due to farming accidents, the Ossyrians had eschewed all human contact.

Micah heard the shouting before he arrived in the square in front of the Council Chamber, the only place where daffodils grew in the Esperian Spring, genetically modified by the Genners to survive the winter's acidic blue snows. The yelling rose in pitch, and he broke into a trot. Rounding the corner he saw the Transpar – Zack – holding the wrist of a farmer Micah barely knew. Erik Fornasson, his resident reminded him, a wizened man with wild grey hair like a scouring pad, framing hollow cheeks and blazing eyes. Fornasson pounded the transparent man made of alien glass with his free fist and his dusty boots, to no avail. Micah slowed to a brisk pace, cutting through the growing crowd of bemused and angry people.

Micah caught the eye of an approaching khaki-uniformed constable and then stepped into the zone surrounding the grappling pair.

Zack had been Micah's friend, and Blake's best friend, and had sworn vengeance on Louise after her last attack, but had been the first casualty of their trial by the Tla Beth. He was no longer human, instead a cipher made of flow-glass, but with enough of Zack's memories that his wife Sonja would rather have him than nothing. Most of the community shunned Zack and pitied Sonja, and nobody talked to him except the original team who'd been out in the Grid: himself, Sandy, and Blake. Micah hadn't seen him for over a year.

Fornasson spied Micah. "Hey, get him the hell off me. I have rights, don't I?"

Micah considered it for a moment. Two more constables arrived, taking up the rear. "Release him, Zack. That's an order." He had no jurisdiction over Zack, but he hoped the military style of his command would have an impact; the original Zack had been a soldier all his life. With an inward shiver Micah realized Zack had not aged in any appreciable sense in eighteen years.

The head of glass swivelled in Micah's direction, eyes crystal clear like an ice sculpture. He regarded Micah for a second then opened the hand holding Fornasson. The farmer made a fuss of rubbing his wrist and glaring at the Transpar.

"Now, if nobody minds, I'll get back to my animals, they need milking, and –"

"A couple of questions first, please." Micah barred his way, as the constables moved a measured distance behind the farmer. He noticed other farmers, friends of Fornasson most likely, edge towards the front of the crowd. Several had their staffs with them. They stood tall, outnumbering Micah and the constables three to one.

Fornasson puffed out his chest. "I don't have to answer any questions from you, Mr. President. In fact, I heard you resigned last night, so I'll be on my way." But he remained where he was.

Micah nodded absently. He addressed the small crowd, focusing on the farmers. "Four spiders were burned to death yesterday in their home in Shimsha. It was arson."

People shuffled, murmured to each other. A few of Fornasson's friends glanced to him, then to one other. Fornasson glared. The embers of hatred evident in his eyes and the lack of surprise told Micah all he needed to know.

Fornasson glowered. "Can't say I'm too upset about that. More than a few of my cattle have disappeared through the years."

It was true. Micah had pressed Blake on the issue but had never gotten a satisfactory answer. But equating the sentient spiders to cattle spoke volumes about how Fornasson viewed humanity's alien neighbours. Micah turned to Zack, who hadn't budged a millimetre since releasing the farmer. "Why did you seize this man?"

Zack answered in a voice that tinkled like wind chimes. It was pleasant on the ears, but Micah missed Zack's booming baritone. "Forensic evidence: spider DNA strands, fuel oil residue on his palms, smoke particles in his hair consistent with the crime scene, psychological profile and reactions since capture."

Micah didn't know Zack's capabilities; nobody did, not even Sonja, who wouldn't tell if she did. He had no doubt that Zack was right, but the crowd wouldn't see it that way, and there was due legal process to be followed; Micah's process, in fact.

"Mr. Fornasson, I'm afraid I'm going to have to ask you to accompany these constables to the police station."

A young farmer stepped forward, planting his staff in the ground. "Erik is right. You are no longer President. And these spiders – why should we care if they had an accident and a few of them died? What did they ever do for us?"

In part Micah sympathised with the latter argument. Over the years he'd entreated Blake and Glenda to work to bring the communities together. But the spiders didn't trust humans. Whether it was a self- fulfilling prophecy, or an accurate judgment of human characteristics, was moot right now. Micah was amazed they had all gotten this far without incident.

"As a citizen, and on behalf of Captain Blake Alexander," Micah said, knowing that most citizens still held Blake in high regard, "I'd like to ask the constables to question this man and the Transpar." *There, that should do it.*

"No." Zack's gaze locked onto Fornasson.

"Zack," Micah started, but didn't get time to finish. The nannites in his brain shifted gear to quick-mode to take it all in. The young farmer swung his staff upwards to strike at Zack's groin. Another farmer behind Fornasson took out a short pulse pistol from his pocket. A third, seeing the constables distracted, let his weapon – a stun rod – drop into the palm of his hand. Zack moved like a blur, the young farmer's staff finding empty air until Zack's hand sliced through it, chopping it in two. Zack sank to the ground, his right leg stretching out horizontally behind him at calf level as he spun around, sweeping both farmers off their feet, snatching the pistol out of the second farmer's hand in mid-air. Zack rose again, and with a flourish of his fingers flicked a globule of his own glass flesh at the third farmer's forehead, then returned to exactly where he'd been, in time to seize Fornasson's wrist before the man had time to move away. The two farmers hit the ground with a thump. Micah's resident flashed "1.1 seconds" in his left eye.

The young farmer was on the ground, staff snapped in two, the other farmer, pistol-less, rolled into the dust clutching a mangled hand. The third wavered as if stung, as his weapon dropped from his limp hand to the floor. A small coin-sized glass disk adhered momentarily to his forehead. As it fell off, the man collapsed onto all fours, the disk rolling in the dust towards Zack's foot where it was re-absorbed. Zack passed the pistol to one of the constables. It had been crushed beyond repair. The constable took it gingerly, his eyes wide, staring at the Transpar.

The crowd caught up with these lightning-fast events, shuffling backwards. Two of the constables dragged the unconscious farmer away, confiscating his illegal stun rod. But the peace didn't last. Other farmers helped up their comrades, then as one advanced on Zack.

Shouting and arm-waving resumed, farmers jostling with the two remaining constables to release Fornasson from Zack's grip. Micah knew the time for reasoning, always short with a mob, had passed. Not for the first time, he witnessed fear overtake people's rational minds   as they fought against the Transpar, something alien, ignoring the man buried deep inside who had fought so hard and sacrificed everything to save them. The crowd grew larger, which in Micah's experience rarely improved the situation. Against his better judgment, nannites poured into his hands and feet, increasing their tensile strength tenfold. Zack's crystal head pivoted in Micah's direction. Micah wondered how much Zack sensed.

The whine of a transport sled screeching to a halt interrupted the melee. The crowd broke apart, those at the front craning their necks to see who had arrived. Micah watched the two Ossyrians dismount from their hover-chariot.

People turned to see the pure black faces like Alsatian dogs, Pharaonic head-dresses of horizontal gold, jet and lapis lazuli stripes, and dazzling white knee-length tunics concealing black furry limbs.

The Ossyrians, Level Eight doctors who had eradicated every ailment from cancer to the common cold, had ministered to the populace whenever in dire need. All diseases had been purged permanently, to the point where Ossyrian appearances had become a rarity. One walked with a dancer's gait up to Fornasson. It lifted a scanning device that swept invisible waves up and down the farmer's body. The Ossyrian placed a paw on Fornasson's chest. The farmer tried to back away but Zack held him firm. From the Ossyrian's limb a needle emerged and punctured the man's sternum. No blood appeared. Fornasson became still. So did everyone else.

The Ossyrian opened his jaw, revealing the mesh of pale blue fibres within. A few in the crowd placed their hands over their ears again,   as the voice emanated like a choir of fingernails scratching down a chalkboard.

"Did you kill the spiders?"

Fornasson's body shuddered as if due to an internal struggle, then became calm. "Yes."

Again the grating voice. "Did you have help?"

Fornasson's body was almost as still as Zack's. "No." The syringe retracted and the Ossyrian lowered his paw.

"Wait," Micah said. He walked up to Fornasson, who looked groggy, as if waking from a dream, his calm features crumpling into a frown as he realized what he'd just confessed.

"Fornasson," Micah said, keeping anger out of his voice. "Erik. Why? Why did you do it?"

The man's features twisted and curled, and he turned sideways and spat on the floor. "It's just a matter of time. A few cattle, a few people go missing. We're on *their* world, Micah. You and Blake brought us here, thinking it was empty, but it wasn't. Sooner or later, it'll be us or them. Any sane person can see what's coming."

Micah turned to the Ossyrian. He had to move on, because he knew that even the more rational people around him had at one time or another wondered the same thing. Hell, even he had. "What happens now?"

The Ossyrian uttered a squeal that made Micah and everyone else flinch, and the Transpar led an unresisting Fornasson to the sled, the farmers backing away, heads down, few meeting the eyes of their comrade. Anger and resentment were one thing, apparently, pre-meditated murder another.

The Ossyrian addressed Micah. "You are also coming with us. You are responsible for your people."

Micah's eyes widened a fraction, then he nodded. "Of course." He addressed the crowd. "Go home, all of you." Then he added to the farmers. "I'll see Erik Fornasson gets fair treatment." Without waiting for a reaction, because he had no idea if he could deliver on that promise, he called to Zack. "Tell Blake what happened, where we're going." He'd almost forgotten. "And tell him Kilaney is coming."

The Transpar stared at Micah.

The crowd shuffled backwards as Micah and the Ossyrian boarded the sled. He stood next to Fornasson, who scowled.

"You should've stayed out of this, Mr. ex-President. Your time is over. You led us to this point, you and your damned liberalism, and were about to walk away. Well, now you can't." He looked Micah in the eye. "You're an analyst, as we've all heard before. So, I know I've committed a crime, and I'll pay, but you, you can trace it all the way back to its causes." He looked forward again. "Might not like what you find – who you find – if you do."

Micah dismissed the idea. Long ago he'd learned the difference between a cause and a contributory factor, and the role of individual choice in separating the two. However, there was a trace of guilt, though not for this crime. "You're *mostly* wrong, Fornasson. What I should have done, as an analyst, is seen this coming."

Zack appeared next to Micah so silently it made him start. "Bill Kilaney?"

Micah nodded. The Transpar's face was like a child's, completely innocent. Without another word the Transpar turned and started walking towards Hazzard's Ridge.

The Ossyrian sled lifted knee-height off the ground and thrummed through the streets, the cool morning breeze brushing against Micah's cheeks. Once outside Esperantia, the crystal pyramid gleamed up ahead in the distance. Despite the circumstances, Micah smiled. It had been a long time since he'd been inside the Ossyrian ship.

Out of the corner of his eye he saw something charging up the hill to his right, a trail of dust behind it. It was the Transpar, running. God it was fast! Micah smiled again. *Go, Zack, go!* He wished he could be there to see Blake's face when he heard the news.

CHAPTER 7 – SUPERNOVA

Pierre's father had often told him the smart ones hide right out in the open. Still, where they were about to go was hard for him to accept, even with his Level Ten intelligence rating. Sitting next to the reptilian Ranger Ukrull in their cramped craft that smelled like a swamp, he stared through the front viewer, his nannites adjusting to the glare so he didn't have to squint.

"You're sure about this?" he asked, knowing there was really no need for the question, for two reasons. First Ukrull, at Level Fifteen, had a kind of telepathy, advanced neurological scanning senses that could detect and process thought patterns from an array of stimuli. Second, Ukrull was always sure. Still, Pierre had never seen the inside of a supernova before, and felt the occasion merited the question, even if he knew Ukrull would not deign to answer. Telepaths didn't appreciate rhetoric.

The blaze of raw power in front of them across the entire spectrum screamed at any normal being to run like hell, whether intelligent or simply endowed with basic survival instincts. Pierre hadn't felt anything like fear for a long time, but he had to admit this situation had his full attention. Ukrull, however, didn't even acknowledge the question with so much as a grunt. Instead he kicked a control and their ship lunged forward into the hidden homeworld of the Tla Beth.

As they slipped though the cauldron's edge of the slowly exploding star the ship's scanner blanked, unable to process brightness on such a scale. This time Ukrull grunted. "Fix later."

Pierre had asked him years ago why he didn't have a bigger, better ship. The Ice Pick, as Ukrull referred to his stubby vessel, effectively his home for more than ten thousand years, wasn't top of the range by Grid standards. Ukrull had gone unusually quiet, and his scaly tail had for once stopped thrashing. "Acquired second-hand. Gift. Don't make like used to."

Ukrull had never revealed who the gift was from. The ship's hull creaked despite the null field around it, made the grinding whine of an animal in pain, and shuddered. The Ice Pick had to be Tla Beth tech, Level 17.

"Eighteen," Ukrull corrected.

Pierre turned to stare at his mud-coloured, amber-eyed reptilian companion, whose upper incisors curled down his lower jaw like mini- tusks. Level Eighteen were a mystery, confirmed extinct. The Kalarash, having nurtured them for millions of years, had suddenly and inexplicably wiped them out. Pierre wondered how old Ukrull really was. He didn't believe telepaths were beyond telling lies.

The screen stuttered awake again, and Pierre felt a jolt. They had landed. On what he had no idea, because all he saw forward was a uniform purple sky.

"Outside," Ukrull stated, as he nudged the airlock control, adding, even before Pierre thought his question, "Safe."

In many respects it was the inverse of a Dyson Sphere. Humanity had long ago conceived the idea of constructing a sphere of immense diameter around a small star, creating a self-contained world within the Dyson shell, with infinite energy supply. The Tla Beth had gone one stage further and built a home inside a dying sun. He knew that two billion years ago the war between the Kalarash and Qorall had involved using stars as weapons, so perhaps they had developed counter-measures, maybe involving phase-shifting – Pierre could only guess. Still, superlatives failed him. He gazed upwards towards the reflective shield, indigo in colour, shading their inner asteroid-sized planet in permanent twilight. He had no idea how it worked, but as a defence it was ingenious; even star-breaker weapons were unpredictable against a supernova, and Nova bombs would be a self-evident waste of time and energy.

The ground was smooth as glass. With each step its marbled yellows and greys swirled, as if the floor was alive, reacting to him. He intuited what it meant. The entire surface was receptive, recording and processing everything. Ukrull had once told Pierre that the highest intelligence was pure perception, though Pierre found that difficult to accept. But evidently the Tla Beth placed a high value on data and information.

He'd expected a grand city, at least some spires and exotic aerial vehicles. The Tla Beth were legendary in Gridlore, and also mysterious, leading to many fables and artistic renditions of a fantastic crystal metropolis in golden skies where they might live. But after half an hour of walking, something he relished after being cooped up in the Ice Pick for months, he had seen no structures whatsoever.

"Tla Beth energy creatures, phase-shifters. Can live, function, hide in Transpace. Self-sustaining. Entire planet tech. Planet has Makers. If need, supply. Power no problem here," he said, flicking a claw skywards.

Pierre filled in the rest: the inner core of the small 'planet' must include exotic matter, so the 'Makers' could fabricate anything – ships, weapons. The planet would then shrink very slightly, as matter was converted during the process, and local gravity would be updated. No, he thought, the Tla Beth themselves were probably tolerant of massive gravitic shifts – it wouldn't matter to them. He gazed down at the whorls around his feet and understood. The flooring was creating local gravity for him and Ukrull. It represented yet another defence mechanism against uninvited invaders.

"Correct."

This time it wasn't Ukrull. A Tla Beth had buzzed in front of them. Pierre had the curious feeling he should bow, but restrained himself. The creature was the shape of a rounded hourglass encircled by a dozen vertical metallic rings, hues on each one shifting like oil on water into infra and ultra frequencies. Pierre adjusted his eyesight so he could pick up all twenty-seven official Grid colours. It was impressive, mainly because he knew these rings were processing terabytes of data every second; the light show was a side effect.

The top and bottom parts of the hourglass – the Tla Beth's 'body' – were black and white, like a version of the yin-yang symbol, ubiquitous in more than a hundred Grid sub-cultures. The top half was mainly dark with smatterings of white, the lower half the reverse. Drops of white – whatever they were – sifted through the Tla Beth's hourglass 'waist' like liquid sand, altering the balance of black and white.

Pierre focused. This was a War Council meeting. Ukrull delivered his briefing, and Pierre watched as holos flashed at an almost subliminal rate: star charts, figures and casualty statistics, attack formations, dark worm incursions, strategic assessments, all silently transmitted between Ukrull and the Tla Beth. Pierre couldn't follow all of it, but the net result was plain; they were steadily losing against Qorall.

Abruptly the transmissions stopped. The Tla Beth's upper half was almost black, a single white dot in its centre. It spoke to Pierre in flawless English.

"We have located one of the Benefactors, a Kalarash."

Pierre knew better than to ask where; undoubtedly the information had already been uploaded into the Ice Pick's nav-mind. The Tla Beth answered the next questions before Pierre had finished thinking them.

"The second one. Tla Beth and Kalarash have uneasy relationship. Yes."

Pierre tried to catch up fast, reverse-engineering his questions. *The one that left the galaxy, or its mate Hellera, who was still somewhere inside the galaxy?* Next. *Why send us, why don't you go find the Kalarash?* Next. *Is it because of what happened to the Level Eighteen race?*

Pierre nodded, but the Tla Beth and Ukrull had gotten bored waiting and were conversing again, using some kind of 'picting', symbols appearing and dissolving in the ether between them.

Pierre had never been very emotional, having been raised by two scientists, even before his father had interfered with Pierre's genetics, mutating his intelligence at the cost of his ability to love. Or so he'd thought until his brief affair with Kat. Since then, after the Ossyrians had tried to help him change and his nannites had spiralled out of control, catapulting him to Level Ten, he'd lost almost all emotional feeling. He'd never looked back. It was a scientist's dream to become more intelligent, to understand so much more, to travel the galaxy and see its wonders first-hand, in the company of someone even more intelligent. A scientist always needed a challenge, and for Pierre finding new questions motivated him almost as much as deriving answers.

But he *had* thought of Kat over the years, wondering what had become of her and the daughter he'd abandoned shortly after her birth. Sure, he had bigger things to attend to. But recently – and he was convinced this was somehow Ukrull's doing – he was almost remembering how to feel, how to care. And he 'felt' something now. He tried to remember which emotion it was, what label to apply. To know was to quantify, so he made an instantaneous assessment, even though he knew that such numbers were neither stable nor independent. What he 'felt' was 41% anxiety, 27% concern for two people he'd not seen in eighteen years and – this was the one that surprised him – 32% indignation at the way the Tla Beth and Ukrull were ignoring him, and the fact that they'd lost touch with the Kalarash in the first place. The 32% increased, polarising him into a state of something approaching anger.

The picting stopped. Ukrull turned toward Pierre. The Tla Beth had a helix of white coiling in its upper half. It was hard to tell when Ukrull was grinning, but Pierre reckoned he was. The Tla Beth spoke.

"You are right. We became complacent, arrogant. We felt we did not need the Benefactors anymore. And your next question: can a single Kalarash defeat Qorall and his ever-growing army? Unlikely. But she must try."

For a split-second, white surged into the Tla Beth's upper half, swirled, and then squirted back into the lower half, the rings all turning a pale green. Pierre had no idea what that meant.

The Tla Beth continued. "If you are unsuccessful, we will consider surrender. Too much of the galaxy has already been lost."

Pierre's quicksilver eyes narrowed. "But..." He gazed first at the Tla Beth, then Ukrull. Neither said any more.

Pierre bowed to the Tla Beth, and then nodded to Ukrull. "Then let's go." He recalled what Blake, his former commander, used to say. It seemed appropriate.

"Time's burning."

Pierre ate a small plate of nutrients as he and Ukrull hurtled through Transpace toward the Diamond Nebula where the last Kalarash known to exist in the galaxy, Hellera, was reportedly hiding. The food was the perfect mix for his health, and had a bland, metallic taste. He hadn't changed his weekly 'meal' for ten years. Ukrull chewed noisily on a bone, occasional crunching sounds preceding a spray of gristle and reptilian saliva that Ukrull would leave for the Ice Pick's cockpit microbes and fauna to digest and reprocess into amino acids, including some of those Pierre was eating. Pierre forced down his last mouthful with an audible gulp, then made sure he got to the waste recycling closet before Ukrull. Pierre could mentally disconnect his nasal senses if he chose to, but he simply preferred to be first.

Afterwards, Pierre decided he needed some privacy. He slipped into an inner trance to take stock of events and his own situation. He and Ukrull had seen first-hand Qorall's strategy, brilliant in military terms, and utterly ruthless. But Pierre felt he was missing something, something obvious. For eighteen years he had had no truck with something as fuzzy as intuition, and yet he couldn't deny he was uncomfortable with the Tla Beth's plan.

For the first time in years, he wished Kat were there to advise him, he would welcome her instinct. But at Level Ten, he could do the next best thing: he focused and recalled every aspect of her, every conversation, inflexion of voice, eye movement, pupil dilation... In his mind an avatar of Kat arose, facing him in a white room.

"Hello, Pierre," the avatar said. "Platinum suits you. It's your colour."

Pierre felt pleased at first, then caught himself – was he pleased with the simulation, or to see her again? Just an avatar, he reminded himself – let's try to keep this scientific; clinical. He addressed the slim, short-haired brunette with the grey eyes and crooked smile. "You have access to all my premises. We go to meet the female Kalarash known as Hellera. What do you advise?"

She cocked her head. "I missed you. I thought it would go away; you know, fade. It didn't. Not much, anyway. Not nearly enough."

He had an urge to clear his throat. This wasn't going to plan. He thought about removing some of the emotional algorithms his brain had engineered into her avatar, but of course that would affect her intuition. He had to play along.

"I... missed you too, in a way."

She glanced away. "Whatever. Your daughter – Petra – of course you remember her name, it's the last word you spoke to me. She's grown up into quite the young lady, but she's never even met you, her father." Her eyes flashed dark. Anger, he realised. But she continued, waving a hand dismissively. "Okay, back to your agenda. You're seeing something that the Tla Beth are missing, but you're also avoiding an obvious solution." She folded her arms, stared at him.

Pierre knew the first part, what he was seeing. "That Qorall is evil." To the Tla Beth such a concept would be seen as too vague and superstitious, foolish even. Pierre considered it, letting it 'run' in his head. The Tla Beth thought Qorall wanted to overtake the galaxy, to be its supreme commander. That made sense to Grid Society and its masters, who valued intelligence above all else, and ultimately order through control. But what if Qorall wanted revenge? What if he was not only intelligent, but consumed by two billion years of rage against whatever the Kalarash had done to him? The thought stream and all its implications condensed into fact in his mind. "Qorall wants to *destroy* the galaxy? But why?"

She walked up to him, held his shoulders. It had a curious effect on him, and he didn't understand why, since both his image and the avatar were figments of his mind. Still, he didn't shrug her off. Her hands felt warm. He remembered Kat's touch, a long time ago, when he'd been a different Pierre. It had meant so much to him then. She let go. He felt a pang. *Why did she let go?*

"Pierre, this galaxy was nurtured by Qorall's nemesis, the Kalarash. It's their garden, it means something to them. He wants to hurt them. Maybe he's only pretending to take over the galaxy. He'll leave nothing but cold rock, no light, no stars left burning."

"Like last time," he said, recalling the legends of the War two billion years ago that had left the Jannahi galaxy dead.

"Petra has your eyes. Well, not those ones obviously, not silver, but you know, like you had before. It's why I could never forget you."

Pierre felt unbalanced, disturbed. But he resisted the urge to tamper with her algorithms, because he hadn't yet seen the solution she'd mentioned.

"Show me those eyes, Pierre, then I'll tell you."

He felt something, a shade of an emotion. Indignation, he recalled. "This is a little absurd, you know you are an avatar."

She shrugged. "Humour me. Or yourself. I'm a construct of your mind. Maybe you're trying to answer more than the question you think you are interested in."

Was it possible? He made an adjustment to his matrix, his silver eyes rippling to be replaced by his old human ones. He still stored their DNA signature. He thought it would make no difference, this was all inside his mind in any case. But it did. He saw her differently, as if she really were Kat, not just an avatar. She gazed at him. A smile, a non-crooked one, broadened her lips. He felt an urge to mimic the gesture.

"Thank you," she said. She broke off her gaze and turned away, speaking to the nondescript, out-of-focus walls in his mind. "You go to seek Hellera as an ally, to fight Qorall."

"Yes."

"But the Tla Beth think she will not be enough on her own to defeat him."

"Yes."

"Then don't see her as an ally."

Pierre still didn't get it. How was this possible? What was the point of being Level Ten if a normal human could see something he could not? He suddenly wondered if she were really an avatar, or something else. But that wasn't possible.

She said nothing further. He played back her words. Hellera. Ally. The antonym of ally would be enemy. Not an enemy. Wrong track. Defeat. Synonym of defeat is surrender. No. Something else. Third way. Not defeat. Qorall more powerful. Capitulate. Placate. Hellera..."

Kat turned back to him. "There, that wasn't so hard was it?"

He stared at her. "You think we should capture Hellera and hand her over to Qorall?"

"He wants to hurt someone." She walked up close to him. "Pierre, you're still a good man, it's why you haven't thought of it, but it's an option you must consider."

"For the sake of the galaxy?"

She shrugged. "You called me here to dig up what you didn't want to face. You now have more cards in your hand. It's just an option, you don't have to take it."

She looked small, human, fragile. He placed a hand on her shoulder, then another. She looked up at him. He pulled her towards him, felt her warmth against his cool platinum skin. He let her avatar fade from his arms, dissolving her construct.

Pierre returned from the depths of his mind to the surface, back inside the Ice Pick. The Hohash had been active, he noticed, but it went dark again. Ukrull was gazing at it. Pierre assumed he'd been interfacing with it for some reason.

Pierre wondered whether to tell Ukrull about this potential game plan. He didn't know how far the Ranger's telepathy could penetrate. Too far, probably.

"Ukrull, we have to talk."

The Ranger pulled back from the controls, clasped his fore-claws together, and faced Pierre with a hard stare. He then leaned forward, close enough that his breath made Pierre recoil.

"What?" Pierre said.

Ukrull leant back in his chair, and snorted. "Okay. We talk. First, what wrong with your eyes?"

CHAPTER 8 – INTERROGATION

Louise no longer liked what she saw in the washroom mirror when she got up in the morning. She'd just finished her daily physical training routine and showered. The face was still pretty enough, her body trim and fit, but her expression betrayed a wrong turn she'd made somewhere along the line, a sacrifice that went against her inner nature. She continued to stare as she stood in the full-body dryer, warm jets of air rippling her supple skin. She reflected that her life split neatly into four parts.

Before Earth's Third World War she'd been 'normal', a teacher. Louise could barely remember what that even felt like, who she was back then: naïve and dumb, asleep, drifting through life. The War changed her forever; signing up then getting captured, tortured and raped every day for a year before their camp was liberated and she took her revenge. She'd joined the Chorazin, the global Interpol, fought against the bad guys – though it never really mattered to her who they were – alongside Vince.

She stepped out of the dryer enclosure, put on a string and donned her one-piece black uniform with its Chinese collar, Qorall's vermillion circle insignia above the left breast. It reminded her of the Chorazin outfit, and of Vince. Those had been the good times, when work and love came together in a resounding, satisfying collision. Except she outgrew the Chorazin and became a double agent for the Alicians. Her third phase. She still could have recovered at that point, but then Micah came along. Louise brushed her teeth. Micah had gotten Vince killed on Esperia, while trying to kill her. She spat out the frothy foam, rinsing her mouth. That had been the sharp point of inflexion on the curve of her life, into a downward spiral. She'd ended up irrevocably pitted against humanity, whom she now despised and believed should be eradicated. But her 'career path', ending up working for Qorall in her fourth phase, had also left her at odds with Sister Esma and the Alicians, her only remaining 'family'.

These last eighteen years had been intriguing and fascinating, exploring the Grid and all its species. But lately it had all been ultimately unsatisfying. What was the point? Rather, what was the point for her, personally? She'd had a few lovers here and there, the Mannekhi being the closest physically, but no one that mattered. So, where the hell was she going with her life? It reminded her of one of those pathetic job questions during her annual appraisal back on Earth: "Where do you see yourself in five years time?" She quit the bathroom.

Louise walked to Kat's room. Aramisk, the stocky, dark-haired Mannekhi girl with an impudent tongue that would get her killed one day, sat staring at a pad beside the twitching body of Kat. The Hohash mirror was locked in a rectangular brace at the foot of Kat's bed, active but unable to leave.

"Is she still in the dream, Aramisk?"

"Yes, Arctura."

Even her Q'Roth name now sounded wrong to her. She studied Kat. This had been Qorall's idea. Let her rampage through the info-streams till she dug up something from Qorall's enemies about Hellera, the missing Kalarash, or the other one, Kalaran, who left the galaxy just before Esperia's quarantine. The Kalarash were the only real potential threat to Qorall, but he couldn't locate them.

Louise reluctantly acknowledged she liked Kat, or at least respected her, which put her in a very select but important category in Louise's world. It was probably because Kat had never truly given up her struggle since her capture two years ago. Similar to Louise in that enemy camp back in Thailand, Kat was biding her time, even now trying to play both sides, pretending she was working for Louise and Qorall. A little naïve, but at least she had integrity, a quality few possessed, no matter their Level.

But this controlled dreaming procedure, and its next interrogation phase would almost certainly kill her. Louise kept her voice flat. "How are her vitals?"

"Within tolerance. The human psyche is complex and maladaptive; her subconscious knows she is being manipulated even though her conscious mind doesn't. That creates physiological stresses that most higher-level species have outgrown. In her case it will eventually trigger cardiac trauma and irreparable dysfunction." Aramisk watched Louise's reaction. "I'll do whatever I can to keep her alive... if that's what you want, I mean after Qorall has the information."

Louise cleared her throat. "Yes. Do that. She may prove useful afterwards."

Aramisk glanced at the Hohash. "That, however, I have no control over whatsoever. The connection between them runs deep. Psychophysiologically it connects to the node in her head, but over the past two years bridges have built inside her brain from the frontal lobe and hippocampus to the brain stem, the reticular formation."

"Your point?"

Aramisk glanced back towards Kat. "I believe it could kill her if it chose to do so."

Louise didn't need the rest spelled out. The Hohash clearly had a strong link with Kat – it also 'liked' her, for want of a better word, and was protective towards her. Hohash were always destined to be servants to somebody. But its higher goal would always be to protect its creators, the Kalarash. So, today they would test its loyalties to the limit.

"Proceed. Let me worry about the Hohash, you focus on Kat. Does she have the information yet?"

Aramisk nodded. "Yes, I can't see it of course, but there was a spike five minutes ago, consistent with our objectives."

Qorall was monitoring this as well, from the other side of the galaxy, wherever he was – Louise didn't want to know. But if this went wrong, if they failed to retrieve the information, it would go badly for her. Louise's "where do you see yourself in five years?" question would change its parameters to "five minutes", the most likely answer being "dead". Qorall didn't tolerate mistakes. Her own loyalties would also be tested today.

Louise pulled up a chair. "Wake her."

* * *

Kat had been dreaming of Pierre. It had seemed so real. She stirred, but restraints held her body down. She snapped fully awake. Louise was sitting next to her.

"Louise – Arctura – what the hell is going on?"

Louise didn't look happy, but said nothing. On the other side of Kat's cot, Aramisk tended a drip feeding into Kat's left wrist.

Kat grew suddenly desperate. "Jesus! Aramisk, let me go!" She turned back to Louise, noticing the Hohash at the foot of her bed. It was in some kind of metal brace. "Arctura, please, why are you doing this? I said I would help you."

Louise spoke. "Where is Hellera?"

Kat was nonplussed. "Who? How would I know?" But with a shock she realized she did know. The dream she'd just had; somehow...

"Qorall is devious," Louise said. "I met him once, after a fashion. I wish I hadn't." She turned away.

Kat had never seen Louise look afraid before.

Louise turned back to her. "He doesn't have anything like a Hohash, but he can access your node, and you can access the Hohash." Louise leaned forward. "He's been looking inside your head, at least part of him has, following your 'research'.

98

Shit! He's been ghosting me! Kat wondered what he had seen. The encounter with Micah and Antonia? Qorall wouldn't care about that. Finding Kilaney? Maybe. Pierre and Ukrull? Definitely.

"During your last 'trip', your drug-induced dream, he managed to trick your Hohash into accessing the one onboard the Ranger's ship. Kat, make this easy on yourself, because he will get the information from you, one way or another." She leant back. "I have no desire to see you hurt."

At first it sounded like what any torturer might say, but something told Kat that Louise actually meant it.

Kat tried to stall, knowing that this information was of incredible importance, perhaps enough to tip the balance of the entire war forever into Qorall's favour. "My mind's foggy, Louise, I need some time to think."

Louise nodded, tight-lipped, and stood up. "Have it your way." She turned to Aramisk. "Do it."

Kat's head swiveled in the Mannekhi woman's direction, but her all-black eyes didn't meet Kat's. She turned a valve on the transparent tube, opening it fully. Louise spoke from the doorway. "Call me when it starts."

Once Louise had left, Aramisk faced Kat, her eyes intense. She whispered. "You will dream, Kat. There will be terrible pain. Just remember that whatever happens, it is not real; your body remains here. Do you understand? Try to remember: your body is here."

Kat decided to do something else instead. As drowsiness washed over her, she accessed her node and linked to the Hohash. Her mind was growing fuzzy, heavy, but she communicated, not hiding her distress or sense of panic. Erase Hellera's location from my mind! The Hohash burst into life, like a fireworks display at close range.

Aramisk leapt to her feet. "What are you doing? By all the Gods! Arctura! Come quickly!"

Kat tried to focus, to stay awake long enough to let the Hohash do its job. She felt a slash inside her head, like a razor cut, and through pain-slitted eyes saw the Hohash vibrating, rattling inside the brace.

Louise raced back into the room, took one look, and then glared at the Hohash. "Oh no you don't!" She pulled out a pulse pistol and put it next to Kat's temple. The Hohash stilled.

Kat communicated again with the Hohash. *Don't stop. Make her pull the trigger.* But the Hohash remained calm. Kat's eyelids grew too heavy to stay open, and she slipped into sleep.

Kat felt her mind falling out of her body, as if she'd become a ghost, Hades pulling her down through the floor. It was as if the ground no longer had substance for her, or else her mind had lost its grip. Kat wanted to scream, but couldn't breathe or speak. Amidst her terror, she remembered how Einstein's theory of relativity said that no object could move faster than the speed of light. But a mind is not an object. She swallowed, and fell faster.

Beads of light streamed past her, with occasional violet and pink flashes of nebulae, and Kat had the sensation of travelling impossible distances in the blink of an eye, of her mind being whiplashed halfway across the galaxy. She guessed the Hohash had something to do with it. Pierre had once told her he believed them to be incredibly advanced artifacts, designed by the Kalarash themselves, and that even the Tla Beth did not know their full potential.

The light show slowed, and blackness loomed. She saw a swirl up ahead, and at first thought it was the rings of a gas giant, but at the centre was a darkness sucking everything around it into its core. The perfectly round edge of that mouth folded inwards, as if it might swallow itself. Futile as it was, Kat flailed her limbs, trying to turn back, to stop herself tumbling into the black hole.

She tried to remind herself that she was physically safe – her body was still back on Louise's ship, and her mind had no gravity, so a black hole couldn't hold her. But inwardly she screamed as she was swept into the pitiless blackness. Just as it had almost engulfed her, she saw a spherical ship beneath her, stationary near the event horizon, resisting the terrible gravitational forces streaming past it, like a pupil in the black hole's eye. She fell straight through its outer hull.

Everything was red. It reminded her of a vid she's seen as a kid, of Dante's Inferno. She had already guessed whose ship it was, and doubted

Qorall would want her to see the real ship's interior, so she persuaded herself to try and relax and 'enjoy' the show.

Kat tumbled through a sky that was aflame, through clouds that twisted and wrenched amidst tornadoes of fire, and fell directly into a volcano's mouth vomiting molten rock. She drifted in boiling gelatinous magma, crushing sound surrounding her, like bubbling thunder. Every contour was soaked in shades of red: vermillion and crimson the hottest zones, deep russets the slightly cooler ones. Kat could no longer feel any part of her body, had no sensation of limbs, torso or head, and bobbed along in the currents. She reckoned she was okay as long as she knew this was not real, or rather, that she was not really there. She could treat it as a dream.

No sooner had she thought it, than her mind became groggy, and she could no longer see clearly. Shit – he's playing with my mind. She focused: this is a dream, this is a dream, this is...

The lava surged along with her for hours. Something writhed in the distance, though she didn't understand how she could see, encased as she was in a river of scarlet mud whose temperature she couldn't begin to imagine. But whatever it was, Kat had the impression of size, that what she witnessed was titanic, though there was no point of reference. It reminded her of a cubic frame, but each strut was a massive limb, a bone covered in purple flesh sweating rivulets of ice despite the heat. There was no obvious head. The cube-frame moved awkwardly, spasmodically, an upper joint opening, allowing it to rock forward, as another bone- like limb pounded onto the superheated silicate terrain of the ruby island surrounding it. Qorall.

A split opened up on one of the upper limbs. A roar bellowed across the lava sea, blowing waves across the molten rock's surface. The sound was terrifying, but agonising, too. She sensed bitter loneliness, and a pit of rage against injustices of the past. The creature howled for revenge.

Kat still had no sensation of her body, but felt her fugue receding. She couldn't remember how she'd arrived, or precisely where she'd been before. Then she recalled falling through the hull of a black ship on an event horizon, so everything around her must be some kind of vast ship, where the sky must be the roof; a hollow asteroid, maybe. She wanted to get the hell out of there, but had no control whatsoever, no idea where in the galaxy the ship was, nor how she'd gotten there. The next question was why she'd been kidnapped.

The eddies buffeted her along a channel where the lava flowed faster, away from the creature. She sped past a shore of rust-coloured rock, towards a pulsing ovoid, textured like smooth heart muscle. She tacked toward it then veered away in her river of magma.

Kat floated like this for several more hours, coursing along, occasionally meeting organ-like masses that she supposed were part of this vessel's anatomy. But she was losing her sense of self, and found it harder to think, as if her consciousness was only capable of perception. She didn't tire, which made her worry she'd be trapped there indefinitely, a speck of consciousness wandering forever in a ship from Hell. Then she saw something, a faraway blue dot. She'd become so used to perceiving myriad shades of red that she'd forgotten other colours existed.

Up ahead, the dodecahedron of blue crystal sat motionless amidst the surging fluid. She picked up speed, accelerating toward it. Her mind raced, too, knowing this was somehow sanctuary, but she feared she would be dragged away again, doomed to swim endlessly inside the volcanic tides. It got closer, and she dared to hope. She slowed down, and bumped into its exterior, which wasn't hard as she'd expected; it was spongy and sticky, a glistening membrane. It held her in check. There was a sucking sound, and Kat squeezed through. Incredible pain, like being dropped from an oven into a glacial lake, saturated her mind, as her body was reborn inside the sphere.

She lay on the transparent floor, naked, short of breath, her skin goose-bumped. Shivering, Kat drew her knees up beneath her and curled into a foetal position, forehead against the cool, glass-like floor. She was relieved to have a body again, and listened to her own breathing, waited till it calmed, then stood. It was like being inside a child's marble, terrible heat and power coiling outside.

Interrogators back on Earth for centuries had used nakedness as a form of humiliation to beat down their male or female captives. Kat stood up, chin lifted, hands on hips, the way she'd done back on Earth during a gay pride march during her University days following a threatened post-War resurgence in homophobia. This time, however, she didn't have 'Look me in the eye' tattooed across her breasts.

But her body felt younger, too perfect, and she worked out it was merely another illusion. No bruises, burns or lesions. The mole on her inner left thigh told her that this was no simple avatar simulation – someone, or rather something, had created a damned good simulacrum. Then she remembered who that 'someone' was.

She doubted her lava trip was an idle gesture, or to impress, and guessed that while in that state of almost pure perception, the rest of her mind had been accessible; she'd been violated, interrogated without her consent or even awareness, as easily as she might download and review files on a holopad. That raised the further questions of why she was still there, or alive at all, and what Qorall was searching for, and why he couldn't find it. She had no idea what it was.

Kat blinked and suddenly her sister Angelica was there, dressed exactly as she had been at Kat's going-away party, the night before Kat had joined the Eden Mission Academy. Her heart skipped a beat, then her fists and teeth clenched. Her sister was long dead. But it looked like her, even smelled of her sister's favourite perfume, Orsex. Kat almost cried out, and had to hold herself back from jumping up to hug her lost sibling. Instead, she stayed put, lips zipped, waiting for whatever it was to speak.

"Where did Pierre go?"

It sounded just like Angel's luxurious throaty voice, the one that used to fondue boys' hearts. Kat closed her eyes, but they opened again, against her will. Trying to turn had no effect either. She glared at the apparition. "If I'm right, you've already been inside my head, so you should know what I know."

Angel wore her signature 'whatever' smile, the same one that, along with her athletic figure and Nordic looks, made boys awfully stupid around her. But this wasn't Angel.

"It's what you don't know you know that interests me." Angel winked. "Let's try something else then. What were you doing in Esperia's caverns when Louise found you two years ago?"

Good question, but she had nothing to offer there that Qorall didn't already know; that was why he'd sent Louise there in the first place. "Curiosity. I'd never been to those caves, where the spaceship had been. You know, the Kalarash. A pal of yours I imagine –"

Kat's left arm burst into flame, but she couldn't move. She tried to curse but blinding pain overwhelmed her. She screamed as she watched her skin crackle, warp and spit, her cry choking on itself as the pain blurred her mind and vision. Inside she shook, gasping for breath, hot tears running down her cheeks, but her body remained upright as if suspended by a hook. Her head turned against her will, eyes clearing so she could see the blue flames burn down to muscle, blackening bone. What was left of her arm crumbled to ash on the floor.

Abruptly Kat collapsed, dizzy, convulsing, knowing she should have blacked out, that no one was meant to experience such pain. She bit down on her right knuckle, tried to control her breathing. Her heart had gone into overdrive, felt like it would burst through her chest.

"What did you find down there, Kat?"

"Nothing." Yet even as she said it, she knew for the first time that it wasn't exactly true. Something she'd forgotten, or not really seen at the time, but had been there, before Louise had arrived. Something else lurking in the cavern directly above the underground ocean. But Qorall didn't wait. Her legs were next.

Kat's breath came in jagged, laboured rasps. With her one arm left, she clawed against the floor, tried to move away from her captor. She had nothing in her mind except the desire for no more pain, or to die, she really didn't care which. She reached the wall.

"Go screw yourself," she said, then closed her eyes tight, waiting.

Angel crouched next to her, and whispered in her right ear. "This isn't going to work, is it? Let's try another way. Let's see how resistant you are at age fifteen."

Kat's former fugue returned, blanking all thought until only perception remained, and then she fell asleep.

* * *

Louise was pacing. "Her vitals?"

Aramisk raked a hand through her thick black hair. "We almost lost her, but her signs are calming down a little. However, he's taking her to a deeper level." Aramisk dropped the pad onto the bed. "She won't survive the next one, Arctura."

Louise bit her lip. "Then wake her."

"What?"

"I said wake her, bring her out of it. Now!"

"Qorall will kill us!"

Louise's voice steeled. "I'll think of something."

Aramisk shook her head in disbelief, then picked up and tapped at the pad. She frowned. "It's no good, Arctura, I can't break the connection. Qorall and the Hohash are each accessing her node, and neither seems inclined to let go. She's locked in, and they're pulling her mind apart."

Louise stared at the Hohash, its flashes and vibrations at fever pitch. "I'll be back shortly, Aramisk, and she had better be alive when I return."

Aramisk nodded, then leant over to Kat's contorted face. "It's a dream, Kat, remember it's just a dream."

* * *

Kat lay face down on the beach, the sound of the surf roaring in the background. She wiggled her toes, trying to dislodge the wet sand stuck between them, towel damp underneath her after the last frolic in the waves surfing with her sister. When she was on the longboard behind Angel, nothing else mattered, not her damned exams, not even her uncle's odd behaviour toward her; the way she sometimes caught him staring.

Some boys were playing football close by; there were always boys close by when Angel was around. Kat had zero interest in boys, and looked the other way whenever her sis kissed one of her many boyfriends. Angel said Kat's time would come, but Kat was already fifteen, and reckoned her hormones had other avenues in mind.

Kat was starting to burn; she knew she should really turn over, or get into the shade. But she wanted a deep tan like her sister. Besides, the sun could block out all kinds of things. She heard Angel stir, and cracked open an eye, squinting in the blazing sun, to see the silhouette of her sister standing above her, squirting sunscreen into the palms of her hands. Angel straddled Kat's lower back, and began rubbing oil into her. Kat had seen Angel do this routine before with one of her vivacious girlfriends, but never with her 'little sis'. It was the first time Angel had treated Kat as someone approaching an equal, one of her entourage. Kat decided to play along.

She moaned as Angel's hands rhythmically pressed down into the grooves either side of her spine, kneading the warm oil up and over her shoulders. "Oh God, Angel, that feels good!"

Angel varied her massage routine, eliciting more pseudo-groans from Kat. The boys stopped their football. She leaned forward, close to Kat's ear, lingering for effect. "We're giving them long-shower material." They both burst out laughing. Angel dismounted, and sat cross-legged next to her.

Kat turned over, propped herself up on her elbows, letting her head roll back, feeling the sun beat down against her small breasts and her throat. "You're killing them, Sis."

Angel laid a hand on Kat's stomach, and drew circles with her finger, and winked. "But what a way to go, eh?"

They both laughed again. Kat lay down flat, feeling as light as the cirrus clouds wisping across the azure sky. She shaded her eyes to spy a gull soaring overhead, shrieking for its mate.

"You miss him, don't you?"

Kat did. She hadn't talked about it, not to anyone else. "Like hell," she said. She turned toward Angel, saw the frown. The boys were calling lewdly to Angel, but she never took her eyes off Kat. Abruptly Angel's head turned to face the sea.

"He had no right to just dump you like that."

Kat's lips tightened. She didn't like to talk about it; but she'd never seen her sister so concerned for her before. Their whole family was pretty stunted on the emotional register. She'd not even talked about it to her new best friend at school, Louise, or that strange new girl that had befriended her, Aramisk. "Pierre had to leave, you know that."

Angel turned back with a flash of anger, opened her mouth as if to say something, then shook her head. "I know, I've just never understood."

Kat sat up, moved closer. Angel had always comforted her, been the big sister, stood in for their mother who'd died when Kat was barely two, and had protected her from her God-awful uncle when their father had gone off the rails and drunk himself into oblivion. But now Angel was in pain. Kat stretched out her arm and, hesitatingly, placed it over Angel's shoulders. Angel folded into Kat's embrace, the first time their caring relationship had ever reversed direction. Kat felt her eyes water. The boys quietened, and moved further towards the breaking waves.

Kat needed to talk about it; had needed to for a long time. She drew in a breath. "Micah said Pierre's gone to get help." Her head started to ache; she should get out of the sun, it was so damned hot. She played with her straw hat, but didn't put it on.

"Where on Earth is he going to get help, with the storm that's coming. Don't be naïve, Kat, he's dumped you, that's all there is to it."

Kat felt as if she'd been slapped. What had gotten into Angel? "I don't know any more than what Micah said, I'm not even sure he knows, but –"

Angel broke out of Kat's arms. "Listen to yourself. It's pathetic. Men stick together, cover for each other. Micah, Pierre, they're all the bloody same. Christ, I should know." Angel dug into her bag and fished out a cigarette, lighting it with a fluency that looked so adult. But Kat hated it when Angel smoked. She only smoked when she was angry – no, when she'd been let down by somebody.

Kat looked away. The boys had moved closer again, yelling something. Suddenly a ball thudded right next to Angel, showering them both with a hissing spray of sand.

Angel was on her feet in a second, shouting. "For God's sake piss off and leave us alone." She picked up the ball and gave it an impressive drop-kick into the ocean.

She took a long drag, glaring at the boys till they ran off to retrieve their ball, looked down at Kat, and then dropped the cigarette into the sand, burying it.

She knelt down next to Kat and put her arms around her. "Sorry, Sis, I'm being a real bitch today. Forget about it, just forget the whole damned thing."

Kat shook; if Angel wasn't there for her, she wouldn't – couldn't – cope. But Angel hugged her tight, rocking her. She thought of Pierre, how he'd left, deserted her. But she couldn't be angry with him; he wasn't the first to leave her, everyone did sooner or later. Yet she believed he would come back. Why? She tried to focus. Why would he come back? She flinched at a stabbing pain behind her eyes. God, not another migraine! And her heart was thumping, which was odd. Must be the heat. She wanted to get in the water, put her head under, but she didn't move.

Angel released her from the hug. "I hope he does come back, Kat. For you."

Something clicked in her mind. "Not for me."

Angel opened her palms upwards. "Meaning what? Don't tell me he's got a crush on me, I couldn't –"

"No, no," Kat said, with an urgency to verbalise the revelation while it hung in her mind. "Something else! The Kalarash were here on Esperia for half a million years." Kat found it hard to concentrate. The sun, this sudden stabbing pain. Wait a minute. Esperia?

Angel rolled her eyes. "Everyone knows that, Kat. But Louise told me Micah searched all the caves, the oceans even. Nothing. Gone, the same as Pierre."

Kat gave her a quizzical look. "How does Louise know Micah?" Angel put on her cynical face.

"Oh, I see." Kat felt her face flush. "Well, anyway. The Kalarash did leave something behind."

"Besides a few Hohash, you mean?"

Kat nodded, but pain lanced through her left eye. She cried out, cupping a hand over her face, squeezing both eyes closed. Angel moved toward her.

"Come here, let me see." She pushed Kat's hand aside. "Open your eyes."

Kat tried, but couldn't open the left one.

"Open it!" Angel shouted, her voice sounding odd, distorted.

Through her right eye, Kat saw dark shadows as the boys gathered around them. The pain grew, as if someone was pulling a needle through her left eyeball. "Angel, help me, please! Call an ambulance!" The boys closed in, pinned her down, their hands rough claws.

Angel's voice hardened, sounding masculine. "OPEN YOUR EYE!"

Kat squirmed, trying to escape the boys' grip and the blinding pain; she felt her left eye boiling inside its socket. Angel's fingers became talons, trying to tear open Kat's eyelids, but they were glued shut. Through her other eye she saw the gull circling above, framed against a sky of pure fire. It dropped down, wings fluttering, until just above the boys' heads. It landed on her chest.

"Get it off me! What the fuck is going on? Angel, please!" Kat glanced up at Angel, who was busy clawing at her left eyelids, teeth bared with the effort. The gull leaned closer, its own blood red eyes peering into Kat's. One of the boys behind the bird unsheathed a knife, and passed it blade-first to Angel, who loomed closer.

"Now we'll see what you're hiding, Katrina." She raised the knife high above her in a closed fist, then slammed it down into Kat's chest and raked it downwards, carving a fissure in her ribcage. Amidst the spray and spume of blood, something stirred within Kat's body, and then a small, black, four-legged spider emerged.

Kat screamed and screamed again, until she fell backwards out of her body. She felt her mind being tugged back across huge distances by the Hohash, back to Louise's ship. Her last thought before her consciousness dissipated was that she'd never thought she'd be glad to get back there.

* * *

Aramisk studied the pad next to Kat, a finger on her carotid pulse. "She's alive, barely, falling into a deep coma, there's nothing else I can do." She stood away from Kat's bed, staring toward the other end of the room. "Qorall's not going to be happy with you, Arctura, though I think he got the intel just in time."

A smoking multi-barreled rifle hung from Louise's right hand, as she also stared at the molten mess at the foot of Kat's cot, a hole scorched right through the Hohash. It was dead.

Louise inspected the rifle. She hadn't been sure it would work against a Hohash, even though the weapon had a Level Twelve rating – Qorall had sent it to her five years ago as a reward after she helped bring down an entire enemy star system. Louise lowered the weapon. She'd grown too attached to Kat, even though she wasn't Alician, even though Louise wanted all other humans dead, gone. Kat was the closest person she could relate to. Louise had been too long on the road, spent too much time with aliens. She knew Kat wasn't a friend – quite the opposite, Kat would probably kill her if she ever got the chance – but Louise found she couldn't stand by and watch Qorall literally frighten Kat to death.

She made up her mind. "The Hohash self-destructed, Aramisk. Understood? They've been known to do that. It sensed Kat was about to betray a Kalarash secret, and shattered. Tell the others."

"Yes, Arctura."

As Aramisk left, Louise called after her. "It's just 'Louise', now. Tell the others that, too."

Aramisk gave her a searching stare, then left.

Louise considered her options. She had to get out of Qorall's service, she'd had enough: endless killing and espionage, all the time away from her own kind, serving Qorall, always his agenda. That wasn't who she was. She had dared to ask to be released, but he always demanded one more task first. She knew better than to press the issue. As for where she would go if he did allow it, there was really only one option, given that the Mannekhi or a hundred other species she'd met held no interest for her. It would have to be Sister Esma and the Alicians.

She glanced down at Kat, her short hair matted with sweat; she didn't smell too good either. Louise stroked the woman's damp forearm once. "I will take you with me, if you don't disappoint me. If you ever wake up."

Her wristcom buzzed, a coded Largyl 9 message, an advanced Q'Roth dialect that Mannekhi could never decrypt. Qorall had the information he wanted. Louise was to destroy the Hohash, and go at once to Esperia and obliterate it, leave no trace.

Afterwards, she decided, she would leave his service.

Louise smiled. She picked up the pad on Kat's cot, and while checking that Kat's vitals had stabilised, noticed her own reflection. It was more like her old self. She spoke to Kat's comatose frame. "Within a week, you're going to be the last human alive. I will kill all of them. Don't worry, I'll get you upgraded if I have to do it myself." As she walked away from Kat's bed with a lighter step than in years, Louise killed the lights, and added, "Sweet dreams."

CHAPTER 9 – BETRAYAL

The Ossyrian chariot skated just above the ground towards the pyramid-ship. Micah and Fornasson stood rigidly side-by-side behind their canine-like chauffeurs. Strands of the Ossyrians' manes, jet black and shiny, flailed in the wind, whipping against their white tunics. From the corner of his eye Micah noticed Fornasson gaze out to a hillock beyond which his farm lay, then stare at the ground rushing past. One of Fornasson's hands let go of the railing, and his body tensed. Micah seized the man's wrist. "Don't even think about it," he said. "How far do you think you'll get, assuming you survive the fall?"

Fornasson grimaced, grabbed the rail again and stared straight ahead.

Micah let go of his wrist.

From afar, the pyramid glistened silver, but as they approached and began to decelerate, Micah noticed that he could see the Acarian mountain range straight through the three-hundred-metre-tall pyramid as if it were transparent. He knew it was no such thing: the outer layer was stealth tech. From space it would not be detected at all, and would look like a shimmer of heat haze on the desert floor. It reminded him that the Ossyrians, a medical race bred to heal, weren't naïve – even doctors needed defences, and in their case, that meant formidable bio-weaponry. None they would share – their convoluted equivalent of the Hippocratic Oath had been made quite clear on that point on numerous occasions, though as President he'd pushed hard. It was one reason he'd not been allowed back inside the ship for over a year. Officially he was here to see that Fornasson got proper justice, but he also needed to talk to Chahat-Me about defences once the Ossyrians departed, and promised reinforcements. The news from Kat had reminded him just how vulnerable Esperia was.

The chariot stopped slowing down. Fornasson fidgeted and glanced nervously at Micah, who looked straight ahead, hands firm on the railing. Images of the burned-out husks of the spider family flooded back into his mind, making him want to punch Fornasson. Yet he feared what the Ossyrians would do, how they would mete out justice as they saw it.

"Bend your knees a little," Micah said.

A glass ramp appeared, extending down to ground level from about a quarter of the way up the pyramid. They hit the bottom of the ramp smoothly and shot upwards into the Ossyrian space vessel that hadn't moved an inch from the ground since it had first landed. Despite knowing better, Micah braced himself for some kind of impact, but they simply stopped, as inertia-controllers relieved them of Newtonian momentum. Micah stepped off the chariot as if he did this all the time.

The room was cylindrical in shape, as were many in the pyramid whose Ossyrian name could not be pronounced with human vocal chords, but which they'd translated as the *Pteraxia*. The Ossyrians had never explained the name's origins or significance; as usual they were very private about their past, as if they had something to hide. The floors, ceiling and walls were glassy, a shifting sea-shell collage of pastel pinks, tangerines and lilacs, but opaque all the same. There was a faint smell of rose petals.

Micah didn't look at his kinsman. "Fornasson, you can get down." His voice came out crisp. In his time as leader on Esperia there had only been three murders, and he had opposed the death penalty each time, carrying the vote against several respected Council members, even though prison was difficult to maintain in such a small society. The community of Esperantia had mercifully escaped anything like a serial killer.

Micah knew that if he himself had done something so heinous against the spiders as Fornasson had, he'd expect and accept the worst. But he hoped for redemption in others. Micah tuned out his anger and studied Fornasson, the creases on his face, the hooded look around his eyes and hunched posture. Was remorse setting in, or was Fornasson just sorry he was about to be punished? Micah couldn't tell. What he did know was that although he personally wanted to drag Fornasson back to the scene of the crime and hurl him into the midst of the carnage and cindered corpses, instead he'd defend him, and argue for humane treatment.

Their Ossyrian chauffeurs stood in line with two others. One of them had more horizontal golds than reds, blues and blacks in the head-dress, which Micah knew signified her as the leader of this party. Micah had never seen a male, and had begun to wonder if they existed at all, or had been side-stepped somewhere along the

Ossyrians' evolutionary trek, their procreative function supplanted by medical ingenuity.

Fornasson stepped down and stood in front of Micah. He stuck his chin out and held his chest proud, as if ready to take responsibility for his actions and accept his fate; Micah decided that whatever Fornasson had done, he deserved some respect, and fair treatment. He also realized that he was the only person present who was going to stand up for Fornasson's rights. He'd seen enough domestic justice situations over the past years, but he'd never had to defend a murderer before. The Ossyrians had already extracted a confession from Fornasson, and he suddenly wondered if there would be any trial at all, or if they would simply dispense punishment – whatever that might be – on the spot.

Micah made to speak, but felt a pricking in the back of his neck, and suddenly he was unable to move. His eyes waxed into a kind of stupor, and he realised his hosts had just anaesthetised him. Micah felt a sense of outrage, violation even, but his physiology failed to react – there was no blood rushing to his head, he couldn't clench his fists or even glare. He beckoned his resident, but the Ossyrians had somehow deactivated it. His fingertips tingled, and Micah knew that it was his nannites; they were still active, awaiting his command.

In his peripheral vision he noticed Fornasson shift from one foot to the other, fists by his side, then take a step back. Micah saw why. Three spiders came into view behind the Ossyrian line-up, sturdy, silent and quick. The Ossyrians parted to allow the spiders through. Micah's fingers itched, but the paralysing drug was too strong. The tingling shifted to his lips and throat. He tried to find a voice, yet still nothing came and he couldn't move, except the muscles in his chest and diaphragm allowing him to breathe.

The spiders circled Fornasson, who remained as still as he could, given that he was shaking from head to foot. The bands around the spiders' bodies pulsed scarlet and black. One at the front advanced, nudging Fornasson back towards the entrance, and it was clear they were going to take him away.

The implications of what was about to happen burst into sharp relief in Micah's mind. Despite Fornasson's crime, there were enough Steaders who would sympathise with him to cause problems, and a summary execution would fuel long-harboured fears about their alien neighbours. Fornasson's crime would be forgotten long before the fact that the spiders killed him in revenge.

Micah made up his mind. It was a long shot. His nannites complied, and surged around his torso, locking his diaphragm muscles. He reckoned he had twenty seconds, tops.

As one, the four Ossyrians turned towards Micah, just as his vision fazed and he slumped towards the floor. An Ossyrian moved so fast it was a blur, catching him before his head hit the ground. The Ossyrian's quicksilver paw morphed into a needle and punctured his sternum. Micah gulped in air and arched his back, his body control returning. The Ossyrian released him, and Micah rolled over and promptly threw up, the acid taste of bile lingering in his throat. Still on the floor, he turned to find that Fornasson and the spiders had stopped and were staring at him.

Another Ossyrian entered: Chahat-Me, the Ossyrian contingent's leader, the only one who spoke any decent semblance of English through their musical windpipe system. Her voice sounded like a synthetic choir.

"Micah. What are you trying to achieve?"

He got to his feet, and bowed to Chahat-Me. The Ossyrians never expected any such deference, but Micah always gave it, out of respect and gratitude, and in her specific case because Chahat-Me had helped defend humanity when they had been on trial.

He wiped his mouth on his sleeve, aware he must look a mess. "Fornasson is our responsibility. Justice should be served according to our rules."

Chahat-Me looked toward the spiders. Her mercurial eyes flashed a tight band of colour at one of them, the laser-light ricocheting to the others in their cascading instant mode of communication.

There was a pause, and Micah felt that everyone, especially he and Fornasson, held their breath. The three spiders then moved in front of Fornasson. Light shone into the man's eyes. Micah went to move towards him but Ossyrian leader's arms held him where he was.

"Be still, Micah," Chahat-Me said. "They are showing him his crime."

Micah stood transfixed, as Fornasson hung there, rigid, spellbound, fingers flexing as if he were being electrocuted. It lasted long, torturous minutes. The man's mouth was agape, as if shouting, but no sound issued forth. Suddenly, Fornasson dropped to his knees, the light beams still pouring into his eyes. One of his hands shot to his mouth, knuckles first, and Micah saw him bite down hard. Micah glanced at Chahat-Me, but she shook her head.

The light beams shut off. Fornasson's head bowed to the ground, and Micah saw drops of blood drip to the glass floor as the man's upper body shivered. The spiders shuffled past him and left, disappearing down the ramp.

Micah was released, and he rushed over to Fornasson, grabbing him by the shoulders. His face lifted, and stared vaguely in Micah's direction.

"Micah, is that you?"

It took Micah a second to realise what had been done. He helped Fornasson to his feet, and faced Chahat-Me. "They blinded him?"

Chahat-Me nodded. Fornasson was in a daze, staring at the floor – no, Micah realised, staring at the images left there by the spiders.

"You could cure him," Micah said. "You are doctors."

One of the other Ossyrians took a step forward, but Chahat-Me stalled her with a gesture from her right paw, not taking her eyes off Micah's.

Chahat-Me approached Micah very close, her snout centimetres from his face. Her jaw opened, the mesh of blue and white fibres tightening and vibrating as she spoke. "Be quiet, Micah. Do not say anything in the next minute." She turned her head to Fornasson. "Erik Fornasson," she began. "They have taken your eyesight away as punishment, but spared your life." Chahat- Me raised a paw and three toes leant on Micah's chest just below his throat to enforce his silence. "Erik Fornasson. Do you wish us to restore your eyesight?"

Micah stared at Fornasson, who looked as if he'd been broken on the inside. The farmer lifted his head, managing to stare in the rough direction of Chahat-Me. He raised himself up, swallowed hard. "Their judgement," he began, but his voice cracked. He coughed, cleared his throat, and shook his head.

The toes on Micah's chest stayed him a little longer.

"We need to be clear," Chahat-Me continued. "Do you wish us to restore your eyesight?"

Micah watched the man's eyes mist, his jaw clench, but he stood proud again.

"No."

Whatever Micah had thought of saying deserted him. Two Ossyrians escorted Fornasson back to the chariot, and they departed.

Micah had a hunch, knowing from Petra of Chahat-Me's compassionate side. "Will he really stay blind?"

Chahat-Me lowered her voice. "In ten years the effects will wear off and he will see again. The images of what he has done will staywith him till his end. The spider representatives agreed with this sentence. Erik Fornasson was lucky. The spiders are one of the most pacifist and forgiving races we have ever encountered. Most other species would have killed him, after long and painful torture."

"Including yours?"

Chahat-Me's mercurial eyes stayed unusually still. The other three Ossyrians left. She laid a paw on his shoulder. "Micah, we must talk."

Micah was suddenly tired, then had an idea, mundane as it was. He needed to get the sour taste out of his throat. "Kat told me once that you make a mean Cafarino."

Chahat-Me's eyes glittered.

They glided through triangular corridors proceeding upwards, though a locally-controlled gravity gradient made it feel like he was strolling across flat ground. Ahead, pulsing rainbow shades invited them into a voluminous domed chamber. The bitter aroma of bubbling Cafarino, a coffee substitute derived from a local mountain herb, quickened his pace. They emerged into the vast, kaleidoscopic atrium where

Ossyrians milled about, clustered in small groups around tall, narrow racks of tubes from which the Ossyrians sipped the grainy purple liquid, all the time 'talking' with their quicksilver eyes, shapes rising and falling in complex, almost subliminal patterns. His vision cast around; still nothing resembling a male, not that he was sure how they would look.

Chahat-Me paused at the entrance, and shook her head. "Kat introduced Cafarino to us, contaminated us with it. It is not so good for human physiology, worse for ours." She made a movement with her shoulders, resembling a shrug, and led Micah to a free rack. Micah closed his eyes as he sipped, savouring the clove and cinnamon melange in his mouth, then swallowed, careful not to crack down on the small grains. His head warmed and cleared at the same time, and he felt a trickle   of energy run down his spine as his tension released – this blend was good! Within seconds he felt more alert than he had for days – years, he decided. Whatever they had added to it had an almost narcotic effect, and he felt his shoulders relax, his chest open. He licked his lips afterwards, and found himself grinning at Chahat-Me. Then a gong sounded, and the atrium quickly emptied. His good humour dried up, knowing the dispute he was about to have with Chahat-Me. It wasn't that they were running out of time; rather, to Micah, it felt like they had all been standing still for a whole generation, and now time was rushing towards them.

Micah paced up and down the only square room in the pyramid, one the Ossyrians had fashioned for the yearly meeting held with the human Council, to make them feel more at ease. But after three hours of debate he grew increasingly frustrated, not helped by the withdrawal from their damned spiced coffee. He smacked his hand down on the table.

"What was the point of saving us, keeping us alive, if you desert us now? We could be annihilated in days. Are they out there, now, waiting? Can you at least tell me that much?"

Chahat-Me and three other Ossyrians sat in their golden, high-backed chairs, front paws folded in their laps. The others had evidently decided to leave the talking to Chahat-Me, but he had no doubt they understood every word, nuance and inflexion, even if they couldn't formulate human speech properly themselves. He pushed. "We have two ships, one is a transport, the other a Q'Roth Hunter Class vessel. Not exactly a fleet, is it? How long do you think we'll last? Where are the reinforcements you promised?"

Chahat-Me glanced at her colleagues, flashing the ultra-rapid communication mode that only Pierre had ever mastered.

"We have been recalled, Micah," Chahat-Me answered. "The war is going badly. We requested your extraction a year ago, but you must understand there are other priorities."

Micah threw in his ace, courtesy of Kat's message. "Qorall is headed here, isn't he?" He noticed the other three ruffle their manes.

Chahat-Me touched something on her armrest and an image appeared, a holo. Micah stared at it; his anger stalled, then freefell.

Ossyria was one of the most beautiful planets he'd ever seen, unique in the whole galaxy, a giant marble divided into ten horizontal slices that rotated at different speeds. Three of its five turquoise oceans were bisected, and cumulous cloud layers swirled at the edges, and would have created permanent hurricanes were it not for advanced weather control systems. The re-designing of their original planet, which had taken thousands of years to implement, led to unlimited geothermal energy, feeding the continent-sized hospital and city-sized clinical research complexes, the medical engine underpinning Grid Society.

Yet what Micah saw now was a charred, shattered, lump of rock, its horizontal fault lines cracked open by crust-breaker weapons. Their homeworld had been destroyed. No wonder the Ossyrians had been pre- occupied these past months, as Qorall's forces had drawn ever closer.

"I don't know what to say, other than to express how deeply sorry I am for you all. You should have told me earlier. You have other planets, right?"

One of the other Ossyrians made a noise like a snarl, and Chahat-Me turned to her, silencing her with a quicksilver look.

Micah felt he should add more. "It must have been difficult for all of you, being here while this was ongoing."

The one who had snarled stared at him, her quicksilver eyes unmoving. Micah didn't know what that meant.

Chahat-Me closed down the holo, much to the relief of everyone in the room. "We have all been recalled. Two ships sent for your extraction have been destroyed en route."

Micah stared at Chahat-Me. "I'm sorry for those aboard. Does that mean – "

"We have no information on who destroyed the ships. Debris from a Q'Roth vessel was found at one of the sites."

"But they are on your side – our side – surely, they are fighting against Qorall, aren't they?" This news quickened his pulse.

"We do not jump to conclusions, Micah, they could just as well have been defending the Ossyrian ship. Nevertheless, it has given us cause for concern for your welfare."

Micah sat down on the bench on one side of the room. Q'Roth, again, waiting to finish the job? His voice sounded flat. "What do you propose?"

"We leave in two days. Fill your transport vessel. It will take half the population. They can follow us, we will protect them. For the rest – "

An oval door irised open out of the far wall. Petra stepped through, short but like a cat ready to spring, followed by Gabriel. They both wore combat fatigues, Gabriel's famous long blond curls shorn. Around his left eye was a fresh tattoo, a darker, curved maze. Micah didn't like the look of it.

"I have a better idea," Gabriel said. His hands were closed by his side. He opened them, and two small metal balls fell towards the floor. Micah didn't hear them hit the ground.

Micah awoke with ringing in his ears. As consciousness returned fully, it rose to a screeching din. He made to get up, but couldn't decide where 'up' was. But that made no sense: he could see Gabriel and Petra standing at a console in front of a luminous window, but his inner ear was playing havoc with his sense of balance. He manoeuvred into a sitting position, and placed a finger behind each ear, pressing. A buzzing ensued as his nannites got the message.

He looked around. Three Ossyrians lay slumped in a pile a few metres away. One loosely held something in its front paw, a weapon drawn too late. With great relief, Micah saw their chests rise and fall beneath their tunics. He crawled on all fours toward the weapon.

"Told you."

He could barely hear Petra's voice through the high-pitched whine. Micah reached the Ossyrian, and sat back on his knees. He had no idea what the weapon did, and didn't much care. Slipping the loop off the Ossyrian's wrist, and expecting to get shot by Gabriel at any moment, he turned around and levelled his arm at Gabriel who, together with Petra, stared at him, arms folded. Micah tried to speak, but couldn't hear himself properly, and gave it up. Gabriel didn't budge, so Micah pulled what seemed to be a trigger. Nothing happened.

Gabriel walked over, crouched down, took the weapon from Micah, and mouthed two words. Micah frowned, and then got it the second time. *Like this.* Gabriel flicked some kind of switch on its handle, and fired point blank at Micah's leg.

Pain exploded in Micah's thigh. Agony accompanied the crackling blue electric arcs that engulfed his leg, then spread upwards to his waist. His eyes rolled back, but through the haze of electrifying shock he saw Petra walk over, snatch the device and do something to it, then fire at him again. The pain shut off as if it had never been there.

The screeching lowered in intensity. He could make out a few words as Petra spoke close to his face.

"... injured two of us ... icah ... ship ... ours. No Ossyr... dead ... sthetised. They can mo... ery fast."

He felt an itching behind his right ear, then a crack, as if a bone had just snapped back into place. Suddenly he could hear.

"... coming down in ten minutes. Then –" "No need to shout," he said.

Petra grinned. "Told you, Gabe. Better watch him." She strolled back to the console.

Gabriel scrutinised Micah. "Pierre. Pierre did something to you, didn't he, before he left?"

Micah struggled to his feet. "Gabriel, listen to me."

"We were listening, Micah, all three hours of that field-manure. Petra bugged you."

Micah felt he'd been slapped. He thought about it: *when she'd hugged him on the back of the skimmer.* Petra didn't turn around, instead studying a display in front of her. Micah stowed it for later. Gabriel continued.

"They're screwing us over, Micah. Not necessarily the ones here, but their lords and masters. 'Following orders. A question of priorities.' Do those refrains sound familiar? And you, no disrespect, but you have no leverage with them, do you?"

Micah glowered. "What did you do to them?"

"Sonic grenade, adapted to their physiology." He turned his head slightly, and Micah noticed a small disk in his ear.

"Not sure how *you're* conscious, though, let alone standing. Petra said you were special."

Micah got up, and they both joined her at the console. The flat part, at waist height, was fluid, shifting braids of colour. Petra's hands glided over them, tightening reds with one hand, blues with another, then sent them twisting around each other into one corner of the display. Micah had no idea what the console did, what she was doing, or how she knew what to do.

As if sensing his question, she spoke. "Chahat-Me used to bring me up here when I was a kid. The others scolded her, but she had a soft spot for me."

Micah remembered something he'd heard. "But it shouldn't work for you. The ship's controls are genetically coded for Ossyrians." Then he recalled. "Ah... the climbing accident?"

She nodded.

He remembered it well. It had nearly given him a heart attack. Petra had been just six years old when she'd skipped school and accepted a dare to free-climb the Eastern face of Mt. Cerebus. No one had managed it yet, and Petra had almost made it. When the Ossyrians got to the site, Petra's skull was literally cracked open. Chahat-Me had used some of her own flesh and blood to heal her on the spot.

"Nice way to repay her," Micah said.

Petra's head dipped as she peered deeper into the display.

"Don't be too hard on her, Micah. This was my plan. We're doing this to save everyone, Steaders and Genners alike." Gabriel cocked his head at Micah. "You taught us how to fight, how to strategise, remember?"

"Done!" Petra announced. A wave of fluorescent orange swept from one end of the display to the other, rebounded and headed back to its origin. The entire display flickered and went off, revealing a dull metal surface.

"What just happened?" Micah asked.

Gabriel patted Petra on the shoulder. She tensed, almost flinched. Gabriel withdrew his hand. "Petra has primed the barrier for de- energising. Once the tip of the ship reaches it, we enter the access code. No more quarantine."

Micah stared in disbelief. "What? You're insane! We'll be defenceless!"

Gabriel shook his head. "No Micah, for the first time we will have the ultimate weapon."

Micah thought about it. The timeworn weapon of choice when faced with a larger, more powerful foe. Surprise. If there was an enemy waiting, all they'd observe was an Ossyrian ship departing, a bunch of harmless medical doctors. He had to admit, right now he didn't have a better plan, and the Ossyrians were only capable of taking half the human population, something few people including himself were likely to accept. Still, he felt like they were all groping in the dark, unknowing of who or what lay just outside scanning range.

"How long have you been planning this?"

Petra answered. "Two years, Uncle. Fornasson gave us the distraction we needed, saved us manufacturing one. Twelve Genners are aboard. We have control and access to Ossyrian bio-weaponry, as well as delivery systems."

He stared at her, feeling like a father who has just realised his daughter is grown up and about to leave home. She held his gaze, raised her chin a little, then turned away.

A radio message filled the silence, using Genner click language. Micah's resident translated: *Gabriel, two parties are headed our way, fast: Vasquez and Blake.*

Gabriel clicked back a receipt of message, and then addressed Micah. "Time for you to leave."

Micah folded his arms, splaying his legs. "I'm not going anywhere. You're going into battle. You're smart, but still inexperienced. Besides, I have someone to look after. I made a promise to both her parents."

Petra didn't turn around.

Gabriel faced Micah. "Give me one good reason why I should allow you to stay onboard."

Micah studied the young man, a born leader, a natural hero. But there were nasty, treacherous minds out there. "Who do you think we'll find waiting for us, Gabriel? I assume Petra told you about Louise."

Gabriel nodded. "And I predict that Sister Esma will be there waiting with her, too."

Micah nodded absently. "Ah, so you see you do need me. If they are both there, that could actually be better than one of them alone."

Gabriel's brow creased.

"I think he's got you there, Gabe. As Ramires always said, know your enemy. Micah knows them both, especially Lou –"

"Thank you, Petra," Micah said.

Gabriel eyed him then nodded. "So be it. Take us up, Petra. And Micah, don't try anything. You might beat me in a holosim, but in a fight you'd be no match at all."

Micah willed his nannites to stand down. "Agreed."

Petra touched a control and the panel flooded with a sea of blues. She sank her fingers knuckle-deep into a gelatinous part of the display, and then lifted them out slowly, blue slime cloying to her fingers. The pyramid, stationary for eighteen years, rose into the air as smoothly and silently as a weather balloon.

Micah walked around the console and leaned forward against the glass to see his town, the one he had founded and led through so many crises. He'd never seen it from the air. In that moment, Micah realised how much he cared for it, for his people. This is all that's left of us, he thought, small and fragile, driven by love and fear in equal measure, desperate to survive. Only twenty thousand souls remaining out of almost seven billion. As the Pteraxia rose higher and faster, and stars pierced the darkening sky, it felt like seven billion pairs of phantom eyes waiting in the darkness, watching.

As they ascended and the sky grew darker, Micah switched into assessment mode. Worst case scenario was Sister Esma and Louise having somehow teamed up, lying in wait just outside the Ossyrian ship's sensor range. Best case scenario was nobody there, except maybe a grinning General Bill Kilaney in a warship come to defend them. But Micah had heard nothing further from Kat, no news via the Hohash, and in this case no news was bad news. The best news of all would be the Kalarash known as Kalaran, accompanied by Jen and the others, returning from wherever the hell they'd been. A Level Nineteen ship could see off the Q'Roth and Alicians, no trouble. But that felt like pure fantasy.

Micah had thought Kilaney long dead; it would be good to see him and find out where he'd been and what he'd been up to all these years. But the likelihood of him being already out there seemed remote; the Ossyrians would have detected his approach. The outcome of his assessment veered back towards pessimism.

He turned around to Gabriel. "Okay, tell me about the weapons we have aboard. All of them."

CHAPTER 10 – SECRETS & LIES

Kilaney had been busy since his forced departure from the Ngank's surgery vessel. He and his commandeered Mannekhi ship lurched back into normal space-time, still a couple of hours from Esperia. He'd dragged all twelve unconscious crew members onto the Bridge, carrying the three females – he was 'old school'. He sat in the command chair, waiting for them to wake up. His sweat smelled less acrid than when he'd been human first time around; the Ngank had done a good cosmetic job, but on the inside he felt a powerful panther-like strength and focus, a legacy from his Q'Roth days.

He ran his hands over his face – he'd always hated mirrors, even before Sister Esma had converted him into a Q'Roth warrior, and wasn't going to start liking them now. Hair was beginning to grow back on his head; it felt soft, downy. That was going to be downright embarrassing if he managed to meet up with Blake. He had eyebrows, and – it brought a smile to his lips – he felt the prickle of stubble on his chin. He'd never worn a beard. Maybe it was time.

Kilaney observed his captives, who were about to be freed, after a fashion. All of them were fit and young, one or two a little more mature, but no show of grey hair, if indeed they greyed with age. Staring towards their closed eyelids, he knew that underneath was the only overt way to distinguish them from humans. Long ago he'd tried to find out if humans and Mannekhi were in some way related, but the relevant files in Grid Central Archives were classified Level Fifteen. He'd asked Ukrull about it during his short stay aboard the Ice Pick, fully expecting no answer, or at most a grunt. Instead, he'd gotten the longest sentence he'd heard from the reptile. It was partly why they now lay on the floor alive.

Their long, deep breathing rate shifted, became shallower. Good, he was beginning to think he'd have to find a bucket of cold water. Within minutes the first two stirred, and they quickly woke the others. He watched the order they chose, inferring the crew hierarchy. The first one they woke, evidently their captain, stood apart, facing Kilaney, while the others busied themselves, checking instruments, navcom, weapons capability, life support. A nod or two from the captain here and there. Two males went to the weapons locker and withdrew four pistols, arming two other crew members as well as themselves. They didn't give one to the captain, but he was the one who spoke.

"You're in my chair."

"That's not how it is," Kilaney replied.

One of the females moved in Kilaney's direction, but a glance from the captain stopped her.

"Then tell me how you think it is."

"Ask your crew."

Without taking his eyes off Kilaney, the captain called out to his key officers.

"Siltern."

"Sir, Navigation is locked, control encrypted, we're heading toward a planet in the Quintara sector, the human one we were briefed on. A Level Twelve barrier shields it. Arrival in two hours."

"Arnter."

"Sir, half the ship's spines are prepped for penetration mode, the other half for hellfire beams. We're going in hot."

"Gallas."

"Long range comms has been disabled, encrypted with a Q'Roth Largyl 6 cipher. I can break the code, but it will take longer than two hours."

"Fentra, something good, please."

The female withdrew her face from an enclosure screen, and gave Kilaney a long hard look. "He's a hybrid. Human and Q'Roth." One of the men's pistol arm went rigid. "I wouldn't do that, Tolbar," she added. "He's injected us all with a Kelleran bloodworm. He has the mother."

Kilaney shrugged. "I found them in your Medlab. I'd heard about them, though I'd never seen them up close before. Pesky little critters. Is it true what they say about them?" He knew damned well, as the Mannekhi used them on prisoners, but he wanted to hear the captain say it, to acknowledge the status quo.

The captain folded his arms. "You die, we die. You hurt, we hurt.

You're still in my chair."

Kilaney got up, gesturing to the seat. As the captain took it, Kilaney added, "You have a fine crew, captain."

The captain looked taller now, sitting in the command chair. "What is your name?"

"Does it really matter?" Kilaney didn't want to give them his Q'Roth name, they might well have heard of Jorann, and decide that bloodworms or no bloodworms, he had to die.

The captain spoke while he called up holos showing the Esperian system. "Names are everything. Our lineage matters deeply to us. I am Xenic, of the clan of Karanashak, wardens of the twelve jewel planets of our Eastern sector for fifty generations. I am the first of my line to be captain, all my ancestors were traders, many of them in the Orrat, the resistance, thirty-three of them put to death at the hands of our patrons. I know all their names. If you ask any of my crew, you will hear similar heritage." His all-black eyes bore down on Kilaney. "Names are important to us. When you are born into servitude, history becomes your lifeline. Our progeny know our names, and we will live on through them. We are a proud people, and are not afraid to die. So, tell me, what is your name, your heritage."

Kilaney felt stung. He'd slaughtered so many Mannekhi in battle, yet had never met one before. He drew in a breath. "My name is Bill Kilaney, I was a general back on Earth, our only planet, destroyed by the Q'Roth." He hesitated. He'd never told anyone the rest, except his wife Sarah, back on Earth decades ago. "My father was a petty thief who deserted me and my mother when I was still a child. I found out later he died in a bar fight. My mother became a prostitute, and at first cared for me, but the drugs she took to cope with what she did stole her from me, bit by bit, until she died in a fire in a cheap motel. I had one lucky break serving as a grunt during the War, when I took a knife missile in the gut intended for a Colonel, and still managed to rip the assassin's throat out with my bare hands." He looked down at his fingers. There had been so much anger in him back then. He looked back up. "Life turned around after that, and the Colonel promoted me fast through the ranks, even if he didn't make it through the war himself. My ancestors... I know little of them, the rest of the family shunned me, more so after I became a General." He stared at the floor, then looked directly at the captain. "I'm still a soldier. I have nothing else. I have no children. My wife is dead. I have to say I envy you your ancestry. All I have lies on the planet we're bound towards, and I am here, you are here, to protect them."

"Protect them from what, exactly?"

Siltern spoke up. "From a Q'Roth Crucible."

Kilaney continued. "It is indeed your chair. I could not operate this ship on my own, certainly not in a battle. The Q'Roth are your sworn enemy, and –"

Xenic held up his hand. "What was your Q'Roth designation?" Kilaney chewed his lip, then answered in a quiet voice. "Jorann."

One of the younger females walked up to him, and with speed and power that surprised him, punched his jaw. Kilaney stood and took the force of the blow, while all of the crew except the captain gasped at the shared pain. The girl herself grunted with some satisfaction, and walked back to her station, nursing her chin.

The captain spoke, as the rest of his crew stroked their jaws gingerly. "Thank you, Tessia." He stood up. "Siltern, you have the Bridge. Kilaney – that is what we will call you, or else we will all have very short lives – walk with me."

They left the Bridge, and Kilaney followed Xenic to the observation deck, letting Xenic speak first.

"You took quite a gamble, especially telling us your Q'Roth name, hated by so many Mannekhi. You know the bloodworms are cyborg, and their power sources have a short duration, just twelve hours. They also have a limited range. I could put you in a pod and eject you into space, to rot."

Kilaney had thought of it. "I would self-terminate if you tried it."

"So ready to die?"

Kilaney gripped the rail and stared toward the slightly brighter star he knew to be Esperia's sun. He turned to Xenic. "My people are in mortal danger. Imagine how you would act if all Mannekhi were in jeopardy?"

"But humans are not *my* people."

Kilaney drew in a deep breath, then told him what Ukrull had said.

Xenic and Kilaney re-entered the Bridge. "Gallas, set up General Kilaney a tactical console, with external comms." He paused. "With weapons back-up access." The entire crew turned to stare at their captain. "We are going to take out that Q'Roth vessel. Kilaney has defected, and has their defence codes."

The crew nodded, turning back to their stations. The Bridge lights shifted to red, battle mode, and Kilaney felt rather than heard the engines increase their output, spurring the ship onwards, faster.

Kilaney realised two things about Xenic: first, the Mannekhi captain knew how to lead, and second, that he was a damned good liar.

* * *

The Shrell leader Genaspa, at the front of six phalanxes of her most trusted warriors, stared straight ahead with all six eyes and twelve sensor ridges, through the eddies of Transpace to the Quintara sector, where the spider world lay, where she would lead the unhappy mission to poison space within that entire sector. She already knew all the details, but wasn't going to miss an opportunity to train her protégé, Nasjana.

She thought-directed "Tell. What you see. What you propose." Nasjana shifted up a gear, flapping her tech-augmented wings faster, and moved forward from her phalanx of fifty, her Second taking her place. She drew alongside and slightly behind Genaspa, and addressed her First. "I see the two-mooned Katha Class planet the indigenous natives name Ourshiwann, that the humans call Esperia. I see two other planets, one further in to its Giver, and one further out, both without intelligent life's seed. There is also a thin asteroid belt from a former planet, and the ice-scratch of a past comet with a return cycle of two thousand years. I propose standard spatial necrosis treatment: three opposing Shrell teams at right angles to the Giver, twenty light minutes apart before we commence the run."

Genaspa sent a sinusoidal frisson down her right wing, a sign of approval.

Nasjana did not return to her team.

"You have a question?"

Nasjana dropped slightly behind. "I have a doubt."

Genaspa's wings took on a more rigid motion. She'd been expecting this from one of her team leaders, though not Nasjana, her Second. Or maybe, she reflected, that was why she had chosen Nasjana as Second. "Tell."

"Where you lead I follow. What you tell, I do. As do we all. But this... We only poison space when absolutely necessary, to avoid dangerous space-rift expansions, or to corral errant races."

Nasjana's thought stream had come out fast, urgent, and Genaspa realised she was worried. But they were short on time. They must be in formation, in every sense of that word.

"Tell true, Second." She had to wait a full flap-beat for the response.

"Why do we follow the orders of Qorall? He has brought the *Xenshra* inside the galaxy, those despicable inter-galactic worms. I fear we will never get them out. And Qorall has caused more space damage than in recorded Grid history."

It was a good question, but not the whole reason Nasjana was daring to doubt her First's judgement.

"Tell deeper. All."

Nasjana wings trembled, slowing her until with an effort she caught up. "My husbands. I fear many will perish today."

Genaspa forced herself to concentrate on the flight. A First must never waver. Tell true, she had instructed, and yet *she* had not told her team-leaders the whole. None of the husbands would survive the day. Genaspa and three hundred Shrell would enter the system, she and fifty would return, all female. This was a high price. But only Genaspa knew that Qorall held fifty thousand Shrell hostage – a tenth of their entire nomadic population – in a faraway quadrant, lured there to shore up the damage done when he and his worms breached the galactic barrier eighteen years earlier.

This was not what Nasjana and the others needed to hear, nor would it necessarily convince them – it did not persuade her, either, since Qorall might decide never to free his captives, or to feed them to the worms.

Genaspa knew the other team leaders would have one or two eyes and ridges focused on this little exchange, wondering if Nasjana would persuade her to call it off. Not this day.

"Nasjana. This is for you alone. When Qorall asked – demanded – I sought a second opinion."

Nasjana broke protocol and jumped in. "But who could you possibly –"

"Hellera, the last Kalarash left in our galaxy."

Nasjana winged forward, taking her eyes off their target, a dangerous move at this speed, and stared at her First, then dropped back just behind Genaspa's lead.

"What did she say?" Nasjana asked.

"She told me to do it. That it was necessary for the *long-term strategy*."

"Did she explain that strategy?"

"No. Nor did I expect a Level Nineteen being to indulge me, a mere Level Nine." She swivelled three of her eyes towards her Second.

Nasjana drew back. "I... I apologise, my First. I understand if you wish to name a new Second –"

"I do not."

Nasjana blinked all six eyes at once, for a full flapbeat. "With your leave, I shall return to my position."

"You will signal to the other leaders and instruct them and all the husbands that what we do today is of the utmost importance for the survival of the galaxy."

"Such a message should come from the First, not me."

No, Genaspa thought. I may not survive this run. They must begin to hear from you as a Leader.

Nasjana hesitated, then began to fall back.

Genaspa listened to Nasjana's pronouncement. She would make a good leader one day, a good First. As the thought streams rippled through the ranks, Genaspa felt their swarm's wing pulse harmonic grow stronger. But she herself did waver, thinking of her own former husbands, lost during a similar run two thousand years earlier. It was why she was First, because she made the necessary sacrifice, knowing that the husbands' life force would be bled away from them as they ripped spacetime, curdling its quantum foam; that was the energy exchange needed to inflict such damage. She had cherished each of her six males, and had not taken a husband since.

Abruptly she made the decision. She slowed down, decelerating at a breathtaking pace, as if rearing up against a wall. With no small pride she observed all six phalanxes stay in formation, even the husbands. The entire swarm stopped, panting, awaiting her command. The eddies of Transpace scattered around them like tornadoes of orange steam, blown away into wispy nothingness.

She turned and addressed them all. "We will pay a heavy price today." Her thought-stream flickered for a moment, then regained its true. "You are the best, that is why you were chosen. Many of us will not return." She let her eyes swivel to take in every individual Shrell, including the males, who blinked all eyes in return. "I wish you to say your goodbyes properly, as you see fit. You have one hour." She turned her back on them, and quietened her form-sensors so they could have their privacy.

A single ship threaded above her, the Mannekhi one her flock had overtaken earlier. She watched its ripples flourish then diminish, twirling in its wake before dissipating. Go ahead, she thought, do whatever it is you have to do, you have little time. She spied another ship on the other side of the Quintara sector, a Q'Roth Marauder, also heading in at terrific speed. She reflected that so many beings – the Rangers an exception – rushed around in their short life-spans, generally making things worse. Shrell were different, they were gardeners, conserving natural space – in normal situations, of course, though not this time.

Genaspa heard the cries of ecstasy behind her. Good, she thought, in a year there will be new Shrell to replace those we lose today. Her eyes and all twelve sensor ridges fixed hard on the distant planet, the object of so much sudden attention while at the war's front another planet fell every few days. We do this for you Hellera, not Qorall. You had better be right. I hope that whatever is in that system is worth it.

CHAPTER 11 – THE PLIGHT

The Crucible Class Q'Roth vessel hung dark and silent in stealth mode, two million kilometers across the system from Esperia. Sister Esma stood close enough to the battleship bridge viewscreen to scratch the outline of Esperia with her fingernails. None should ever have escaped. Nearly two decades earlier she'd underestimated a single outlier factor – Micah. Two and a half more days and she would flatline the curve, close the coffin lid on an inferior humanity's dead-end history.

But that wasn't the only reason she was here. If it had been purely a mission of revenge, of eradication of the dwindling embers of humanity, she'd have sent her Principal, Serena, to do the job. No, the plight, that was why she had to oversee this job personally, why she had left high level war-room talks with the Q'Roth Supreme Commander. By a cruel twist of fate, the future survival of her beloved Alicians hinged on mankind. She needed to take back a handful of humans, the only question being how many; no Genners, that much was certain. Once she had that figure, which should arrive any minute, the human cargo could be extracted as soon as Quarantine came down. Then the rest of that dustbowl planet and all its inhabitants, including the Ossyrian guardians, would be exterminated, leaving only cinders.

Behind her on the bridge of the three kilometre-long Q'tarin, two elite Q'Roth warriors stood draped in blood-red cloaks. They each held in their possession one half of the genetically coded key to arm the Inferno Class planet-cutter, whose tightly-coiled tendrils occupied four- fifths of the ship's length. She longed to see the Crucible weapon in action, unfurling and embracing the planet, its eight finger-thick lance- wires stretching tens of thousands of kilometres from high orbit down to the planet's surface. The wires would cut their way through enough of the planet's crust to begin irreversible magma spouts and disintegration. Esperia would boil in its own lava. The Crucible was aptly named.

She stood next to her command chair, the only seat on the bridge, while her elite Alician bridge crew manned their consoles standing up as was traditional on all Q'Roth vessels. She rarely sat in that chair, knowing the Q'Roth would see it as a sign of weakness. Despite her height in heeled boots, the two warriors towered a good metre over her. But to the rest of the Alician crew there was never any doubt as to who was in charge. That was necessary: in order to stay at the top in Alician politics there could never be any sign of weakness or doubt about a leader's command capability. Otherwise an assassination attempt was likely; that is after all how she had finally risen to the position.

Ten years earlier Sister Esma had traded her jet black hair for a golden Q'Roth skull cap descending to the nape of her neck, shrouding her cheeks, and drawing anyone's attention – Q'Roth or Alician – to her wide black eyes, hooked nose and thin lips that rarely smiled. Her whole demeanour sent a message – she was deadly serious. Though to her people back home she could occasionally exhibit kindness of a sort, in battle, and particularly in front of the Q'Roth, she was always ruthless.

Her left arm ended in a blue-black, lobster-like Q'Roth claw, capable of shearing through metal. Most believed she had taken it willingly – true to a degree – but it had also been a punishment by the Q'Roth Queen after her High Guard suffered an embarrassing defeat during humanity's trial. The Q'Roth surgeons had also rendered Sister Esma sterile, though she would live another seven hundred years. The claw hung motionless at her side. During eighteen years it had seen little action. For Sister Esma it had only one purpose to serve. She wanted it to close around Micah's throat.

A year earlier, she had ambushed an Ossyrian relief vessel en route to the planet, and information gleaned from the wrecked pyramid ship's data-core had shown the pathetic progress Micah had made in all this time; a sprawling tinpot town fringed by scraggy farms, almost no transport infrastructure. It was a travesty compared to the Alician new homeworld Savange, with its silver-spired central city, tethered spaceport and Level Five ship-outfitting industry. The Alician spaceport harboured the ships of two other species as well as the Q'Roth, earning their place in Grid society rather than cowering under a shield and Ossyrian skirts.

She pictured Savange's three moons, its shark-grey mountain range with peaks reaching twenty kilometres, counterpointed by nutrient-rich purple oceans. Alicians were not lowly farmers; they were traders and tacticians, participating in the war effort, assisting in numerous battles, aiding the Q'Roth in strategy and logistics. She'd seen a Level Eight report which had mentioned the bipedal newcomers, stating that the Alicians showed promise, that "they had an edge".

The praise had not gone unnoticed by her patron, and two years earlier, the new Q'Roth Queen had offered Sister Esma her arm back. She declined. It was a symbol to others, and hardened her purpose to the very core. Maybe after humanity had been erased. Instead she had traded the rare opportunity of the Queen's goodwill for a succession of missions, first to discreetly prevent relief from arriving at Esperia, and then to extinguish humanity once and for all. The Queen had agreed, although there might be repercussions afterwards, sanctions even, from the Tla Beth or the Ossyrians. But in the heat of the War it would be forgotten quickly, and Sister Esma had promised to make it look like an accident, a freak interaction between the engines of the departing Ossyrian ship and the quarantine barrier, resulting in a devastating chain reaction. In any case, the Queen also wanted to see humanity squashed, after the humiliation of the trial. As for the Tla Beth, they had quarantined Esperia more out of necessary legal protocol rather than actually giving a damn about the upstart race called humanity. Removing humanity from the Grid map would secretly satisfy all the parties remaining, and afterwards, all would simply move on.

Glancing down at one of the emerald screens, she watched the Q'Roth data scroll past, its writing filled with barbed and jagged serifs; Q'Roth script looked as if it would cut clean through any paper it landed on. One field was a countdown till the quarantine shield came down. Fifty-six hours. But her eyes latched onto another icon; the analysis she had been waiting for was complete. She swung around, walked between the two guardians and barked two names.

"Serena; Casteur."

An athletic blonde and a middle-aged, balding man quit their stations and fell into step behind her. As they marched through a maze of twisting, jade-coloured corridors, Sister Esma recalled her conversation with her chief medical advisor Beatrix three years earlier...

"It is as we feared, Your Eminence. The Mannekhi genetic infusion did not take. The results were... abominations. All have been destroyed, along with the Mannekhi prisoners. There is only one option left, difficult as I know it will be to accept. The Ossyrian medic has confirmed it. She has agreed to aid in the genetic transfusion process, under duress. No one else knows of these results, they have been encrypted for your sole –"

Sister Esma knew she should not have had Beatrix executed. Shooting the messenger was a human reaction, beneath Alician standards. But the news had been terrible. How had nine hundred years of careful planning derailed so completely? Negligible statistical collateral, she'd said to the Q'Roth Queen when Micah, Blake and twelve thousand humans had escaped the Cull. The Queen's slits had blazed scarlet. Culls must be total, she'd replied. And yet if humanity had not escaped, the Alicians would have no future. It had been the cruelest of jokes, but now Sister Esma was determined to deliver the final punchline.

Casteur, Serena and Sister Esma arrived outside a sealed room, the narrow glass pane in the door revealing a lone occupant, an Ossyrian doctor, sitting upright, her quicksilver eyes oddly calm, forepaws bound in magnetic cuffs. Sister Esma held up the amethyst amulet that always hung from a gold chain around her neck, and the door swished open. The female Ossyrian doctor's snout pivoted towards her, though she did not rise from her bench.

"Are you ready for the humans?" Sister Esma enquired.

The Ossyrian bared her jaws as if to speak, then closed them again. She nodded towards the far wall. Sister Esma followed her gaze to the rack of empty stasis drawers from floor to ceiling which she knew ran five deep behind the wall. She raised her wristcom to her lips, staring directly at the Ossyrian, searching those silver eyes.

"Lieutenant, transmit a message to Savange, to my aide Nera. Pick one of the Ossyrian's offspring..." The Ossyrian was suddenly on her feet, and Serena leapt in front of Sister Esma, weapon drawn, aimed at the Ossyrian's head. Sister Esma did not blink, and continued with the instruction. "The youngest is to be released. Leave her in a war zone near the front, where an Ossyrian support vessel will find her. Remind her that if she breathes a word, her siblings and mother will be executed after long and painful torture."

"Understood."

Sister Esma lowered her wrist. The Ossyrian hesitated, then bowed. Serena kept her weapon drawn. Sister Esma noted that throughout the exchange, Casteur had remained behind her, near the door. Still, he had his uses, and it was the price she had to pay for executing Beatrix. She left the room, Casteur trailing in her wake, Serena backing out, not holstering her weapon till the door was sealed again.

After re-tracing their steps through the long, low-lit silent corridors, they reached Sister Esma's briefing room behind the bridge, and went inside. An array of weapons including gun-helmets and flow-metal armour decorated the ebony walls, all taken in battle from deceased foes. Sister Esma wasn't afraid to bloody her own hands; many of the bladed weapons were stained with varying hues of it. One in particular, an ivory- coloured fire-sword, had a faded spray of her blood spattered along its matt-black edge. She resisted touching the scar on the right side of her abdomen where it had slashed her open. Her own counter-strike at the exact same moment had found her combatant's throat. In battle and in life, choosing the right target had always been her way.

She perched on her chair carved from finest Savange forest oak, facing the two Alicians. Casteur was almost four hundred years old, and looked around fifty. Serena was technically eighteen, but now, with Q'Roth surgeons at Sister Esma's disposal,

Alicians matured faster in the early years, so that the girl had the looks and demeanour of a thirty year old, and now her ageing process would pause for hundreds of years.

Serena's head was bowed slightly, whereas Casteur's wasn't. He had the arrogance of many doctors she'd encountered, irrespective of species. No matter, he had learned much from the Ossyrian. But she was in no mood for bad news.

"Doctor, I understand your analysis is complete."

His chin lifted slightly, his grey eyes meeting hers. "The originals will serve our purpose. Fifty will do, but I suggest we take one hundred. The others, the ones who call themselves the Genners, are not useful."

She remembered why she tolerated Casteur; he was more politically astute than Beatrix had ever been, and knew which details would please, factoring in how she despised the Genners to the point of outrage; they had not earned their upgrade the way the Alicians had. She gave him the barest of nods. This time he bowed, then left.

She studied Serena. Young and beautiful, as Sister Esma herself had never been. But she had sharpened Serena like a razor, fashioned her as she once had Louise. The thought of Louise distracted her a moment. So much time and effort invested in that one, only to lose her, for her to turn renegade. This time there would be no mistake. Besides, Serena was one of the few Alician offspring to survive the plight.

"Serena, you know your mission."

The girl raised herself up, pride lighting her eyes. Her voice was smooth, self-assured, but respectful – no, Sister Esma thought, something better – she was loyal.

"To capture one hundred human adults, fifty male, fifty female, of fathering and child-bearing age, and bring them aboard, anaesthetized. No Genners. Every other creature encountered to be culled. My troops are prepared. Six of my fellow Achillia, fourteen Q'Roth guardians, seven Raptors fuelled and tooled. My raiding party will have one hour before the planet-cutter initiates." She dared a smile.

Sister Esma knew from bitter experience that where humans were concerned there could be unaccounted-for variables. "Practice again. Use the Tla Beth battle simulator set to 'unpredictable'."

Serena's smile broadened. "Of course."

"This time, with the holographic simulation safety protocols switched off."

Serena's eyes widened a fraction, then settled. She waited a few moments for any further instructions, then bowed and left.

The door sealed, and Sister Esma leant back against the chair. The plight: a genetic mutation, a reproductive fault. Their and the Q'Roth's doctors, and two kidnapped Ossyrians, had not been able to solve the problem. Ninety-nine per cent of Alician children were stillborn or died within a few days. When first told by the lead Ossyrian doctor that this situation was not curable, she had lashed out with her claw, decapitating the dog-faced doctor, and then turned to the other one, daring her to come to the same conclusion. A year later it had been pronounced that there was a solution, after the imprisoned Ossyrian had managed to have a consultation with a Ngank surgeon passing through the sector.

Since Earth's fall, the Alician population of five thousand had only grown by fifty, even after an intense breeding programme initiated by Sister Esma's decree. She eventually quashed it, as the infant death rate was intolerable for her people. Artificial attempts to stimulate birth success fared even worse.

She rose and moved to a shelf and poured a glass of Vintnarian Brandy, watching the blue, syrupy liquid roll around the glass, inhaling its minty vapour. She drank it down in one go, as was custom even though it seared her throat, and then hurled the empty glass into the far wall, striking and shattering against the cutlass that had almost claimed her. She retook her seat.

Beatrix had been right, of course. Unless Sister Esma's Alician flock found a compatible source of genetic material, they would become completely sterile as a species in two generations. Genetic obsolescence. A problem in their DNA re-sequencing, another unaccounted-for variable. The problem had not shown itself on Earth while the Alician Order had slowly grown over the last millennium – something in the environment had masked it, or most likely prevented it. But now Earth was a charred lump of rock.

Sister Esma noticed her claw was cutting into the armrest of the chair. Standing up, she walked to the porthole and stared towards Esperia's orange disk. The proposed solution had almost made Sister Esma kill the second surviving Ossyrian doctor. An infusion of original human genetic material. Her claw closed, and she rammed it fist-like into the hull, sending a deafening boom around the room. Those on the bridge would hear it, too.

Let them.

The Ossyrian doctor onboard had been pregnant when captured by an Alician elite squad, her litter of six children now hostages back on Savange, so Sister Esma knew she could count on her. Releasing one of the Ossyrian's daughters would guarantee her obedience. A camp had been prepared fifty kilometres outside Savange's capital, a kilometre underground, to house the humans. The infusion process would take fifty years, after which the genetic mutation would be resolved. During that time, infant survival would start off close to thirty per cent, rising to ninety-nine within five years, where it would plateau. The saving grace in all of this was that the required human genome served only as a catalyst: all the newborns would be pure-bred, fertile Alicians. Initially she would let the humans live their lives underground, but if they proved difficult they would be kept in stasis except for short periods to take part in the infusion process. After the fifty years the surviving humans would be put down.

Sister Esma turned away from the portal and closed her eyes, instructing her resident to show the year-old detailed holos and intel on humanity's population, demographics, weapons and ship capability, as well as the Ossyrians in their pyramid ship. Nothing would be left to chance this time. Onboard and primed were the countermeasures against Ossyrian bio-weapons that all Q'Roth ships now carried, in case of accidental exposure during battle against Mannekhi and other Qorall allies. More importantly, she also had the Mannekhi weapon used to destroy pyramid-ships. Most Ossyrian vessels had been upgraded a year ago with their own defences, but not the one on Esperia. The Ossyrians would be added to a long list of unsung heroes, and the human quarantine experiment would soon be forgotten, buried in the ongoing avalanche of daily War statistics. And the Ossyrian doctor onboard would know nothing about the fate of her comrades, confined as she was to a secure and data-dry area of the ship. No one was going to get out this time, just her ship and the hundred who would ensure the Alicians would live to see their rightful place in the galaxy.

She instructed her resident to show the latest data on the War, in particular where the front-line had reached, and re-calculate her prime inquiry, the one she checked every day. The answer had not changed. At the current rate of progress, the War would reach Savange in two years. Sister Esma opened her eyes, the resident auto-shutting off, and gazed out at the stars, finding the twin yellow epsilon pulsars, a signpost to the Alicians' new home with its grenadine sunsets in winter-time. She pictured the Terosh, dinosaur-like winged reptiles that swooped down from the cliff-tops, calling to their young. No matter that she was sterile and could never have offspring; her people, they were all her children.

Two years until the War arrived. But she doubted it would last that long. The Tla Beth were tough, but not stupid, and were running out of options. Rumours of the Mannekhi being favoured by Qorall gave Sister Esma hope. New alliances could always be made, if necessary bowing to a higher order. The Q'Roth might fight to the last warrior's dying breath, but that instinct had been bred into them by the Tla Beth themselves; the Alician way had always been one of cunning. Sister Esma didn't think big, she thought long.

Her claw relaxed. The objectives and priorities were clear: the hundred, Micah's head, and Esperia blitzed into an asteroid belt. She returned to her chair, and activated a small control with her right hand. A melody issued forth, a little night music. She remembered Amadeus, so full of life, his hands so expressive, that candle-lit evening in Vienna. She began to hum.

A thought intruded: no Alician musician had surpassed this human genius, despite their upgrade. Never mind, she thought, we have other talents more useful in the Grid. She closed her eyes, remembering his touch, no matter that he slept with others. She'd whispered to him afterwards that he was Level Five, but he had laughed, dismissing her fanciful ideas, and gone back to his composing. She'd watched him work till the first rays of morning, his shoulders hunched and twitching as he raced to write down the wonders in his brain, as if his subconscious sensed he was short of time. He and Leonardo had been the only two humans who had made her wonder if her strategy had been wrong during all those centuries. But the music lulled her, and she remembered watching him conduct the piece in a packed music hall. At one point, he had looked up and fleetingly waved to her with his baton.

For the first time in a week, Sister Esma fell asleep.

CHAPTER 12 – DEFENCELESS

Blake powered down the skimmer at the edge of Esperantia, dust whipping around him and Zack's Transpar. They dismounted and walked over to meet with Vasquez and Ramires, neither of whom looked happy. An ebony, dread-locked Genner stood apart. He wore desert-style ultra- light combat fatigues, and rested on one bare foot, the other planted firm on his standing leg's inner thigh, holding a steel halberd in his right hand, its foot-long curved blade glinting in the afternoon sun. A scarlet, semi- circular maze-like tattoo skirted the boy's left eye and temple, marking him out as one of Gabriel's top Youngbloods. There was something odd about the blade, the way its edge glimmered even though the young warrior held it perfectly still.

Vasquez stood rod-straight as usual, his shock of short white hair making him look fitter than his age deserved. Ramires, the last Sentinel, whom Blake had not seen for five years, had greyed, even his moustache, but he still moved like a leopard; you would never hear him coming up behind you. Blake noticed the waist pouch that contained his legendary nanosword. So, it was serious.

Both men nodded to Blake without indulging in pleasantries. Blake was glad for that. He took command. "Zack said Micah went to the pyramid, but something tells me more is going on."

Ramires clicked something in Hremsta to the Youngblood, who lowered his foot to the ground, and turned to face Blake, with a pinched, almost surly expression. Clearly he didn't want to be there. Ramires clicked faster, almost spitting. The warrior raised his chin.

"Gabriel, Petra and twelve others have seized the Ossyrian ship," he said.

Blake stared from the boy to Ramires, to Vasquez, their looks confirming it. He ground his teeth, trying to remember not to beat up the messenger, who obviously wished he were with Gabriel right now. "To what end?"

The young man stamped his halberd into the dust. "To defend ourselves, of course! You of all people should understand. I..." He stopped shouting. "We revere you, Commander. All Genners have studied your battle strategies. But you have been absent, and Micah has become a politician. You have all grown soft." He pointed to the sky. "We believe our enemies are up there. Perhaps they will not even wait until Quarantine comes down. We must seize the advantage."

Blake simmered, wondering whether it were true; had they gone soft? He'd not been able to face people after Glenda had slipped away. Nor could he sit in endless Council meetings, debating meaningless minutiae. Micah was welcome to it.

He addressed the boy. "What's your name, son?"

"Marcus," he said, standing firm, then added his lineage as all Genners had been taught, "of Chris and Mary Ellen Arvine."

"I remember your father and mother, a forthright couple if I well recall." Blake noticed the boy's shoulders relax a little. "So, tell me, what's Gabriel's plan, and what are the rest of you supposed to do now?"

Marcus glanced sideways at Ramires. Blake knew that Ramires had always been the closest link with the Youngbloods, training them in martial arts and mental discipline.

Ramires addressed the Youngblood. "Marcus, you said you studied Blake's strategy. Very well. Tell me, what is the quickest way to disable a defence capability?"

Marcus looked at the dusty ground. "Inner divisions," he said quietly, dark eyes peering through his dreadlocks, straight at Blake. "Gabriel will take the ship into orbit then disperse Ossyrian genetically-coded mines there and at the edges of the system, neutralising any non-Ossyrian, non-human or non-Genner who enters our space."

Vasquez interrupted. "That's a war crime. Tell me he's going to post warning beacons, at least?"

When Marcus didn't answer, Blake pursued. "The Ossyrians – Chahat-Me – will never agree to this."

Ramires shook his head, kicked at the ground. "Petra," he said. "She has the Ossyrian gene, and knows her way around that ship."

Marcus said nothing more.

A booming, grinding noise caused Blake to turn around. Zack's Transpar already faced the pyramid, three klicks away, half-way between them and the mountain range. The Ossyrian ship's vertex had the same apparent height as the Acarian peaks. At first nothing happened, but then the pyramid slowly lifted from the desert floor.

Blake heard shouting from the other direction, and had no doubt that people in Esperantia would be watching in disbelief, the massive vessel that had been a landmark for eighteen years finally departing, abandoning them two days early.

Clouds reflected off the ship's mirror-like surface as it rose, sand and earth tumbling from its base, forming small dust-clouds, but otherwise no jet engine or obvious source of thrust. Anti-gravity, a trick humanity hadn't yet learned. Abruptly the sound ceased. The pyramid flushed   a deep blue from top to bottom, then began to rotate. When it was a hundred metres from the ground, it became fully transparent, no longer reflective, almost invisible except for a slight rippling of the sky behind it. Blake knew that if he took his eyes off it he would not find it again. Stealth mode. Gabriel and Petra were smart, at least.

Blake had never trusted the Ossyrians, even though they'd cured Glenda's cancer and many other illnesses, and never harmed anyone, never interfered in human politics, and never asked for anything. But he couldn't forgive them for their role in the Genning, in forever dividing human parents from their children. He'd always kept his distance from the dog-like aliens, and a part of him was glad to see them go, captives on their own ship, even if it made humanity more vulnerable. While he didn't condone Gabriel's actions, there was a taste of justice about it: *you reap what you sow.*

When the pyramid ship could no longer be seen, he turned to Marcus. "So, what are you supposed to do now?"

Marcus shifted his feet. "We were to take the Q'Roth Hunter vessel into low orbit." He glared at Ramires.

Ramires cocked his head to one side. "That's where Vasquez and I first found Marcus and three others trying to break into the secure area around the ship."

For the first time, Blake noticed a light bruising on Ramires' forearms. The holster clasp on Vasquez' sidearm was also undone. "The other three are in the infirmary, right?"

A wry smile cracked under Ramires' moustache. "Two of them; not the girl, Virginia." He raised an eyebrow. "She's very tough, that one."

Blake eyed Marcus. "We've not gone completely soft, then."

Marcus bristled. "Our role was to protect Esperantia and all the Steaders in case of attack. Others were to stay here in case of ground assault."

"Goddammit, boy," Vasquez interrupted, "we don't even know if anyone is up there. Council has discussed this over and over. The Ossyrians promised – "

"To leave!" Marcus flared up again. "I know... all Genners know that none of you have forgotten what the Alicians did. And we understand Grid Law, we learned all the rules from the Ossyrian classes in school, about the different Levels, rules of engagement and inter-alien conflict protocol, what a crime is and what the punishment is, all of it. But we also know that there is a war going on out there. So, you tell me, Commander, do people ever play by the rules in a war? And you, Colonel Vasquez, have the Ossyrians left us with any real technology to defend ourselves against a Level Six attack? And you, Ramires, the last living Sentinel, you are sworn to avenge your fallen brothers and sisters. You knew Gabriel's true father, the ultimate Sentinel assassin, killed by Sister Esma herself. You have trained us since we could walk, to fight, to kill, to defend ourselves. Can you not hear your slain Sentinel brothers and sisters screaming from their graves to act, to take the fight to our enemies?"

The three older men looked at each other, Zack's Transpar remaining immobile behind them. Blake couldn't refute any of it, and wondered why they hadn't come to the same conclusion. Council was mainly farmers and small-minded politicians, the military sidelined long ago. That was probably why Micah resigned; his hands were tied behind his back. But Blake realized he should have come back long ago instead of burying himself. He stood straight. "You trained them a little too well, Ramires."

Vasquez jerked a thumb behind him towards Esperantia. "The Council –"

"Irrelevant now," Blake said. "This community has committed an act of aggression, that's how the Grid will see it, and they won't split hairs between Steaders and Genners. These kids – excuse me, Marcus – have made the first move. It's not the way it should have happened, but it's done. We need to stand behind them. If there's no one out there, fine, Council can do what it likes with Gabriel. But if there *is* anyone waiting, they are sure as hell going to react now, so we'd better be ready."

Marcus thumped the end of his halberd into the ground, twice. "Then you will release my colleagues and we will take the Hunter vessel –"

Blake raised a hand. "I don't doubt your intentions, nor your courage, Marcus. But we're not helpless sheep. Gabriel has given us a wake-up call – one we clearly needed – but from here on we work together."

Ramires nodded eagerly. "This will only work if you are seen to take the lead, Blake. Maybe we should let Marcus take the vessel?"

Blake turned and laid a hand on the shoulder of the tall, all-glass shell of his former best friend, who had hardly moved nor said a word during the entire exchange. "Actually, I have a better idea." He then turned to Ramires. "But first, tell me about the halberd. Is it what I think it is?"

Vasquez rubbed the stubble on his chin, then smiled. "It's been our little secret, Blake. What do you think we've been working on for the past ten years? I only wish we had a nano-pistol, but we could never get one to work."

Ramires nodded to Marcus, and walked a few paces away. "Last time we met the Q'Roth in battle, only my nanosword and Earth's nukes could kill them." He dug into one of his pockets, and pulled out a blue- black object. Blake recognized it as a thumb from a Q'Roth claw.

"A memento from my last encounter with one." Ramires shrugged off an inquisitive look from Vasquez. "The head was a little too heavy to carry." He tossed the thumb into the air. In a blur, Marcus flourished the halberd and struck the normally impervious Q'Roth flesh, cleaving it in two with a metallic twang that reverberated in Blake's ears like a high-pitched gong.

Blake stared at the halberd. "Sweet." He could imagine Glenda's reaction. If she had been there, she would have told Ramires that Blake wanted one. In that moment, he knew why he'd been hiding away with the spiders for so long. It wasn't just about Glenda. It was about him as a soldier. Soldiers should be able to defend those they care about, fight for what they believe in. But he'd felt their cause was futile; they had nothing to fight back with. Maybe their town would be wiped out from deep space, in which case such a weapon was useless. But in his experience, sooner or later, wars came down to decisive battles, and battles always came down to infantry, to hand-to-hand combat, to staring your enemy in the eye and knowing that one of you had to die. Glenda was right; he damned well wanted one of those weapons.

Ramires patted Marcus on the shoulder. "You were wrong when you said I was the last Sentinel. You, Marcus, and Gabriel, and all the Youngbloods, you are all strong enough, and skilled enough. You are worthy to bear that name."

Blake looked up at the sky, wondering how many ships might be waiting for Quarantine to fall. Or there might be no one, the rest of the galaxy too busy or uninterested. But he recalled what his mentor General Bill Kilaney had once told him: "If you don't prepare for something, you are prepared for nothing." *I hope what I heard is true, my old friend, that you are out there, too. We could use a hand.*

He turned to the other three, who were waiting for him to speak, and moved to one side and gestured for the Transpar to join their circle. As he told them his plan, Blake felt a cold fire he had thought long extinguished ignite in his veins. And as they discussed tactics and scenarios, he sensed a fifth presence, and imagined the touch of Glenda's hand on his shoulder, happy for him, glad that he was back in the game.

✳ ✳ ✳

The truce between Gabriel and Micah hadn't lasted long. Petra had never enjoyed watching men argue.

Micah shouted, even though Gabriel was right in front of him. "Do you have any idea what the Tla Beth will do afterwards, when they find out you've deployed mines? And you're betraying our only ally!" His hands balled into fists.

Gabriel's shoulders tensed. "The Tla Beth are otherwise engaged, Micah. And the Ossyrians were about to become an ex-ally."

139

"Rubbish!" Micah's fist slammed down onto the top of the console. "Since the previous two back-up missions failed to arrive, Chahat-Me has negotiated a relief squadron of Level Seven Wagramanians to be here in three months, they will install orbital defences. The Alicians and Q'Roth can't ambush them, they're too strong, especially now they're forewarned."

"All the more reason our enemies will attack as soon as the Ossyrians leave. From orbit it would take Sister Esma thirty seconds to wipe Esperantia off the face of the planet!"

"You're obsessed with that woman. For all we know she's long dead. She killed your father, and I'm sorry for that, but don't you think it's clouding your judgment?"

"Sharpening it. It's your judgment that's clouded, Micah. Why did you really resign as President?" He didn't wait for an answer. "It's because you know deep down that we've become completely reliant on other races, victims in waiting; sheep, Micah. And you have led us to this point. Your guilt over our situation, our complete inability to act, made you resign."

Micah turned away from both of them.

Petra touched Gabriel's arm. "Don't be too hard on him, Gabe. We wouldn't even be having this conversation if it wasn't for him."

Gabriel shrugged off her touch. "Past records don't always make for current success. It was time for Micah to step aside, and he did. And here we are."

Micah spoke softly, still not facing them. "It's Louise we should be worried about. I've seen her in action, Gabriel..."

Petra tuned out the verbal fencing, watched it from a distance. She'd been expecting Micah to turn on her; after all, she had betrayed his trust. But he hadn't, except for one long, hard look before he'd embarked on this tirade against Gabriel.

She wondered if she should have warned Micah. But then Micah would have found some way to tear down their plans, and she believed Gabriel was right – that even if there was a remote chance a hostile force was waiting for Quarantine to come down, then they had to strike first or risk being exterminated in a matter of hours.

But Gabriel himself was also a reason. He wasn't hers, but she had made herself important to him, and *she* was on the ship with him right now, not his girlfriend Virginia, who would be with Marcus in the Hunter. She mentally kicked herself for being so pathetic, so Level Three.

Petra watched the two men she loved: Micah, the father figure, and Gabriel, beautiful Gabriel, whose arms she longed to feel wrapped around her. But a flicker caught her eye, from a bank of screens showing various chambers where the Ossyrians lay unconscious. Chahat-Me was awake. Petra didn't see how that was possible. She tapped the console and saw her Ossyrian godmother pacing in the cell, occasionally glancing towards the camera, appearing to look directly at her. Petra felt a little sick; too much betrayal for one day.

Micah and Gabriel were still arguing. She didn't need to listen, all the arguments had been played out over and over by Genner discussion groups during the past year; the Youngbloods had frequently met intense resistance from other Genner groups. As required by their Genner-optimised process, she'd taken alternative sides during fierce debates in Hremsta, and the answer was always the same: Gabriel's solution carried least 'cliff-edge' risk, least chance of total annihilation. The other Genner factions had accepted the verdict, and despite misgivings, had not warned any of the Steaders. She took some comfort from that.

Petra manipulated the controls with practiced ease as they ascended into orbit – they'd made a simulation of the Ossyrian console from hacked schematics and her memories from when Chahat-Me had brought her onto this very bridge at the age of four, along with Kat, her mother. Her thoughts stilled and dwelt on Kat. Petra wondered if her birth-mother would be proud of her, of what she'd become, of who she was, and what she'd decided to do right now.

Many Genners had grown cool to their parents over the years due to intellectual superiority, though such phrases were never spoken outside of Hremsta. One had even told Petra she was in some ways lucky, that absence made the heart grow fonder. But Petra had always been more emotional than other Genner kids, a trait that had pushed Gabriel away from her, as if she seemed needy. So she'd played the tough girl with her peers, the one with a cutting tongue and sharp nails. If you can't get love, she'd decided, respect was the next best thing. She hoped her mother would understand.

"... what about you, Petra? Petra?"

They were both staring at her. She'd tuned out, but with a mental flick she replayed their entire conversation, analysed it and formed a response. "You're both wrong."

Micah folded his arms. "Which part, exactly?"

"None of *that*. You are both wrong because you stopped trusting each other years ago. Genners and Steaders. That says it all, doesn't it? We're a divided community. We have to re-integrate. Now would seem a good time to start."

Micah ran his fingers through his mat of salt-and-pepper hair. He sighed, and turned to Gabriel. "I can never win with that one."

Gabriel turned to his console. "Tell me about it," he said.

Petra smiled. Now *that* would have made her mother proud.

"It's time," Gabriel said.

Micah spoke more softly than before. "Once you take the shield down, there's no fast way to get it back up. Are you sure about this?"

Gabriel turned back to Petra. "Anything on long range scans?" She shook her head.

"How long will it take to deploy the mines?" Micah asked.

Gabriel touched the console panel in front of him. "Araik and the others below are preparing them. The first batch is ready." He turned to Micah. "You're not going to try and stop me?"

Micah leant against the hull. "I want warning beacons in Grid Standard posted at all entry points, including a subspace one to alert ships in transit."

"That will alert the Tla Beth, or at least the Rangers."

Micah pursed his lips. "Zack used to say something: the deeper you are in the shit, the cleaner you'd better dress."

"Very well," Gabriel said. As soon as deployment is complete. It will add another hour."

"What about the Ossyrians?"

Petra joined in. "We release them, of course. I'll talk with Chahat-Me. But the mines are going to be locked in stealth mode. They won't be able to undo them."

"The Tla Beth will," Micah said.

Petra thought Micah was taking this well, all things considered. She still expected his tone to be harsh with her, yet it wasn't. "That's where you come in, Uncle. You can blame us Genners – "

"I won't do that."

"You could, though, Uncle. The Tla Beth made you accept the 'upgrade' of all human kids. You had no choice. Anyway, by the time they get here we'll either have destroyed the enemy or we'll all be dead, and if nobody's out there we'll have had plenty of time to think up excuses for deploying mines. You're good at that."

Micah uttered a short laugh. "Thanks, I'm sure."

Gabriel addressed her. "Take the barrier down, Petra."

She stared at the button. Eighteen years of protection. They'd thought about trying to keep the barrier up beyond its fixed lifetime, but it had proven well beyond their technical know-how, even that of the Ossyrians, apparently. The Level Twelve shield's make-up was founded on a strict energy decay cycle that would need a transfusion of fresh barrier energy to replenish it and keep it going, none of which existed on the planet. The only solution had been to bring it down early. That had always been an Ossyrian option in case of catastrophic events either on Esperia or in its solar system. Now the option was theirs, the Genners', and in that precise moment, it was hers. Having decided everything logically, still a part of Petra's emotional mind had doubts. She prayed they were doing the right thing, and held her breath. Her finger hovered, as if questioning, then she pressed it down firmly, and entered the command. She gazed out the viewscreen at the starlit sky.

There was a shimmer for a second, and then it was as if a thin film dissipated. The stars looked brighter; she was sure she could see more of them now.

Inside the ship, a screeching noise began, rising in intensity. She glanced back at the internal scans and saw Chahat-Me's snout in the air, her jaw open, the blue fibres within stretched taut; she was howling. Not only her; Petra saw that all the Ossyrians had woken, including the three they'd removed from the bridge, all of them were screaming the same high-pitched, single word. The grating sound jangled down her spine. Reports came in from all over the ship, from Gabriel's people, trying to speak above the din. Abruptly it stopped.

Gabriel moved over to Petra's console. "Are they all still contained?"

"Yes."

Micah came over to them. "What did they just shout, Petra?"

Her hand trembled, the one that had tapped in the final command. "It was a single word," she said, forcing herself to keep her voice steady. She prayed they hadn't all just made a fatal mistake.

Gabriel placed a hand on her shoulder. "What did they say, Petra?"

She hoped her mother Kat would return soon, not caring if Louise was with her. She looked into Gabriel's eyes. "They said... that is... they screamed... 'No'."

PART TWO –
BATTLEFIELD

CHAPTER 13 - KALARASH

Jen watched their ship's entrance into the Hourglass Galaxy, courtesy of the scout-drone sent ahead. In the pure darkness of the inter-galactic void, a ruby gash opened in the fabric of space. The tear widened, like a bloodshot eye, an obsidian pupil irising open at its centre. The Kalarash ship, the *Memento*, her home for the past year, emerged, shaped like   an elongated crossbow. Metallic hues of aquamarine and scarlet rippled back along its ten-kilometre shaft. Her two comrades Dimitri and Rashid had gotten bored watching these events – it was their thirty-third galaxy after all – and busied themselves elsewhere. Jen never missed one. The eye-like portal blinked and was gone, space around it snapping closed as if the portal had never been there. They were in.

The *Memento* hung outside the shimmering galactic barrier that billowed like a giant, translucent sail, buffeted by dark energy riptides. Sitting in the arrowhead fore-section, Jen stared in awe at the tumble of stars speckled with orange and azure nebulae, the galaxy's tightening 'waist' visible as a brightness that hurt her eyes after nine more days inside a trans-galactic shunt. The ship's fourth occupant, and its Master, Kalaran, was elsewhere and everywhere, his mind long since melded with the ship's organic-metal physiology. She saw from the console that he had sent the access codes, but the barrier stayed up.

On instruction, Jen fired the quantum-tunnelling syringe into the barrier, and it set to work, quiet and invisible. She imagined it chewing its way through the barrier's epidermis, numbing the galactic sheath as it bit deeper, to prevent alarms being raised. She confirmed that the hollow moon they had hauled all the way from the Silverback Galaxy – which she'd known since a child as the 'Milky Way' – was intact, and remained masked in its null-entropy field. Kalaran hoped he wouldn't need it, but it was insurance; none of them were prepared to return empty-handed.

Jen put her feet up on the console. They had some waiting to do, especially as during the previous thirty-two visits they had had no response. Kalaran was looking for the Kalarash known as Darkur. Considering there were only seven Kalarash left in the entire universe, they were pretty anti-social and good at covering their tracks. Still, Kalaran believed that this time he would be there.

She trawled her hands through her hair, and wondered how things were going back home. Intergalactic time dilation was a tricky business, especially using these shunts, and whenever she asked Kalaran what year it was back 'home' he'd answer the same – he could only tell her when they headed back. But she knew his agenda was getting tight. In fact both their schedules converged on the same point – Quarantine disablement. For her, her lover Dimitri and comrade-in-arms Rashid, they wanted to be back in time to help protect whatever had become of humanity from those Alician bastards and their Q'Roth locust friends. For Kalaran, he wanted to save Hellera – though she hadn't talked to him for half a million years – and defeat Qorall. It all came down to the spiders, apparently, and having at least two Kalarash ships, ideally three. Hellera no longer had one, and so Kalaran needed to borrow one.

For Jen it was more personal. She had never fit in socially, and had burned most of her bridges with people back home. But the one anchor that kept pulling at her was Gabriel, the namesake and son of her dead brother. She wondered if he was a tall boy by now, or even a grown man, how he looked, if he had his father's voice...

She got up and paced. As if on cue, Kalaran spoke to her. As always, he used her brother's voice, sometimes an avatar of him. She both hated and loved it; hated it because Kalaran manipulated her, was assured of her complete attention and compliance when he took her brother's form, and loved it because it was just as if her brother was alive again.

"Are you okay, Jen? I picked up a drop in your psycho-emotive state."

"Uh-huh. Like I'm ever stable for more than five minutes. What do you really want?"

"Darkur is here. He's coming. Get ready. Tell the others."

He 'choired' the last four sentences so they hit her all at the same time, something he'd been teaching her since he 'messed with her brain' as she put it, trying to advance her to Level 5. He'd asked her at the time if he could quash some of her emotions to make room for higher order thinking. She'd told him to fuck off. He'd inquired as to whether that meant yes or no. Jen always had to remind herself to be careful whenever communicating with Level Nineteen beings.

She whirled to the comms station he'd created for her, and connected the neural interface. "We've found Darkur. You guys better get up here." She used the interface to scan the other side of the barrier – and felt, as well as saw, the bow-wave of

Darkur's crossbow ship, sleek, elegant, subtly muscled with space-field manipulation weaponry that even Qorall didn't possess. It reminded her of her martial arts training years ago, when she studied the classic Art of War by Sun Tzu and the Book of Five Rings by the most famous swordsman of all time, Miyamoto Musashi. The first rule was 'ground'; you should know the terrain you are fighting on. And if you can control it, all the better. The Kalarash could alter space and gravity fields. With that kind of power, they didn't need conventional weapons, though they could make them on demand. Unfortunately, Qorall had those damned dark worms...

Dimitri arrived first, his large frame, goat-black hair and huge smile tumbling into the cockpit. She grinned.

He saw the interface node clipped to her right ear, and beamed. "Oh, how marvellous! You finally got it to work! How I hate you!" But he swung her into his arms and lifted her feet off the floor in an embrace, kissing her fully. She closed her eyes, wondering how she had ever even thought of giving him up back on Esperia when she'd gone off the rails. He put her down, but still had his burly arms locked around her. "I'm handling the stent. I want to be able to tell Micah and Blake when we get back that I broke through a galactic barrier!" He laughed and she had no choice but to acquiesce.

An Indian voice intruded. "Then I will monitor the moon. Please, excuse my interruption."

Jen disentangled herself from Dimitri's grasp. "Thanks Rashid, that leaves me with comms, and my new toy." She tapped her ear, smiling.

Rashid took the third station. She briefly studied his thin frame, tight black curls, and gleaming white-toothed smile that was the most genuine she had ever encountered. But it was the eyes that drew her. All black. Rashid had been blinded during the escape from Earth, in the initial assault by Louise. When Rashid had joined her and Dimitri just before Kalaran departed Esperia, Rashid had been wearing a 'dolphin', a rainbow-hued band of metal around his eyes and head that acted as a 'sensurround' system to replace normal vision. A month ago Kalaran had given Rashid new eyes, but they were all black, like the Mannekhi. Kalaran didn't say why, only that it might come in useful later.

Kalaran's voice spoke just to her, via the interface. "Jen, I'm going to be communicating with Darkur. I'm going to give you filtered access so it does not hurt you or scramble your brain. You'll also pick up thought remnants – filtering such communications all the way from Level Nineteen to Level Five is messy, but this means you will feel some of the context as well. Is this acceptable?"

"Are you kidding me? I get to see inside your head, what you're thinking?"

"It will be a gross translation, that is all. Our thought patterns are far too nuanced for you to ever fully comprehend."

"I'll take it," she said.

She sat down, leaned back in her chair, beaming. Dimitri glanced at her. "What's going on, my love?"

"Oh nothing much," she lied.

* * *

After reaching the age of two and a half billion years, Kalaran had hoped he was done with arguing. But within the first pico-second of his former colleague arriving at the other side of the barrier, the bickering began. Kalaran had at least expected a "Hello". The truth was, when there were only seven of your species left in the entire universe, each in its own adopted galaxy or like Darkur and two others, itinerant, and all of them leagues ahead of every other registered species, privacy became a premium, irritability a reflex.

He didn't stop Darkur's thought-probe from interrogating every facet of the ship, including downloading the entire thought structure of the three humans onboard. As if that wasn't rude enough, Darkur refused to follow protocol and drop the barrier. The Kalarash species weren't big on reunions, and evidently a ship-to-ship meeting was off the agenda. But Kalaran relaxed – Darkur's scans failed to detect the moon, which now drifted a couple of hundred thousand kilometres away in the starless void. *Darkur – your complacency will be your undoing.*

Kalaran was tired from the long journey – he'd had to fight off dark worm attacks in the interstitial void whenever there were breaks in the shunt system. He had certain visitor's rights, however, and demanded linear communication. It would vex Darkur, but after a year of talking to Jen, Dimitri and Rashid in human language, he'd gotten used to it.

"Whatever you want, the answer's *no*," Darkur grumbled.

Not exactly a good start. "I've come a long way, Darkur. At least hear me out."

"Kalaran, this distraction has just cost me the Saccardian Sector rebellion. I'd been keeping an eye on them. It's cusp time. Two thousand years of careful social manipulation are now careening down a black hole! Literally!"

Kalarash made it a policy of never saying sorry. They did what they did and accepted responsibility for it, unless they decided not to, of course. Being at the top of the species pyramid had its perks.

Kalaran took advantage of the few nanoseconds' pause that followed to make his case personally. "Qorall is winning the War in the Silverback galaxy, and racking up an impressive death toll, even by our standards." "Kalaran, when will you ever learn? We've seeded hundreds of galaxies. Some work, some fail. You're losing perspective."

148

Or finding it again. "Qorall is our responsibility. We set him on this path." That was below the belt, but true enough.

Darkur sidestepped it. "What's with the low-bred company you're keeping? They're barely Level Four."

Kalaran didn't have a good answer. There was something about this race calling itself 'human'. He'd always been a sucker for the underdog, and humanity had lost everything, including its home planet. But Darkur had a point – why should he care? There were millions of races scattered across the universe, most of whom were more intelligent than this one. But even a Level Nineteen race such as the Kalarash had to rely on instinct once in an aeon.

"What exactly is it you want from me, Kalaran? I'd like to get back to my work and see what I can salvage in Saccardia."

Kalaran aimed high. "Recall the others. Fight Qorall, destroy him once and for all."

Darkur's voice lost its grumpiness. "Not sure we can *destroy* him anymore. We could defeat him, maybe. But the others are busy and will be less hospitable than I. Also, if we did wage war on him again, the galaxy likely wouldn't survive – you do remember what happened last time?"

Kalaran considered the Jannahi galaxy: dark, inert, devoid of life, its stars extinguished.

"Kalaran, tell me your mind hasn't entered the scattering stage. You must have anticipated my answer. In any case, why don't you talk to Hellera? Rumour has it she's in your precious Silverback galaxy at the moment."

Kalaran would have kicked something if he'd had a foot handy. "We're not talking at the moment." He reflected that in this case, 'moment' signified half a million years. Kalaran wondered if he had more in common with these humans than he'd thought.

But Darkur was right, he had considered that he would get no personal help. He checked the moon. Rashid was ready, Dimitri, too. "Darkur, I need to borrow your ship."

The expletives that followed had no human equivalent.

Kalaran's scanners snapped into action, latching onto the comms spike on the sub-space frequency used only by Kalarash. He located Darkur's ship on the other side of the barrier. He primed the moon, then hesitated, deciding to try one last time.

"Darkur, I'll have it back before you know it."

"I swear you've really lost it this time, Kalaran. Aside from Hellera, who likes hanging out in nebulas, we haven't been separated from our ships for two billion years! Not since we defeated Qorall last time, back when your little human friends were amino acid goo waiting for something special to happen. The answer is – "

Kalaran's mind unleashed a set of synchronous commands: the syringe punctured the barrier; a liquid diamond stent widened it in nanoseconds; gravitic hooks leapt through like gossamer lampreys, fixing onto Darkur's hull; the moon catapulted forward through the fissure, its mass used as the counterweight to pull Darkur's ship through the other way. Last, an extraction program Hellera had first used on Kalaran several million years ago stripped Darkur's mind and physical correlates from his ship and deposited them inside the moon. Kalaran smiled – as far as his residual anatomy would allow – a trick he'd learned from his human associates.

The moon drifted along the inner edge of the galactic barrier. The stent collapsed. Kalaran knew that Darkur would waken soon, really pissed off, so much so that he might actually chase him all the way back to the Silverback Galaxy. But first he'd have to build another ship. Until then, the hollow moon would do – Kalaran had made it Kalarash-friendly, even tearing out some of the guts of his own ship to make the moon comfortable and functionally advanced. He instructed the moon's navigational array to head to Saccardia at maximum speed.

It was done.

* * *

Jen, Dimitri and Rashid all breathed out at the same time. Jen smoothed her brow with a clammy hand. After a year of waiting, it had all happened so fast.

"Three point eight seconds," Dimitri confirmed.

Jen's head ached, but she didn't want to click off the interface just yet. She felt elated and groggy at the same time. It had been like watching two Gods play zero-G tennis.

She tried to contact Kalaran. "That didn't take long. Which plan are we on now, B or C?"

"Would you like to pilot one of these ships? Darkur's is known as the *Duality*. He's always hated black holes."

She was on her feet in an instant. "Hell, yes!" she shouted Dimitri and Rashid turned to her. "What, Jen?" Dimitri asked.

She walked over to him, kissed him, held his face with trembling hands. "Love of my life, when I tell you, you must promise not to kill me..."

* * *

150

Kalaran's mind held all the data of their thirty-three trips, exact local times including gravity distortion effects, and plotted the trip home. He didn't calculate as such. Instead, his mind, distributed over the ship, perceived all the parameters and coalesced an answer that required no further checking. It would be tight, but they would arrive back just before Quarantine came down.

Even with Darkur's ship, it was still a long shot. He'd have to find Hellera after all, though she might side with Qorall just to spite him, or quit the galaxy.

Kalaran whisked all three humans into the control centre of Darkur's ship.

He'd hoped to stay longer, to catch up, but this had always been a flying visit. He sent an avatar over to Jen and the others to instruct them on how to manoeuvre the ship, though their task would be much easier: all they had to do was stay within his slipstream. He would handle the worms.

He'd run many simulations since leaving, predicting what would happen on the small world where the humans had been quarantined; most of them resulted in catastrophic outcomes. The ones called Micah and Blake were predicted to hold things together, just. But he knew that as soon as the quarantine came down all prediction confidence was lost in an uncertainty cascade. Humanity had a score to settle against the Alicians, and all simulations predicted that humans would pursue this vendetta even at the cost of losing the galaxy to Qorall. Moreover, even when he biased the statistics to gain a positive outcome, it required humans and Alicians to work together, and put aside their lethal feud. As Jen would say, fat chance.

Jen signalled 'ready'. His ship turned and accelerated away, Jen's in tandem.

While his avatar indulged the humans who were having a great deal of 'fun', he focused his mind on the task at hand. He had one ally remaining in the Silverback galaxy, the Hohash. Those omnipaths, servants of the Kalarash and no one else, had nearly been lost. The eldest survivor had transmitted disturbing signals across the void: a new variable, one tending to worsen all simulation runs, an Alician female who had joined forces with Qorall. He had no idea why she should do so, nor did Jen, other than that this woman named Louise was a 'queen bitch', as unpredictable as she was dangerous. Normally this would not even be on his sensor grid, but Louise had kidnapped one of his Hohash, and if it fell into Qorall's clutches...

Kalaran considered that this was all a suicide run, given that Qorall had been preparing for a very long time, and that he should turn around, explain to Darkur that it had all been a bad joke, or else high-tail it to a new galaxy on the other side of the universe. Jen and the others had already said they'd understand if he didn't go back. Kalaran recalled that in his long history, at one point he'd been technically dead for a million years, and had found the experience unmemorable, definitely not worth repeating. But he'd fought Qorall once before, stared into those nova eyes. If Qorall won this time, aside from taking revenge on Kalaran so that he would be truly gone forever, he wouldn't stop there: he'd target other galaxies, those harbouring the remaining Kalarash and their progeny. On impulse, Kalaran sent a sub-space comms message ahead of him, addressed to Hellera, via all Hohash, in case she still had one: "We need to talk."

He activated the portal, an oval patch of space blinking open, latticed by lightning bolts that sparked then vanished, revealing the blue and white vortex that was their route home. The first batch of dark worms smeared into view, blockading the shunt gateway. They'd arrived quicker this time. He readied the anti-matter and spatial distortion defences, but knew that it would take all his mental effort to outrun them. It was a welcome relief. Jen brought her ship up close behind his. *Good girl.*

Kalaran erased all the simulations. In a matter of local human days they would be back, just before quarantine came down, and then they would see. In any case, as Jen would say, it was all now in the lap of the Gods. He smiled again; it felt good for a Level Nineteen being to consider that there might be a higher order.

But it was time to focus. Kalaran's consciousness spread out to all parts of the ship and its Hades Class weaponry, and he got down to business, tackling the writhing, dark energy creatures who could swallow both ships whole.

CHAPTER 14 – STRATEGIES & TACTICS

Sister Esma got the call from Serena, leapt out of her bed, still fully clothed, and for once broke her own protocol and ran all the way. She calmed her breathing just before arriving, then swept onto the bridge. "Report!"

Serena was ready for her. "Quarantine is down, two days early. The Ossyrian pyramid ship is about to leave orbit. The single Q'Roth Hunter Class vessel is still on the ground."

"Long range tactical?"

Serena tapped a screen. "A Q'Roth Marauder is inbound, no callsign registering –"

"Louise," Sister Esma interrupted. "Interesting." Louise had always been a wild card. That had been advantageous when she'd controlled Louise, but she didn't anymore. Sister Esma drummed her fingers, wondering what she was up to. Then she caught Serena's expression. "More?"

"Yes – ah – good, they're in sensor range now." Serena touched the console and a starchart holo appeared, showing Louise's Marauder and another vessel almost in-system. Serena put her finger against the moving blob on the 3D display. "A Mannekhi spike-ship is coming in fast, again no callsign but that's to be expected; we cannot decode enemy insignia. We only picked it up three minutes ago."

Sister Esma moved towards the display, inspecting a blur like a faint comet's tail approaching from the same direction as the spike ship. "And what, may I ask, is that?" It looked like the wake from a craft, but there was no vessel at its head.

Serena pursed her lips. "We don't know. The Q'Roth don't either, it seems. It's not in their database."

Sister Esma surveyed the sector holo, Esperia and its two moons dead centre. Bringing down the barrier early was a smart move she hadn't given them credit for, but it would make no difference. The fact that the Hunter was still on the ground suggested that either they were not expecting attack, or the vessel itself was disabled, or else they had been divided concerning this action – perhaps the Ossyrians were called back early to their new base planet. Again, it changed little, and the Hunter was not a serious threat against Serena and their smaller but faster Raptor craft.

Louise – if it was indeed her former protégé – could prove to be an asset or a distraction. She had to admit, though, that she would like to have Louise back after all this time. True, she'd tried to have Louise killed after the sacking of Earth, but Louise was Alician, and would see the larger picture.

The Mannekhi Spike-ship, however, could prove to be a problem. She decided to delay the launching of the planet-cutter tendrils until its motivation had been discerned – spike-ships were unpredictable, as were the Mannekhi generally. The space anomaly – that was a known unknown, a risk that would need to be handled tactically as it developed.

The assessment had taken her five seconds. She dismissed Serena back to her station. She turned to address her crew and the two Q'Roth warriors.

"This changes nothing, our strategy remains the same. First, the absolute priority is to take fifty to a hundred captives from Esperia to restore our future survival prospects. We will not under any circumstances attack Esperia before those people are secured. Second, we disable and preferably destroy the Ossyrian vessel before it can transit out of the sector, and neutralize the Hunter vessel once airborne – it is too close to their precious Esperantia at present."

"Third, we destroy Esperia using the planet-cutter as agreed with the Q'Roth queen, to make it look like an accident –" she bowed slightly to the Q'Roth warriors, who remained immobile, "– unless this becomes difficult, in which case we launch missiles to obliterate Esperantia and most of the surrounding continent. If we take that course of action, we, the Alicians, and I personally, will take full responsibility for our actions, absolving the Q'Roth of any and all complicity." She stared at the two warriors. "Is this agreed?"

The two simultaneously clicked their mid-claws together twice, fast.

Sister Esma turned to the rest of her crew. "Is any of what I have said unclear? If so, speak now, for mistakes will not be tolerated once battle is joined."

Serena studied the rest of the crew. "I believe everything is clear, your Eminence."

Sister Esma took her command chair. "Do we have a clear shot at the Ossyrian pyramid ship?"

"In five minutes," Serena replied.

"As soon as we are ready, take us out of stealth mode, and open fire."

* * *

Kat awoke in darkness, and could still see what she'd just been dreaming. Six Q'Roth letters. She knew a little about Q'Roth script, but to her it didn't make any word she recognized. It blazed in her mind like an after-image, ivory figures against the indefinable blackness of night. It felt like she had been staring at them for hours whilst asleep, which made no sense.

"Lights," she said, and her room was bathed in Q'Roth standard mustard light. At least she wasn't restrained anymore. She lifted her right wrist to her mouth, too weary to get out of bed or even lift her head.

"Aramisk? I'm awake. Can you help me, please?"

She lay there trying to work out what had happened before, but it was all mixed up in her head, and her mind felt as exhausted as her body.

As soon as Aramisk entered, Kat interrogated her. *How long? Where are we? Where are we headed? Where is the Hohash? What is Louise's plan?*

She didn't care much for any of the answers she received. If Louise teamed up with Sister Esma, Micah and the others wouldn't stand a chance. Everyone she knew would be killed. Kat thought her nightmares had been bad, but this felt like endgame. Her stomach knotted.

Aramisk was unusually quiet, even for her. Kat guessed why. "What will happen to you, Tarish and the others?"

Aramisk's face clouded over. "She said she will take us with her."

Kat said nothing, she didn't need to join the dots for a Mannekhi.

"What does Tarish say?"

Aramisk looked even less happy, if that was possible. "He says we are bound to her, we must do her bidding. If she disposes of us, which is his and my prediction, then so be it."

"So, you let her kill you? Just like that?"

Aramisk's voice grew harsh. "No, not 'just like that'. You know nothing about us, our history... what we've been through. Besides, Louise carries that damned rifle with her all the time now. We've never encountered anything so lethal."

Kat remembered something. "What if I could distract her, get her away from the Bridge?"

Aramisk regarded her with suspicion. "How?"

Kat wanted to keep it to herself for the moment. "Can't you trust me?"

Aramisk snorted. "No. Mannekhi live and die as teams. We don't hide anything from each other. That is our code. Tell me now or this conversation goes no further."

"But then you will tell Tarish, and he'll inform Louise and I'll be dead within seconds."

Aramisk paused. "You need my help or you wouldn't be asking." She got up and walked a circle. "There is a blood debt between us: I owe you for saving my life at the forest planet." She stopped. "Very well, speak now and I may decide to delay telling Tarish."

"Christ, remind me never to haggle with one of your kind!"

Aramisk waited.

Kat tried to sit up, and Aramisk came over to help her. As she held Kat in her arms, their faces neared, and Aramisk kissed Kat, locking her in an embrace.

Kat was completely surprised, also because Aramisk was one hell of a kisser. "What...?"

"Do you think your species is the only one to have same-gender attraction? My own lover was killed in action four years ago." She released Kat, and stood. "Your plan, please."

Kat swallowed. At least it had got her blood flowing again; she felt her face flushing. "Right. Um..." She briefly imagined Micah and Antonia witnessing that kiss – the tables turned. But thinking of Micah brought her neatly back to her plan. She cleared her throat. "Last time we dealt with Louise, Micah killed her."

Aramisk placed her hands on her hips.

"Well, to be precise, it was another called Jen, but it was Micah's plan, which is why she hates him so much. Anyway, she had a back-up clone."

"Ah. And you think she has one onboard."

"Definitely. She must go there frequently, at least once every few days, to download recent memories, so that if she's killed –"

"Yes, yes. You want me to find it. I think I already know where it is, as I have access to security logs detailing movements, and there is an area of the ship, a locked room near to where Louise carries out her training regime. But it will require an entry code, most probably her command override code, in Largyl 9." She folded her arms. "Do you have this code?"

Kat recalled the figures she had dreamed, carved into her mind. The Hohash was an omnipath, it could access the entire ship's database and see straight through any code. When Louise had been about to destroy it, it must have sent the code to her, a last attempt to aid her. She felt sorry for it, as if she'd lost a beautiful, trusting animal. She also knew it must have been incredibly old, and now was gone forever.

"Yes," she said.

Aramisk studied Kat, then began to walk in a circle again, hands clasped behind her back. "We arrive in Esperia's system in two hours. The location is deck 4, room alpha 17. If you can disable the clone, and we can get her off the bridge, I might be able to persuade Tarish." She stopped pacing again. "But if he says 'no', then I will not defy him. Do you accept these conditions?"

Kat nodded. Aramisk headed for the door. Kat found herself calling after her. "Wait? Wait a minute, please." She got up off the bed, and staggered toward Aramisk, who met her mid-room, supporting her in her arms.

Kat looked into those eyes, for the first time not repulsed at some subliminal level by their alien nature. "Aramisk, in a few hours we're both likely dead, and if there is an after-life, we'll both be reunited with our lovers."

"So?"

Kat knew it was wrong, but she needed something to get her through what she had to do. "So... kiss me again, one last time? Aramisk, Plea—"

CHAPTER 15 – FIRST STRIKE

Blake felt a chill run down his spine when he heard the ripping sound coming from the sky as the Quarantine shield came down. He stared upwards. A spot of red blazed in the sky's zenith, then stretched into a circle of fire racing outwards in all directions towards the horizon. Thunder boomed across a cloudless afternoon sky, then silence poured in. The other four men all turned as one to him.

"Let's get to the ship. We need to get into the game, and it's going to take place up there."

They ran all the way.

Blake stood at the Hunter vessel's portal, with his back to Zack's Transpar in the pilot's chair, Marcus at the weapons console. He gazed at the screen as their blue-black Q'Roth Hunter Class vessel, shaped like an armoured crab and half the size of a football field, lifted from the ground, retracting its six squat legs. The inquisitive crowd dispersed, ushered away by Vasquez's militia. Vasquez would coordinate Ops – if there were any – from the dome. Ramires, working with Gabriel's partner Virginia, was to set up armed Youngblood trios – they functioned best that way – at each main intersection of Esperantia, while several militia patrols had been dispatched to the farms.

Vasquez had earlier posed a question as he shaded his sight from the afternoon sun, looking towards Hazzards Ridge. "What about the spiders, Blake? Will they join the fight if it comes?"

Blake had thought about it often. In many ways he still hardly knew them – they always seemed non-violent, artistic. They had sacrificed themselves during the previous Q'Roth incursion a thousand years earlier in order to save their unhatched young, not firing a single weapon. In fact, he'd never seen so much as a spider dagger.

"Wouldn't count on it," he'd replied.

Vasquez carried on his preparations. "Should we head out to the hills? From space, Esperantia looks like a big round target."

Vasquez had a point, Blake thought, studying Esperantia from the ascending ship. From above, the town was roughly circular, its rooves glinting from the zinc solar panels, corrugated lines marking out the main streets, pockets of plazas here and there, stubby three-storey blocks on each corner with low-rises in-between.

Five churches, including the Monofaith, faced off each other in Pentangle Square, notable for its minarets and steeples competing for height. The square park on the opposite side from Pentangle, next to the schools, was a soft, easy target, where strafing invaders would reap scattering humans like wheat. As for the Dome at Esperantia's Northern edge, it stared upwards like an innocent, unblinking eye gazing at the sky, inviting a single well-chosen missile. During WWIII Blake had commanded enough strikes on enemy outposts to know how to level a place like Esperantia in short order. He was tempted to shut off the display.

Vasquez had told Blake that Antonia was handling a crisis meeting of the Council, which right now included anyone who could squeeze inside the Monofaith, answering the question of whether they should ship some people out. It would take two hours to reach the caves they'd first found on their arrival, those that led down to the underground ocean. Esperantia had subterranean shelters, Micah and he had seen to it years ago. Yet one serious-sized nuke would finish the town and cremate anyone below ground. So, the big question was how long they had.

Word had been sent to the fringe town on Lake Taka two hundred kilometres away, but there were only two hundred residents in scattered homesteads, those who couldn't take the 'big city life' of Esperantia.

The Transpar lifted them away from the town and Blake spied ivory Shimsha, and felt a pang of regret. He'd sworn to Glenda to protect the spider race, and yet at the first sniff of trouble here he was, backing humanity again.

Sonja's medical team was already gearing up the infirmary, with paramedics ready just in case. Weapons had been dispatched to all able-bodied men, and although Marcus and Virginia had persuaded the Youngbloods to work alongside the militia, they all knew that if it came to a ground assault, each group would fight according to its training and style. Blake consoled himself that, altogether, it wasn't too bad given how much time he'd had to prepare. But then he caught himself – in reality they'd had eighteen years to prepare for this day, and now it had arrived, their readiness was pitiful.

The Transpar accelerated the Hunter into Esperia's deep-blue ionosphere.

"Like old times, Zack."

The Transpar didn't respond, nor did Blake expect him to, long ago having given up the ghost of his friend. "Transpar or not, you're still the best goddammed pilot on the planet." Blake decided there and then, that even if only one per cent of that glass being was still Zack, then that was enough, especially as they were about to go into battle. He decided to call him Zack forthwith.

He glanced at Marcus, who looked uneasy. Blake would have preferred a crew of just himself and Zack, but he needed someone to liaise with Gabriel, if that was possible, someone Gabriel trusted. And he needed a good man at the weapons console. Blake had no doubt Marcus' reactions would be quicker than his own.

"Marcus, can you contact Gabriel?"

Marcus nodded. His hands tapped at the tall Q'Roth console, its green light reflecting off his sixteen-year-old chin, barely registering the stubble he undoubtedly longed for.

"He's not responding." Marcus paused. "Sir."

Blake sat in the forward command chair. "But I'll bet he's listening.

Open a channel, and see if you can bring up a visual of the Pyramid." Blake heard a click and a sound like a distant stream. "Gabriel, this is Commander Blake Alexander. Long time no see. I know what your plan is, and I'm not going to interfere, but we should coordinate our efforts. Do you agree?"

There was no visual; stealth mode, Blake assumed. The sound of trickling water continued. "Is he reading me?"

"Yes, Sir."

"Then you try. In Hremsta."

Marcus clicked for around thirty seconds, while Blake momentarily let his head rest against the back of the chair. He closed his eyes. *Well, here I am again Glenda, sixty years of age and still kicking. Maybe I'll see you soon.* He knew what her response would have been. *Nothing reckless now, you look after that young boy.* He opened his eyes. Fast clicks and guttural noises came through from Gabriel's ship. *Progress.*

Blake was about to ask when the Transpar broke in. "We are not alone. A Q'Roth warship, range two million kilometres, stealth mode. I cannot yet tell the vessel's class."

"Marcus, relay it to Gabriel!"

160

Marcus stuttered the message in Hremsta as fast as he could.

"Blake, this is Micah. We aren't picking up any vessel other than yours."

Blake frowned. *Since when did Micah speak Hremsta?* "Micah, Zack's at the controls, patched into the Hunter's sensor arrays. I don't doubt him – if he says it's there, it's there."

Micah continued. "Okay – Gabriel is going to deploy one of the mines as a missile, please relay us some telemetry – ship codes – anything – so we can target the ship."

"Roger." He turned to watch Zack's crystal fingers blur over the keypad.

Marcus nodded. "Co-ordinates sent."

Blake was thrown sideways out of his chair as their ship lurched to one side. He clawed his way back, struggling against the G-force of intense acceleration, noting that Marcus had managed to stay with his console. "Report," he barked.

The Transpar responded with its cool, tinkling voice. "The warship fired on us and the pyramid too. We took minor damage, and I am executing a fractal defence pattern so they cannot get a fix on us. The inertial gravity will protect you now – my first evasive manoeuvre was a little extreme."

Blake regained his chair. "Show me the Ossyrian vessel, split screen."

The pyramid spun slowly, punched by pulse beams from the warship. Stealth mode had failed, and the pyramid hung like a spinning sapphire in space. Hell's teeth, how could they detect and target it so accurately from so far away?

Marcus interrupted. "Gabriel has launched the Ossyrian genetic weapon. Five seconds..."

Blake waited, then shielded his eyes as space lit up with green saccadic flashes. The Level Eight weapon, refined for the Ossyrians by the Tla Beth, was known and feared throughout the galaxy, employing a gamma-based carrier wave to penetrate hulls and infect non-coded DNA. Yet Blake wondered if counter-measures had been developed during the War – after all, it had not stopped Qorall's advance. The Q'Roth vessel stopped firing, and Blake held his breath. At least the beam pulses had ceased. He prayed Gabriel's gambit had worked.

"Blake," Micah said over the comms, "we took some damage, the Ossyrian shields are still holding, barely. It appears the Q'Roth firepower has increased since this particular Pyramid-ship was last updated."

"Do you have any conventional weapons, beams or missiles?" Even as he asked, he doubted they would help. The Ossyrian vessel might be Level Eight compared to Q'Roth Level Six, but so much time had passed, and weapon-tech had undoubtedly advanced during the ongoing war.

"No," Micah answered, hints of desperation and frustration in his voice.

A yellow pulse beam flashed across Blake's viewscreen, slapping straight into the pyramid. *Dammit!*

"Zack, intercept the Q'Roth ship, full speed with your fractal pattern, don't be afraid to shake us up a little."

Marcus looked up from his console. "Suicide run?"

"Not today, son. Hail the warship, let's see how personal this is."

Marcus tried. "No reply."

Okay, Blake thought, have it your way, strictly professional. "Micah, Gabriel, we're going in. I have a nannite warhead and a nuke. Won't down the warship, but maybe I can take out their beam weapon and distract them for a while." He wondered why it wasn't coming closer, but then why should it, it could do all it needed to from a safe distance. The real question was why it hadn't fired on Esperantia, now that the Q'Roth – or whoever was aboard that ship – knew the barrier must have come down.

Gabriel came online. "Commander. Clearly they want something from us."

Gabriel's last word jarred as Blake saw three pulses smack simultaneously into the pyramid, its own evasive manoeuvres failing to outpace the Q'Roth warship's targeting capability. A blackened smudge scarred the pyramid's mid-section, some of the mirror-like exterior appearing fused and warped. Blake winced; there were casualties for sure.

He stood. "Gabriel, get behind the moon while you still can." But even as he said it, the pyramid vanished, and Blake reminded himself these kids were smart. Sure enough they showed up where he'd advised.

Blake sat down again, and called up the long-range viewscreen. The enemy warship was long, large structures at the front end, engines at the rear, but most of it was uniform, without any gun turrets or obvious function. He frowned. "Marcus, do you recognize that ship configuration from any of the Ossyrian databases?"

Marcus walked down a few steps from his console and stood next to Blake, as if he needed to get closer to the screen to verify what his eyes had already confirmed.

"It's a planet-cutter, Sir, Crucible Class. They haven't been in use since the Eruvian uprising two thousand years ago, except for demolition during solar system re-balancing." He returned to his station.

Blake steepled his fingers in front of him. *Sonofabitch.* Blake had heard about them, but never seen so much as a schematic. So, that was the attacker's plan. Blake guessed it would have to get a lot closer to Esperia to deploy the weapon, so Gabriel was right, whoever was out there wanted something first.

Micah came online. "Blake, we're out of the action for a while. We took heavy damage, and that last jump triggered a general power failure." Micah sounded rattled, though trying to put a brave face on it.

"Micah you take care of yourselves for a while. I always said the best place to have an accident is in a hospital. We'll keep them occupied."

Gabriel spoke, his voice uneven. "Commander, I fear I have misjudged the situation, we –"

"Stow it, Gabriel," Blake interrupted. "You and your Youngbloods were right, and we should have listened." *And I should have been there to listen.* "If you hadn't done anything we'd have been easy meat. You gave it your best shot. Now get that ship back up and running, I'm damned sure we're going to need it active pretty soon."

He turned to Marcus, who was staring at him. "Apprise Vasquez of the situation. Relay him all our telemetry. Tell him to prepare."

"For what, Sir?"

Blake could feel it in his gut; he knew what was coming, though he had no idea what they wanted or why. "Tell him to prepare for ground assault. They'll be coming soon."

Their Hunter zigzagged as sporadic beams from the destroyer tried to target them. Every once in a while the ship was punched sideways as one of the energy pulses struck a glancing blow, but they were steadily closing the gap. He knew no human pilot, not even Zack, could fly like this, anticipating and reacting with lightning speed. Still, it was taking too long. He slapped his thighs. "Zack, can't you go any faster, dammit?"

"Sure, boss."

Blake swivelled his head to face the Transpar. *What did you just say?* Marcus, deep in discussion with Vasquez, hadn't heard it. Blake spoke quietly to his crystal companion. "Zack? Is that you?" But there was no response, the Transpar looking serene as ever, glass eyes glinting and staring straight ahead at the nav-displays in front of him, his fingers dancing over the console, enabling all of them to escape being fried alive.

Blake clutched the edges of his command chair. They were nearly in range, fifty thousand miles from the Crucible. But he detected movement on the mid-range scanner. "Marcus?"

"Sir, seven smaller craft – Raptor Class – just left the Crucible, heading towards us."

No, he thought, they're going maximum speed towards Esperia, though a couple might slow to tackle us en route.

Marcus voiced the question Blake was pondering. "Do we engage them?"

Blake studied the tactical screen, the vectors, the time-to-intercept display. He knew if they went into a dogfight, they could be damaged or taken out – Raptors were short range, more manoeuvrable than a Hunter, harder to hit. He had ten seconds before intercept. If only he knew their mission.

"Zack, slide into their path, so at least the destroyer won't fire on us. Maintain speed but increase spin. Just before intercept, thrust to avoid any grav-mines they deploy and launch port and starboard spikeshot... well, you know what I want, right, a dead-man's flourish?"

The Transpar nodded.

Marcus interjected. "What you're asking is impossible! Even the Transpar can't – "

Blake raised a hand, and Marcus cut off the rest of his words. They both watched the screen. Blake brought up the aft viewscreen, too. The tactic was the equivalent of an old-style Uzi machine gun being whirled around to catch anything in its spray: the Hunter would spin and jettison HB-enhanced proton-heavy clusters – shot, in layman's terms – into the enemy's pathway. The Raptors' own speed would magnify the kinetic energy of the impact, their normal bow-wave deflectors overwhelmed by the super-dense material. If enough made contact they could tear a ship apart. That was the theory, but in practice it was very difficult due to the relative speeds. It was like firing a rifle at a rider galloping past a narrow window, the shooter using a microscope for a lens. Time to see what the Transpar can really do.

On the forescreen, seven pinpricks of light blurred large then were gone. At the same moment on the aft screen, seven blobs flashed down to nothingness, but then two of them flared into a shower of red sparks before vanishing.

Marcus was speechless, though he let out a short laugh. His right arm tensed, as if he was going to punch the air, but instead he faced the Transpar and bowed deep, a fist over his heart.

Blake smiled, but knew what was coming. He turned to Zack. "Well done, buddy. You'd better increase our defence moves, whoever is on that Crucible is going to be pretty pissed."

Blake was proven correct almost immediately. A lattice of pulse beam tracers lit up space all around them, jarring the ship. Zack's frame leaned forward, zen-like concentration smoothing his face so that his nose seemed to recede and the eyes grew larger, as they dodged a hailstorm of fire from the Crucible.

Blake watched the Transpar, wondering if it could sweat, feeling proud of what his erstwhile friend had done. But the growing density of enemy beams told him they'd never reach their target in one piece.

"Turn about, Zack, use fractal dodge but stay in the Raptors' slipstream, chase them back to Esperia."

He walked up to Marcus' station. "Think we can target any of them?"

Marcus hit a pad and a 3D image of a spherical grid showed the five remaining Raptors closing on Esperia, the Hunter lagging well behind. Marcus' brow furrowed. "Not till they decelerate outside Esperia's atmosphere, if that's what they intend to do. Even then we'd risk striking Esperantia ourselves if we missed."

Marcus laid his right forefinger along his nose, studying the Raptors' flight pattern. It was a gesture Blake had seen Genners do when they concentrated: considering all the eventualities, playing them forward in probabilistic time. He recalled the chess matches Micah had instituted to check the children's development, and how the really good adult players had learned to hate this forefinger habit, as it was usually shortly followed within a few moves by checkmate. Blake recalled the bitter rows over the Genning of the children, how he'd fought and lost against Micah on that issue. Now, maybe for the first time, he realised its advantages.

He stared at the pattern too, but there were too many unknowns for him to handle: the enemy's intention, including their identity, their pattern when they decided to attack, and their armoury capacity... All he knew was that humanity had one vessel against five Raptors; he had to even the odds.

"You have an idea, Marcus?"

He nodded. "Yes, but very risky."

Blake assumed they were on the same track. "How many could we take down?"

"Two, maybe three."

"Are we still alive afterwards?"

Marcus' eyes met Blake's.

Blake nodded, then returned to his station. He punched a control. "Gabriel, Micah, Vasquez, you're all on comms. We'll be coming in hot behind the Raptors. My guess is they're on a ground assault. Don't know why, but that Crucible can only be here for one reason, to destroy Esperia. We're going to try and take down a couple of the Raptors. Vasquez, get everyone prepped down there, they'll be coming in in five minutes. Gabriel, Micah, do you have jump capability?"

"Blake, it's Petra, Micah and Gabriel are busy. Negative."

"Then damn well get it back, and get Chahat-Me to call for –"

"The Crucible is jamming everything."

So, a surgical strike, whatever it was, then a clean-up operation. No witnesses. And it meant he had no real strategy, just tactical manoeuvres. That had implications for chain of command. "Vasquez, you're now in charge."

There was a pause. He knew Vasquez would catch the implication that Blake and the others might not survive. A second later, Vasquez replied, his voice firm. "Good hunting, Sir."

"Marcus, tell Zack what you need him to do."

As he listened to Marcus' words, he smiled. It was brilliant, and yet underlying it was a very old strategy, one he'd heard from Bill Kilaney forty years ago during close combat training. Bill had simply said, "If you don't want to miss, make sure you're touching your opponent." He'd called it the bayonet strategy, after the ancient horrors of the First World War trenches, when young men had to learn to kill others directly, pushing cold steel into their enemies' bellies and hearts, prising the life out of them. Fear made most men do it, because if they didn't, they'd be on the receiving end instead. Being in ships, fighting with energy beams and missiles made it feel more distant, less personal, but in the end it wasn't. You lock onto your enemy, you touch him, and then you kill him, you tear his life from him. That was war. That was what you did to protect those you loved. Glenda was far from his mind when he was in this mode, and he knew she found it difficult to accept, it being the one sore point in their long marriage they'd argued over countless times.

But then, he figured, in about five minutes he'd have plenty of time to explain.

Marcus came and stood next to Blake. "It's all set. Four minutes, Zack and I will coordinate on tactical, you, Sir, just..."

"I promise not to touch anything."

"Commander. Us Genners... I feel we've been foolish. Thinking we're so much smarter, and yet we're only a level or at most two above you, and out here, that means little."

Blake nodded. "Enough foolishness to go around." He turned to Marcus, still a boy, as proud as any sixteen-year-old would be. The Genners had become distanced from their parents, they'd lost something. If Glenda was there, she'd have wrapped her arms around the boy, and hugged him.

"Take your station, Marcus."

Marcus obeyed. Blake stared into the viewscreen, the dot dead centre where Esperia would suddenly grow large in about four minutes. Glenda, he thought to himself, I'm bringing some friends home. Despite facing almost certain death, he smiled.

CHAPTER 16 – HISTORY LESSON

Pierre had spied the majesty of nebulas from a distance many times before, their swirling scarlets, violets and Prussian blues a semi- transparent palette against a canvas of stars. But being inside a nebula was different. Ukrull's Ice Pick whorled through curtains of energy and dark radiation that made the small ship vibrate. The viewscreen showed vermillion veils buffeting them, and showers of purple super-charged exotic particles that spattered like hail on the hull's shields. Blood orange lightning stretched thousands of kilometres into the endless distance, only serving to emphasise the strangeness of what was known as the Diamond Nebula.

For Pierre, sights such as these were what he lived for. They more than compensated for the loss of emotional connection with his former companions, including the first and only woman he had ever loved, and the baby he had never seen grow up into the eighteen year old girl she was by now. To him, that whole period had been *before*, the dark, chaotic and mostly unhappy life of a socially-inept scientist staggering blindly on the hazardous spaceway of complex human social interactions. That was before his nannites interacted with an Ossyrian medical intervention, sending his intellect rocketing from Level Four to Ten.

But Pierre wanted to help his former associates; he felt he owed them that much. Having finally met the Tla Beth, the incumbent rulers and administrators of Grid Society, he and Ukrull were about to meet a Kalarash, the most intelligent beings in the known universe. The one emotion he still allowed himself to manifest was the unbridled and pure scientific joy of discovery, of wonder. A thin smile decorated his flow-metal face.

Ukrull said little, navigating as if bored, searching, hunting according to no discernible pattern. They had come to find Hellera, officially the last Kalarash in the galaxy, given that Kalaran had left eighteen years earlier. He wondered about the relationship between the two, if there was any. The Tla Beth wanted her aid, though the avatar of Kat had suggested a more sinister tactical mission. He'd dismissed it; aside from the very idea that he could capture a Level Nineteen being, it felt...wrong.

He still didn't know how far Ukrull's telepathy could penetrate, whether the reptile had detected this other option of trying to kidnap Hellera as a future bargaining chip with Qorall. If so, Ukrull had kept his own counsel. There was no point in Pierre trying to conceal a thought from the Ranger, which Pierre presumed would only serve to amplify it. Next to the currently dormant Hohash mirror was a holo-display that tapped into the Tla Beth Grid-net, requiring a sub-vocal guttural command for activation. Pierre uttered the grunt, much to Ukrull's amusement judging by the bout of hacking and spitting that followed, and regarded the display of the galactic war's progress. Half the galaxy glowed red, including that half's spiral arms. The inner core blazed white, since there was nothing worth conquering there. The war front was like an unstoppable tsunami wave, tongues of flame licking outward, enveloping systems one by one. Esperia lay like a dusty pearl in its path.

Six months, Pierre judged.

"Your offspring there," Ukrull grunted, tugging with a claw at something the colour of spinach caught between two giant stained incisors.

Pierre said nothing.

"Two days," Ukrull continued.

Two days till Quarantine came down. Pierre didn't need reminding. He wondered again how Kat and Petra were doing, and Micah and Blake, and the Genned children. But it seemed pointless to speculate, and he'd left it all behind. He noticed that the thought had wiped the smile off his face. Perhaps it was time to carry out another emotional thought-pattern purge.

"Miss them," Ukrull pursued.

Pierre turned to face Ukrull. Telepaths could be quite annoying, evidently, probably why they never settled down with a mate. "Why are you so talkative all of a sudden? And this flight plan is ridiculous. We'll never find her."

"Not flight plan; dance."

Pierre wondered if his companion had inadvertently drugged himself somehow. Before he could continue, Ukrull took up the lead again.

"To find something must know what looks like."

Pierre's mouth opened, but his thoughts overtook him: Ukrull talkative; erratic flight plan; know what you're looking for; Level Nineteen race...

"*Hellera?*" he ventured.

Ukrull sat back, and his yellow eyes softened as he folded his fore- claws across his ribbed, sand-coloured underbelly. He – or rather she – seemed to be smiling. "Ukrull gave me permission."

Pierre stood, despite himself. "How long?"

"A day."

"Telep –"

"Naturally."

So, Hellera had been watching him, seeing the Tla Beth plan in his mind, maybe the other one, too. Now she had made her presence known, she faced him square, held his gaze the way Ukrull never did, and had that unperturbed confidence of a superior being. Pierre wanted to know how she could inhabit Ukrull's body and mind, and where Ukrull was exactly, but all of that was secondary – while she was there, he had more important questions. His excitement ramped up inside himself, unchecked. He was smiling again.

"Will you join the fight against Qorall?"

Ukrull's voluminous rust-coloured tongue flicked out and rolled over his eyes. "My effort alone would make no substantive difference."

"Then what is your plan?"

Ukrull made the grunting noise that controlled the galactic display, which shifted into the centre of the cramped cabin, and hung between them.

"History lesson," Hellera said, "of life in this galaxy. Tell me what you understand."

The swirl of stars turned slowly about its axis. *Time.* She was showing him time speeded up at an incredible rate. He calculated the galaxy's rate of turn and converted it – a million years per second. Nothing happened for a while, then a spark flared in a spiral then snuffed out, signifying a civilisation flourishing and fading into obsolescence and extinction. Several more peppered the display, each one barely registering before fading. For a few seconds, an entire spiral waxed red, and then thousands of star systems glowed violet, indicating a terrible and all-consuming war, then faded to black, a few star systems hanging on before reverting to grey, indicating their civilisations and grand empires had decayed into oblivion.

And so it continued. He worked out where Earth was, and kept half an eye on it, but knew that at this rate of time lapse it would not even show up as having produced sentient life and civilisation. Then a swelling ring of stars lit up around the inner hub, inward of the spirals, flickered precariously, and remained bright. The Grid. The interstellar highway that had fuelled and cemented a galactic society. It lasted a full ten seconds, rippling out to most of the spirals, then froze. *Today.*

He wanted more. "Hellera, can you fast-forward, please, mostlikely prediction."

The reptile's yellow eyes blinked lazily one at a time, so Hellera never took an eye off him. The stars all returned to their silver-grey pinpricks, all civilisation extinguished, and then the galaxy split apart, shattered into myriad motes losing cohesion, imploding, becoming dust, the dark matter and energy forces that bind a galaxy together depleted. *Just like before*, Pierre thought, according to the legends of the war two billon years ago in the Jannahi galaxy when the Kalarash last joined battle against Qorall.

Pierre sat back. She had asked him to say what he understood, but the shock of knowing the likely end numbed him.

Hellera spoke, the harshness somehow removed from Ukrull's larynx. "The time between enduring civilisations is very long. You should know this from your own history – four billion years – and humanity has only evolved in the last couple of million, the beginnings of civilisation just dawning before almost being erased."

She stood, Ukrull's long tail swiping slowly side to side. "We Kalarash get terribly lonely in those times of darkness. We see the same mistakes over and over again."

Pierre sensed the despair of a goddess whose children were forever doomed. He wanted to counter this pessimism. "But this is different, Hellera. The Grid is something spectacular, a glue to fix society into the galaxy's fabric, make it sustainable, and Qorall threatens it all. Why? And how can you not fight him, while there is still a chance, even if remote?"

Ukrull's head shook. "Listen to yourself. You are supposed to be Level Ten. Do you care for the ants around your feet?"

"I might if I had cultivated them for generations."

She snorted, a stream of salty snot issuing forward from one nostril, drenching a console that immediately exuded a resinous cleaning compound. But she grew more serious. "We fought his race, killed all of them, Qorall is the last. It takes a long time to get to Level Nineteen. As you already have guessed, the higher the species, the lower the successful reproduction rate – the maturation takes so long, too many mutations along the way. A natural negative feedback loop." Her voice became distant. "Your Level Three companions might consider it God's little joke on us, perhaps, and maybe just as well, we are not easy to get along with. Still, Kalaran and I tried..." Her tail swished out and struck a boxed equipment item, denting it. "Qorall cannot create mates or his own kind. But he can exact revenge."

"Yet he doesn't target you directly." But Pierre already understood. Qorall wanted to make the Kalarash suffer first. And yet it still seemed wrong, as if Qorall had another agenda. Something Kat had said a long time ago. Pierre needed to backtrack. He didn't know how much time he would have with Hellera, and sensed her growing impatience, perhaps boredom. After all, he was effectively just another ant. "Why did you go to war with Qorall the first time?"

Ukrull's tongue flicked over his eyes again, as the large reptile settled back into its chair. "Guess."

Pierre went straight at it. "The Level Eighteen race. It's to do with them, isn't it?"

"You are quite smart for a Level Ten. But there is a piece you have not yet understood, a key question you have not yet asked. What would Kat ask if she were here?"

It seemed such a non sequitur, but Pierre obliged, not hiding the fact that he thought the question derisory. "Well... she'd probably ask what you looked like."

"Yes, she would. Not quite the right question, though. It does not concern what *we* look like."

Pierre's sight went black, before him a uniform darkness. Something blue and metallic began forming out of the ether in front of him. Two bars extended horizontally, an oval ring above them at their mid-point, with a long stalk protruding downwards. The ring, shaped like the outline of a hood, contained a thin stretched film of rapidly changing colours, moving faster than his sight could follow, not unlike a Hohash display. Suddenly the flickering colours stilled into a single ivory and blue eye, which vanished.

What remained before him, blue-silver, was a shape familiar to any historian back on Earth. It was the ancient Egyptian ankh symbol of life and water. But it wasn't only a shape, he could sense an order, a way of thinking; the only analogy he could bring to mind was an old-style computer operating system.

His eyes opened again. *So what?* It was interesting, but what was so significant about this shape and its underlying 'programming'?

"Template," Hellera said. "Basic form, instinctive reactions and thought processes." She sighed as if Pierre was a dullard. "Inter-species genetic paradigm."

Pierre's mouth fell open. He closed his eyes and called up every alien image he'd studied in Grid history, mapping them against the physical and cognitive ankh template, humans included. He integrated all available information about their thinking strategies up to Level Ten, as he couldn't comprehend beyond that point. Still, he tried to extrapolate all the way up to Level Seventeen. The template was like a genetic prime number. One species stood apart. "Tla Beth," he said.

"Changed now, originally they fit the template." "Qorall?"

"No. He is from a distant galaxy, his species brought back by a travelling Kalarash named Bareel."

Pierre pondered the implications. She'd somehow moved into Ukrull's mind. If most intelligent life in the galaxy had been seeded by the Kalarash, probably after watching it stutter and stall too many times on its own, then it would also give the Kalarash a way in, like a DNA key, to any of those species. A control mechanism, bringing order. It was also a failsafe device in case of rebellion. He recalled what the Grid races called the Kalarash – the *Progenitors*. How apt. It made it clearer why Qorall would be content to destroy all life in the galaxy.

Pierre tried again. "The Level Eighteen race?"

"A particular brand of machine intelligence."

Pierre nodded. He'd often wondered about the Tla Beth's imposed limitations on drone intelligence. "Went bad?"

Hellera cleared the other nostril. "That adjective doesn't really cover it."

"So, your plan?"

"To leave."

Pierre had hoped for more, and let the disappointment ring loud inside his mind, in case it would have an effect. It did. She was gone. He knew it even before Ukrull started growling, and then howling with a deafening roar, the din ricocheting off the walls, making Pierre clamp his hands over his ears, his nannite-enhanced physiology not protecting him as it usually did. Hellera's doing, he assumed. His entire skin tingled from head to toe as if ants were crawling over him and chewing at him with formic-acid-coated mandibles, and he wondered how long Hellera would make it endure. After a minute it abated.

"You dumb!" Ukrull said, kicking a range of controls that sent them spinning back towards the nebula's edge. "Why ask wrong questions?"

Pierre scratched the last itch from his chin and managed not to glare at Ukrull. "What would you have asked?"

Ukrull leant back, and held his fore-claws above his rib-cage, as if holding a ball. "Why Esperia?"

Ah, yes, that question had been on his list.

"Doesn't matter, know now," Ukrull said.

Pierre looked at his companion. "You do?" He could never tell when Ukrull was grinning, but a couple of larger incisors thrust out beyond the Ranger's mangled mud-coloured lips more than usual.

Ukrull grunted a command, and a new holo popped up between them. He muttered something and an image of Shimsha from Hazzards' Ridge arose. Pierre watched the spiders milling about. Okay, what was so special about the spiders? *The template.* They didn't fit the template, neither in shape nor in thought format. "Wait, you mean they've evolved here separately?"

Ukrull did the eye-licking thing, which Pierre presumed equated with eye-rolling. Then he got it.

"Not from this galaxy," Ukrull said. "Kalaran brought spiders here."

Pierre sat back, reeling from the implications. "But they are only Level Four! They have no weapons, no real tech, how can they help? What threat can they be to Qorall?"

"Level only meaningful inside template. Spiders outside. Qorall knows now they are threat. Will destroy them, autopsy later. We get back first. Find out."

At that moment the Hohash flashed into life, and they both turned to stare at its display. Pierre's heart, such as it was after so much physiological evolution, sank at what he saw in Esperia's sky, evidently viewed from a Hohash still on the planet. The quarantine barrier shimmered and effervesced, and then it was gone. *Early. They've taken it down early.* "How fast can we get there?" Pierre noticed his physiological components were erratic... as if he was worried.

Ukrull growled. "Will be late. Maybe too late."

Pierre stared at the viewscreen. He suddenly, ridiculously, felt like a father on a business trip who was going to miss his little daughter's birthday party. Hellera had augmented his emotions, that much was certain, perhaps in retaliation for his daring to try and make her feel remorse. He stood and kicked at the equipment.

Ukrull turned his yellow eyes on him, cocking his head. "Never kick my ship. Only I kick. You sit. I make us go faster. Will hurt. Want?"

Pierre sat down, and nodded. His lover, his daughter, images and projections of what Kat and Petra might look like now, flooded his mind. He'd abandoned them... for what? To look at pretty nebulae? He felt an old enemy emotion wash over him – *guilt*. But the underlying feeling stressing his entire system was worry, concern, and... with a sinking, defeated feeling, he realised it was *love*. He watched and felt Hellera's handiwork, like a virus sweeping over eighteen years of careful cognitive management and emotional excision. There was nothing he could do to stop the onslaught, the re-writing of his mind's software, and the longer it went on, the more he knew he would not want it to stop. His whole being wanted to be there on Esperia. Despite all his Level Ten processes, all he could think about was Kat and Petra, Micah, Blake, and all the others. His people were in terrible danger.

Ukrull gave him a long, searching look, growled, and entered his claw into a recess on the console, and pulled hard. Pierre's vision blurred momentarily then cleared. Sound seemed suppressed, and he had to force himself to keep breathing, his mind fazed. He shook it off, willing his nannites to compensate, and glanced at one of the console indications that registered speed, noting that it was already off-scale.

Pierre had not felt such strong emotions since the changing, his 'evolution'. Anger at Hellera for what she had made him feel was submerged by guilt-fuelled rage at himself. How could he have stayed away for so long? *Give me pain, Ukrull, bring it down on me. Go faster, warp spacetime as much as you can.*

A headache started, and Pierre felt as if his flesh was being boiled off his skin. But he sat, refusing to move, his jaw clenched shut. *Petra – Kat – hang on please, I'm coming!* Against the invading silence, Ukrull stood and began to roar, tilting his head back, holding out his right claw, his bass voice shaking Pierre's bones. Pierre got up and clasped the reptile's wrist and joined in, venting his sudden outpouring of concern and frustration in a tenor scream of anger, their voices mingling in an unholy choir as the ship ripped through subspace at an unprecedented rate. Pierre's body began to convulse, but he held on, and everything around him turned blinding white.

* * *

Hellera watched them go. She gave the Ice Pick a helping shove, having earlier added a Level Nineteen protective membrane over its hull so the shear stresses of travelling through a hyper-conduit wouldn't eviscerate the occupants. "Ants," she thought, though not unkindly. She gazed to the far side of the galaxy, fixing her vision on a spot that was as unremarkable as it was dark, a hidden inter-galactic portal where she had last tracked her former mate.

Hurry, Kalaran, or you will be too late.

CHAPTER 17 – DISTRESS

The acrid smell of burnt equipment and flesh woke Micah. He gazed forward blearily towards the jagged, charcoal hole into open space, wide enough to suck out a hovercar, framing a black-suited Petra who manned the console. She worked feverishly within arm's reach of yawning vacuum, protected by a pink-tinged emergency force field. It shimmered every few seconds, indicating the precariousness of its power supply.

Everything sounded to Micah as if his head was underwater, a bubbling diffuse noise that only served to make what he saw more surreal. Sparks rained down from shattered, fused equipment. Frayed cords hung and swayed as the ship was rocked by small explosions and decompressions, occasionally touching the force field keeping them all alive, sending electric blue arcs skittering across the gossamer energy skein. Death was knocking, trying to open that door to cold relentless oblivion. One more hit...

He tried to get up, to move, but nothing happened, the only sensation something trickling from the left side of his mouth down his chin. Gabriel came into view next to Petra, agitated, shouting, waving his arms. Micah swallowed with effort, thought about speaking, gave it up, then looked down. A rod-like chunk of blue ceramic material protruded from his navel. He gripped its smooth surface, slick with his own blood, and dared to pull. It was stuck fast.

Gabriel came closer, singed hair and blackened tattoo, frowning. He said something but Micah couldn't untangle the words. A black-haired snout appeared, quicksilver eyes shifting rapidly. Micah placed a listless hand on Chahat-Me's shoulder and nodded, held his breath. One of her paws morphed into a syringe and pierced his sternum. Gabriel's palm braced against Micah's left shoulder as he wrenched the ceramic rod from Micah's body. Micah's jaw clamped down on the scream exploding inside him, and he rolled his eyes back into his head, arms shaking, then he dared to look down again. Blood gushed out, but Chahat-Me stemmed it with a paw morphed into a flat disk, generating a rising heat that grew and grew, accompanied by steam tainted with the smell of cauterised flesh. Chahat-Me put something in Micah's mouth and he bit down hard, his voice finding itself in gasping, spasmodic growls, fists squeezing rhythmically in time with tremors of pain in his abdomen. He glimpsed Petra turn towards him, horror plastered across her face. Gabriel yelled something at her and she turned back to her station.

Micah tried to move but Chahat-Me's paw rested firmly on him. From his sternum, where her syringe still penetrated him, a trickle of cool rain fountained through his body, and he slumped back with relief when it reached his head. Gabriel tossed the blue bar aside, said something to Chahat-Me, then moved out of view.

One of her paws extended something into his right ear. It felt and sounded odd, as if someone was rummaging about inside his head, nudging flesh and bones out of the way. She tugged at something, there was a snap, and suddenly sound flooded in: hisses, alarms, clanks, thuds, and a gushing noise he knew to be the Pyramid's circulatory self-healing system channelling liquid nannite polymers to bolster and repair damaged areas and equipment. It sounded like it was in full flood. Beneath it he heard not-so-distant cries of agony, some human. Ossyrians called to each other in their high-pitched wails.

"Are we still behind the moon?" he said. Chahat-Me nodded. *Thank God.*

"Make me mobile," he said. Her eyes quivered, and Micah guessed she had other plans, to put him into stasis, to kill the pain. "I prefer to die awake, fighting."

Chahat-Me stood, and he noticed something different about her, she was suited in black, tight around her, the normal headdress replaced by a smooth hood, also black, down around her shoulders. Pierre had once told him that the Ossyrians had originally been violent warmongers until the Tla Beth had tamed them and changed their orientation. *Now would be a good time to resurrect those traits.*

Chahat-Me said something to two other Ossyrians, also black- clad, who came over and clamped something to Micah's forearms, then manoeuvred a rig underneath him, one of them wrapping a thick band of material around his waist. That was when he realised he couldn't feel his legs.

They harnessed him into a kind of anti-grav chair. Micah suppressed the worry that he might be paralysed from the waist down, on the basis that their survival prospects were bleak anyway. He needed to get back into the battle. There was a joystick by his right hand and he played with it once the others moved back. Rising from the ground, he lurched around and moved in fits and starts, then more gently as he got the hang of it, and headed towards Petra. She turned as he approached, her face blanching before she set her chin and braved a smile.

"About time," she said.

He remembered why he cared so much for her. "Status," he said. "Like you, Uncle, pretty messed up." She smiled again, then grew more serious. "Ninety dead including six Genners, 47% of the ship exposed to space, life support functioning in four main areas, 30% of the ship fused and impenetrable. No jump capability, no comms outside local, energy reserves will last a few hours, shields and stealth tech down."

Micah turned to Chahat-Me as she joined them. "Weapons?"

Chahat-Me stared through the hole. Her left paw delved into the plasma console and the ship rotated slowly, accompanied by a shuddering that made Petra grip Micah's arm for support. Esperia loomed into view, looking equally peaceful and defenceless. Micah spotted the five points of light flashing across the gash of space, inbound to Esperia. *Dammit, Gabriel had been so right.*

Gabriel joined them. "We're dead in the water, Q'Roth Raptors inbound to Esperia, Blake in hot pursuit. From the stealth-sats we launched just before jumping here, we know the Crucible is moving this way, backed up by a Q'Roth Marauder we just detected entering the system. The Crucible is almost certainly here for a clean-up job after whatever it is they plan on Esperia." He cast Chahat-Me a harsh look. "They won't leave any survivors."

Micah understood Gabriel's frustration, and his implicit blaming of the Ossyrians for leaving them defenceless. But he also knew Gabriel's genned instincts would kick in, and decided to nudge them in the right direction.

"Chahat-Me, do you have nothing else we can use in a fight? You're Level Eight, Q'Roth are Level Six, there must be something?"

She stared at the console, then resolutely outside, toward Esperia. "Nothing," she said. "Two Hohash scout ships. One two decks from here. The other one the Genners below could reach. They are in danger. Decompression will come soon." She showed Gabriel the location of the second Hohash vessel on a schematic, then addressed the human contingent. "You should abandon ship. We Ossyrians will stay."

Gabriel clicked in Hremsta through comms to his Youngbloods to get to the craft, then paused, facing Chahat-Me, his face softening a little. "I am sorry it has come to this, that you must pay the price as well. Micah, I will check out the nearer craft. Maybe we can do something about the Marauder when it arrives."

Micah watched him go, knew it was a long shot; Hohash craft had no weapons capability. Still, he could imagine how hard it must be for a young warrior like Gabriel to be left adrift, far from the battle, waiting to be taken out by a single energy pulse once the Crucible had line-of-sight.

Something about Chahat-Me wasn't right. Micah had been surprised about the two Hohash craft, a well-kept secret for the past eighteen years, but that wasn't the issue right now; the Ossyrians probably considered the Hohash tech too advanced for humans, genned or otherwise. Micah had come to know Chahat-Me's inflexions, and there was something defiant about the way she had earlier said "Nothing". He decided to probe.

"What do Ossyrians do when faced with certain death? Do you have some rituals? Petra is effectively your goddaughter, your *Chorana-Wa*. You adopted her as part of your family. How do you say goodbye?"

Petra flicked a hand at his elbow. "Uncle, what do you think you're doing?"

Micah stared at Chahat-Me, her snout resolutely pointing outwards, her silver eyes quiet.

He pressed harder. "Apparently you were once fierce warriors, worse than the Q'Roth, before the Tla Beth modified you."

Another klaxon burst forth, which Petra quickly silenced. She spoke in a small voice. "I'm sorry Chahat-Me, we just lost emergency shielding in section 12. There were six Ossyrians in that compartment." She thumped the console. "Just lost comms connection with Esperantia."

"Chahat-Me," Micah pursued, knowing it was unfair, "there must be –"

Micah found himself shoved backwards in his anti-grav chair against a bulkhead, an Ossyrian paw morphed into a rounded claw squeezing his throat. Chahat-Me's eyes were unmoving. Her jaw opened, the blue fibres drenched in spittle as he'd never seen before. She spoke, or rather, seethed one word – "Watch!" – as another of her paws syringed into his right temple, and his resident spurred into action.

In his mind's eye he saw space littered with broken ships, some defunct, cracked open, alien bodies drifting, a fleet dismembered. Something moved between the ships, like black fireflies – his resident informed him they had been highlighted, as they would not otherwise be seen. One large ship lumbered forward, particle beams lashing out wildly as if trying to swat invisible mosquitoes.

The image zoomed in on a cluster of the fireflies making their way to the ship. Tight-suited, hooded aliens with something sleek on their backs for propulsion. Each held its gloved paws above its snouted helmet, as if diving, gripping a metallic hemisphere in front. They cored straight through the ship's hull, into the decks, as half a dozen Q'Roth warriors were sucked out into space. The pack of Ossyrians were wolf-like, feral, working in trios to tear down Q'Roth warriors, spraying a directed mist from their paws that caused Q'Roth flesh to bubble and disintegrate. The Ossyrians always attacked the head first, blinding their opponents. Micah guessed it was a genetic nannite, very aggressive, coded to Q'Roth DNA. The Q'Roth warriors, once attacked, thrashed about wildly, but within seconds their heads were reduced to an ugly, rust-coloured, fizzing and quivering husk. Despite his hatred of the Q'Roth, Micah wanted to turn away. But he couldn't.

The onslaught was relentless, and if an Ossyrian was cut down another took its place. The view shifted to a pack in the engine room, then another in the command centre, as coordinated teams sent the ship's systems into irreversible overload. Just before the detonation, the three Ossyrian packs onboard all suddenly stopped what they were doing and sat, raising their snouts in the air, emitting a piercing choral howl that grated Micah's skull, seconds before the ship tore itself apart, incinerating all aboard, Ossyrians included.

Micah was shown land invasions, ground assaults, and witnessed the terrible violence of the Ossyrians. Interjected behind these scenes were short info-spurts, showing how the Ossyrian 'plague' as it had been called over fifty thousand years ago, had rampaged across one sector after another.

Many species had feared these wild creatures, until the Ossyrians' 'taming' by the Tla Beth. High level Grid Council hearings had called for the Ossyrians' outright extermination. The Tla Beth solution had been clever, gradually assuaging the hatred as the reconfigured doctor-race saved trllions of lives across the Grid.

The scene shifted, and he saw Ossyrians more like the ones he knew today, doctors, parents with their children, whom he had never seen, schools where young Ossyrians were shown their awful heritage. He hadn't known Ossyrians could cry. The last images, his resident informed him, were secret, never shown outside Ossyria: scrupulous genetic testing and termination of any embryo or child showing any retroactive tendency toward their more aggressive past. The intrinsically more violent males were genetically bred out of Ossyrian society. That had been a necessary condition for Grid Council's acceptance of the Tla Beth solution.

Miach's resident shut off, and he opened his eyes. Chahat-Me released him, and he manoeuvred his anti-grav chair towards Petra. She studied him, waiting, but he found nothing to say. He held back from pushing Chahat-Me further, feeling he had no right; the Ossyrians had been through too much. Besides, they were all now trapped in a lost cause. What would it gain?

Gabriel re-entered, booting a pipe leaking yellow bile out of his way. "The rest of the Youngbloods have found the Hohash craft on the lower level; they're inside, awaiting instructions. The one two levels up is prepped." He folded his arms, a wry smile on his face. "Well, Micah, you never programmed *this* in your little simulations, did you? It seems the only option is to wait around and then try some kind of distraction tactic, most probably a suicide run. Even so, I doubt it will affect the overall outcome."

Petra stirred, as if she wanted to say something. A frown crossed her face, then evened out. "Gabe, I'm sorry you can't be with Virginia."

Micah stared at her. *Why do we do this? Even when there may be minutes left, why don't we speak the truth?*

Gabriel nodded to her. "Thanks Petra, maybe at least she'll get to fight them."

Misplaced anger boiled up inside Micah. "Gabriel, you know for a Genner you're pretty –"

Another klaxon cut him off. Petra was on it. "Another ship has arrived. Two!"

Gabriel was next to her in a second, and Micah moved back, letting them work together.

Gabriel called out the intel. "The Q'Roth vessel we detected earlier, Marauder Class, and... a Mannekhi vessel. The Marauder is inbound for Esperia, the Mannekhi Spike-ship is on an intercept with the Crucible." A voice crackled into the air around them. "This is General Bill Kilaney, can anyone hear me?"

If Micah hadn't been supported by anti-grav, he would have fallen over. "Bill? Is that you?" He whooped. "My God, you are most seriously welcome here. We're under attack, Esperantia is –"

"We've got it all Micah, these Mannekhi have damned good scan- tech, I have to say. We're going to engage the Crucible, we're too far out to reach the Marauder in time, never mind the Raptors, but watch out, that Q'Roth Marauder is carrying some pretty heavy ordnance. Micah, you need to do something to stall it or else we'll arrive too late. Got to go, it's about to get hot here. Godspeed."

Micah turned to face Chahat-Me's unwavering eyes. "I'm sorry, Chahat-Me, but it has to be done."

Gabriel cast a look at Petra, who shrugged.

He pressed one final time. "We're out of time, we need to act oryou might as well kill your god-daughter yourself in a humane way."

"Steady, Micah," Gabriel said. "What's going on?"

Micah said nothing. Chahat-Me brushed past him and stood closeto Petra. Two of her paws morphed into a crude approximation of human hands, and took Petra's small fingers and clasped them. "Forgive me," Chahat-Me said, then added, "for you, daughter."

Still holding Petra's hands, Chahat-Me leant her head back, raised her snout in the air, and emitted a deafening howl that made Gabriel and Petra flinch, but Micah found himself smiling grimly. The howl continued across a shocked silence for a full minute, before several other Ossyrians entered the Bridge, staring at their leader. Then, one by one they joined in, and Micah heard it elsewhere throughout the ship via the local comms. It lasted another full two minutes before the coordinated howl shut off, leaving a ringing in Micah's ears.

"Thank you," Micah said, and bowed first to Chahat-Me, then the other Ossyrians on the Bridge. She nodded, and they all left.

Gabriel leant back against the console, a wry smile of his own. "Micah, we Genners hate being out of the loop."

Micah explained the Ossyrians' history. "We're going to abandon this vessel, and inflict damage on whichever ship comes our way. Petra, use thrusters to get us as close to interception point as possible."

She watched him a moment, then began activating controls.

Micah studied her, knowing that despite this sliver of hope offered by Kilaney's arrival, their end was likely approaching. Of all people, he knew what it was like to love on a one-way street basis. He turned toward the Youngblood leader.

"One more thing, Gabriel. I need you to do something."

Gabriel allowed another smile. "Sure, you're the man with the plan, Micah. Name it."

Micah folded his arms. "Kiss Petra."

Petra's hands froze on the console. Gabriel laughed. "What?"

Micah stared hard at him. "We're all likely to be dead in the next fifteen minutes. Kiss her."

Gabriel's smile caught. He turned to Petra, who was stone. "Petra, what's he...?"

Micah watched them as if in slow motion, happy that even if Genners were emotionally stunted, they weren't stupid. She cracked, and tears raced down her cheeks when Gabriel placed his hands gently on her shoulders and turned her towards him. He looked her in the eyes, then lifted her chin gently, and kissed her once. Not truly a lover's passionate kiss, but it hardly mattered. Petra buried her head into Gabriel's shoulder, one hand around his waist, and with the other she reached out to Micah, who clasped it. The three of them stayed like that, Gabriel hugging her tight, whispering softly to her in Hremsta, until Chahat-Me reappeared with three suits, followed by the remaining Ossyrians, a predatory crouch in their stance, as if they were once again capable of a viciousness that had in former times made many species' blood run cold.

Good, Micah thought. Now we're ready. Now we're a team.

CHAPTER 18 – GROUND ASSAULT

Blake had almost forgotten what it was like to be in command of a tactical space vessel. The black, crab-like Hunter stole after the Raptors inbound to Esperia, the single rectangular viewscreen hunting its prey. He searched the growing disc of Esperia for the after-burner lights of the Raptor craft, used for rapid ground troop dispersal, imagining them full of deadly Q'Roth warriors. Truth told, he still did not know the Q'Roth mission objectives, or if Alicians counted in their number.

Five orange lights blazed above cloudless Esperia as the Raptors braked for atmospheric entry. The Hunter accelerated, and he gripped the arms of the chair as he, Zack and Marcus tore towards the planet's atmosphere with no intention of slowing down.

"Four minutes," Marcus shouted as the ship shook violently upon breaching the outer atmosphere. Four minutes till ground impact. Within a precious twenty of those seconds the Hunter's outer corona glared orange on the viewscreen.

"Integrity?" Blake dared to ask. He glanced at Zack's Transpar, who gazed calmly ahead.

"Barely holding," Marcus replied, "but we're closing on the three rear Raptors, they're slowing down to avoid damage – we won't be able to go back into space again." He uttered a mirthless laugh. They all knew this was a one-way trip.

"Catch them my friend," Blake said quietly, turning to the Transpar, knowing he could hear far better than any human. The Hunter accelerated again, pushing Blake back into his chair. A keening noise rose steadily in pitch, and there was a flash of white as something tore off their outer hull and disappeared into their wake.

That was when he saw the first Raptor, dead ahead, its two wings like curved swords, its box-like rear tapering to a stubby snout at the front. With its silver and ice-blue hull, the Raptor reminded him of the Trevally fish, a predator that hung out with sharks, often taking the first taste of blood that would unleash a feeding frenzy. "Prepare the grappler," he shouted, but Marcus was already readying it for deployment.

Blake fired the Hunter's energy beam, but as they'd feared, the enemy ship slipstream diminished the pulse, or else the Raptors had new shielding; possibly a mixture of both. It meant he couldn't take the Raptors out easily, and once they'd decelerated through the outer atmosphere the Raptors could work together and eliminate the Hunter, and then carry on with their mission. Marcus had been right: his gambit with the grapple was their only option to eliminate one or two of the Raptors, evening the odds for the ground troops in Esperantia.

The Raptor immediately in front veered to starboard, revealing the lead vessel. "That one," Blake said, pointing. "Chase it down, Zack. Marcus, be ready, we only get one shot."

The Raptor that had dodged sideways slowed, aiming to get alongside the Hunter so it could get a good clean shot. *Just as Marcus had planned.* Feigning the chase of the lead Raptor, Blake waited until the sidelong Raptor was nearly in optimum firing range. "Now!"

The Hunter sheared sideways and accelerated, narrowly missing the slowing Raptor. Marcus fired the grapple harpoon and snagged the parallel Raptor's main engine housing. Blake held tight in his chair as the Hunter slewed violently, handcuffed to the Raptor in a deadly spiral dance.

Zack's Transpar stood, his glass arms lengthening down to the console. His feet morphed outwards like crampons, anchoring him to the floor.

The scene in front of Blake spun wildly, as the two ships careened downwards, trailing after the lead Raptor. Blake knew better than to watch the main viewscreen when in a spin; it was too disorientating. He called up an 'outsider view', the holo showing the Hunter and the tagged Raptor spiralling towards Esperia. The chained Raptor fired wildly, trying to hit the Hunter or the grapple connection. But Zack worked the thrusters and the coupled momentum to their advantage; the Raptor couldn't get a clean shot. Blake saw two other Raptors falling back to engage, and Zack executed Marcus' stroke of genius. The Hunter pumped up its main engine and shot downwards after the lead ship. The other three Raptors, fearing for their leader, moved in to intercept in an offset pattern that meant they would not hit each other in the crossfire.

"Sixty seconds," Marcus shouted.

Blake chewed his lower lip. It was getting close, but he couldn't give the instruction; only Zack's calculative powers could pick the perfect moment. After five agonizing seconds Zack pulled a hard turn and jettisoned the grapple.

The suddenly released Raptor spun out of control and hit one of the other Raptors, shattering its engines before both ships exploded into fireballs of burning debris. Blake heard a shrill whine as Zack strained the engines to their limit, bringing the ship out of a deadly tumble. An explosion in the next compartment threw Blake out of his chair.

"Main engines offline, thrusters still working," Marcus confirmed.

Blake got to his feet. No more fancy manoeuvres; only one course now. He turned to Zack. "Well done, my friend. Now run that sonofabitch down," Blake said, pointing again to the lead ship.

Energy beams strafed the Hunter, and explosions echoed from the outer decks as the other two remaining aft Raptors fired non-stop. But the Hunter's slipstream vortex diluted their weapons-fire, and Marcus successfully targeted two enemy homing missiles, nearly gaining another kill as the Raptors got too close to their own missile detonations.

"Thirty seconds!" Marcus shouted.

Blake returned to the main viewscreen, now stabilised, and watched as Esperia's desert landscape filled it, the Acarian mountain range clear as a scar on a man's face. A small patch glinted in a valley – Esperantia. The Raptor in front bucked this way and that, but its pilot was no match for Zack. Blake knew many in mankind's last city would be staring upwards, witnessing the screeching chase bearing down on them. Abruptly the Raptor, evidently realising its fate, swung about and fired point blank on them – Blake respected that. The viewscreen whited-out, and the sound of metal tearing off their ship made him wince. Then there was the unmistakeable grinding sound of the two ships colliding, and a heavy clunk as the Hunter's forward grips clamped onto the Raptor.

Blake recalled Kilaney's counsel: if you don't want to miss, touch your enemy, then kill him.

"Goodbye, Boss, it's been an honour."

Blake whirled around to see Zack move towards him, as if to embrace him, like they'd never done. But instead, the Transpar's features blurred, its body becoming fluid. It advanced on him before Blake could react, enveloping him completely in a warm liquid cocoon that quickly hardened into an external shell that felt very dense. Blake could see clearly, but could neither feel nor hear anything external, only his heart beating once, slowly, reverberating like a drum through his body. The blood swished around his arteries, into his head. It didn't make any sense, unless...

With an effort Blake turned his head and stared forwards. The screen in front of him splintered in slow motion, cracked and then burst apart. Shards showered past

Blake at the speed of falling snow, a few glancing off the hardened glass case tightly wrapped around his head and body, though he felt nothing. The hull ripped slowly apart, revealing the Raptor's glowing fore-section, the cockpit and its two pilots – Alician, he realised – eyes wide with fear. There was a bump and they were tossed upwards from their seats like toys. The Raptor's hull warped and buckled, a metallic ripple sweeping towards the pilots who raised their arms in slow motion, unable to defend themselves against the compression wave that pulped them both at their mid-section, their necks and eyes suddenly going slack. Behind them a Q'Roth warrior was running, again in slow motion, straight towards Blake. Still unable to move or speak, Blake watched the warrior, in an incredibly brave move, dive over the crumpling metal and shoot across the compacting ship straight at him. The warrior's serrated foreclaws stretched out for Blake's head but glanced off his protective shell – what was left of Zack's Transpar. The warrior's trapezoidal head with its six bleeding vermillion eyes hit Blake's face straight on, ruptured and split in two. Blake got to see what a Q'Roth brain looked like up close.

Through blue-blooded smears Blake stared as the Hunter worked its way through the Raptor, its momentum crushing the smaller ship. Marcus' body flew forward like a rag doll, gashed by the jagged hull, mashing his body... Blake closed his eyes.

Zack, what have you done? But he knew, though he had not known it was possible. Marcus had asked him what Level the Transpar had been, but they had never known, only that the Tla Beth had fashioned him from an impervious flow-material. Transpars were technically 'evidence' used in Tla Beth courts, and as such had to be permanent, almost indestructible. He recalled that Vasquez had once commented that if they could somehow replicate the material, it would make impregnable armour.

Blake heard the hammer-strike of another heartbeat and surmised that the process had quickened his mind, so that everything around him appeared to move slowly. That would also make sense for a being whose primary function was to be an unbiased witness: events could be observed and absorbed in good time, dispassionately.

Blake opened his eyes to find the fused ships, what was left of them, burying themselves into a crater of hard rock. Solid stone and bedrock ignited and split apart with the power of their impact. He thanked Zack for managing to miss Esperantia.

Closing his eyes again, he thought of Zack at his wedding, of heady nights in Thai bars during training, of firefights and battles when they lost count of saving each other's lives, and inevitably of Kurana Bay. The glass Blake was encased in, the Transpar's body that Blake now knew had enveloped him just before impact with the Raptor, wouldn't let the tears he felt inside form. He guessed Zack wouldn't have wanted it any other way. *Goodbye, my friend, may you rest in peace at last.*

He opened his eyes. Everything had stopped moving. It was dark but there was light from somewhere behind him, so he figured he was in an open crater. Flames licked all around him, but still he couldn't move. Blake guessed the protective casing would wait until things cooled down.

There was no urge to breathe, but he wanted to get out of the crater. The two remaining Raptors would be executing their mission, whatever it was. He became impatient, though he knew it would do no good, that he would be released as soon as it was safe; no point surviving the crash only to be burned alive.

After a few minutes some movement returned, but he was like a man covered in thick glue. He fell over, then crawled to Marcus' mangled body and smashed head, and sat for a while cradling the boy, stroking his matted, burned dreadlocks. One eye socket was burned out. Blake closed the other. *Glenda, take care of him.* He laid the boy's remains down with tenderness, then stood up, able to balance this time. Sunlight glinted down towards him through twisted metal, revealing the smoking crater's rim, thirty metres above. He began to climb. As he passed Marcus' station, he noticed something glinting blue, trapped in the carnage. It was the blade from Marcus' halberd. He prised it free. The shaft had snapped in two, but the nano-edge shimmered. "Thanks again, Marcus," he said, picking the active half up as he resumed his ascent, Zack's residue dripping from him with every step like morning dew.

* * *

Virginia, Ramires, and six Youngbloods sprinted toward the still- smoking Raptor just landed in Pentangle Square in front of the Monofaith, as four Q'Roth and a tall, slender woman leapt down from its aft hatch. Virginia noticed straightaway the woman's air of confidence, as if she was about to go for a stroll – Alician for sure.

Two teams of Vasquez's heavily armed militia converged from opposite sides of the plaza. The blonde in the midst of the Q'Roth held up a silver ball above her head, then let it go.

"Down!" Ramires yelled, but only he and Virginia hit the ground fast enough. A carpet of emerald flame lasered outwards with a sharp wasp- like buzzing sound across the plaza, cutting all the other Youngbloods and militia in two. Virginia watched in horror as her brothers' and sisters' heads and torsos toppled to the ground, sliced in two at their waists, twitching and arching, gurgling noises coming from bursting throats, hands and arms reaching out in spasm before stilling.

Not like this!

"Be still!" Ramires hissed at her in Hremsta. The flame layer hovered above them, still fizzing, and Virginia knew he was right – they were still far enough away that the raiders might think they were dead. Through heat-hazed air she saw four Alicians leave the Raptor and head into the Monofaith, accompanied by two of the Q'Roth warriors, leaving one pair and the blonde.

"I take the warriors, you take down the woman," Ramires said. That was fine with her; that bitch was dead meat.

"Vasquez," Ramires whispered to his wristcom, "we need a distraction, fire a shell right in front of the Monofaith."

Virginia surveyed her target and calculated the distance, the time, the wind direction. Six seconds. Her muscles tensed, she lifted her abdomen slightly, dug the toes of her boots into the ground, and placed her palms next to her chest. The Q'Roth and Alicians had just entered the Monofaith's wooden archway doors when the shell hit. Virginia sprang forward as soon as the woman's head swivelled to see the blast of dirt, like an upside-down volcano. *One.* She took the giant silent strides like she'd been trained to, straight towards the woman, who had lifted something silver and stubby in her right hand. *Two.* In the corner of her eye, she saw Ramires cut left to go around the other side of the Raptor to take the Q'Roth warriors from an oblique angle – God he ran fast! *Three.* She unholstered her pulse pistol, felt its warmth in her hand. *Four.* She took aim, still running. The woman's head turned and saw her. *Five.* Virginia fired, but the woman had flung herself backward in an arc, twisting in midair. Virginia's right leg caved beneath her as a stab of heat lengthening up her torso and down to her right foot told her she'd been hit. She tried to get off another shot but her right hand instinctively went down to the ground as she pummelled headlong into the dust.

Virginia tried to roll but a boot connected with her cheek, and she tumbled to a stop, a deft hand snatching the pistol from her. The right side of her vision was blurred, but she sprang up onto her good foot, the other dragging on the ground. She wiped blood from her chin, and unsheathed the dagger from her belt.

The longhaired woman in front of her had a smile on her face – something about it told Virginia it was always there, mocking life. Virginia spat blood into the air then leapt forward with the dagger in a feint followed by a thrust. Dammit, the woman was fast too, clearing the rapid, deadly sweeps and lunges by millimetres, as if dancing, or simply walking out of the way. Virginia heard the sound of Ramires' kiai shout and the ring of metal, then the sound of a nanosword slicing through tough flesh. *Good, kill them Ramires!*

After a vicious knife thrust that Virginia felt sure would strike home yet again failed to find its target, pain exploded in her right elbow. The other woman had neatly snapped it, the compound fracture spattering drops of Virginia's blood onto the woman's cheeks. Virginia's dagger skittered into the dust.

Virginia found herself on her knees. *Sorry Gabriel, not going to plan.* She tried to kick off and lunge at the woman but a foot struck her chin and flung her down. She struggled for breath, arcing her back in pain on the floor.

Metallic clangs and Ramires' shouts echoed around her; he'd obviously caught the first Q-Roth warrior by surprise, the second was going to be more troublesome. Virginia knew she had to distract the woman, give Ramires more time. Through gritted eyes she saw the bitch standing above her, looking down. She spoke, her voice serene.

"We wondered how the Genning had gone. Not that impressive, really. Can't beat a bit of Q'Roth DNA, you know." She walked away, toward Ramires and the Q'Roth.

Virginia crawled with one hand and one foot toward her dagger, sending bolts of pain shuddering throughout her body. She glanced up and saw the woman standing with her back toward her, studying the fight, head cocked to one side, as if watching a vid. But then her head turned slightly, listening. Virginia made one last stretch and gripped the dagger's hilt. She thought of Gabriel, of them entwined in each other's arms, of his laugh so few ever saw or heard, and struggled to her knees for stability. The woman was still listening. Virginia's semi-functioning arm aimed, retracted, and then... stopped. The dagger slipped from her fingers. The breath went out of Virginia and she smelled burned flesh.

The woman had turned, a small weapon in her hand, a sliver of smoke rising from its stubby barrel. At least her smile was gone. Virginia's neck slackened and her head dipped down, and she saw the cauterised hole in her chest where her heart should be. *Gabe*, she thought, and died.

∗ ∗ ∗

Serena mentally filed away the notes on the Genned girl's fighting prowess and resilience. She had actually been impressed: another ten years of training and they would have become formidable opponents. Sister Esma would want a full report later.

This one, though, the way he moved, incredible, always out of reach of the Q'Roth's deadly claws and serrated legs; she herself would not like to go up against a Q'Roth warrior. And he had cut down the first warrior, caught it by surprise – unheard of! She'd missed that manoeuvre, distracted by the girl, but would find out how exactly he had pulled it off from the Raptor's allcam replay later. He had the nanosword, but Sister Esma had forewarned the Q'Roth, and each had a truly expensive and rare *Shrike*, a hyper-dense lance, its regenerative blade capable of blocking such a weapon. The Q'Roth howled with rage and frustration as the man ducked and dodged, but she saw sweat pouring off the human's forehead; the Q'Roth had more stamina, and would prevail.

She spoke to her comms piece around her neck. "How goes it?" "We have thirty, bringing them out now."

Serena kept the gun in her hand, just in case. She heard something new, and a belt device around her waist confirmed it with three sharp pinpricks, their location and intensity on her waist telling her the direction and distance of inbounds. She whirled around and fired three times in less than a second, sending three bodies crashing into the dust at the edges of the plaza. Serena always hit the heart. She spoke again. "Number Four, how's the Dome?"

"Neutralised. We are securing the second batch into the Raptor now."

Sixty, that was all they could carry. But Casteur, the Alician Chief Medical Advisor, had said fifty would be enough. She walked to the aft of the Raptor, then spoke in Q'Roth to the warrior, raising her weapon at the blurring fight. "Move aside so I can shoot him."

The Q'Roth growled, refusing to move out of her line of fire, instead increasing the fury of his attacks, driving Ramires backwards. *Your choice.* She lowered the weapon, and stood in the shade of the aft ramp into the Raptor and tapped at a control panel. Her waistband started pricking her from all directions. Too bad, she thought, glancing at the Q'Roth. *Collateral.* She hit a button and a green arch-shaped corridor flashed out from the Raptor's rear entrance to the Monofaith steps, just as the four Alicians and two Q'Roth herded the thirty people down the steps. Red spots crackled on the force-field near her body as newly arrived militia fired continuously from the edge of the plaza, trying to break through. She didn't move, instead glancing to her left, where the Q'Roth had knocked down Ramires and was trying to kill him, stamping down with his legs like a scorpion, but that man, who in the galaxy was he? And then it came to her. A *Sentinel*, maybe the last one alive. She considered how Sister Esma would prize him, and for a millisecond thought about taking down the barrier to capture him, but no, too risky.

"Come on!" she shouted as her compatriots hustled the people, wide- eyed and fearful, past her into the caged section in the Raptor's belly. It would be tight, it was meant for twenty. She smiled as they filed past, downtrodden, defeated, angry, confused. *Genetic material, that's all you are, but you will cure us.* She tapped a control and the corridor sealed at the other end and began retracting, even as militia advanced, still firing. The last two to board were the Q'Roth warriors, who hesitated, looking to their colleague.

She spoke clearly in Largyl Six, the official Q'Roth language. "We leave now. He stays. You don't." Her eyes fixed on their slits until they boarded.

The ramp closed and the ship swiftly rose amongst a sound like stones pelting their hull; more fire from the militia, of no consequence given the Raptor's shielding.

Serena stood in front of the cage bars, staring at the humans until the noise abated. "My name is Serena. You are prisoners, but we will not harm you." Murmurings grew, things were said, shouted. She ignored it all, waited, and searched among them to see who were the strong ones, the ones who watched carefully, saying nothing. It quietened down. "You are coming back to our homeworld. We need some of your genetic material." Another outpouring of anger, more insults, still Serena held her breezy smile. A Q'Roth informed her in Largyl Six that both ships were aloft now and out of harm's way. She didn't nod acknowledgement, but addressed the caged crowd again. "We will treat you well. You will live out your lives as a small community of sixty people, isolated but in good conditions. Once a month we will extract genetic material, that is all. You will not be permitted children. If you rebel, we will induce coma and take what we need from your limp, unconscious bodies. It is your choice."

Somebody tried to throw something at her through the bars, a dagger. She didn't flinch, calculating in an instant that it would narrowly miss her head. The Q'Roth warrior behind her caught it in midair, and advanced. She stilled him with a flat palm. Silence followed, and as one all the humans stared at her. "Is there a leader amongst you?" Even as she said it, she gazed at an auburn-haired woman, in her early forties she judged, who moved toward the edge of the bars, the others parting before her, chin held high. *Such poise, someone I can deal with.*

"What is your name?"

"Antonia."

"Well, Antonia, calm your people, we have a long voyage ahead of us."

"What of Esperantia? What of the others?"

Serena's smile stayed in place. "We have all that we need."

Antonia's eyes drilled into hers.

Good, she can smell a lie. Serena raised an eyebrow, and Antonia said nothing more, her lips tight. Perfect – political acumen, too – she cares for the others, doesn't want to panic them, possibly wants to bide their time so they can escape.

Another, blonder woman, a little older, pushed her way to the front and stood next to Antonia, scowling as she spoke. "If you turn your back, bitch, even for a second – "

"That won't happen. We'll talk again soon. I'm afraid all of you must sleep now." She touched a control and the entire cage shimmered, all the people inside frozen in stasis. Serena made her way to the cockpit and took the rear command chair. She tapped the console. "Sister Esma, two Raptors en route, sixty humans, one Q'Roth left behind presumed dead by now – the humans have some basic nano-weaponry." There was no oral acknowledgement, simply a message 'received'. Serena didn't need gratitude or appreciation. She had gotten the job done, even if the loss of five Raptors had been well outside predictions. But the lack of a personal response from Sister Esma, a rebuke even, made her wonder if something else had happened back on the Crucible. Serena knew she would find out soon enough, and so leant back against the hull, and smiled. She had never seen a planet-cutter in action, and was looking forward to it.

* * *

Blake sprinted across the plaza, overtaking the militia, as the human cargo was herded into the Raptor, but he was headed for Ramires. He couldn't bear to see another comrade cut down, and the man was already on the ground dodging pounding Q'Roth feet for his life. Blake ran full pelt toward the fizzing energy shield, gambling that it would retract before he collided with it and was vaporised. It did. As soon as it was out of the way he saw Ramires pinned down by one of the Q'Roth's legs, the warrior's head leant back in a roar of victory, an upper leg raised high for the kill, its body lit up by red pulse fire from militia, none of which affected it. Blake, still running, raised the halberd's shortened shaft in his right hand then hurled it tomahawk-style at the Q'Roth's back. The effort tripped him but as he crashed down into the dust he heard a spinning sound and a crunch choking off the Q'Roth's howl. Blake skidded to a stop and dared to look up. The halberd's hilt was sticking out of the warrior's back, the tall Q'Roth wavering, blue blood spurting from the fissure in his spine. The drone of the Raptor taking off was accompanied by a sirocco of dust, and then a boom rang out around the plaza as it shot upwards.

When the dust settled, the warrior was on the ground, twitching. Vasquez hurried over to Ramires, Blake too. Ramires was in bad shape, but he pointed to the nano-sword hilt a few metres away. Blake retrieved it and passed it to him. Vasquez supported the wounded Sentinel while other militia gathered round, accompanied by people pouring out from the churches, and trios of Youngblood warriors. Ramires took the sword and hobbled over to the dying Q'Roth, refusing further assistance from Vasquez. He knelt on its chest, ignoring the blue blood bubbling from its gash of a mouth. Ramires activated the nanoblade, and placed the point on the creature's neck.

"Bring Virginia here."

People around stared at Ramires and then at Blake. He nodded to two militiamen who fetched her body. Blood and sweat stained Ramires cheeks, and tears joined them, a few lodging in his matted moustache, one or two falling onto the Q'Roth's blue-black heaving ribcage. Ramires breathed in laboured rasps. Blake and Vasquez took Virginia's limp frame and held her close to Ramires, guessing what he wanted to do.

Ramires took her dead hand and placed her fingers around the hilt. He looked up, addressing everyone, his voice carrying around the entire plaza. "This is for you,

Virginia. This is your kill," he said, and thrust the blade down, and then with an anguished cry cleaved the warrior's head in two.

The militia, the Youngbloods, and everyone around began stomping their feet in unison. It grew until it echoed off all the churches. Blake and Vasquez took Virginia's body and handed her to several Youngbloods, who lifted her high and took her away.

Blake helped Ramires to his feet, and the stomping died down. The three men leant on each other, and Blake quietly spoke what they were all thinking. "It isn't over."

CHAPTER 19 – CRUCIBLE

Genaspa saw that all were ready. Six team leaders along with their wings of forty-nine Shrell males and females. The teams waited at six equidistant points around the edges of the Quintara system comprising Esperia, its sun, two smaller barren planets and an asteroid belt. She gave the signal, and the run began. Genaspa watched Nasjana's wing as it broke formation, splitting into ten packs. Nasjana led her four husbands on a direct intercept toward Esperia, while four other packs headed laterally in the four directions of the outer-spherical compass. Those packs would circumscribe the Quintara sector, creating an outer shell of poisoned space, preventing any ship from fast entry or escape, and shattering any ship traversing the sector via Transpace. The density of micro-rifts inside the shell would be highest around the inhabited world Esperia, as demanded by Qorall, and requested by Hellera. Despite the environmental harm, Genaspa's wingtips twitched with pride; it was satisfying to watch her teams in action.

The remaining packs coiled inwards from the perimeter in a fanning helix pattern, into the Quintaran sector, crisscrossing its inner space with trip-wire sub-spatial fractures, invisible ruts that would derail anything travelling at light or a decent sub-light speed.

Genaspa knew that Qorall, and Hellera for that matter, both wanted this sector locked down, presumably for different reasons, given that they were blood enemies. By the time the run was over, this area would become a general travel hazard, to be avoided at all costs, lighthouse- marked for Level Six and above.

In the longer term, a thousand years or so, the damage would affect the sun itself, which would slip into red dwarf state without going nova, and its three planets would lose orbital cohesion because of the ensuing gravity shifts. By a slow process of attrition due to the subspace rifts, the planets would disintegrate, until all that would be left would be asteroids and dust. The sub-space damage would remain an open wound.

An unpleasant frisson traced down her wing edges. As soon as this was over, she would demand the release of the Shrell captives held by Qorall in the Syntaran sector.

Extending her sense ridges Genaspa felt Nasjana's efforts as she drove her husbands onwards. The males tried to resist, as they had been trained, the push-pull tension of acceleration against the brakes causing subspace around them to vibrate. Nasjana's team made the first incision like a sharp hook in the curtain of space. The resultant ripping etched barbed scars in the subspace fabric behind them as they spiralled towards Esperia.

Genaspa watched the trail, knowing that mixed in with it was the males' life essence. The run would bleed them of energy. They would end as husks, before dissipating, dissolving into the sea of sub-space.

From a strategic point of view Genaspa knew she should stay at the outer edge to supervise, waiting for the run to be completed and for her females to return before the voyage home. Shrell rarely concerned themselves with the trials and tribulations of other species, preferring to live in isolation except when called upon by the Tla Beth or Rangers for their services. But this time felt different. The sacrifice would be significant today, and she wanted to know what was so important on Esperia that it should be entombed and doomed to eventual annihilation. She signalled to her team-leaders that she was joining the fray.

* * *

"Fire," Xenic commanded.

Kilaney, in his former capacity as commander of a Q'Roth battle cruiser, had been on the receiving end of Mannekhi whip-arcs often enough. But he had never seen them from their point of origin aboard a Mannekhi Spiker. Purple fire boiled into a plume at the end of three spikes then whiplashed towards the Crucible ten kilometres away. He flinched as the pulse beams pounded the enemy ship, knowing the savage punch it would deliver as well as the high-energy radiation, knocking the occupants off their legs then incinerating them wherever the beams could penetrate the hull.

Curling residual blue energy arcs fizzed down the Crucible's long fuselage, but they had not yet inflicted serious damage. He itched to destroy the ship, but Crucibles were very tough by design. Their shielding was far heavier than any normal warship. It had to be to withstand the tremendous energy forces executed by their crust-dissolving tendrils, as well as the frequent hailstorm of rocks and magma spewed out into space by any planet on which a Crucible operated. Kilaney racked his brains for a way to get past its defences.

He caught the eye of the female Mannekhi Fentra, who was manning weapons, and pointed. "Aim for the fifth juncture back from the main front housing."

She stared at him.

"Do it," Xenic instructed.

Kilaney wondered why the Crucible didn't return fire. They had standard weapons, though usually an escort destroyer as well. Then it hit him. "They're going to jump," he said.

"Keep firing," Xenic instructed. "Track them, Siltern."

Sure enough, just as the purple beams lashed out again, theCrucible vanished.

"Siltern?"

But Kilaney had already guessed where it was headed.

"They are closing on the planet, Sir, near the larger of Esperia's two moons."

Kilaney was impressed – in-system jumps were very tricky, and this one had been spectacularly precise. "There are more than Q'Roth aboard that vessel," he said, glancing to Xenic.

The tall, black-haired, red-suited commander nodded. "Bring us about. Prepare to –"

"Sir, wait," Fentra shouted, "there's something..."

Kilaney looked over to her, saw her eyes go wide, just before she leapt in front of him. He had no time to brace himself. Suddenly he was flung forward, and flew with alarming speed toward the viewscreen a few metres away. Fentra arrived first. He pummelled into her, unable to do anything except knock the wind out of her, his temple striking a glancing blow on hers. There were thuds as more crewmembers hit the wall. He gathered his breath, and pushed himself into a standing position, trying to help Fentra recover. Others around him groaned, though no one looked seriously hurt. All of them rubbed their left temples where his head had connected with Fentra's.

He supported her in his arms, but as she recovered she shoved him away, glaring. "Get off me, Jorann. As soon as that bloodworm inside you is dead –"

"Enough, Fentra," Xenic said from somewhere behind them. "Stations everyone. Siltern, what just happened?"

Siltern regained his post and pored over his console. "We hit a tripwire of some sort... oh no!"

Xenic waited.

Siltern called over to Fentra, who had regained her post. "Check the Nara-wavelength."

Xenic pursed his lips, then walked over to Fentra's station and stared over her shoulder. "Shrell," he said, and all the crew turned as one to him.

Kilaney spoke up. "That's impossible. Why would they –"

Xenic addressed him. "It does not matter. We Mannekhi have prior experience with the Shrell. After the Yenshra'ta rebellion the Tla Beth ordered Shrell to poison two sectors of our space." Xenic hung his head for a moment. "It is a terrible punishment to endure, a lesson that worsens through successive generations."

The way Fentra looked up at her commander at that point told Kilaney that Xenic's ancestors had personal experience, and Xenic himself had been scarred by it. It also told him that Fentra and Xenic were perhaps more than colleagues. But the captain collected himself and returned to his command chair.

"Siltern, is it a full run?"

Siltern tapped his console and a holomap of the sector appeared. Kilaney saw gossamer threads slowly coiling inwards from an outer ball of spider-web lines. It was as beautiful as it was deadly. He knew they'd been lucky: the Mannekhi vessel had been moving slowly when they had struck one of the space-furrows. The Crucible had been luckier still, having jumped just in time.

Xenic asked what Kilaney was thinking. "Is there a safe window through?"

Siltern nodded. "Micro-jumps, but we have to be quick. I can get us close but we'll be delayed."

Fentra broke in. "We'll never get out. We should leave while we still can. We don't owe this system anything. I'd rather die fighting for our own people."

Xenic walked to Siltern's station and placed a hand on his shoulder. "Plot it," he said. He turned to face the rest of his crew, as he pointed to one of the screens showing Esperia. "Helgothora, the Eleventh Tribe."

Fentra laughed, a few others joining her. "You can't be serious? That's just a legend we tell our children after the Slapping."

Kilaney had no idea what they were referring to. "The Slapping?"

"Tell him," Xenic said. "He needs to understand."

Fentra folded her arms, the humour in her voice transmuting to cold metal, her smile replaced by a somber look, even by Mannekhi standards. "We Mannekhi are born into servitude. When any child reaches the age of four, when we consider them independent decision-makers, they go with their parents to the Municipal Hall where others gather in front of one of our sponsor races' Ambassadors. The Ambassador asks the child to do something..." She looked sideways, presumably remembering what it had been for her.

Kilaney felt sorry for Fentra already.

"For example," she continued, taking a breath, "to run through my brother's hand with a knife." She straightened up. "The child refuses, of course. Then the parents – first the father, then the mother – slap the child across the face, hard. Most children do not cry, Kilaney, Jorann, whoever you are. It is their parents who weep later. Some people never –" her voice cracked, she cleared her throat "– have children, just to avoid this scarring that keeps us forever in our place."

Kilaney could imagine how it would be one of a number of acts to break the spirit. He began to count up all the Mannekhi ships he had destroyed in the past ten years, estimating how many Mannekhi had been killed under his command.

She continued. "Six thousand years ago, the Eleventh Mannekhi tribe, called Helgothora, escaped. They were tracked down by the Q'Roth and annihilated, but a story lingers that one man, Corakadahn, a geneticist, managed to send a Seeder to a neo-fertile barbarian planet inhabited by bipeds. Every child and every parent knows this story, a dream of a Mannekhi strand that escaped and grew up free." Her eyes burned into his.

Xenic stared at Fentra, then Kilaney. "Look at him."

They did. Fentra folded her arms.

Xenic added spark to the tinder. "The humans built pyramids nearly five thousand years ago."

Now the crew stared harder, their all-black eyes less harsh and more inquisitive. Fentra continued playing devil's advocate while Siltern worked fast on the console behind the Captain. "Did the Ossyrians come?"

Xenic nodded. "Five thousand years ago. I have checked the Grid database records. The humans have the ankh."

She unfolded her arms, her voice quieter. "Most races have the ankh."

"They have ours, the cruciform one, blue steel."

Siltern drew back. "We are ready, but we must go quickly."

Xenic looked around at his crew. "I want you all behind me on this one. If anyone disagrees we turn around and leave."

Kilaney decided he had best stay quiet. But one by one they nodded assent, until the vote came to Fentra.

Fentra gave Kilaney a hard stare. "If the others are the tribe, we can save them... cherish them. But this one... You, Kilaney – Jorann – you must die for your crimes."

Kilaney nodded, not breaking her gaze. "I've paid that price before."

Xenic turned to Siltern. "Execute."

* * *

"Damage negligible, Your Eminence, hull plating around the engines is intact, planet-cutter functional integrity one hundred per cent. It will take some time for the Mannekhi vessel to find us again."

Sister Esma made no acknowledgement. The Mannekhi vessel was no match for a Crucible. While she would have relished dissecting their Spiker, time was of the essence. However, their presence signified both a threat and an opportunity. She clicked a message in Largyl 6 to the red-cloaked Q'Roth Commander at his console.

His blue-black head swivelled toward her, all six vermillion slits waxing, but he made no reply. Nevertheless, she saw on her console that he had transmitted the message to the Krishtach Q'Roth destroyer on standby two sectors away, to approach in case of need for assistance or extraction. Hubris was a human affliction; Sister Esma knew how to hedge her bets.

She then turned her attention to the secondary screen in front of her, scratches like cobweb strands hanging in empty space. "Shrell, you say?" The Q'Roth commander confirmed it. It was going to be hard getting out. She turned to one of her lieutenants behind her. "Is Serena aboard yet?"

"Both Raptors have just docked, Your Eminence."

It was tempting to turn and go right then, and leave Esperia to its own fate amidst increasingly poisoned space. Certainly no races would be coming to help them now, and Qorall and his worms would eventually arrive and finish the job.

But Sister Esma didn't believe in leaving loose ends, and hadn't gotten this far without attention to detail. Besides, she'd been waiting eighteen years to crush Micah and humanity's remnants. "Can we reach the planet to activate the cutters?"

The lieutenant stared deep into his console before replying. "We risk being trapped there if we approach closer, Your Eminence, Shrell activity appears highest around Esperia."

Sister Esma's fingers curled, her sharp fingernails pressing into the softer flesh of her palms. They were behind the moon on the night side of Esperia, with Esperantia on the dayside. She could not target the city with an energy beam. Her dark red lips whitened, tightening to a thin scratch.

A door swished open behind her, and Serena waltzed onto the Bridge, beaming more than usual. "We have sixty humans. They are being processed now, and will soon go back into stasis for the trip home."

"I asked for one hundred, Serena. And you have lost five Raptors, not forgetting a Q'Roth Legate."

Serena's smile didn't falter. "They *are* resilient. I took notes of the Genners' abilities, not to mention the last Sentinel alive." Serena glanced at the screens in front of Esma. "The moon," she said.

"Excuse me?" Sister Esma parked the reference to a Sentinel for later. As for the moon, she guessed what Serena was referring to, and should have already seen it herself.

Serena continued. "I was listening to comms while coming here. Break up the moon – it's a much quicker job, and it will rain asteroid- sized rocks down on Esperia for weeks. Even if one doesn't strike their excuse for a town, the impact craters and dust clouds will plunge the planet into winter darkness for decades. They will perish, especially since no help will arrive."

Sister Esma gazed up to the Q'Roth Commander, his trapezoidal head bearing down on her. "Do we have time to do this and find a conduit out of here?"

"Esss," the Q'Roth Commander hissed, raising a claw from under his cloak. A hooked digit slid into a recess on an inert panel in front of him. Mustard lights and lettering lit up all over the panel, accompanied by a grinding noise.

"Come," she said, gesturing to Serena to join her at the front so as to have a prime view.

Together they watched the eight tendrils rapidly uncoil from the long fuselage, reminding her of an octopus getting ready to devour its prey. All the filaments unfurled and spirited outwards as they commenced their deadly embrace around the moon. After several minutes the Q'Roth Commander's inserted claw flicked sideways. The threads coated in super-charged plasma flashed yellow, then orange, red, violet, and finally black and blue, the Q'Roth signature colour. *A nice touch.* The grinding noise on the bridge segued into a deep hum, throbbing in time with the energy spikes.

The gaps between pulses decreased, like a heartbeat speeding up, and the tendrils glowed across space to the moon. Sister Esma approached the screen, content that Serena knew not to follow without a further invitation. The hum's heartbeat sped up further.

The flashing cords that had latched onto the moon's mountainous surface began carving out ridges, cheese-wiring their way down towards the crust. One of Sister Esma's staff brought up a smaller screen showing a close-up of one of the tendrils in action. It had already cleaved a mountain in two, and now burrowed deep beneath the surface, its fierce blue glow still detectable beneath the smoking lava-red fissure left in its wake. Rocks and slag billowed out, plumes of steam from deep perma-frosted water flashing into the vacuum of space. Abruptly the entire left side of the terrain shifted angle, caving in, signifying that the tendril had cut through the outer crust. The split mountain shuddered and cracked, slow motion avalanches of massive boulders tumbling down its sides. The rift snaked towards the horizon like an open wound. The image zoomed out, revealing other angry scars spreading across the moon's surface. It was breaking up.

An alarm intruded, and Sister Esma returned to her command chair. "Report."

"It's the Mannehki vessel," Serena said. "They've found us."

Sister Esma never hesitated, particularly in battle. She addressed the Q'Roth Commander first. "Separate the ship, so the cutter can finish its job. Set it to auto-destruct in fifteen minutes."

She addressed Serena. "Take the tactical station. Bring us about, all weapons ready."

Serena leapt up the step to the central console, the lieutenant there hurrying out of her way. Sister Esma heard but ignored Serena's whispered remark, "About time."

Sister Esma noted the Q'Roth Marauder was now in-sector, and wondered when Louise was going to bother to contact her, and whose side she would be on, aside from her own. But Sister Esma would wait. Patience wasn't a virtue, it was a strategy, one that had never failed her.

CHAPTER 20 – MUTINY

The only weapon Kat could find was a knife. She didn't know if it would be enough. Eighteen years ago, after Louise had sent one of the four refugee ships from Earth into the heart of a star, taking two thousand souls with it, Micah and the others had developed a plan to kill her if she ever attacked again. She did, and they succeeded. But Louise had arranged a back-up clone that had sprung to life almost immediately, more enraged with humanity than ever, making Louise a permanent threat. All Kat knew about the process was that there could be only one clone, as otherwise the memory back-up process became unstable. Aramisk had figured out where the clone lay hidden, inactive. All Kat had to do was kill it so that it could never activate automatically in the event of Louise's death. No big deal, she told herself, as she perspired, scurrying through the lower corridors of the fourth deck, the sheathed knife tight in her white-knuckled hand. Kat would have complained about the complete ineptitude of the plan if it hadn't been her own.

Arriving at the door, she found the keypad and recalled the Q'Roth six-character code the Hohash had embedded in her memory. Half- wondering whether it would work, and no small part of her hoping it wouldn't, she waited after entering it. Nothing happened. About to try again, she stopped herself. Level Five and Six didn't make mistakes such as simple slips of the finger or claw, and if she entered the code a second time it might trigger an alarm or worse. After a few more seconds the door slid open, and Kat stepped inside. The door swished closed behind her.

Inside the square chamber the smell of astringent disinfectant washed over her, blue light seeping out from an open sarcophagus raised on a plinth. Kat spied a pulse pistol on a rack near the door. It made sense – if Louise was killed, the clone would auto-activate and might well need a weapon. Kat stuck the sheathed knife in the back of her waistband and picked up the gun, checking its charge. She almost

201

tiptoed over to the large bath-like basin, filled with what she guessed was Q'Roth blue amniotic fluid. Underneath the surface was a human outline, but she would have to reach in to pull out the clone's head in order to kill it. *What made me think this would be easy?* At least there were no ripples, not even bubbles on the liquid's surface. Reluctantly, she rolled up her left sleeve, took a breath and slid her fingers, hand, and then her entire arm into the body-temperature fluid. It was deeper than she'd hoped.

When the liquid was almost up to her shoulder, she touched soft flesh. Her fingers skirted around, finding a nose and closed lips. Kat needed to reach deeper to get her hand around the back of the clone's neck to pull her out, but she'd have to put the pistol down and hold onto the edge with her right hand, and she was on her toes already. Kat cursed, but there was nothing else for it, so she laid the pistol where she could grab it in a hurry, gripped the side of the bath, took a breath and leant a little deeper, the side of her chin dipping into the syrupy fluid, praying that the clone was inert.

Her left hand slid behind the clone's neck and, using her right hand as anchor, she began to tug the clone to the surface. As Kat hauled herself back, so that her feet reached the floor again, she grunted with the effort to raise the clone's head completely out, against the sucking effect of the gelatinous liquid. Her right hand groped for the pistol.

Just as the clone's face broke surface, its eyes opened, followed by its lips. Kat grabbed the gun but Louise's arm whipped out, catching Kat's at mid forearm, killing her grip. The pistol rattled to the floor.

"Hello Kat," the clone gurgled, blue liquid oozing out amongst the words. "How long can you hold your breath?"

The clone's hands snapped around Kat's neck and dragged her down into the sarcophagus. Kat's entire body tumbled in. Her eyes and nostrils burned, and she thrashed about, trying to break the clone's grip. She suddenly remembered the knife, and reached back with her right hand. At the same time, the clone's arms straightened, its hands squeezing tight, strangling Kat. The pressure on her carotid arteries triggered dark patches in her already-blurred vision, almost making her drop the knife. But the straight-arm stranglehold gave her the room to manoeuvre. With a bubbling grunt, Kat swung the knife straight up into the underside of the clone's jaw, driving its long blade up through the clone's throat and into its lower brain.

The hands around Kat's neck stiffened, spasming, then went slack. Kat didn't bolt for the surface. Instead, bracing herself against the clone's forehead, she withdrew the knife and then slit the clone's throat from ear to ear, just to make sure.

Kat breached surface, gasping and coughing, then clambered out, slopping out of the ooze, and sat shaking on the floor, her back against the sarcophagus, in a large blue puddle. She tossed the knife, sending it skittering across the floor. "Longer than you think, bitch," she said, then spat out some more of the fluid.

* * *

Louise was losing patience. "Why can't we go faster?"

Aramisk said nothing, busying herself with the navigation console, feverishly swiping strands of black hair out of her vision. Tarish spoke, fingering his white goatee as he stared at the viewscreen depicting a normal star view, with Esperia's small rusty disk dead centre. "There are Shrell here." His voice sounded reverent. "They are poisoning space in this sector. If we move any faster than Aramisk can navigate with our scanners, our ship will be sliced in two."

Louise didn't know how Aramisk was tracking the Shrell, particularly as her own screens showed nothing; rumour was that these insular, Level Nine ray-like creatures lived in subspace and Transpace rather than normal space-time. In her years travelling the Grid she'd had plenty of time to catch up on its history; fully a tenth of Mannekhi territory had been devastated by Tla Beth-sanctioned poisonings, retribution for rebellions. She had little doubt the Mannekhi had developed ways to fathom the creatures' pathways.

Louise activated a Level Six tracer in the ship's data-core to see how Aramisk was tracking the Shrell, then addressed Tarish. The black Gel- suits they wore, prepped for battle in case of hull breaches, made Tarish look younger than his two hundred years.

"Can we fire on the planet from this distance, through these fractures you insist are there and my scanners cannot see?"

Tarish's voice remained calm. "That would not be prudent. We can only detect the wake of a Shrell, some minutes after they have passed. There would be a risk of detonation due to collision with a fracture, perhaps close to our ship. I do not need to remind you –"

"No, you do not. Any change in the other three ships' status?"

Aramisk answered from behind her console, voice taut. "The Mannekhi Spiker just came in range of the Crucible, which is decimating the moon. The Ossyrian vessel is nearby, but adrift and heavily damaged. The two Raptors returning from Esperia have berthed inside the Crucible." She chewed on a knuckle, her face lit up green by the Marauder's tactical displays. "I could finish off the Pyramid with an interceptor, if you wish."

Louise studied the diminutive Aramisk, her thick black hair shrouding her features, making her look as if she was hiding from the world. She was the most talented but also the most unpredictable of the crew, and had been spending too much time with Kat for Louise's liking. Aramisk clearly had no love for the Ossyrians, but that could be a feint; maybe she was looking for a way to help her Mannekhi colleagues in the Spiker ship move against the Crucible. In any event, Louise cared little for Ossyrians; they were of no consequence, and their ship would not survive long. *Avoid secondary entanglements*, Sister Esma had once counselled.

Louise strode toward the bridge exit. "Leave them. Their ship is no threat. Call me when we have a clear shot of the planet. Until then, no contact with any of the three ships. We destroy Esperia, then we leave, understood?"

Tarish and two of the others bowed. "As you order." Louise hovered in the doorway, waiting. "Understood," Aramisk added.

It sounded genuine to Louise, for a Mannekhi at any rate. She quit the bridge.

As soon as Louise left the bridge and was alone, her mood brightened. It made her realise how sick she was of her Mannekhi crew; she could never fully trust them. They were from a culture born into Patronage, taught from early childhood how to hide their true feelings. The only interesting companion had been Kat. Even if Kat wanted to kill her, at least she was honest about it. As she walked through the ship Louise realized she was sick of it, too, having spent seven years aboard this particular vessel, after the previous one was destroyed in an ambush by the Q'Roth Ninth fleet. Qorall's forces had saved her life that time, rescued her from capture. Even if it had been to gain information on the former whereabouts of Kalaran, the fact was that he'd saved her.

Louise paused mid-corridor. For a moment she thought she heard something, maybe Kat, who'd been recuperating from her coma; but then it went quiet. She continued walking her thoughts. Trading the past seven years of her life against Qorall's self-serving act of saving her – it was no longer enough. The trouble was, there was no glory in Qorall's war: those conquered were afraid, broken and subdued, and most of those not yet conquered were simply afraid. She had been a maverick for too long. She wanted a cause again, like she'd had as a Chorazin agent with Vince, and as an Alician with Sister Esma. Now, there was a cause; screw looking for Hellera. Her step lightened. She should get Qorall working for *them*, helping the Alicians. Now, *that* would be motivating. For the first time in weeks she felt clear, energized. Now would be a good time to update the clone's memory core, just in case.

Arriving at the lower deck area, she saw the dried blue footprints on the floor, and sprinted to the chamber, found the room and entered. She touched a panel area and the body began to rise to the surface, and stared at what had to be Kat's handiwork.

Louise lifted the listless, blonde- haired head toward her, its lifeless innocent eyes open wide, a gash across its throat. Louise studied the face awhile, remembering who she used to be, a lifetime ago. Each time she'd tried to find her way back there... no matter. She let the head back down gently. There was no time to grow another one.

Kat. Probably aided by Aramisk or even Tarish. She kicked the sarcophagus. Why did everyone betray her? Leaving the door open, she headed to the unoccupied secondary battle bridge. En route, she lifted her wristcom to her lips. "Where is Kat?"

"Unknown," came the synthetic Q'Roth computer reply, "Sensors are not functioning normally."

"Internal or external problem?" If the former, she would choke the life out of Aramisk personally.

"Unknown."

Louise gritted her teeth and broke into a run.

* * *

Kat arrived at the bridge, bedraggled, her forehead and armpits perspiring, her hair still damp and sticky and no doubt coloured blue. She'd nearly bumped into Louise en route, and had then taken a tertiary pathway to get to the bridge. Once Louise had passed, Kat had sprinted all the way. She hated running: it sped up her pulse for all the wrong reasons – *fight or flight*, she knew Pierre would have said. For her it always seemed to be both. But she didn't feel well. Dizziness threatened, and her neck hurt.

Kat raised and steadied her pistol arm. The four Mannekhi turned one by one to stare at her. All of them looked her up and down.

"Where's Louise?" Kat croaked, addressing Aramisk.

Aramisk walked toward Kat but a raised hand from Tarish stopped her. He placed himself in the firing line, taking command.

"She left five minutes ago," he said, arms folded.

"You're injured," Aramisk said, peering at her from behind Tarish's gaunt frame.

Kat leant hard against the wall, catching her breath. *Don't pass out now!* She waved the pistol at Tarish. "Seal the Bridge, the Battle Bridge, too."

Tarish nodded to one of the other Mannekhi to execute the request. "Such measures will not keep Louise out for long."

Kat shrugged. Her attention fell on the viewscreen split in four sections, showing Esperia and several ships she didn't recognise, except for the disabled Ossyrian pyramid drifting in space. She kept the gun levelled on Tarish. "Looks like I need an update." Her head began to throb hard, almost making her eyes water. She stumbled, her legs almost buckling, but regained her balance.

Aramisk sighed, snatched a small case from the wall, brushed past Tarish and ignored the barrel shifting in her direction. "What you need is medical attention, right now, before your carotid fails and you stroke or die or both." She knelt down at Kat's feet and opened the case, fishing around until she found what she was searching for. "This may hurt," she said.

Kat laughed. "What, more than it does already? Don't see how that's –"

Aramisk sprang to her feet and plunged a syringe into Kat's neck. Kat shook violently, a feeling of ice flooding into her neck and head, freezing the back of her eye-balls. She gasped, placing her left hand on her right wrist to steady the pistol, eyes misting with pain. Tarish didn't move. Kat's strength ebbed as the coldness flushed down her arms, and then her legs gave way. Aramisk caught her, lowered her to the floor in a sitting position, and held her there. Tarish had already snatched the pistol, moving faster than his age would suggest likely.

"Wait," Aramisk said to Tarish. "I've been in communication with the Spiker Captain. It's Commander Xenic. He just sent me a file."

Tarish loomed over her. "That was not your place."

She shrugged. "Check your console. You won't believe it, but you'll want to."

Louise's voice cut through the Bridge. "Open the door down here. Now!"

Tarish pocketed the pistol, and moved to the access control panel. Aramisk placed both palms over her heart. "Check your console, Tarish! *Please*. Kat is of the Helgothora. I've verified the Captain's analysis. It's *Xenic*, for the Ancestors' sake. My father fought alongside him in the Cretachian Campaign. We can trust him!"

Tarish's brow furrowed, then he regained his composure, moved to his console, and spoke in measured tones to Louise as he scanned the file. "Commander, Kat is here, she tried to take the bridge, but we overcame her." His all-black eyes suddenly widened and he turned from the console to stare at Kat, then Aramisk. His voice betrayed nothing of the revelation. "However, she temporarily locked us out of certain command functions. Aramisk is working on it as we speak."

Louise's tone sharpened. "You have five minutes, after which I will decide you are liars and mutineers, and I will kill you all, do you understand? I have already segregated the ship and still have control over the Nova bombs, and a way off this vessel."

"It will be done." Tarish cut comms. He spoke as if to himself. "She will not wait five minutes."

Kat shivered. With a grunt, she tried to get up, and slipped. Aramisk caught her again and helped her upright. Kat felt her pulse slowing, steadying; her right carotid ached, and the puffy swelling around it was tender to her fingertips. "What was in the file? What just happened?"

Tarish looked over his Mannekhi crew, then back to Kat. He took her hand, held it as if it was priceless, and smiled. "For all the good it might do, Katrina of Earth and Helgothora, daughter of the Eleventh Tribe, we just changed sides."

* * *

Louise had been considering her next move – after Esperia's destruction – for some time. Qorall had her running errands, and it wasn't her style. After so many years on the move she wanted a 'centre', a home of sorts. No matter which way she played it over in her mind, it always came back to the Alicians. She believed in their cause, and she was still Alician.

She reached a secondary communications room and activated short- range comms, directing an encrypted beam at the Crucible. "Sister Esma," she began, "I know it's you. This is Louise."

The lack of reply was expected, so Louise raised the stakes. "I have seven Sclarese Level Nine Nova bombs onboard, and I only need one to finish off Esperia. If you do not respond I will target your vessel."

Louise tried not to react when she saw the golden skull cap framing Sister Esma's angular face, her high cheekbones guarding a hooked nose. Her former mentor had aged. But that wasn't all of it; she was diminished somehow, the years had taken their toll on her. In the background of the holo she heard the dull sound of explosions. Sister Esma's large black eyes darted over unseen displays. "Louise, this was expected, but I am a little busy right now. What is it you want?"

Louise found the words didn't come so easily. But she was running out of time. She recalled she'd never seen the new Alician homeworld. "I've heard Savange is beautiful at this time of year."

Sister Esma's head swung towards her former protégé, raven-like eyes probing. "Are you serious? After all this time you want to come back into the fold?"

Louise nodded, becoming more convinced of it with every second that passed. But she had other reasons, too, which she had discussed with nobody, ideas concerning Qorall.

"Your crew?" Sister Esma asked.

"Not invited. Clean slate."

Sister Esma's thick lips curled into something approaching a smile. "Fire the weapons at Esperia, then join me as fast as you can. Once we have destroyed the Spiker, we depart."

Louise nodded again.

"One more thing, Louise." Sister Esma's eyes appeared to soften. "It *is* good to see you."

Louise stared at the blank screen, wondering how it could all have been so different if she'd have stayed with the Alicians from the start, what she and Sister Esma could have accomplished together. There was still time. She raced down to the space deck, issuing a Commander-priority override to the Marauder's control-mind on the way. By the time she arrived at the hangar where five Raptors lay, six of the seven Nova bombs had been loaded onto one of them; the seventh would detonate with the Marauder when it self-destructed.

She didn't need to check the time to know that five minutes had already elapsed. The fact that Tarish and the others had not communicated with her was as clear as an outright admission. As she boarded the craft, her one regret was that she would have to leave Kat behind; she'd grown to like her. But betrayal was betrayal, and according to Q'Roth and Alician tradition, there was only one punishment fitting for treachery.

The Raptor powered up as she checked that the Shrell decryption algorithm had been downloaded from Aramisk's console. The map of Shrell wires, as she thought of them, might not be fully accurate, but it should be good enough to get within firing range of Esperia and then reach the Crucible.

Once outside she sent the auto-destruct codes back to the Marauder. The ship's self-destruct was intended to stop it falling into enemy hands, and would cripple the ship. But the Nova bomb left onboard would vaporise the Marauder and anything else in range.

Clean slate.

Heading towards Esperia, Louise dodged the Shrell-wires using manual control rather than autopilot. While doing so, she weighed the choice she had just made, the implicit contract with Sister Esma, who had originally saved her and then condemned her to death. Yet there was mutual respect. Besides, after such a long time, Louise wondered what it might be like to be amongst her kind again, even if she had too much Q'Roth DNA in her ever to be considered a 'normal' Alician. But she hoped to turn the Alicians to Qorall's side – the winning side – when the time was right.

The Raptor's onboard computer mind signalled that she was within firing range, and plotted six independent trajectories to see the bombs through. Probability of at least one getting through – and she only needed one to strike the planet – was 99.786%. Probability of two bombs getting through was 91%. *More than adequate.* She decided to keep one on board, as an insurance policy.

Micah, I was hoping for this to be a little more personal, but never mind. She touched a panel and then counted the five rapid zips as her cargo left for Esperia. Then she swung the Raptor hard about and aimed toward the Crucible. Space lit up behind her as two of the Nova bombs snagged Shrell-wires, the shock waves catapulting her Raptor forwards. Louise executed a series of manoeuvres requiring all her enhanced Level Six reflexes to avoid being sliced by the wires, and then the ship came back under control. Another ignition buffeted her craft, and then quiet. The remaining two intelligent missiles would learn from their fallen comrades, and would proceed slower, but reach their target.

Louise thought about her ex-lover Vince, how often they'd had close calls like that one. But Micah and the others had stolen Vince from her. She smiled, embellishing one of Blake's favoured aphorisms: *You reap what you sow, humanity.* Accelerating, Louise slalomed through the wire mesh towards the Crucible, wondering what Savange would look like at this time of year.

* * *

Aramisk bowed her head over her console, her voice resigned. "Louise has activated the Marauder's self-destruct sequence."

Kat moved next to her. "Can you disable it?"

She shook her head. "Louise convinced the ship's mind that her crew has mutinied." She cast Kat a look. "Five minutes, just long enough for her to get clear. And she wasn't joking about segregating the ship, there's no way to reach the Raptors. We wouldn't have time anyway."

Kat thought hard, wishing Pierre were there: he would think of something. But she hadn't gotten this close to Esperia – to Antonia and Petra – to be blown to smithereens when practically in orbit. She slapped the side of the console. "We need to think outside the cube," she said, as much to herself as to the others. *And fast!*

"Curious expression," Tarish said.

Dammit! These Mannekhi – so detached... But something snagged her mind. *Outside.* "How far do we have to be to avoid the blast?"

Aramisk frowned at Kat from beneath her dark fringe. "With a Nova bomb added into the mix? About twenty kilometres. Wait, you're not thinking...?"

But Kat had already moved to the rack of helmets and began tossing them to the four Mannekhi, picking up a Gel-suit for herself. "Select two Raptors, instruct them to depart and pick us up outside."

Tarish caught the helmet, and stared at it. "Your plan won't work."

The others, including Aramisk, looked towards him, but no sooner had a klaxon begun its Q'Roth countdown than Aramisk spoke. "We have to try."

Kat stepped into the self-applying space suit, feeling the cool, wet, chamois-like material race up over her one-piece and exposed flesh. She held her breath momentarily as it slowed then stopped just beneath her chin, then slipped the hood-like helmet on, feeling it connect seamlessly to the gel material. Air breathed into the suit and helmet, its black exterior toughening while remaining smooth and flexible on the inside.

Tarish placed his helmet on Louise's chair and walked calmly to Aramisk's station. "One of us must stay. You are relieved."

Aramisk met his eyes, then took his hand and bent her forehead to touch his upturned palm. "Walk with the Ancestors," she said.

Kat decided not to intervene. She squeezed his arm as she walked past him.

"Go, all of you," he said. "I will direct the Raptors, and will signal Xenic. I will also try to warn anyone else out there as to what Louise is about to do."

Kat considered that she was just buying time, getting a better view of Esperia being obliterated. Nevertheless, she and the others hurried to the airlock behind the bridge. As the inner hatch sealed she watched the tall frame of Tarish at the console, and for the first time decided she could maybe get to like the people she'd been stuck with the past nine months.

Aramisk activated the depressurisation sequence, then sighed. "Problem," she said, her voice transmitting clearly into Kat's helmet.

"What?" asked Kat, aware how fraught her voice sounded.

"The depressurisation sequence will take thirty seconds, but the ship will detonate in one minute. We'll still be in the blast zone."

Kat studied the airlock control scripts. Louise had taught her how to use them a year ago in one of her rare, kinder moments. "Tarish, emergency decompress in five seconds. The Raptors will have to work fast and deploy gravitic scoops." Kat looked at her three helmeted companions. "Take a breath."

It was like a fairground ride in the dead of night, a rollercoaster that at the height of its pitches and rolls flew off its rails. Kat spun wildly, saw the Marauder tumbling silently around her, glimpsed one of her Mannekhi colleagues head-strike an antenna and career off in another direction, a white puff of gas from his or her helmet billowing around the head, arms and legs flailing uselessly. The sound of her raspish breathing accentuated the whirling vista, and she tried to count down. The suit's thrusters engaged, and stabilised her, the ship rolling into view, already a kilometre away, fish-shaped and muscled with gun ports. A grey dot loomed in front of her – one of the Raptors – and the gravity net scooped her up, hauled her into the cargo bay and flung her next to another suited colleague. The aft doors started to close as the Raptor accelerated away, leaving the Marauder behind to shrink to a dull point of light.

Tarish spoke softly from the Marauder via the suit-com. He sounded so close. "Goodbye Katrina, I wish we had known who you really were. I wish I could have known you better. You have no idea what you mean to us. Live."

Through the final chink between the closing bay doors, harsh white light spilled into the bay where Kat and one other survivor lay.

Goodbye, Tarish. Wish I could have known you better, too. I've never trusted father figures, but you... What a waste of the nine months she'd had onboard with them. Kat kicked herself. But maybe she could honour him. She tried to think like a Mannekhi, knew they would simply move on. Antonia, Petra, even Micah; she had to contact them somehow.

A chime told her the bay was pressurized, and she removed her helmet, as did the other survivor.

"I'm glad you made it, Aramisk," Kat said.

From the cockpit they tried for ten minutes to raise the other Raptor, finally detecting a small debris pattern.

Aramisk spoke, her voice monotone. "Where now?"

Kat knew they wouldn't get within a hundred klicks of the Crucible without an approach code, and they would be too far behind Louise to catch her. Besides, her mind brimmed with thoughts of Antonia and Petra.

"Esperia. If it's still in one piece."

Aramisk nodded, and the Raptor veered towards the planet.

Kat bit down on her lower lip, staring at the orange dot dead ahead, willing it to survive, trying not to think of it glowing nova-white, incinerating everyone she cared about.

Not quite everyone. *If you're out there, Pierre, now would be a bloody good time to intervene.*

But as the craft powered toward Esperia, Kat noticed that her companion was frighteningly still, as if she might crack. Mannekhi hid their emotions well, but she knew they weren't made of stone. Kat draped her arm around her rigid shoulders. "Aramisk, tell me about Tarish, and about the Eleventh Tribe. I've never been good with relatives, but it's never too late to learn."

Aramisk turned to face Kat, face blanched behind strands of unruly hair, lips trembling as if struggling to let the words out. Then the façade she'd built up all her life split wide open. Kat held her, and while she rocked Aramisk gently, uttering soothing nonsense, all her own anger, fears and pain breached the surface too.

CHAPTER 21 – TIGHTENING NOOSE

Jen's exhilaration at flying the Kalarash ship had long since evaporated. She'd handed over control to Dimitri, Rashid operating tactical, sweeping aside dark worm debris as Kalaran ploughed through the latest, thickening wave. Just how many were there? Qorall had evidently been breeding them somewhere, or genetically manufacturing them, but that would require bio-farms on an almost unimaginable scale.

She tugged at her hair, let her forehead dip down and bump the console in front of her. "This is taking too long!" The other two didn't hear her, they were both immersed, their minds hooked into the ship's functions. Jen was supposed to be resting, not having slept in two days. Instead she accessed the *Memento*'s long-range scanners, but didn't like what she found.

Jen had asked Kalaran if he could see what was happening back home, and without another word he'd let her look. Four Hohash were in the area: two on Esperia, two on the pyramid ship. These omnipaths relayed information to the *Memento* as it battled to enter the galaxy through the portal blockaded by Qorall's forces. Due to the gravity weapons Kalaran was using, there were temporal effects in the data-stream. Images arrived in pulses, flashes of vision. It reminded her of old-style radar, where every sweep would give an update of what had just happened, and then fade. The gap between the updates was around ten minutes, though back home they were being transmitted every second. She'd asked Kalaran once if he could go back in time. He'd said no, but that it was possible to slow time, or give that appearance. In any case, ten minutes was up.

With a mental flick, the image arose in her head again through the neural interface. She filtered out the deepening lattice of Shrell filaments– a quarter of the males were already dead – and focused on Esperia's predicament. The Hunter vessel was a burial mound of twisted metal, and sixty captives had been taken – she didn't know why. The pyramid was listing badly and looked good for only another fifteen minutes or so. That was where she kept staring, because Gabriel was onboard. Images of him stole her breath away – God, he looked like his father! Micah seemed to be badly injured, but at least the Ossyrians were patching him up.

The Crucible had lacerated the moon, and in about one local hour an avalanche of rock would start its fall towards Esperia, burying it under a hundred metres of meteoric rubble and dust. The Hohash had uncovered who was running the ship via a decoded transmission between the Crucible and the Marauder. Jen wasn't surprised. How could humanity have such awful luck, with Sister Esma hell-bent on its eradication and Louise riding shotgun? The only active deterrent was Kilaney onboard the Mannekhi spiker; she'd never met him, but his reputation preceded him. The info-pulse faded, normal vision flooding back.

Jen stood up and paced, tugging at her hair again. She kicked the side of a console. "Kalaran," she shouted, "let me *do* something! I can't just stand by and watch them all die." There was no answer. He was busy. They all were: Dimitri's shut-eyed expression was deadly serious, his large hands twitching feverishly over the multronic navcon keypad. Rashid's body was perfectly still except for his fingers dancing inside a football-sized holosphere, each tiny movement whipping out hellfire beams from the *Duality* to fend off or slice through enemy flesh. Beads of sweat clung to his temples. Hold it together, Rashid!

Jen turned on her interface again and switched back to short range, seeing an augmented forward view from the *Memento*. There were three more enemy waves inbound, combinations of ships and worms, enemy vessels attacking as soon as they emerged from the ruptured portal. Where the hell were they coming from? Jen didn't want to distract Kalaran, so left him to try and scorch a way through. But the tactic was obvious – Qorall wanted to delay Kalaran's return, to ensure that Esperia fell. Not that he gave a damn about the humans. The spiders; Qorall now knew they were a threat, despite not knowing why or how. Join the club; Kalaran wouldn't tell her either. Jen resorted to her favourite way of killing time, a karate kata where she could flex her muscles and utter a heartfelt 'kiai' at its end.

Ten minutes up, she switched on and stretched the scanner scale out again, in time to witness Louise's Marauder detonate in a shower of white shards, two Raptors surviving, one headed to the Crucible, one to Esperia. She was unsure who had made it off alive. But just before it exploded the last occupant had broadcast a message that Louise had Nova bombs and was going to fire them at Esperia. If any got through, the spiders and all of mankind would vanish, boiling to death on an imploding world. If that happened, she wondered if Kalaran would cease the fighting and turn back around.

"No." Kalaran used an avatar of her father this time – she'd asked him not to use her brother anymore, not with the real Gabriel – his son, anyway – out there fighting for his life.

Jen was relieved to hear it. "But without them you can't win, can you?"

As was more often the case, Kalaran answered a different question. "Hellera is still there. Qorall has found her hiding place."

"Kalaran to the rescue, eh?"

Her father's face turned to her, a flash of displeasure – she hated the way Kalaran could mimic people from her memories so damned well. "Sorry," she said. As if to try to change the subject, not wishing to lose his attention and end up pacing alone again, she asked the question in the back of her mind. "Why did they take the hostages. I mean the Alicians, why did they take sixty people?"

Kalaran's borrowed face smiled, the way her real father used to when he was humouring her. "I'm Level Nineteen, Jen; I always know what you mean."

She shrugged, folded her arms. "I'm not distracting you am I? You know, from more important things?"

Kalaran's smile broadened. "Ninety-nine and a half per cent of me is locked in battle, but the rest of me needed a small break, a diversion."

"I'm flattered," she said, failing to sound sarcastic, because whenever she got his attention, particularly using her dead father's image, she never wanted it to end.

He opened his hand, and moved it as if tossing something into the air. A series of small linked balls appeared. A molecule. She'd studied chemistry, and every night Kalaran had been sleep-teaching all three of them advanced sciences, but she didn't recognise it at first, except that the way it twisted, it could only be a DNA strand.

It rotated in midair while Kalaran spoke in her father's grainy Irish voice. "It is tempting to imagine that one can easily move up a Level." He said no more.

This was how it worked between them, the way he taught her. Intelligence is never about facts, he'd once said to all three of them; it is about the way you think, the questions you frame. Jen knew she had to make the leap to the next point, see the link. "The Q'Roth... they upgraded the Alicians in a matter of centuries..." Her eyes widened. "You mean they got it wrong?"

"They missed something. I had one of the Hohash run a deep bioscan of the Alicians who raided your new world." The atomic-level model shrank into nothingness. "They will die out without this molecule in its natural state. A reproductive imbalance."

Jen snorted in disbelief. "So, if none of us had escaped..." She shook her head. "Life can be a sardonic bitch, eh?"

214

Kalaran grew serious. "That has been an especially hot Level Nineteen discussion topic for eons, Jen. One of our koans, you might say."

Kalaran didn't usually talk more than a few sentences. She capitalised on his mood with one of her long-harboured questions. "So what do the different Levels really represent?"

"Species think that they can advance by learning a trick or altering DNA, but it takes thousands, sometimes tens of thousands of years, and for higher Levels, millions. They think it is like a simple musical scale; you just need to go up a notch."

"It's more like harmonics, isn't it?"

Kalaran stared at her a moment. But he suddenly seemed distracted, as if seeing something elsewhere, and was gone.

"See you around Kal. Nice chatting. I know, you're busy." But he'd given her an idea. The Hohash... Jen walked to one of the glass spheres the three of them used to move around the vast ship. "Take me to the Hohash." There was a pause during which the sphere remained stationary.

Kalaran spoke to her without appearing. "Why do you want to see the Hohash?"

"I have an idea. Best if I don't tell you, though."

The sphere dropped through the floor into a vast, lilac-tinted empty space, making her grab onto a waist-high rail despite the gravity stabiliser, as she free-fell past the smooth, asteroid-sized globes whose function remained a mystery. Dimitri had described them as God's marbles, as usual seeing wonder in everything. The mercury lake was five kilometres below, and she plummeted towards it. This area had been out of bounds for the past year. As it rose up towards her she realised how vast it was, its surface rippling, swirling currents underneath. She held her breath and grabbed the rail again. *Are you going to stop?* It was getting really close – she could see the reflection of the sphere, getting bigger. *Kalaran, please!*

It stopped a foot from the surface; she felt no deceleration, and stumbled out onto the squidgy surface, her heart thumping in her chest. *Thanks, I think.*

Jen had never stood on it before, and didn't know if it was actually mercury or not, but decided it was best not to slip.

The Hohash she had seen only once before – Kalaran was a bit protective about it – was waiting for her. Instead of a golden rim like others she'd seen, this one's rim was a deep red. But it was the mirror itself that was mesmerising. Most Hohash had flat mirror surfaces, and she'd found one in the caves where she'd first encountered Kalaran that had its surface divided up into eight segments, almost like a jigsaw puzzle. But this one had five concentric ovals, making her feel drawn in, as if, like Alice, she could step right through it.

Jen had one thing, and only one thing in common with Kat. Jen had a node, however her success in accessing any Hohash had been pitiful compared to Kat. Kalaran had told her it had nothing to do with her node, rather that she had 'issues', a darkness inside her the Hohash didn't appreciate. She'd sulked for a few days after that little gem, not missing the irony. But she needed to try something. Closing her eyes a moment, she reached out, trying to open her mind to it. With a shock she was 'in' – this had usually taken ten minutes, or much longer, and occasionally forever.

Opening her eyes, she placed the 'call' as she thought of it, letting the Hohash know whom she wanted to communicate with – Hellera – knowing it was a ridiculous idea. Why would Hellera even acknowledge, in her eyes, such a lowly being? But with trepidation that had her biting her lip and gripping the Hohash's rim, Jen knew that the link from this Hohash to Hellera's was 'open'. Jen saw nothing, but spoke anyway. She had a pathetic urge to start with "Your Majesty..."

"Hellera, my name – "

"Is Kalaran there?" The voice was synthetic, cold.

"Yes, he..." The connection broke, leaving a stinging sensation in her head. *Great.* Not for the first time Jen wondered what on Earth Kalaran had done to Hellera. Dimitri had offered a few bawdy suggestions, but Jen seriously hoped that by Level Nineteen beings would have risen above such behaviour. Try a different approach, she told herself.

Hellera.

The sting was more intense this time, making Jen's eyes water.

"I can have the Hohash in front of you eviscerate your brain. Be concise and then do not contact me again."

Jen thought quickly, then spoke three words.

Jen escorted the Hohash back to the cockpit control area Kalaran had created for his three human guests. She counted down, then accessed the scanner again. Three of Louise's Nova bombs had detonated as they snagged Shrell filaments. Nothing else had changed appreciably. She flicked to short-range, the view ahead of the *Memento*. A crimson glow mushroomed behind the enemy worms and fleets. Abruptly, ships exploded as a ruby cloud engulfed everything in its path, scattering worms and flinging space vessel debris in all directions. As the cloud faded to pink, and then the blackness of space washed back in, a single ship emerged, its deep red arrowhead facing the *Memento*.

Dimitri and Rashid both disengaged from their immersers, and glanced at Jen.

"The cavalry," she said. "I thought it was about time."

Kalaran's voice entered the room. "You called her. What did you say?"

"I said, 'Kalaran needs you'."

Kalaran didn't do pauses, but Jen was sure there might have been a tiny delay, probably in the nanosecond range.

"How did she arrive so quickly?"

Jen shook her head. "Maybe I should look over your intellect rating system. Your entire template seems to neglect emotional intelligence."

Kalaran laughed. "As you would say, Jen, I get it. She was already on her way."

The three Kalarash ships slipped through the portal amongst fleeing dark worms, entering the Silverback galaxy unobstructed, shoving away the debris of mashed warships. For Jen and the others it had been a year, though eighteen had sped past on Esperia. She'd heard no more from Kalaran, other than an image relayed on a central viewer showing the nebula where Hellera had been hiding until very recently, or rather, what was left of it. Dimitri reckoned it was a white hole. Jen didn't know what that was exactly, except it was blinding white and everything in that sector had shredded and was breaking down at the sub-atomic level. The radiation was off the scale, exotic particles spilling outwards at sub-light and lightspeed. Dimitri had a hard time conceiving its power; undoubtedly one of Qorall's secret weapons, probably not his last. Hellera had gotten out just in time.

The scanner saccades were coming more regularly now they were inside the galaxy, as they slowly segued towards 'normal' time. Jen's expression grew dark, events unfolded rapidly on the pyramid ship. She called for Kalaran. "We need to get there faster, or slow time more, so we arrive before it's too late, preferably both."

There was no answer, so Dimitri filled in the gap. "We cannot do both, my love, you know that."

She whirled around to her lover, her chest heaving. "But I don't want to watch him die, all alone, when we're so damned close!"

Dimitri deflated, offering her his hand.

Hellera's ice-cold voice spoke, sending a shiver down Jen's spine, making Dimitri and Rashid jump. "There is a way. Tell her, Kalaran. Or else I will."

CHAPTER 22 – NOVA STORMERS

Micah staggered like a drunken spider, ricocheting from one side of the corridor to the other. Petra folded her arms tight, as if hugging herself, biting her lower lip.

"Stop clowning around, Uncle."

"Not funny," he managed, smiling through pain-clenched teeth. He knew that when Petra resorted to humour like that, she was really concerned. Chahat-Me, on the other hand, watched dispassionately, along with two other space-suited surgeons who'd just implanted the bio- mimetic spinal shunt. He still couldn't feel his legs; that would require more intensive surgery. For now, Micah just wanted to be on his feet when he faced the inevitable.

One of the two Hohash craft had returned to Esperia carrying three Youngbloods and several wounded Ossyrians. Chahat-Me suggested he go with them, but the look he'd given her needed no translation, and ended any further discussion.

He stumbled again, trying to convince himself he was less wobbly on his feet. This field op was only possible because they had hotwired his resident to the shunt's neuro-cluster. But every time he thought he'd got the hang of it, he veered off in near-collapse, groping for support.

After a further minute of embarrassing himself, smoother muscle control returned. Standing straight, he turned, and walked towards Chahat-Me. Relief flooded through him at simply being able to walk with normal steps, though a deep throbbing pain lurked in his lower back. "Thank you Chahat-Me." He gazed into her quicksilver eyes. "And I'm sorry for... earlier. All of us owe you so much. These past years you've looked after us, I'm not sure we earned that."

Petra joined him, hooked her arm inside his, and leant her head against his shoulder. "It's nice when you're not being a pain in the ass, Uncle."

He squeezed her hand, wishing there was somewhere safe he could send her. But there wasn't; the whole Esperian system had become a battlefield. Blake had once told him this was why loved ones should stay at home, away from the killing zone – otherwise soldiers couldn't concentrate, and could easily be undone. Micah knew Petra was his weak spot.

Chahat-Me touched Micah's right temple, and his vision switched to black. A flood of images poured forth through his resident, making his legs tremble. Petra supported him. He saw ancient Egypt, the construction of the pyramids, Ossyrians walking in palaces, teaching basic medicine before they departed. Then he was shown flashes of humanity's medical development throughout history, from leaches, blood-letting and trepanning the skull to 'let the bad vapours out', to Pasteur and penicillin, the cure of malaria and the defeat of the nano-plague in 2038; human doctors working tirelessly. Micah guessed the Ossyrians respected this aspect of mankind's progress.

Micah witnessed the time Kat saved Chahat-Me's life and prevented a catastrophe, and the scene on Ossyria Prime where Pierre had given the Ossyrian High Council slender hope of reaching Level Nine status. Finally, there was Micah's recent wake-up call for Chahat-Me to be prepared to fight once again, which she now accepted. He understood from the transmission that she saw it as a necessary precarious step to overcome their current predicament, despite its attendant risk of species regression to a more hostile state.

But there was more: he saw secret Ossyrian debates – his resident providing a basic translation – that had recurred throughout millennia, over whether to 'reintegrate' their original aggressive nature with their now more disciplined minds, to reach natural Level advancement. They had been holding back, out of conservatism and fear of Tla Beth retribution. Micah realised he had forced their hand, and now Chahat-Me embraced it.

The freeflow shut off, and Micah blinked open his eyes. Frowning, he said "Some steps forward can't be retraced," thinking again of the human predicament, but then he smiled, and placed a hand on Chahat- Me's shoulder, leaning on her for support. "You've just added a bit of yang to a lot of yin. Better that way."

His back pain eased off, his nannites having finished some local re- engineering, and he straightened. Gabriel was two decks away prepping the Hohash craft. He turned to Petra. "Which Q'Roth ship should we head for?"

Petra studied the console displays. "The Crucible is closest. The Marauder is still far out, though... oh crap!" She raised her wristcom to her mouth. "Gabriel, a Raptor has just left the Marauder, headed for Esperia." She glanced nervously at Micah, then listened again. "I just intercepted a broad spectrum message from someone named Tarish onboard the Marauder. It's set to self-destruct. Louise is aboard a Raptor loaded with Nova bombs, and..."

She turned to Micah, her eyes pleading. "Kat!" she said, gripping his shoulders. "My mother must be on the Marauder, she was with Louise."

Micah weighed the risks: if Louise destroyed Esperia, they were all doomed anyway, and if the Marauder was on self-destruct then going there would only add to the casualty list, even if they could get there in time to help, which was doubtful. He ignored Petra's pleading eyes and put his hand at the back of her neck, pulling her face into his shoulder as he spoke into his wristcom. "Gabriel, go, stop Louise's Raptor any way you can."

Petra's fingers dug into his flesh. He held her tighter. He whispered, trying to soothe her. "Kat's a survivor, Petra."

A klaxon sounded, and Petra pushed off. "Life support's failing. The pyramid is dying."

Chahat-Me confirmed it. "Time to leave. You come with us. Attack Crucible."

Petra drew in a long breath. "You're damned right, godmother. Whoever they are on that ship, we're going to fucking tear them apart." The Ossyrian leader's quicksilver eyes drew back, narrowing, a snake-like yellow tinge backlighting them. Micah was suddenly very glad the Ossyrians were on his side.

* * *

Gabriel stood legs splayed aboard the small saucer-shaped Hohash craft, and activated the gravitic brace that would secure him in place against any radical manoeuvres. Relaxing his vision, he accessed the neural interface developed by Virginia when she was just fourteen years old. He felt a sudden pang, wondering how she fared down on the planet – he didn't believe in intuition, but he also couldn't ignore a deep foreboding chewing away at his insides.

The Hohash on the craft sprang to life. In the few times back on Esperia when he had 'connected' with one during flight training, it had felt impersonal, like using a passive tool. This time there was a rapport, a synergy, and he realised they were a team – and more – he sensed the Hohash had its own ideas.

The saucers were slow but could execute micro-jumps, and Gabriel's mind reached out, piggy-backing the Hohash sensors. At first it was too much information, and he was reminded how sophisticated these ancient, enigmatic artifacts were. Focusing on the region around Esperia, his Hohash-enhanced perception clarified. It wasn't that he *saw* the Crucible, the Spiker, the Marauder and the lone Raptor heading for Esperia, rather he simply *knew* where and what they were, in their relative positions, like knowing where your limbs are in the dark, and what they were capable of.

Louise's Raptor fired five of the infamous Sclarese Nova bombs. Even one of them would make light work of Esperia. He initiated the first jump to halve the distance between him and the missiles. A moment later as he returned to normal space-time, two of the bombs ignited simultaneously, which he felt through the interface-Hohash medium as heat rather than the blinding light he knew they would create, effervescent suns snuffing out within seconds. His ship lurched sideways but the brace held him in place. The Hohash remained stationary and flashed a lattice of silver threads across its mirror-like face. Gabriel had no idea what it represented.

Gabriel's genned mind could truly multi-task, and he calculated and executed the next jump while simultaneously trying to understand what the Hohash was showing him. He didn't get it until it showed a picture of the creatures laying the gossamer trails. Executing the jump, he perceived three remaining missiles snaking their way to Esperia. At least they had slowed down – presumably trying to avoid the threads – they were Level Nine missiles, after all. Louise's ship doubled back, making steady progress toward the Crucible.

The image on the Hohash of the creatures laying down the threads mesmerised him. Like every Genner, Gabriel had studied Earth's entire catalogue of life-forms, including marine varieties, and he was reminded of a ray as he watched a group of five blue-and-green spotted creatures swimming through space. Their wings were lined with semi-organic tech whose edges fizzed and glimmered with a rainbow sheen. The leader was smaller, and each of the others, in a tight square formation, exuded a thin white thread, spindling it between them before letting it stretch and drag behind. He had no idea whether this was good or bad news. Maybe it would impede the Crucible; but that made no difference if even a single bomb got through.

Gabriel jumped his ship, calculating that he could only reach one of the bombs in time, and even then it was not clear how he could stop it. When he came out of the jump, space as shown on the Hohash didn't look normal: no pinprick stars or sprawling distant nebulas. Instead he saw fuzzy blobs of washed-out grey against a background of bulbous pockets of sepia and black. Further behind, shadows waxed and waned... Gabriel wondered: dark matter? Dark energy? Am I witnessing subspace? Genners had speculated that the Hohash could transit through subspace. But why was the Hohash showing him these images, when it had never shown anyone before?

Just as he was about to jump, the Hohash plucked his mind like a guitar string, commanding him to watch. It flicked to a normal space view superimposed on what he was now convinced was subspace. The third bomb exploded: hotter and closer, casting a normally unseen web of orange 'feelers' out into space, trying to make contact before they fizzled into oblivion. One of them encountered a trail of white threads from the rays, and raced along its length until it found the Shrell quintet. Gabriel winced as the five rays glowed red, blazing before effervescing into a shower of sparks. They were gone.

The Marauder, far behind him, engulfed by its own self-destruct system boosted by a Nova bomb, exploded in a flash of white. Two small craft fled from it, one caught in the explosion's wake that he felt like a burn on his skin. He prayed Kat was on the other one, for Petra's sake. He suddenly thought of their kiss. She'd cared for him – in that way – all those years, and never once said anything... But there was no time.

Two bombs left. He had to make a choice. Only one way to stop it. Jump right in front of it so it would detonate, taking him and the Hohash craft in the explosion. So be it. He thanked Ramires for preparing his instincts all these years, preventing him from hesitating when it most mattered. For the first time in a long while he thought of the father he'd never known, and had a Steader-like desire to make him proud. He shook it away. Picking one of the bombs, he calculated the required jump, which had to be absurdly precise, taking into account a dozen parameters shifting every millisecond. This time it required his full attention.

With the remainder of his mental capacity, Gabriel considered his existence, about to be lost. Images of Virginia, Petra, Sandy and Ramires flickered through his mind's eye. But he found himself again thinking about the father he had never known, and realised why.

Sister Esma had killed his real father, and now he too would die, but without achieving the revenge for which he had prepared and trained all his life. It was a failure, and even his last act might prove futile if the other bomb got through, as was likely. Yet he had to try, for all the people down on the planet, and – he couldn't ignore it – for the father he'd never known. Many Genners didn't believe in an afterlife, but for the first time he wondered if there was one, in which case he might finally get to meet the legendary Sentinel.

As soon as the calcs were done, he didn't waste a second, and executed the final jump. But even as he did so, he felt what could only be described as a mental jab from the Hohash, nudging one of the jump parameters by an almost infinitesimal amount. He glared at the mirror. *What have you just done?* Gabriel held his breath.

* * *

Genaspa flapped her broad wings together so hard they slapped, sending a frisson through her body. Four teams had already been taken by the Nova bomb's leakage into subspace. She thought-commanded: "Nasjana, all of you, stop the poisoning immediately! Retreat from the planet, return to the system perimeter."

But five teams were already too close to Esperia, too enmeshed in their own webs. If one more bomb ignited... she had known the males would be lost, but not the females – all of who would be pregnant now... Curse these missiles, this interaction had never been seen before, never predicted. She watched the small craft sliding across hidden space toward one of the bombs. Very well, she decided, and headed for the other, the one closest to Esperia.

Nasjana thought-directed her: "First, what you do today – "

"Listen clear, Nasjana. Qorall holds the entire thirteenth and sixteenth Shrell flocks captive in the Syntaran sector. Tell Hellera they must be freed."

Genaspa used Nasjana's shocked pause to concentrate, drawing up close behind the missile, zooming in with her senses to see Esperia's landscape take on detail, a scab-like mark on the Southern continent indicating a town; no, two, side by side. She thought-directed to all remaining Shrell: "Nasjana is First now. Tell true, tell all Shrell of today."

With a painful effort she thrust ahead so she could glide, and then emerged into normal space. It felt heavy, thick, impure, cluttered. But Genaspa knew it was transitory. Wrapping her wings around the missile casing, she enveloped it, her flesh impervious to its temperature, though she could not survive long in this embrace with the bomb's intense radiation. She exhaled a glistening cocoon, drawn from her own intestines, which billowed around her and the missile. Genaspa slowed its progress, but it had too much momentum for her to stop it in time. Far below, using her long-vision, buildings became visible, small human figures in between, running around; as if anything they could do would ever matter in the larger scheme of things.

Continuing to exhale, folding her life force around the missile, she dragged it into subspace. It was then that she felt something watching her. *Impossible, we cannot be seen here.* Her body shook, still continuing the outbreath, her life force failing, her body crumpling as the sheath solidified around the bomb. But the sense-presence, the basis of thought- directed communication across subspace, was irrefutable. Just before she and the bomb passed straight through the planet's crust, she saw the spiders standing atop a ridge, watching her.

So, Hellera, this is what you lock down, this is what you protect. It was her last thought.

* * *

Nasjana and two other teams found the missile sailing onwards, a turquoise sheath covering it, all that remained of their First. Nasjana collected her flock and informed them their mission was over, that it was time to go home. She instructed two teams to tow the missile back, so as to preserve Genaspa's remains all the way to their domain, and because Shrell did not leave dangerous weapons floating in subspace.

Nasjana had learned something on this mission: that a First does not tell all. She pondered the news of captive Shrell being held by Qorall, and Hellera's involvement in the poisoning of this sector of space. Such elevated species would never normally listen to Shrell, let alone entertain demands.

As the remaining, worn-out teams found their rhythm under her lead, leaving the Esperian system behind, Nasjana considered that in their entire history, measuring millions of years, Shrell had never coveted anything from normal space-time, least of all a weapon. But this missile – still functional – might be useful somewhere in the near future. Nasjana had lived by two maxims all her life, as had her forebears and peers: *Tell true; Tell all.* Now she added a new one, by which she vowed they would make a stand, no longer idly serving the whims of their masters: *Tell hard.*

* * *

When Gabriel emerged from the jump the craft was darkened, violet-lit. It was exactly where he had been a moment before and yet felt completely different. He took a step back, his shoulders nudging the small ship's hull. The lozenge-shaped Nova Stormer filled the length of the Hohash craft. It hung a metre off the floor, its surface difficult to focus on, like morphing shades of grey – some kind of stealth camouflage. He blinked several times but could not resolve it. It was within arm's reach, except he wasn't sure where its surface was exactly, as if there was a translucent shell around it. He realised it was making a bass humming noise, just within his enhanced range of hearing. The pitch rose an octave; his instincts told him that wasn't good.

But what unnerved him were the yellow ellipses with black diamonds inside – like eyes – that kept opening on its casing for a few seconds then disappearing, only to appear somewhere else on its shell. Sensors. Tearing his sight from the missile's mesmerising body, he glanced towards the blunt end, a mosaic of palm-size triangular mirrors resembling Ossyrian schematics he'd seen, ion thrusters for fine manoeuvring.

Gabriel glanced at the Hohash mirror – it was vibrating – no, it was shaking. Its mirror face swirled with purples and mauves, bathing the entire ship in eerie light. He wondered if the intelligent missile realised it had been captured. The Hohash was making a supreme effort to hold the missile there, probably confusing its sensor array, and the missile's intelligent defence systems were fighting back. The two devices were locked in a titanic, invisible struggle.

Gabriel decided to put them all out of their misery, unholstered his pulse pistol and aimed at the bullet-nosed front end. But a pain stabbed behind his eyes, and the gun fell from loosened fingers. The Hohash: he hadn't disconnected from the neural interface, and clearly it wanted him to do something else. Looking up, he saw blueprints flash across the Hohash mirror's face.

"Are you serious?" he said, even as he memorised the translated instructions. One line struck him – the gamma radiation output and dosage bands for one of these missiles once launched – well beyond human tolerance levels. At that point, he knew he was dead already – or would be within an hour. He thought about Virginia in that moment, wishing he could hold her one final time. But the missile's pitch kicked up a note, pulsing with a deep throb, and he let the thought go.

Gabriel considered what his father would have done, and went to find one of the external encounter suits, donning it to increase the amount of time he could work, and then approached the missile's nose. A cracking noise made him turn around. With alarm, he saw a hairline fracture on the Hohash mirror's surface. He placed a gloved hand on the artifact's outer rim. "I'll work as fast as I can."

The missile's shell near his hands glistened, and then a hole opened up, the size of a man's head. The hole's edges crackled, spitting sparks, as if the missile's defences were trying to close it, and several eyes opened up on the casing, remaining open just beyond the hole's perimeter. He reached inside with his right hand and touched the metal casing, but it felt like mud. He pushed through, until his shoulder brushed the fizzing edges of the shield, making him flinch.

Another splinter cracked on the Hohash, even as the missile's pitch rose again, pulsing faster. But he found the device he was looking for, a studded metallic ball he needed to rotate in a series of precise movements. His hand was getting hot, even inside the suit's protective glove. He tried to distract himself from the pain, using Genner concentration techniques, but he knew his body and brain were being irradiated, and it would soon affect his cognitive functioning. Curiously, it made him smile. *Well, Micah, soon I might get to feel what it's like to be a Steader.* His smile froze. A whirlpool of emotions washed through his mind. He had always stayed away from Steaders, kept a distance, even from his parents. Too late now, and no time to indulge in remorse, or to change who he had been all his life.

The heat became too intense, and Gabriel, beginning to smell his own flesh burn, pulled his right arm out. Extracting his hand from the confines of the suit, ugly blisters laced his bloated fingers, and brown fluid oozed from his knuckles. The suit was constraining him too much. He climbed out of it, and thrust his left arm deep inside the body of the missile, searching by feel for the initiator, his head an inch from the energy field, tingling his scalp with static. At last he felt a sucking then a 'plop', and the ball released. He kept his thumb pressed down on a stud.

He tugged the ball through the mud-like body and it came out clean. Gabriel was surprised to find it was like a baseball, shifting grey and white hatching all over its surface, certainly the most beautiful explosive device he'd ever seen.

A few deep breaths weren't enough to recover. He felt dizzy, and lay down on his back, unsure if he'd be able to get up again. The Hohash shook violently, a chunk of its mirror face fallen onto the floor, a web of fractures smothering most of its face.

The missile's tone had risen to a screech, and its skin was covered with elliptical, accusing eyes. He kept his forefinger on the deadman's trigger, and gathered himself. If he let go, the device would explode – not a nova-level detonation by any means, but enough to do some serious damage.

White light flashed into the room, and when it washed away, the neutralized missile was gone, he presumed back to normal space. He rested the device on his stomach, and rolled his head to see the Hohash. For a fraction of a second he thought he saw an ivory and gold eye staring back at him through the shards; most likely a radiation-induced hallucination.

The Hohash rested on the floor, wavering like he'd never seen one do. At least it had stopped shaking. The interior lighting returned to normal. Gabriel struggled to his feet, and went over to the console. Screens were working again, even if the images were scratchy. But they seemed more complex than before, and as he tried to lay in a course of jumps, there was a fog in his mind – he couldn't remember how to do it. He addressed the Hohash, tapping its frame gently. "You know where I want to go, right?"

Gabriel staggered to the exit portal, his left hand holding the device, his right arm hanging limp by his side. Blue, ivory and gold reflections played on the exit before him, but he was too tired to turn around. "Jump," he said, "quick as you can."

As everything turned quicksilver, signifying the first of a series of mini-jumps, he recalled Sandy telling him that he had an aunt, Jennifer, who had disappeared with the last Kalarash before his birth. He'd have liked to have met this woman, even once, to hear more about his father. He wondered where she was, and found himself feeling an unfamiliar emotion – he hoped that wherever she was, whatever she was doing, she was well. The feeling spread out to all he'd known, not only his Genner Youngbloods and his family, but all the Steaders, too. *So, Micah, this is what it is like to be a 'normal' human.* Gabriel knew for a fact Steaders didn't feel like that all the time, but still. *Maybe Blake was right, Micah, you sacrificed a lot when you agreed on our upgrade.*

But he focused on the task at hand, clutching the detonator, though he could barely stand. *Sister Esma, I have something for you.*

CHAPTER 23 – BREACH

Kilaney was the only one not sweating, yet he knew the Mannekhi tolerated heat better than humans. The Ngank surgeon had said he'd made some refinements, and Kilaney once again wondered what else he had inherited from his former Q'Roth physiology.

"We're losing this!" he shouted above the din of successive energy pulses thudding then sizzling across their battered spherical hull, the Mannekhi shields close to failing. A distant explosion signified the loss of yet another of the ship's spikes. The stocky lieutenant with jet-black hair, Fentra, glared at him, then she and the eleven other crew-members on the Bridge turned to their Captain.

Xenic sat tall and stern-faced, his all-black eyes somehow darker than the others, never shifting from the battle-screen. He addressed his navigator. "Siltern, remember Astravia III?"

Siltern's head jerked back as if stung then nodded and dipped to his console.

"Suits, everyone," Xenic commanded, though he didn't move from his chair.

Kilaney saw from one of the screens that their own energy pulse weapons had breached a section of the Crucible's hull, but it wasn't significant, a few square metres, barely a body blow.

Fentra tossed him one of the deep blue suits. "You suffocate, we suffocate, remember?"

Feeling bad about the bloodworms, he struggled into the self-sealing suit. Fentra sighed and came over to help him with some unfamiliar connections. "Don't get ideas. You're a dead man as soon as this is over."

He made up his mind there and then, just as another thunderous boom told him they were running out of time. Reaching inside his suit he pulled out a rack of small vials. Breaking them off one by one he handed them to each of the crew, Fentra last.

He forced a smile. "You don't think the Q'Roth developed an antidote for bloodworms? We've had it for three months. I made up this batch before you woke. It's not refined. You'll feel pain if I die, but you'll live."

Fentra stared at the vial and then looked to Xenic. Without hesitation the Commander pressed it to his neck. A short hiss issued the contents into his bloodstream. The others followed, including Fentra.

She whipped out her pistol, shoving it up underneath Kilaney's chin. "How fast does it work?"

"Fentra!" Xenic said.

Kilaney held her gaze. "Immediately, though I haven't verified it personally."

She rammed the muzzle up higher, lifting Kilaney's chin.

"*Fentra!*" Xenic stood, donning his suit.

She stared into Kilaney's eyes, her lips curling downwards into a grimace. "Quattrail Vortex, five years ago, you led the assault, Jorann. My mother and brother's Spiker was destroyed, but they made it to an escape pod just in time, as did dozens of others. Your forces – your command – blasted every last one of them. Do you know what it's like to die in space, oxygen ripped from your body, your blood boiling in your veins?"

He did. How could he forget? "Go ahead, you deserve revenge. I'd pull the trigger if I were you. I'll make it easier for you." He closed his eyes.

Fentra's heavy breathing competed with the thuds and crashes from the deck just below. The Bridge would be next.

Siltern interrupted. "Ready."

Xenic shouted. "Helmets, everybody. Fentra, decide now!"

Kilaney felt the gun barrel's warm nozzle leave his throat as a helmet was rammed into his stomach. Opening his eyes, he watched her don hers, never taking her sight from him. He sealed his own helmet, hearing Xenic's voice clear as day.

"Spike 17 everybody. *Run!*"

"Follow me," Fentra said, as she turned and bolted from the Bridge, grabbing a heavy duty weapon as she passed the rack, as did the others. Kilaney had only his pulse pistol.

Sprinting along twisting corridors, he didn't turn around to see the stuttering detonation that made his ears ring; it could only have come from the bridge. There was a flash of silver that caught him mid-step: a close-quarter jump! The Spiker's auxiliary control system had executed

Siltern's command and jumped into the Crucible, Spike 17 pricking its hull through the breach made earlier. It was going to be tight. Kilaney sped up, weapon drawn.

* * *

Sister Esma's claw smashed into the battery officer's neck. There was a gurgling noise as the Alician slumped to the floor. She moved above him, her boot finishing him off with a sickening crunch. The rest of the crew first stared at her, then their consoles; all except Serena and the lone Q'Roth warrior.

"We've been boarded," Sister Esma said with an air of disgust. She addressed the Q'Roth warrior. "Kah-Reich, you'd better go and make sure the cutter finishes its job, the Mannekhi are headed to the auxiliary control centre. Serena, go check our precious cargo in case these insurgents get curious."

Kah-Reich's scarlet cloak whirled behind him. Serena checked her pistol's charge as she broke into a trot to catch up with the Q'Roth Commander.

Sister Esma turned to her communications officer, nudging the corpse with her boot. "Get this off my Bridge. And then get me our relief ship, we cannot jump shackled like this to a *Spiker*." She almost spat the word; she despised the treacherous Mannekhi, they had no honour. Hopefully they would all be eliminated during the war, used by Qorall as cannon fodder on his front lines.

As the Alician body was dragged away, Sister Esma re-took her command seat, her back to her crew. "I need a new weapons officer." She was gratified that there was no hesitation as one of her crew took the station.

"You have one, Your Eminence."

Lorena; she recognised her voice, young and ambitious. "Am I correct in presuming that Louise's Nova bombs have not reached their target?" It was a rhetorical question; they would all have seen the flash and red afterglow had one gotten through.

"Yes, Your Eminence."

Sister Esma wondered if the new girl's talent matched her ambition. "Recommendation?"

There was a pause. "Esperantia is on the other side of the planet, but only by a few hours. I can triangulate its position and send three Leveller missiles on a parabolic vector. They will incinerate everything within a hundred kilometre radius. We'll be in range in fifteen minutes."

"Do it."

229

Sister Esma sat back. Things weren't going to plan, but it was always about resolution, seeing it through. Everything else, the setbacks, the trials and tribulations would soon be forgotten by history. The aura of success belonged to those who *delivered*. In theory she could leave the Crucible, take a Raptor out through the Shrell mesh to meet the Q'Roth back-up ship. But this was also about leadership, and the annals of history always saluted those who stood there at the final, decisive moment. One day, after the war, this particular slice of history would no longer be secret, and the galaxy would congratulate the Alicians for purging yet another weed from its Society. But it wasn't about ego, certainly not about her own reputation *per se*. It was about placing her Alician flock in good stead, a solid reputation in Grid Society. Future Grid leaders – whoever they may be – would know that the Alicians could be relied upon to get the job done.

The moon flickered, the planet-cutter pulsing black and blue tendrils boiling its flesh, nearing the point where it would disintegrate and turn into a hailstorm falling towards Esperia. That would take another hour, by which time she'd be gone. So, the missiles would kill the remnants of humanity, and then the moonrock would bury them forever. Sister Esma would leave nothing to chance this time, and could inform the Q'Roth queen that the human embarrassment had been exterminated once and for all.

Esperia: such a vain name, tempting fate. To her it was a blatant admission of inherent weakness that a race must rely on hope rather than its own resources and strengths. Intelligence and firepower trumped wishful thinking any day. Fourteen minutes, and humanity's entire sorry history would be reduced to ashes, and nobody would weep for them.

∗ ∗ ∗

Kilaney and the other Mannekhi advanced steadily in combat mode through the corridors. At each junction in the dark green maze one of them would bolt to the far side, weapon raised, then signal to the others it was clear, then charge to the next junction. It was Russian roulette; eventually one of them would be fired upon. It came to his turn. He didn't hesitate, despite his foreboding. But he hadn't gotten more than a metre past the corner when he caught sight of a dark blur in his peripheral vision. Instinctively he dived into a roll, firing toward the enemy. Something thwacked into his left thigh, spinning him wildly and sending him sprawling into the wall.

Light erupted all around him, accompanied by a sound like a jet engine, as six Mannekhi burst into the opening using fire-cannons. Shielding his eyes with his forearm, he watched Xenic, Fentra, Siltern and three others hefting heavy guns, spewing white hot plasma-fire down the corridor. Abruptly the beams shut off, leaving a ringing in his ears. Only Xenic and Fentra were still upright. Siltern and three more bodies were on the ground, the tell-tale grey and red feathers of Q'Roth flechette darts protruding from their bodies. One stuck out of Kilaney's leg, but the toxin had not been released, he presumed because the dart sensed his Q'Roth DNA. Down the other end of the corridor he saw a mass of collapsing blue-black flesh torn open, revealing smoking organs the colour of red hot coals, the warrior's carcass twitching despite its head having been split open. It was a beautiful sight.

The cannons hummed, liquid fire dripping from their nozzles, oozing onto the floor into sizzling white-hot puddles. He'd not seen this weapon before, but then he hadn't been in close combat with Mannekhi for years.

Xenic offered him a hand. "The auxiliary control room is this way." Kilaney got to his feet, limping, and looked down at the metal dart sticking out of his thigh. Fentra grasped it and yanked it out. He winced but held in a gasp of pain, convinced she had twisted it.

He moved on to his game plan. "The humans they brought aboard, those you picked up on your sensors."

Xenic nodded to the Mannekhi crew. "The rest of you are with me, we take out the planet-breaker control centre. Fentra, go with him."

"There'll be more Q'Roth the closer you get," Kilaney warned.

Xenic headed down the corridor, followed by his crew, "That's the idea," he said.

Kilaney watched them go. He turned to Fentra.

She nodded at Siltern's dead body, the cannon lying next to him on the floor. "It's yours if you want it."

He bent low and reverently unpeeled Siltern's fingers from the trigger arm. Kilaney heaved the strap over his shoulder, and followed Fentra down a different corridor.

As they rounded a bend they came face-to-face with a lone blonde woman, arms folded, seemingly unarmed.

"Where do you think you're going?" the woman said, a faint smile across her lips, as if asking the time of day.

Kilaney's human instincts not to shoot a woman in cold blood overran his Q'Roth ones to kill her on sight on the grounds she was probably Alician. Maybe she was human, a prisoner from the planet. But then...

Her eyes fixed on Kilaney, narrowing slightly, even as Fentra levelled her pistol, her own mind obviously made up. Fentra's shot found empty air as the woman whirled out of the way like a dervish, two paces to the left of where she had been, her own pistol drawn, the smile gone.

He heard Fentra fall and tried to turn, but instead dropped to his knees, then hit the floor, his head facing his fallen comrade. Smoke rose from his chest, and he knew the smell of burning flesh well enough. Fentra had a fist-sized cylindrical hole where her heart should have been. Her eyes stared at him, their black light fading. She flicked her eyes once in the direction of the other woman, then closed them.

Kilaney didn't move, trying to work out why he wasn't dead. The Ngank surgeon had said something about human physiology being so fragile – no redundancy, too many single critical organs. Q'Roth had two hearts, the main one and a secondary one. The surgeon had said he'd made refinements...

The Alician woman was clearly as fast as she was accurate. He heard her walk half-way towards them then raise her arm. Kilaney had fallen on his cannon, but his pulse pistol was still in his hand. He made an effort not to blink, even though the effects of initial shock were wearing off and pain began to intrude. Holding his breath, he listened to her voice, using his Q'Roth combat training to gauge the required angle of fire without turning his head or moving his upper body. The pain helped him concentrate. With his right hand he slowly angled this pistol, hearing her relaxed tone. He knew he'd get just one shot. Kilaney focused on her voice.

"Sister Esma, the threat is eliminated down here at my end. One Mannekhi and a human. I'm heading back to help the Q'Roth defend –" Kilaney fired. He tilted his head and checked, content to see a blackened hole in the centre of her forehead, a look of surprise on her face, her weapon half-raised. *Always aim for the head*, he used to tell Blake; smaller target, but definitive. She toppled to the floor.

"Serena?" the woman's wristcom crackled.

Kilaney knew that voice. He crawled over to the dead Alician and seized her wristcom. "Hello Sister Esma, remember me?"

There was a pause. "General Bill Kilaney. Or should I call you Jorann?"

"I'm coming for you." He switched it off, removed it from Serena's limp wrist and placed it on his right arm, so he could listen to their comms, maybe distract them. He hadn't enjoyed his only former conversation with Sister Esma, when she'd vented him into space, and he had no intention of starting another.

He inspected the hole through his chest; it was neatly cauterized, but the secondary heart was meant only as a stopgap measure, to keep a Q'Roth warrior fighting a little longer.

Xenic came online on Kilaney's other wristcom. "We're pinned down, a dozen Q'Roth warriors, any aid is welcome."

He glanced at Fentra. *You'll get your wish soon.* Using the cannon as a walking stick, Kilaney trudged down the corridor. But he only got a few metres before his legs gave way and he collapsed, short of breath, his chest muscles cramping, his arms and hands shaking. Kilaney realized he wasn't going anywhere, and would be of little use in a firefight. Reluctantly, seeing no options as a broken, soon-to-be-dead man, he wondered what a Q'Roth warrior would do in this situation. But the Q'Roth weren't known for their creativity; rather they were good at following orders. *Orders.* Kilaney kicked himself for not having thought of it earlier. He began practicing; his human throat was no longer that good at simulating Q'Roth commands

* * *

Sister Esma knew, but asked her weapons officer anyway. "How long?"

"Seven minutes. All is prepared."

The Bridge door swished open, and the corners of Sister Esma's lips lifted. She flattened them before swivelling her chair around. "Louise," she said. Despite being glad to have her aboard, she always maintained discipline and authority. "What happened to your Nova bombs?"

Louise shrugged. "Shrell wires happened to three of them. Two of them were on target, but disappeared just before impact. I honestly don't know. Still, seems like you could use some help here. Your orders?"

Sister Esma knew the destruction of Esperia had become personal, her judgement biased, when it was not the Alicians' priority. But Louise was like her; she would get the job done.

"The human cargo: take them to the relief ship and head to Savange immediately. Take the Ossyrian doctor with you, too. Alanis, go with Louise, brief her on the way. You take orders from Louise now."

Sister Esma met her errant protégé's eyes: defiant, confident. There was something else, too – Louise had grown. Sister Esma wondered what Level she was, knowing that if they both survived there would be a power struggle between them. Good, that was the Alician way; better for the community.

"Good to see you again, Sister Esma, it's been too long," Louise said, then added, "Please crush Micah and the others. See you on Savange, we have much to discuss."

Sister Esma let her smile broaden and watched her favourite turn to leave, interrupted by a blast of Q'Roth clicks flooding the ship-wide comms system; Sister Esma couldn't follow it. She felt a tingling in her spine; there had been more than enough surprises for one day. "What is that?"

Louise, poised to leave, cocked her head to one side. "Largyl Nine, Captain's privilege level for the Q'Roth High Guard."

Sister Esma waited; she didn't know this dialect, no Alician did; except Louise, apparently.

Louise turned to face Sister Esma after the rasping noise shut off. "Problem, I'm afraid."

"Jorann," Sister Esma murmured through tightened lips.

Louise nodded. "He has instructed the Q'Roth Commander to switch off the cutter, using an emergency Tla Beth priority code, which appears to be valid." Louise glanced away.

"The rest; all of it."

Louise wandered over to the weapons rack and pulled out two heavy assault rifles, passing one to Alanis. "They've been instructed to relieve you of command by any means necessary."

Sister Esma shouted at the comms officer. "Block all off-ship comms now!"

"Your Eminence, the only way I can do that is to terminate –"

"Do it!" Sister Esma advanced on the Alician woman's console, standing over her while the terrified woman entered a comms termination sequence at lightning speed.

"Done," she said, her shoulders sinking with relief.

Sister Esma pointed to another crewmember. "Seal all blast doors between the Q'Roth and us, then open the escape hatches to space in the connecting corridors."

Louise armed her rifle. "The Q'Roth will fight to the death against the Mannekhi – too much bad blood between them. It'll keep them both occupied. You could come with us."

Her voice had a trace of concern in it, which touched Sister Esma. "A few things to wrap up here first. We'll be ten minutes behind you in the next Raptor. Go."

Louise stared for a moment then left the Bridge, accompanied by Alanis. Sister Esma retook her chair. She called up a display showing Esperia, Esperantia on the other side relative to the Crucible. Overlaid on the display was a parabolic missile trajectory, the firing window of opportunity through the Shrell mesh drawing closer every second.

For five hundred years she had plotted humanity's extinction, and it would take just another few minutes. Yet her right palm was clammy, and her claw flexed and unflexed, making a noise like grinding teeth. For the first time in centuries she had a bad feeling that her plan might fail. She never second-guessed herself, but this time her Level Five mind began cataloguing the unpredicted variables that had already transpired in the last hours. She shut that train of thought off, a futile weakness. As long as nothing else –

"Your Eminence, there's something odd... off our starboard side."

Sister Esma's voice sounded like a sword being drawn. "If you value your life, girl, be specific."

The woman coughed. "I... I noticed some debris a few minutes ago, which I assumed was from the moon's break up. But it's heading towards us, and... it's accelerating."

Sister Esma clicked her right finger and thumb, and pointed to the viewscreen. The image shifted to space, the lacerated moon glowing behind, rocks of indeterminable size drifting here and there, moving away from the moon, towards

Esperia. At first she didn't see it, but then she detected grains of dust moving like sand beneath a wave, always in the same direction, towards the Crucible.

"Magnify."

She stood and walked closer to the viewscreen. The motes refused to resolve, which could only mean stealth tech. "Target them with charges."

"Our weapons are offline. The Q'Roth have shut them down from their location."

Sister Esma stormed over to the tactical console, the officer there blanching before jumping aside. "Damn them! So be it, they leave me no choice." She began typing a long command code, her right fingers chopping fast at the console.

The tactical officer moved closer, her eyes widening. "Your Eminence –"

Sister Esma spoke calmly, her claw resting on the officer's shoulder, close to her neck. "No one will know." She completed the sequence that triggered a release of Q'Roth-targeted killer nannites into the ventilation system in the planet-cutter control centre and surrounding corridors. She turned to the woman. "Will they?" The officer shook her head vehemently.

One less variable. But the motes in space drew closer. She felt a trickle of ice down her spine, not a feeling to which she was accustomed. Calculating their arrival time at the hull – though she had no idea what they would do then – they would be there shortly after the missiles were launched. Yet still the foreboding hung about her. In her mind's eye, she suddenly imagined seven billion slaughtered humans watching silently, willing her to fail, waiting for her to die so they could lay their bony fingers on her. She shook herself. Action was required; this waiting was unravelling her. "All of you leave the Bridge now. Arm yourselves and head to areas thirty through forty-five, decks seven to nine, in case we are boarded there."

All of them except one grabbed weapons and fled the Bridge.

The tactical officer spoke. "Your Eminence, I would like to stay, to assist, in case..."

Sister Esma looked at her. Young, eager, completely devoted to the Alician cause. It reminded her of her own brief time with Alessia over five hundred years ago, and it comforted her. But then she remembered that Alessia had been slain shortly afterwards.

"Stay," she said. For the first time in her life she didn't want to be alone. No, she realised, she didn't want to die alone. Her right hand slid into her pocket and clasped the wooden chess figure of the queen, given to her all those years ago by Alessia herself.

"Esperia launch window," she said, re-taking her chair. The screen shifted again, and she enabled an audible countdown. *Sixty, fifty-nine, fifty-eight...* She tapped out the last seconds of humanity's existence with her finger on the arm of her chair. *Whoever you are out there, you are too late. I may well die today, but I'm taking all of humanity with me.*

CHAPTER 24 – REVENGE

Gabriel realised he was midway through a subspace jump. Usually it was instantaneous: there was no perception until one 'exited' the transit. Now, every surface of the inside of the Hohash ship was silver, like frozen mercury, except for the wave-like shadows shimmering in front of him on the inside of the airlock hatch. But he couldn't move. A young woman's voice spoke to him, clearly, as if standing right behind him – no, he thought, exactly where the Hohash mirror had been just before they jumped. But the Hohash were mute – weren't they?

"Gabriel, please listen to me."

He tried to clear the radiation-induced fuzz from his mind, and hypothesised: the Hohash belonged to the Kalarash; the voice sounded human, but not with the authority he'd anticipate from a Level Nineteen being; he only knew of one woman linked to the Kalarash. He couldn't turn around, but his mouth and vocal chords worked.

"Jennifer?"

She uttered a noise somewhere between a laugh and a gasp. "You're smart, like... your father." Her voice stumbled over the last two words.

His stepfather Ramires had told him how distraught Jennifer had been when her brother, the Sentinel assassin Gabriel – the father he'd never known – had been killed, and the treacherous path down which it had propelled her.

Hearing her voice, that of an aunt he'd never met, resurfaced long- buried thoughts about his father, emotional dead-ends he'd walled off years ago. Sandy had often said how much he resembled his father, though she'd barely known him herself. Plenty of other kids had lost parents during the Q'Roth sacking of Earth, but they had memories, usually holos too, anchors to cling to. Gabriel had nothing, save his own reflection. He listened intently.

"Gabriel – there's so much I want to say..."

He could sense the pain in her voice. "What was he like?"

There was a pause. "Brave and beautiful. People were wary of him, though; they sensed the inherent danger even in his teens. One of his teachers once described him as an unexploded mine." She laughed.

He smiled, but it stirred the suppressed emotions deep inside him, chipping away at those walls. "Go on," he said, almost a whisper.

"Serious, always looking for a cause, interested in politics when boys his age were discovering girls, though he had quite a few girlfriends in his teens. No-one close. He would come out with these profound but enigmatic sayings. My favourite was *'where there is thought, there is power.'* Kalaran thought that was pretty deep for a human. Sorry, I'm rambling." She cleared her throat. "Your father found his cause, the only one that mattered in the end."

Gabriel felt the need to sit, but still couldn't move. He tried to picture his father as a boy, as a young man back in Ireland before the nuclear devastation had blackened that once emerald Isle. He'd watched the history holos over and over, secretly searching the running, confused, screaming crowds for a face like his own. He'd distanced himself from the Steaders, but if his father had lived... He couldn't see where that path would have led him, but he would have liked to have had the choice. For the first time he didn't discount that Genners and Steaders could co-exist amicably, could make it work better than it had. Maybe afterwards, the rift could be healed – if there was going to be an afterwards.

Jennifer continued. "Ramires probably knew more about him as a man than I did, even though he didn't know him personally – I thought he'd been killed in the first round of nuclear detonations. Apparently, he was the perfect assassin, no ego, played the double agent for the Alicians for years before Sister Esma unmasked him. He died fighting to save us."

Gabriel had heard it said before, but this time, hearing it from family, from someone that actually knew his father, made it resonate. It firmed his purpose. But he guessed there was little time, and that this wasn't purely a social call.

"You want me to do something, don't you?"

Jennifer's voice steeled. "The Hohash is taking you directly to the Crucible Bridge. Sister Esma is about to launch an attack on Esperia. There are only seconds remaining in real time. As soon as you arrive..."

"I'll take my finger off the switch."

Again a pause. "Don't let her talk to you or anything, just – "

"Once I see her, I *will* kill her." He wished he could turn around. He'd seen a holo-record of Jennifer, but wondered what she looked like now. He tried to push such questions aside, to stay focused on the task – to be like his father would have been. Besides, there was something else he wanted to know.

"Jennifer, why is this important to the Kalarash?" He heard a low, grinding noise in the background; Jennifer wasn't alone.

"The spiders, they are important in the war against Qorall, though I don't yet know how; Kalaran won't tell me."

"Can they defeat Qorall? Can... can we *win* this time?"

During the unwanted pause, he recalled the latent taste of defeat inherited by all Genners, the feeling of inadequacy and its allied need to prove themselves. It wasn't even about revenge or justice. They just needed to stand up and fight, to make their mark; to achieve some victory, even if a small one. Gabriel almost laughed – *how human.*

"Maybe," she said. "At least we have a shot."

He relaxed a little. "And us... humanity? Do we figure in the Kalarash plans?"

"Definitely," she said, in a drawn out way. "But it's hard to –"

"That's all I need to know, Jennifer." *That what I'm dying for is worth something, not just delaying the inevitable. If the Kalarash have a stake in humanity, for whatever reason, then we have a chance.* Like his father, he'd found his cause.

"I wish..." her voice cracked.

"Me too," he said, feeling closer to this woman he'd never met, never seen, than most people back on Esperia. But he didn't want to die in a maudlin state.

"Where are you?"

She sniffed, clearing her throat again. "Just inside the galaxy, trying to get back. Qorall figured out where our entrance portal was – we think via Louise's Hohash, which she coerced in some way – and sent an armada of dark worms to block us. We broke through, but they've slowed us down."

The mercurial surfaces began to flicker. Time was running out. "Must this Hohash be destroyed as well? They're not just artifacts are they?"

There was that noise again on her side of the mirror, like a distant rumbling.

"That Hohash is almost depleted, and it needs to be there because I've demanded a favour from Kalaran."

Gabriel wondered how a human could demand anything from a Level Nineteen being. "A favour?"

"Yes. You see, I –" her voice cracked.

A deeper baritone voice spoke. "She cannot bear to see you die, Gabriel. Not again, like your father."

The accent was strange. He recalled a conversation once with his mother about two men reportedly with Jennifer on the ship – Dimitri, her Greek lover, and Rashid, an Indistani. But the man spoke with tenderness; Dimitri then.

238

"We must all die," Gabriel said, "and I am riddled with gamma ray damage. I will collapse within minutes once I come out of transit." He wasn't sure where this was going. Having accepted his death, and that it had meaning, he wanted to get on with it, fulfil his and his father's mission to kill the Alician High Priestess. That was enough. Anger simmered at this pointless exchange. The quicksilver surfaces shivered.

Jennifer spoke again, her composure restored. "Even now, the Hohash is scanning you in ways you can't imagine. At the point of death, in the nanoseconds before you are obliterated, the Hohash will transmit your personality string to our ship's Hohash. Kalaran can restore you... after a fashion."

Gabriel didn't like the sound of it. "Like a Transpar," he said, flat.

"No, much more than that, Gabriel."

The mercury was evaporating fast from the hatch door, the white metal surface peering through. Gabriel simultaneously wondered just how much time had been slowed down, and if what she was suggesting was possible.

"Gabriel," she said, "what do you say?"

"You mean I have a choice?"

"Of course! But please say yes."

The pain in her voice touched him – and he reminded himself she was family, a concept he'd never fully grasped before. He figured his father would want him to try, for her sake. "Okay, Jennifer, but only after Sister Esma is dead." The last traces of mercury shrank into vanishing puddles. "Look after her, Dimitri."

She sniffed again. "Good–"

Gabriel and the Hohash materialised silently onto the Crucible's bridge, the skeletal outline of the craft around them appearing like lines of shadow before the Hohash vehicle disappeared back into Transpace.

Two women were before him, five metres away, one standing at a console, the other sitting with her back to him in a command chair – she had a claw where her left arm should be, and was tapping in time to an audio countdown: "*Thirty-seven, thirty-six...*"

"Sister Esma," he said.

The two women spun around, and Gabriel removed his finger from the deadman switch. Nothing happened. The thought-stream flashed through his mind: *intelligent weapon – knows it has been violated – it is refusing to detonate.* The woman at the console reached for her pistol. Gabriel dropped down to a crouch and flung the studded metal ball at her. It caught her chin with its full force, snapping a vertebra in her neck. She crashed backwards onto the ground.

The claw-arm woman – he presumed it was Sister Esma, had not moved.

"*Gabriel?*" she said, a sneer spreading across her lips. "Ah, his son! Come to watch mankind snuffed out again?"

Gabriel's right arm was useless, so he reached across his body for his right-holstered pulse pistol with his left hand, just as she shot at his chest. The impact of the pulse round lifted him clean off the ground, slamming him back into another console. He ended up on the floor, coughing blood, struggling to breathe. His arm had been in the way of the pulse round and so had protected his heart from its electrical discharge, but that arm was now dead too, and enough damage had been done to his nervous system for him to know he was finished.

She walked over and towered above him.

"*Twenty-one, twenty, nineteen,*" the countdown continued.

Gabriel choked on some blood, tried to sit up, but her heel pushed his barbecued chest down. "You have failed, as your father did before you. Stay there; just a few seconds longer."

Sister Esma walked over to what Gabriel assumed was the tactical console, shoving the other woman's body away with her boot.

"*Fifteen, fourteen...*"

Holding his breath, he concentrated. The missile was probably set to fire automatically; he had to destroy the whole control centre where they stood. But how? Then it came to him: *where there is thought, there is power.* He felt a connection in his mind – the interface with the Hohash was still active, its craft just beneath them in subspace.

"*Eleven, ten...*"

Sister Esma had not paid the Hohash any attention – it was standing upright to her left, behind her.

Gabriel called to the Hohash, trying to communicate directly, thinking at Genner speed. "*You must have a power source. When the Q'Roth invaded your world, many of you self-destructed, shattering harmlessly. But you were commanded by the spiders to do so, not to fight back, because they feared the Q'Roth might find the spider eggs. But now, the Kalarash want this woman stopped, the planet saved –*"

Everything turned a uniform blue. Gabriel felt a floor beneath his feet, but couldn't see it. He had no sense of distance. A Hohash appeared in front of him, undamaged compared to the one on the Crucible, but he guessed it was one and the same. Its surface was blank. Without warning it advanced on him. He blinked.

A vast cavern opened up before him, wide enough to hold ten Crucibles like the one where he knew his real body was dying. Fire-like tongues of coloured light spun downwards, coalescing onto an anvil-shaped plinth in the centre of the cavern floor, accompanied by a roaring sound like a waterfall. He couldn't see upwards, as the brightness obscured his sight, but he could make out giant black, tree-like legs, massive gleaming golden quadruple-jointed fingers, dark grey tentacles, and clutches of transparent filaments that curled and uncurled every few seconds. At one point something like an eye opened, a gold-rimmed ivory pupil within an iris of lapis lazuli. It stared at him a second then disappeared. He couldn't fit the pieces together, and realised he wasn't meant to: Kalarash.

Columns of cascading light bathed the plinth, and he guessed it was energy and information. When the light-feeds snapped off, leaving silence underpinned by a ringing in his ears, he wasn't surprised by what was left on the stone slab. The gleaming, freshly created Hohash lay dormant a while, then lifted off and rose upwards until Gabriel could not see it anymore.

The scene shifted and he witnessed a hundred or more Hohash mingling with reptilian Rangers and other alien forms he didn't recognize, in a vast amethyst city, crystal towers and tubes floating above the cloud layer at sunset, with three moons hanging in a ruby sky. So, he thought, this is how it used to be. The scene shifted rapidly, showing less positive scenes – wars, destruction of worlds, of suns and entire systems. Each time a Hohash was present. Each time they watched, but did nothing. He witnessed a torrent of these scenes, unable to turn away. Last, it showed him the culling of the spider race by the Q'Roth, many Hohash shattering into fragments and glinting shards, their golden frames melting into the ground.

"I get it," Gabriel said, "you're pacifists. It's programmed into you."

He found himself back in the blue space, the Hohash in front of him. Its face swirled and a youngish woman appeared; mousy-blonde hair, a ski-jump nose, and bottle-green eyes. *Jennifer*. But the look on her face was strange. *Not Jennifer*; the Hohash wanted to speak to him through this image.

"Omnipaths listen, record," she said.

"Your masters the Kalarash are in danger, they need you to do this."

"Never kill," the Hohash said through Jennifer's image.

"But this time – "

"You are human," the mirror interrupted, "with no concept of 'never'. It is a very long time."

Gabriel almost laughed. But they had very little time back on the Crucible. "The woman whose form you take is with Kalaran, one of your masters. He needs you to do this. They asked me to kill Sister Esma and stop the missiles. Protect the planet. I have failed. You – "

"Difficult to do that and save you as well; I may not be able to send you to his ship. That was the last order from Kalaran."

Gabriel shouted. "Dammit! *I* don't matter! Destroy the bridge, sever the control connection to the missiles. Protect Esperia! That's the only – "

He was back on the bridge, struggling to breathe. Sister Esma was saying something to him.

"It is about thinking in the long term, Gabriel," she said. "Strategy, that's what counts, that's what wins."

"*Eight, seven...*"

He glanced over to the Hohash. It looked broken, fractured, tired. It was incredibly old.

Sister Esma stared out at the viewscreen and beamed, her eyes widening. She looked happy.

"*Six, five –*"

The Hohash flared a violent red, the heat scalding Gabriel's cheeks, and he knew it had decided to do as he'd asked. *Sorry Jennifer, it would have been nice to get to know you.* He thought of Gabriel, the true father he'd never known, and his stepfather Ramires, who had taught him how to live and how to die. *This is for both of you, for all of us. Let the dead, all those Sentinels and others murdered by her hand, watch and savour this moment.*

Sister Esma's head swung in the direction of the Hohash, a look of indignation on her face morphing into a grimace of rage as she realized her time had come, and that her plan had failed. "NO!" She whirled around to Gabriel. "Not like this!" Her hand dove into her pocket, as if clutching something. "Aless–"

The Hohash's surface went nova-bright. Gabriel watched her flesh ignite, phosphorous-white, a human flare, her Q'Roth claw flailing, the roar of fire enveloping her scream.

Gabriel smiled. *Micah, we're finally a team. I've done my part. The rest is up to you.* He scrunched his eyes closed, as the Crucible's bridge exploded.

CHAPTER 25 – UNDER FIRE

Micah had always secretly feared dying in space. It was worse than drowning, where at least something filled the lungs, rather than having them explode outwards. His hands were shaky and he felt his heart hammering in his chest as he sped silently through the expanse of space between the dying Pyramid ship and the Crucible. He was painfully aware that at any moment a random micro-chunk of fast-travelling space-rock could tear his suit's membrane and introduce him to the true meaning of hard vacuum. He and the rest of the Ossyrian attack party relied on their stealth tech to prevent the Crucible's scanners from targeting them. The one bit of good news was that Kilaney's Mannekhi Spiker had caused a major distraction, and had finally brought down the shields of the Q'Roth warship.

Micah stayed in tight formation behind Chahat-Me's delta wing of Ossyrian commandos, using the auto-thrusters in his suit. His resident, normally in the background unless called for, was fully activated, showing him read-outs of distance and closing speed, plus his own biometric data. Micah tried to ignore his heart rate. He glanced across to Petra on the other side of the wing, but her helmet pointed resolutely toward the Crucible battleship growing large in front of them.

The vessel made him think of a monstrous dragonfly: the tail-end comprising four grey-gold bulbs he knew to be the engines. Next was the spindly octagonal fuselage occupying most of the ship's length, which normally housed the planet-cutting cables currently engaged in carving up the larger of Esperia's two moons. Sporadic flashes of purple reflected on the metallic sheen of the Crucible's boxy fore-section, signalling yet another lunar explosion spewing a shower of rock destined for Esperia.

Petra had calculated that the first barrage of moonrock would break atmosphere in just under an hour, categorizing the projected impact on the planet's biosphere as 'catastrophic'. Micah had been searching for a more Biblical adjective.

Just as he was feeling that anything they did now would be too late, an explosion of white light in the Crucible's front end made him squint. When it faded, he saw a small area of the ship ripped apart, as if a giant claw had torn open the hull, exposing it to space. From its location and ruptured dome, Micah reckoned he was staring at what was left of the ship's control centre. *Kilaney and those Mannekhi are damned good!* He wished he could see their Spiker ship pricking the Crucible's hull, but it was on the other side, only three of the Spiker's black and purple spines visible.

It felt like forever getting there, but as the Crucible loomed up ahead, Micah began to wonder when they were going to slow down. He felt a stab of panic as he realised he no longer had manual control over his suit thrusters, and that the entire Ossyrian attack wing seemed to be accelerating; he envisioned them all swatting themselves against an impenetrable metal hull like suicidal mosquitoes. His suit thrusters aligned him behind an Ossyrian who held one of the disk-shaped 'corers'. A cylinder of light struck out from it towards the hull, ribbons of yellow and red proto-plasma spinning faster and faster until the colours meshed. Abruptly he decelerated so fast he felt his organs shoving upwards, squeezing his throat so he could barely breathe.

Unable to see ahead properly, he gazed across to the lead Ossyrian in front of Petra. Where the tunnel of light struck the hull, the ultra-tough metal caved in like a collapsing cake. He glanced back. At the end of Petra's line of Ossyrians was one holding a similar cone attached to her feet – a plug, he guessed. Without warning Micah found himself inside a glowing red channel of metal with smooth, steaming sides he knew better than to touch. A second later he entered the ship, his thrusters braking and manoeuvring him upright, resisting the rush of air sucking back out into space. He counted – 1 – 2 – 3 – and the last Ossyrian entered, a reassuring clunk sealing the hull breach. His suit thrusters adjusted to local gravity then shut off. A green light on the inside of his visor lit up, as all the Ossyrians removed their helmets.

They stood in an olive-coloured chamber intersected by a corridor. Within seconds Chahat-Me appeared with a small group of Ossyrians, followed by Petra. She looked as relieved to see him as he was her. Chahat- Me produced a black bag and ripped it open. Immediately, small glassy darts took flight and headed in both directions down the corridor. Another Ossyrian laid a disc on the floor, and a holo rose from it. Micah watched it unfold, stretching outwards from a central green point indicating their current position, sketching the levels, corridors and rooms of the vast ship. When one of the darts came upon something moving, it paused. Chahat-

Me touched the corresponding point on the holo, and a close-up grew for a few seconds, until she touched it again and the dart continued on its way. There were heavily-armed Alicians onboard.

One of the images transmitted by the darts showed a man leaning heavily against a wall. "Kilaney," Micah whispered, a smile forming then vanishing as he took in the state of the man. "He looks injured. We must –" But Chahat-Me had already signalled two of her team to go to him. Micah also saw Mannekhi, seven of them, in a standoff against a dozen or so Q'Roth.

Petra spoke softly to Micah. "Dumb question time: aren't the Q'Roth supposed to be on our side?"

"Good point," Micah noted. "Either this band is renegade or they've been misled into this fight, otherwise it's bad news."

Chahat-Me's quicksilver eyes gazed into a floating metal orb, an Ossyrian comms device Micah had seen once before on Esperia, no doubt dispatching other teams to that area. One of the darts picked up a cluster of life-signs. When Chahat-Me enlarged the image, both Micah and Petra gasped. It was a dome, like a giant soap bubble, Inside, fifty or sixty humans stood immobilised in some kind of stasis, frozen, hands by their sides. Many of them wore terrified expressions, their faces taut and lined, others downcast, imprisoned refugees accepting their fate. The one at the front, her chin high and eyes fixed forward, was instantly recognisable.

"They have my mother!" Petra unholstered her pistol, her hand shaking as she checked the charge.

They were about to leave when Chahat-Me expanded one last image. Micah's fists squeezed white. In the frame, a blonde-haired woman spun around just as the holo unfolded. There was a blur of light from her rifle, and then the image blanked.

"Nice shot," Petra said. She looked at Micah. "That's Louise, right?"

He nodded. They could see from the map that Louise was headed for Antonia and the other prisoners. Amongst their raiding party, only Micah knew how truly deadly she was, both individually and for the whole of surviving humanity. Whatever it took, he knew he mustn't let her escape this time. His fear from the space-trip dissolved, and he felt purpose calm his perspiring and shaky hands. He made up his mind in an instant, met Chahat-Me's eyes, grabbed her paw and pressed it to his temple. While Chahat-Me accessed his resident, learning his plan, he heard Petra demanding to know what was going on. He broke the connection, unslung his assault rifle, checked the holo-map once more and bolted down the corridor, joined by two Ossyrians at the second intersection. Petra shouted after him while Chahat-Me and the others held her back.

In his mind were three priorities, in order of importance: kill Louise, free the prisoners, and protect Petra. He would intercept Louise and take her down.

Micah and the two Ossyrians rounded a bend and came across an armed Alician male. Micah dodged sideways, a pulse shot missing him by millimetres, and returned fire. Micah sped past the man's collapsing body even before it hit the ground. One of the Ossyrians had gone down behind him, caught by the man's second shot, but neither Micah nor the other Ossyrian slowed.

His resident had recorded the internal layout of the Crucible based on the Ossyrian darts' intel, and indicated which way to turn at each junction, but as he approached a right-angled bend he heard the familiar pounding of six metal-hard legs galloping his way. Slowing down he hefted his assault rifle, knowing that it might do little good, when the Ossyrian, running dog-like behind him, flicked a paw at Micah's rear ankle, tripping his legs. Micah flew headlong across the intersection, hearing the Ossyrian's war-scream behind him as she slid to a halt to face the approaching Q'Roth warrior. There was a sickening crunch as Micah turned around to see a flurry of black serrated legs slash and chop at the Ossyrian's body in a frenzied attack, almost cleaving her in two, but one of the Ossyrian's paws morphed into a syringe, spearing into the Q'Roth's short neck. The Q'Roth sliced her limb off at the elbow, then crushed her skull, while Micah fired repeatedly at the warrior's trapezoidal head, to no avail.

In the blaze of pulse-fire, the Q'Roth's head turned to look at him, casting aside the shredded Ossyrian corpse. The three metre tall warrior staggered a pace forward, then collapsed onto two of its knees, its other four legs slamming onto the floor. Micah edged backwards and kept firing, but realised it was the Ossyrian who had killed it. The Q'Roth's head began to disintegrate, mustard-coloured acid bubbling on its face, exuding a smell of rotting eggs.

Micah got up, skirted the two carcasses and raced down the passageway. His resident, tuned to Micah's hearing and able to resolve it into sonar-like projections, detected two female humans in the corridor branching off to the left, moving away from him, about fifty metres distant. Micah accelerated, rifle ready. He knew he'd get one shot – but which would be Louise? The one in front because she always led, or the one behind because this was not her ship? He opted for the latter. They were almost at the end of the next corridor.

Taking two long strides as silently as he could, he sprung upwards and twisted, rolling in the air so as to present the smallest target, and fired at the one behind. As soon as he'd pulled the trigger he knew simultaneously that he'd hit home, and that he'd chosen the wrong Alician. Inwardly he cursed, unsure he'd get such an advantage again. Before he reached safety on the other side of his corridor, Louise had spun and fired a weapon he'd never seen before, a multi-nozzled rifle. The corridor lit up and his hand burned. Landing with a thump he searched through blotchy vision for the assault rifle he'd dropped. It sat a metre away, smoking, fused by the energy bolt

Louise had fired. Adrenaline pumped through him; he was up against his worst enemy, without a weapon.

"Your shooting is getting better, Micah." She didn't shout, the tunnel-like corridor channelling her speech perfectly.

He heard her footsteps walking towards him, unhurried, still some thirty metres away. He got to his feet and ran the short distance to the end of his corridor. A blast door stood in his way. In frustration he thumped it, the heavy metal not even registering the blow with anything but a soft thud.

"I sealed it a minute ago," Louise added, sauntering towards him.

Micah's mind raced. He looked around, but there was nothing, not even a metal bar to strike her with. In hand-to-hand combat he wouldn't stand a chance, and she had a rifle. If he dived to the other side of the corridor, he'd be dead before he got halfway. Next to the door was a panel with a Q'Roth keypad. He needed the password. If she'd used a random one he was dead. *Think!* Micah knew she was warped by hatred, and this was personal to her – she would have used something relevant to both of them.

"I'm glad you're here, Micah," she said. "It's good to tie up loose ends."

His resident showed him the translated alphabet, overlaying it on the Q'Roth keypad. It also indicated that Louise was halfway down the corridor. Trying to think straight while fighting off panic, he entered 'Louise'. Nothing happened. 'Micah'. Still nothing. *Stupid! I have to do better than this!*

"Over the years I've thought time and time again of how to kill you, Micah. Mostly it comes down to 'slowly', but I don't have much time."

Micah tried 'Vince', her former partner and lover. No dice.

"So it came down to strangling you, like I..." She paused. "But of course, shooting you will do. I just need to see the light go out of your eyes once and for all."

Micah paused. What had she been about to say? Who had she strangled? He heard her pace increase. Damn it! Who had she strangled, hated almost as much as him? She was almost there. He had seconds.

Micah thought of their last encounter at the trial, the Alician who had betrayed Louise, then tapped in H-A-N-N-A-H. There was a hiss followed by a clunk. Micah heard Louise burst into a sprint, just as the door began to move. *Come on!* It slid to the right and Micah curled around it, trying to get the Q'Roth metal between him and Louise. He grabbed the inner side of the door with his left hand, then a burning sensation exploded in his right shoulder, whipping him into the wall on the safe side of the door. Ignoring the pain he slammed his hand down on several keys in fast succession, letting his resident record the code. The door slid back, almost slicing off Louise's fingers as she tried to prevent it from closing. A satisfying clunk confirmed his safety.

He slumped onto the ground, gasping, willing his nannites to combat the electrical discharge from the pulse round threatening his heart. It was like an intense heat raging across his body, and Micah arched his back in pain, refusing to cry out through gritted teeth; he wouldn't give her the satisfaction. But the nannites created a firewall in his chest, first protecting his heart, then quenching the pulse's dissipating energy. His insides felt as if they had just been cooked, but he knew he was okay for the moment, and closed his eyes, slumping back against the blast door.

Outside there was a loud thunk, then another. Louise shouted through the wall.

"This is only a stay of execution, Micah. I brought back a little surprise in my ship. Once I've left I'm going to send this Crucible nova." She waited for a reply, but Micah didn't gratify her.

"By the way, Micah, do you like my new toy? Present from Qorall's Level Twelve Andhrakian troopers. Highly versatile, very nasty. I'm hoping to bump into somebody you care about before I leave, to try out its full range of functions."

Listening to the silence that followed, Micah clenched his teeth against the subsiding pain. After two minutes he entered the access code. The door wouldn't open. *Damn!* He began searching his resident's map for another pathway to where Louise was headed, but there was no quick route. Micah realised two things: first that he had burned out half his nannites to stop the pulse shot from killing him, and second that Louise would next encounter Petra and Chahat-Me. He thumped against the door again, this time hard enough to get a resounding echo. *Petra.* He'd got his priorities all wrong. Nursing his shoulder, he ran along the corridor in the opposite direction to where he needed to be.

* * *

Petra and Chahat-Me reached the holding enclosure along with only a dozen Ossyrians – the path to get there had been bloody. The area in front widened and Petra gazed into the sepia-tinted glass dome where at least fifty humans – none of them Genners from what she could see – stood motionless, frozen in stasis. It was like a nightmarish version of one of the snow-toys she'd seen as a child, as if all the people – including her adopted mother Antonia – were encased in glass. She wondered what the Alicians wanted with them, but mostly she simply wanted to get them the hell out of there.

One of the Ossyrians stepped forward but was immediately consumed by horizontal intersecting laser beams from the walls. A flash of crimson light triggered black splotches on Petra's retinas. When her vision cleared, she saw that not even ash remained. Clutching at her hair, she stared across to the dome and her frozen mother. "Ideas, anyone?"

Chahat-Me's head twisted to either side of the opening, to where the lasers hid, as if calculating something, then turned to two of her taller colleagues. She gripped Petra's wrist. "Leach lasers," she said, "only one target at a time." The other two Ossyrians advanced outside the inner pair, one of them placing her paw behind Petra's back. They stood at the edge of safety, and Petra was still trying to guess what a 'leach laser' was when she suddenly realised what they intended. Chahat-Me yanked her wrist as the other Ossyrian shoved Petra forward. The lasers flared. Petra landed on the floor next to Chahat-Me, her eyes blotchy from the flash, then craned her neck to see... The other two Ossyrians had sacrificed themselves. *Holy shit!* She couldn't believe what they had just done, so quick to die, without a moment's hesitation or preparation.

Chahat-Me helped her to her feet. Petra knew that saying "Thank you" was futile for the two dead, vaporised Ossyrians, but she said it anyway.

They rushed over to a Q'Roth control panel. Chahat-Me's eyes blurred as she studied it, and then began manipulating its curved, barbed controls. The sepia light in the dome faded, returning to normal. Petra walked toward her mother, who was still paralysed in stasis. The dome's glass prevented her from touching her mother's hand, so she stood next to her, remembering how as a very young girl she had waited after school for her two mothers to pick her up and take her home. Chahat-Me walked around to inspect the far side of the dome.

A sound like a buzz-saw rang out behind Petra and she turned to see a blonde woman firing a strange weapon. Orange fizzing beams arced outwards from Louise's bulbous rifle and found each of the remaining Ossyrians standing on the other side of the barrier. Several of them had managed to return fire but the woman moved quickly, her weapon neutralising the few Ossyrian shots that would have struck home. In one second, all of the Ossyrians were down. Petra didn't raise her pistol, but stared at Louise. *Chahat-Me, stay put till I can distract her!*

Louise walked towards her. *Good, keep on walking!* But she stopped just short of the protective line, uttered some words in Q'Roth, then walked straight through the kill-zone and up to Petra. Without warning, she struck Petra hard across the face with the butt of the rifle, knocking her to the floor. Petra tasted blood, her vision hazy. Louise crouched down, flinging Petra's pistol to the far side of the room. "Who are you? You're a Genner girl, aren't you?" She put down her rifle, and noticed Petra's eyes following it. "DNA-coded," Louise said, "mine."

Petra looked into her unwavering brown eyes, wondered if she could strike Louise fast enough – probably not.

Louise stood. "You remind me of someone." She stared towards the humans, now semi-frozen, their faces and hands beginning to twitch. Her sight alighted on Antonia. "My, my. Well, this is unexpected. So, who's the father?" She squatted again. "Micah, by any chance?"

Petra lunged at Louise with both fists and screamed at the same time. Louise fended off her blows with ease, and struck Petra's windpipe with the blade of her hand. Petra found she couldn't breathe, but it had created the diversion she had hoped for. Chahat-Me came from around the dome, flying at Louise, her wide-open snout uttering a death-roar, her paws extending syringes. Petra lay on the floor clutching her throat, trying to get some air into her lungs as she watched Louise twist with gymnastic precision, using her feet and arms to prevent Chahat-Me from injecting her with deadly toxins. Chahat-Me was wild, utterly feral. The pair were locked together and rolled on the floor away from Petra, back toward the entrance. Petra wheezed in a sliver of precious air and got to her feet. Louise yelled something in Q'Roth just as Chahat-Me was gaining the advantage – one of her paws slipped through Louise's left hand, slicing into her wrist. Petra searched for her pistol, couldn't see it. Louise pushed off with a foot against Chahat-Me's underbelly and rolled again, shoving Chahat-Me into the re-activated kill zone. There was a flash, and Petra stared in disbelief – her godmother was gone, nothing left. She half-screamed, half-yelled and ran toward Louise, aiming to drag them both into the kill-zone. Louise shouted the deactivation code above Petra's yell, her foot simultaneously connecting with Petra's mid- section, sending her flying, back against the dome glass, winding her.

Louise crawled to her rifle, touched a few areas on the handle with her right fingers, and then pointed at Petra and fired. Petra saw a purple flash, then realised that she'd not been killed, merely paralysed, her lungs barely managing to inhale and exhale, air rattling in her bruised throat.

Petra stared, inert like a wax doll, as Louise's left arm turned an ugly dark green colour, all the way up from her hand to her elbow, sizzling from Chahat-Me's poison. One of Louise's fingers, black and bubbling, broke off and fell to the floor. *Good, die you bitch!*

Louise manipulated the rifle's controls again and swivelled it around so it pointed at her own arm just below the shoulder. Holding Petra's gaze, lips squeezed together, she fired. It sliced off Louise's left arm like a focused-beam blowtorch, the rotting limb splatting onto the floor, fizzing as it spread out into a decaying, grey-black, bubbling mess.

Louise dropped to her knees, uttering something between a groan and a yell, propped up by her one good arm leaning on the rifle. Her other arm ended in a stump midway between shoulder and elbow. It looked angry but neatly cauterised. Louise raised her gaze to Petra, eyes narrowed and jaw clenched in a grimace. She stood, leaning against the wall behind her. Wedging the rifle under her right armpit, she fished with a shaky right hand inside a chest pocket, pulled out something, and swallowed it. Petra guessed it was trimorph. Louise swallowed. "Never did trust Ossyrians. This rifle's auto-med function serves me better."

Petra glared, staring at the line where Chahat-Me had vanished, cremated. She'd known Chahat-Me all her life, the alien who had looked after her, shared her own blood to save her after the climbing accident, shown her things she ought not to have, well above Petra's level. While others feared aliens, Petra didn't. Her gaze hardened and swung back to Louise, who was shaking but clearly recovering on the other side of the room, now sitting back against the wall with her knees up, rifle loosely angled towards the dome. Petra had always been compassionate, not sure she could kill another being even if her life depended on it. But now the lust for vengeance ignited and spread through her entire body like a dry forest catching fire. She couldn't move, and satisfied herself for the moment by relishing Louise's intense pain. It helped particularly when Louise glanced at, or felt for, her missing arm.

A tingling in Petra's fingers and toes told her the stun effects of the rifle were wearing off, and her head suddenly pitched forward as her muscles slackened. A knock behind her made her turn, awkwardly at first, to see her mother crouch down, her face at Petra's level behind the thin dome glass. Antonia wore a deep frown, wide almond eyes darting occasionally across to Louise. Petra braved a smile, and put her hand on the glass next to her mother's. Others behind the dome wall were also awakening, shuffling around. Petra recognised some of them, then one came to the fore – it was Sandy. She took up position next to Antonia, glaring pure venom at Louise.

Petra had just levered herself onto her feet when six heavily-armed Alicians arrived – three male, three female – entering from the far side of the room, skidding to a halt as they encountered Louise and an array of Ossyrian corpses.

"Report," Louise barked.

The group exchanged glances, then one of the females spoke, standing to attention. "The Command Centre has been destroyed. Sister Esma could not have survived. All the Q'Roth are dead. There are a few Mannekhi survivors and a lone human with two Ossyrians, but they are all blocked behind several layers of kill-fields – it will take them twenty minutes to get here. The rest of the Ossyrians that we know of are dead. We are all that remains of Sister Esma's crew."

"Thank you," Louise said, "That puts me in charge." She stared them down till they nodded. "Lead these humans to the Raptors three decks below, then put them back in stasis. Anyone offers the slightest resistance, kill them. Leave the Genner girl. I'll join you in ten minutes. We will rendezvous with the Q'Roth destroyer waiting outside the system." She paused. "You know," she said, as if speaking to no one in particular, "I actually liked Sister Esma." She stood straighter, enlisting the Alician group. "We will continue her mission back on Savange."

The six moved past Louise, but she stopped the last pair "Not you two. You," she said, addressing a female, "I need you to do something for me." Louise whispered in the woman's ear. The woman stared a moment at Louise, then ran to overtake the others, disappearing down a descending corridor. Louise smiled at the male. "Bring the Genner girl, and follow me."

Petra whirled around to her mother, unsure if she or anyone else inside the dome could hear any of what Louise had said. Antonia soundlessly pounded against the glass wall as the Alician male grabbed Petra and dragged her away. Petra's last view of Antonia was of her head bowed down, whitened fists against the dome wall, Sandy's hand on her shoulder.

Once they'd turned the corner, Petra spoke up. "Where are we going?"

Louise wasn't too steady on her feet. "We have ten minutes to kill."

* * *

It had taken Micah far more time than he'd wanted to find an alternative route towards the holding pen and retrieve an assault rifle from a dead Alician. His resident picked up something around the next corner but it couldn't resolve an image. Priming his weapon, he gave it all he'd got with a burst of acceleration. He saw Louise ahead and facing away from him. It took only a fraction of a second for him to decide it was her. He opened fire, aiming for her back. *This time!* But the shot passed straight through her. *Shit! Holo* –

A pulse round struck his legs and he went down, another shot hitting his rifle, making it burn red-hot so that he had to let go of it as he crashed to the deck. The hologram of Louise disappeared, as did a chameleogram that was masking the real Louise. She stood legs splayed, the bulky weapon in her hand. Micah was stunned to see her left arm cut off just below the shoulder.

"Hello again, Micah. I wanted you on your knees before I executed you. I also wanted to see if you'd shoot me in the back. Nice to see you've finally grown up. Vince would have been proud of you."

Micah's legs spasmed with cramps as the pulse charge fizzed around them. His resident was trying to regain control over them via the neural shunt. He wondered if his legs would still respond. Normally their neural pathways would be out of action after a pulse hit, but maybe not with the Ossyrian fix in his spine. He had no weapon except surprise; Louise didn't know about the shunt, nor his nannites. He had to stall, give the others time to release the captives. He needed something to ensure she'd respond.

"Would Vince be proud of *you*, Louise?" He didn't know how she felt about Vince after all these years, but if it was anything like before, he expected to experience sudden pain. He raised his head.

She looked relaxed, as always. "You continually underestimate me, Micah. I stay one step ahead of you." She addressed someone around the corner. "Bring her."

Micah's questioning frown vanished as soon as an Alician male marched Petra into view. The man held a pistol to Petra's throat, while another gun sat idle in a side holster. Micah eyed it.

Louise waved her rifle vaguely in Petra's direction. "You dare to ask me about Vince, when it was your plan that got him killed? Does this little Genner bitch mean anything to you, Micah? Because I'd really like you to know how I felt after I lost him."

Petra looked fragile but not wounded. Micah guessed Chahat-Me hadn't made it. Petra looked into his eyes, slightly shaking her head. But he knew Louise better, and she was right, he had underestimated her. Again.

Micah struggled to his knees and readied his resident, hoping his legs would work; he gauged the distance. He stared at Petra, his peripheral vision taking in the man behind her. He instructed his remaining nannites to speed up his reactions, and about thirty per cent of them to steel his left hand. He would have only one attempt; this effort would expend his remaining nannites.

"This girl means everything to me," he said. Time slowed down for Micah.

Louise laughed, began to shake her head, and was about to say something. The Alician male momentarily took his eyes off Micah to glance at Louise. Micah triggered the command, and the shunt sent a way-beyond-tolerance signal to his legs. His thigh and calf muscles almost burst as his feet found purchase and his legs kicked off with frog- like speed and power, springing toward Petra, his left fist connecting with the Alician male's forehead like a hammer, snapping his neck, while Micah's right hand wrenched the pistol from his grip. As they toppled – for Micah in slow motion – he fired behind him to where Louise should still be, but at the same moment another shot lit up the room.

He rolled away from Petra and came up in a crouch, trying to hold the pistol that burned red-hot in his hand. He clicked the trigger but nothing happened, and he flung it from his scalded palm. Louise was on one knee, clutching her scorched left side, grimacing with pain. He didn't know why she wasn't flat on the ground. She stared at the blackened rifle, tried to fire it three times at Micah, but his shot had clearly hit the rifle on its way to Louise. "Sonofabitch," she said, between clenched teeth.

She turned the rifle around and aimed it towards her wound, and for one brief moment Micah prayed she was going to kill herself. But the rifle emitted a blue glow, and he realised it was somehow healing her.

Micah focused on Louise. He wanted to rush her, strangle her with his bare hands while she was wounded. But his legs refused to cooperate; the shunt was either fused or temporarily out of action. "Petra, are you okay?" he asked. The Alician male's twisted body was still.

Petra tried to suppress a groan. "Please just kill her, Uncle."

Without taking his eyes off Louise he crawled toward Petra, his legs dragging behind him. "Where did she get you?"

Petra coughed, clearly in agony. "Belly. Let me watch her die."

He searched for the Alician's back-up pistol, checking back to see that Louise was still in as bad shape as he was.

Louise glared at him through strands of blonde hair, sweat breaking out on her face. "I die, she dies," she rasped.

He found the short pistol tucked under the male's hip. Propping himself up on one elbow, he checked the charge, ramped it up to maximum. "You've both been hit by pulse charges; you're both going to die. But I'm going to grant my niece her last wish." He aimed at Louise's head, his finger on the trigger.

Louise tapped her rifle. "I can save her with this." Louise stood up, partly doubled over.

Micah stared. There should be no way she could stand after a pulse round to the body. He glanced at her rifle, his pistol arm steady.

Louise tossed her head back, swallowed. "You want her to live, you throw your gun over there. I save her, I leave."

"No!" Petra groaned. "She killed Chahat-Me right in front of me!" Her last word choked off as she lay shivering with pain on the floor.

Micah waved the pistol at Louise. "I can't trust you, Louise. You'll just kill us both afterwards."

Louise had regained her composure, the sweat dried from her face. "Your choice, Micah. Your little friend has about twenty seconds of life left. Then you get to feel what I've lived with for the last eighteen years after I lost Vince." She looked him in the eye. "I still miss him, you know."

It was the flash of sadness in her look that convinced him she just might be telling the truth. He glanced down at Petra. He'd lost too many people through the years. He imagined his niece dead, cold, still, silent, then with a growl tossed the pistol aside. Louise angled the rifle towards Petra, stroked her thumb across a patch on its handle, and pulled the trigger. A blue glow encased Petra, then shut off.

Micah bent down towards her, placed his hand on her shoulder. Petra was crying.

Louise dropped the rifle and walked away, leaning on the wall for support with her remaining arm. "Relish the brief time you have left, Micah," she said, and turned the corner.

He recalled Louise had brought back a 'surprise'. No doubt she intended to leave and then blow up the Crucible behind her. That was her style.

Micah cradled Petra in his arms, but although still weak, she thumped his chest as he held her. "You... idiot! You should have killed her. She'll take the hostages. Go after her!"

But although his legs were beginning to recover, he knew he could barely stand let alone walk, his muscles traumatized after that lunge to save Petra. He held her tight, thinking about what he had done. He'd wanted to kill Louise for so many reasons, for betraying humanity, for nearly killing Antonia, for sending two thousand men, women and children into the heart of a sun, and for Hannah, eighteen years ago. And for the crimes Louise was yet to commit, including stealing the human captives away. But Petra had been like the daughter he'd never had, and she was alive, her heart was still beating, her flesh was still warm, and that was all that mattered. She cried some more, and he held her.

After several minutes, two Ossyrians arrived with two Alician prisoners. One of the Ossyrians indicated that they should kill them, but Micah shook his head – he needed to know what this had all been about, where the human captives would be taken. A minute later Kilaney arrived, looking like hell, using his rifle as a crutch. Four Mannekhi accompanied him.

"Micah, you look like –"

"Status?" he said, interrupting someone who far outranked him in every way.

Kilaney raised his chin. "All the Q'Roth are dead. Planet-cutter operations have been terminated, but rockfall on Esperia is in forty-five minutes. This is Commander Xenic, by the way," he said, nodding to the gaunt Mannekhi, "and all that remains of his crew. They're on our side now." He stroked his stubbled chin. "Long story."

Micah struggled to his feet. "We have to go to the Raptor hangar while there's still time." He answered Kilaney's raised eyebrow. "Louise is leaving us a going-away present."

While they made their way along twisting corridors and down several levels via spiral ramps, Petra addressed him sternly. "You made a serious tactical error, Uncle."

Micah didn't stop or slow down. *And I'm going to pay for it very shortly.* "One step at a time. First we have to prevent an environmental catastrophe." He imagined an avalanche of billions of tons of rock sliding towards Esperia.

Micah and the others reached the hangar where three Raptors sat, aside three empty berths; Louise had escaped with the captives. One of the Raptors had a large missile slung underneath it, its external casing glowing violet. Armed, no doubt waiting until Louise and the others had steered a safe distance away.

Kilaney, Xenic and Micah walked over to it. "Any ideas?" Micah said, fully expecting none.

"Only the obvious one," Kilaney offered. "We get the hell out of here."

But as they checked each remaining Raptor they quickly found they had been put into sleep mode – it would take twenty minutes for them to fire up. As the others tried to speed up the start routines, Micah double- backed to Louise's, the one carrying the Nova bomb. Petra saw him and shouted after him but he ignored her. *I let Louise live. This is my responsibility.*

He sealed the hatch and got to the cockpit. His resident translated the Q'Roth console displays, and he powered up the ship. His resident also detected a countdown for the missile: 64 seconds.

On one of the monitors he saw Kilaney and Petra running over but he gunned the thrusters and the Raptor pitched forward, initially scraping along the hangar floor before he got used to the controls. A holo appeared showing fine, white striations in front of him. He had no idea what they were but decided it was wise to avoid hitting one.

Kilaney came on line. "Micah, get the hell out of there!"

"Look after Petra," he replied, and shut off comms; he needed to concentrate and get far away fast. He snagged a filament and heard a grinding noise then a thunk, neither of which sounded good. His resident supplied the countdown so he didn't have to look away from the holomap as he slalomed through the field of filaments into the void of space.

45 seconds.

His hands were steady, not shaking as he thought they might. In his mind images flashed of Blake, his parents, Antonia, Petra, and Sandy. That last face lingered. So much he should have said in the past eighteen years. "Goodbye everyone," he whispered.

30 seconds.

Comms re-activated on an emergency channel, and a voice barged into his thoughts. "Micah, is that you?"

The man's voice was oddly familiar, but Micah couldn't place it; it sounded synthetic.

"Who is –?"

"It's Pierre, Micah. No time to explain. You must eject now!"

20 seconds.

Micah nearly gashed the ship open on a knot of filaments. The resident said he was far enough from the Crucible.

15 seconds.

"Micah, I said eject!"

He looked around feverishly. "I don't see how!"

"Just blow the hatch, you have very little time!"

He swung around to the cockpit hatch release lever.

10 seconds.

"But I don't have a helmet."

A deep, gruff voice he'd never heard before, nor wanted to again, bellowed at him. "LEAVE SHIP NOW!"

Micah grabbed the release.

5 seconds.

He took a breath, squeezed his eyes shut and yanked the lever downwards.

For an instant he heard the roaring noise of decompression followed by an implosive silence. Stinging lashed every millimetre of his flesh, at once both boiling hot and freezing cold. His lungs ballooned inside him, his throat expanded and his eyes bulged inside his head, his elbows and knees bloating with excruciating pain. Air burst from his mouth in an anguished scream that made no sound whatsoever. Then there *was* sound, something snapping closed, cocooning him in darkness, a fraction of a second before incredible brightness flared through his still-closed eyelids.

"You can open your eyes, Micah, you're safe now, you're on our ship. Another second..."

Micah's eyes however, were frosted shut. "Pierre?" He reached out and a cool metal hand took his own. He gripped it with both his hands and squeezed hard.

"Fix him quickly," Pierre said, though Micah couldn't see whom Pierre addressed, and he didn't much care.

The Ice Pick dropped Micah off into the hangar and left straightaway.

Kilaney, Petra and the others were all huddled together.

"Nice firework display," Kilaney said, then placed a hand on Micah's shoulder. "Good job, Micah."

Micah wasted no time. Pierre had told him the Crucible was highly unstable, a space wreck in progress. "Commander Xenic," he said, pointing to one of the warmed-up Raptors, "take that one with your crew, we'll take the other one. We'll all need the tripwire detection algorithm."

Xenic nodded, clearly happy to be given his own ship.

"To what end, Micah? What about the rockfall?" Kilaney asked.

Micah glanced to Petra. "Pierre said he would take care of it."

Petra's eyes grew large. "Did you say Pierre? You don't mean...?"

She couldn't complete the sentence. She'd never met her father, never had the opportunity to even speak to him. Micah held out his hand. Petra moved to Micah's side, hardly breathing.

"I want to watch him... my father," she said, swallowing. Her eyes locked onto Micah's, making it clear she wouldn't take "no" for an answer.

Micah turned to Kilaney and the others. "Change of plan. You're all in the other Raptor. We'll be a while."

Kilaney was the last to board the Raptor. "Don't be too long, you two. Well," he said, "I can't wait to see the expression on Blake's face now that I look younger than him."

Micah and Petra sat side by side in the cockpit, her hand in his. Far away a relentless landslide of rock and dust slid through space toward Esperia. But all the way across its leading edge it was being shaved into a bright swathe of light as a small ship moved almost too fast for the eye to follow, erasing the moonfall's wave-front, leaving glittering sparks in its place.

Petra's head was on Micah's shoulder. "Thank you, Uncle," she said. "Thank you for saving me so I could see this, so I can finally meet my father."

Micah said nothing, just squeezed his arm around her a little tighter.

She pulled away, looked at him hard. "Uncle, despite what I said earlier, don't beat yourself up about letting Louise escape."

He frowned. "Easier said, Petra, and you know it. Antonia – "

"Would thank you, and you know *that*. Kat, too." she said, quieter.

"But you have to get Antonia back, and the others. You know that don't you?"

Micah nodded, and she settled back into his shoulder.

He thought about it. Strategically, letting Louise escape with the prisoners was a disastrous decision. Kilaney and Blake should bawl him out for it, though they probably wouldn't. But together, they'd held Esperia safe. That was the main thing for now.

Silently he swore to get the captives back or die trying, even if he had to damned well do it alone. It would mean going to the Alician homeworld. And why not, he thought. We've always been on the defensive, first on Earth, then Eden and now Esperia. Time to take the battle to them.

Pierre's ship suddenly zipped to intercept a massive boulder the size of a mountain travelling faster than the rest. The Ice Pick vaporised it neatly then resumed at the wave front. "Impressive," Micah said, "nice save."

Petra squeezed Micah's palm, with a gleam in her eyes Micah hadn't seen for years.

CHAPTER 26 – CRACKED SKY

The ground crunched underneath Micah's boots as he made the steep climb up Silent Hill, his breath frosting in the chill air. In the pre-dawn light he was unable to see if anyone else had arrived at what had become a dawn ritual. The sound of a Nightjar, one of the few species of bird rescued from Earth, made him look up, catching sight of the three Kalarash ships close together a kilometre above Esperantia and Shimsha. Pausing, he took in their sleek, elongated crossbow shapes. The three silhouettes resembled the beginnings of an Escher mosaic.

But the Kalarash had arrived too late. Sandy, Antonia, the others... taken to be used like lab-rats; Gabriel, Virginia and Chahat-Me dead. He halted his ascent, squatted down, and dug his fingers into the earth, his breathing laboured. Logically, it wasn't his fault. And yet... He'd let Louise slip away again. She'd never rest until mankind was gone. Micah knew what he had to do. But he would have to hide it from the others, including Kalaran if he got to meet him. Subduing dark thoughts, he stood up and continued his way.

He stared up again to the ships. It was too early to see the colours of their hulls, but he could just make out that one was blue-green – Kalaran's – the other violet-red, housing Jen, Rashid and Dimitri, and the third red- green, Hellera's ship. His eyes slipped back to the stony terrain in front of him; he'd see Jen soon enough at the War Council meeting, hopefully to get some explanations.

On the hill's summit, as he'd expected, a dozen people stood between waist-high alabaster tombstones, and he again felt the heaviness he'd been unable to shake off despite it being eight days since the mass funeral. For him and the others, this daily vigil was important not only to honour the dead, but because the deceased were somehow a link with the living captives kidnapped by Louise, already on their way back to Savange.

Without being conscious of it, Micah went straight towards the plots of Gabriel and Virginia. Small rocks laced with quartz delineated each rectangular grave, but a few days earlier Petra had removed the stones separating those two, so that they merged into one. Everyone understood.

Ramires was already there, Petra kneeling on the damp earth, Blake over at Marcus' grave. A few other Genners and Steaders whispered around the buried ashes of loved ones. Micah placed a hand on Petra's shoulder, and without looking up she laid her fingers on top of his. As one, all those present lifted their gaze as dawn arrived and the sky shifted from dark lapis to aquamarine. Micah drew in a long breath, still not used to what he saw. The sky was cracked, crisscrossed with hundreds of gossamer white lines, as if it had been shattered. He knew they only witnessed a fraction of the extent of the Shrell filaments that stretched all the way to the periphery of Esperia's solar system. Initially invisible, they had been transformed – energized – by the Kalarash ships as soon as they had arrived three days earlier. He didn't know why. It was one of the items on his list as soon as Jen returned.

But he and Ramires had the same priority on their agenda – they wanted a ship to go to Savange, to recover the captives, and preferably eliminate Louise and the rest of the Alicians. Chances of success were remote at best. But since the battle for Esperia had ended, there had been a change in the Steader and Genner populace – there was now far more mutual respect and collaboration. Every day and through the night Genners and their parents gathered in the Monofaith, and... just talked to each other. He'd seen several trios of parents and a Genner child where the young boy or girl was patiently explaining something complex, breaking it down till they grasped it. Petra had been instrumental in this social rapprochement, working with both the Genner and Steader sides, arguing that each had something to offer, that Genners needed emotional intelligence and empathy, too, if they weren't to end up like the Alicians.

One unanticipated outcome from recent events had been a public outpouring of grief, and repeated demands that the sixty captives be rescued. So Micah had heard, when the Alicians had come to take them, many stalwart and well-known citizens had come forward, volunteering themselves rather than letting other more frail or fearful men and women be taken. Micah suspected that had been the case with Antonia and Sandy. The Alicians would have accepted such propositions, yielding stronger stock for their genetic extractions. His thoughts shifted to those two women and their predicament, wondering what exactly had become of them. According to the two Alicians Kilaney had caught, they would be kept alive, though the conditions of their imprisonment were unclear. Micah realised he was grinding the soil with his boot; Petra saw it too, and squeezed his hand, reminding him that this was a burial ground. He stored his anger for another time and place. Blake came over, standing close to him and Ramires. "It's time," he said. Petra got up and led the way back down to Esperantia, and the War Council. Micah trudged down the escarpment, his mood gloomy. He had no doubt the Council would support the venture, even if it was purely a political judgement reflecting the emotion of the moment. But the ones they really had to convince were the Kalarash. Only they could grant them their wish by furnishing them a warship for the voyage, but he couldn't think of one reason why Kalaran or Hellera should oblige. But he would find one.

The Council Chamber, one of the few structures untouched by the Alician raid, was bustling for this time of the morning, hundreds milling about the plaza outside, the smell of fresh flatbreads and clove-spiced Cafarino softening the chill morning air. As the four walked towards the entrance, the chatter around them subsided.

Kat stood in the arched doorway. Micah had barely seen her since her return in the Raptor with the Mannekhi female, Aramisk; Kat spent most of her time since then with Pierre and Petra, and Micah let them be. She kissed her daughter on both cheeks, and then, for the first time ever, gave Micah a hug. She'd not spoken a word to him since she'd heard the news about Antonia, but now she whispered into his ear.

"Get her back, Micah, get a ship from them, no matter what it takes."

She released him. Micah held her gaze a while. Petra had already relayed what Kat had said about Louise's behaviour during these past two years, her actions and decisions increasingly unpredictable, her moods full of darkness, and that she was working for Qorall. Louise was more dangerous than ever.

As they were about to go inside, there was a flash behind them. Where they had walked moments before were three figures: the reptilian Ranger Ukrull, the flow-metal Pierre, silver except for his normal, brown eyes, and Jen. He was struck again by the fact that she hadn't aged due to relativity effects: mousy-blonde hair skirting a shy face with its ski- jump nose and wary, sideways-looking bottle-green eyes. She wore a tan jumpsuit that didn't flatter her figure, and evidently didn't care, which meant she was also more self-assured than when he'd known her before. He reminded himself that she'd been with Kalaran for that year, and almost certainly knew far more than anyone else present, save possibly Ukrull, as to what the hell was going on.

Pierre walked up to Petra and Kat and the three of them embraced as if alone in their home. These past ten days Petra had spent a lot of time with her father, who was apparently better emotionally equipped than when he'd left. Pierre had told him it had been a gift from another Kalarash called Hellera. Ukrull swept past them with his powerful lizard- like gait, his scaly muscular tail flicking from side to side making people stumble out of his way, a smell of rotting grass in his wake.

Jen approached. "Micah, we're ready."

He wasn't quite sure who 'we' included, hoping she represented Kalaran in some way. They all turned and followed her through to the chamber. Micah knew that her two companions Dimitri and Rashid had not yet come down to the planet. Apparently, teleportation was possible, but was incredibly difficult except across very short distances in the vacuum of space, and consumed vast amounts of energy, even for the Kalarash. Their massive ships were said to need a day to recharge after each single teleportation. Blake harboured a suspicion that one or two of the spiders had been taken up to the ships, though Jen denied any knowledge of it.

Vasquez and Kilaney were already seated along with the two remaining Ossyrians and the Mannekhi Commander Xenic. Everyone took their seats, except Micah and Jen. Micah waited until a hush settled over the War Council representatives in the inner circle of twelve, and the packed audience seated behind them.

"Jennifer," he said, "please..." He'd prepared a short speech, but suddenly thought better of it. "Just tell us what is going on."

She pulled something out of her pocket and tossed what looked like a handful of dust and glitter into the air. It didn't fall, instead spreading out as it took the shape of the Milky Way. She had everyone's attention. "Here," she said, moving to a single point of light, "is where we are today." As her finger approached the single mote, that area of the 'map' expanded, and they saw a small solar system: Esperia's sun as an orange ball, a small grey uninhabited planet closer to their local sun, their home Esperia, and one gas giant and an asteroid belt further out.

"This was before. And this is now." She snapped her fingers and the Esperian system suddenly looked as if it had been encased in a   ball of glass and dropped repeatedly on the floor; cracks and fractures everywhere. "As some of you have heard, the Shrell were sent here to poison space. Qorall knew the spider population represented a threat, though he did not, and still does not know the nature of that threat. By poisoning space he ensured their containment and ultimate extinction on Esperia –"

Blake leant forward and interrupted. He was the closest the spiders had to a representative on this Council. "Are you going to tell us what threat they *do* pose?"

Jen stared at Blake, and Micah noticed again how she'd changed from when he'd known her eighteen years ago – more confident, but also less egotistical.

"No," she said. "I honestly don't know if they constitute a weapon, only that they are important to Kalaran's plans to defeat Qorall." She continued. "Louise had been tasked by Qorall with destroying Esperia, but she failed, thanks to the valiant efforts of many of you here today, and a few no longer here." Her voice almost caught, but she masked it by clearing her throat.

Micah knew Jen had been very cut up about Gabriel – in fact no one else had known what had happened to Gabriel and Sister Esma until Jen had arrived five days ago with the news. Petra had been inconsolable for two days, Ramires tight-lipped but proud. Micah felt he owed Gabriel a debt he could never repay.

Jen regained her composure. "However, Kalaran also wanted the Shrell to proceed, because, you see, Qorall's back-up plan was this." She tapped an apparently empty region of space just outside Esperia's system and Micah's breathing shallowed. A slug-like creature undulated, its black hide glistening with deep blue crackles of energy. A darker mouth opened, revealing a hint of scarlet fire deep inside its body.

Kilaney shifted in his seat. "Dark worms, our worst nightmare. We still have no idea how to kill them."

"The Kalarash do," Jen said. "However..." her forefinger traced a circle around the Esperian system and the image enlarged again.

Shit. Micah saw hundreds of worms patrolling the perimeter. He guessed Kalaran's strategy, even as Jen confirmed it.

"Once the Shrell had done their work," she said, "Kalaran's ship and the other one we brought back, together with Hellera's, were able to energise the Shrell network into a defence grid. Before, the worms would have cut through the strands like a whale ignoring a fishing line. Now... they cannot pass."

Micah spoke what he presumed others were also thinking. "Then we, too, are confined here." *Again. And we've only just come out of Quarantine!*

Ukrull grunted something to himself. Jen glanced at him, then carried on. "Not entirely, but getting in and out will be dangerous. Now Qorall knows there are three Kalarash ships here, he will focus efforts on Esperia."

Micah watched Jen carefully. *There's something she's not telling us.*

He walked towards the map. "Show us Savange," he said.

All in the circle leaned forward, Kat and Ramires rising from their seats.

Jen touched a far-flung region of the floating star-map and a blue- mauve planet blossomed out of the star-map. Micah's brow widened, then furrowed. It was beautiful, rich in water and foliage compared to Esperia. Glinting lights told him there were several small but advanced cities and infrastructure scattered along the oceanic edge of the main continent. A single large orbital station hung above the largest patch of light, presumably where they did commerce with other races. They had come a long way in eighteen years, undoubtedly aided by their Q'Roth patrons. He clenched his jaw – it wasn't damned fair! He felt his blood pressure rising. The fact that Sister Esma had been killed wasn't nearly enough consolation. "Close it," he said, his voice stone. Jen obliged, Savange collapsing back into a small point of light.

She raised her voice above the growing chatter. "Here are Qorall's forces." Half the stars in the galaxy – excluding the central orb of light where the stars were too densely-packed for any sustainable intelligent life – turned red, and on a galactic scale they were already close to Esperia. Savange, in contrast, was far away in neutral space.

"This is what Kalaran predicts will happen next," Jen said. Qorall's wave front held off from Esperia but continued around it, like a closing fist. The far edges of the circular front missed Savange, though not by much.

Micah interrupted. "We need a ship, Jen, to go and get our people back. One of those hanging above us right now would do, or else something pretty damned close." Others around him nodded and voiced assent.

She pursed her lips; evidently she had been expecting the question. But she said nothing.

Micah was about to speak when he found he was somewhere else.

He stood on a giant marble, swirling grenadine beneath his feet, mixed with crystalline violet and vermillion striations like blood vessels. Under a pea-green sky he saw other globes, none of them moving. Micah guessed where he was.

"I thought teleportation used up a lot of energy." Micah said it to the wind, not expecting a human voice right behind him, especially not *that* one.

"But then you ain't really here, Micah."

Spinning around he saw Zack standing two metres away: not the Transpar version, but the original burly friend he'd briefly known and cherished after the fall of Earth.

"Zack is that –"

"No, Micah, he's gone, but I chose this form – forgive me – because you trusted him, and I need you to listen carefully."

Micah wanted to shake his hand, even hug Zack, but Micah knew he was being manipulated. He stood back. "I'm listening."

Zack squatted. "To defeat Qorall requires an intricate strategy. A rescue mission to Savange would risk everything."

Micah squatted too. "I was expecting Jen – or in this case, you –   to say that. The bigger picture, sacrifices must be made, etc." Anger simmered inside him, stoked up by the images of Savange. He tried to keep his voice even. "I – and we, the people of Esperia – don't care. Help us to do this if you expect cooperation from us."

Zack's bald head swung in Micah's direction and gave him a searching look. Micah saw through those eyes and Zack's expression the sad wisdom of a truly ancient being, one who had seen it all before, countless times. "Micah, is it worth risking trillions of beings' lives, possibly mine as well, in order to bring sixty souls back, when they may well perish here anyway? The Alicians will side with Qorall under Louise's leadership. Your friends may be safer there."

Micah stood up and walked away a few paces, biting down on his lip. He turned around, folding his arms. "A ship, that's all we're asking. One ship. We can't desert them. We've already lost too much." Micah felt his muscles tense; he wanted to strike something, but there was nothing to hit. "First, our entire race is almost extinguished. Then we barely make do on a difficult world, scratching out a living on an almost barren planet, and then we're attacked again, all the while co-locating with a species we can't relate to who obviously have more importance in your grand scheme than us. We're just a damned pawn –" He stopped himself, aware he was ranting, unfolded his arms and put his hands in his pockets. The real Zack wouldn't be impressed, even if he understood Micah's anger. Kalaran had indeed chosen the best personality from Micah's mind for this 'interview'. Micah tried a different tack. "If they had been killed, or were going to be killed, it... it would be easier in some respects." He withdrew his hands, and pointed away from him. "But they're not dead. They're out there, they'll be kept alive for decades as genetic factories, allowing the Alicians to procreate so their progeny can come back one day and finish off the job they started." Micah softened his voice, stared directly into Zack's eyes, trying to reach the super-being behind the façade. "If one of yours was taken – a Kalarash – wouldn't you go after them?"

Zack stood up, gazed out to one of the distant spheres, and spoke. "What do you think?"

Micah was nonplussed until he heard another voice, distant, distinctly female, an unholy choir whose intonations were all off-key. It didn't sound human.

"Show him," the unseen female said. "He needs to see it."

Zack pointed to the floor beneath Micah's feet. As Micah looked down, the swirling cocktail haze cleared into a black space. But it wasn't empty. He saw a ball, dull ochre in colour, drifting towards a green planet. Micah's resident supplied a name and details for the indigenous species – Wagramanian, Level Seven, forest-dwelling tripeds, famed artists, fierce soldiers. He recalled that this race were to be the relief for Esperia in three months' time. Micah saw gigantic ships like indigo fir trees on intercept towards the ball. But he guessed they should turn about and flee.

"They never run," Zack said. "Even when they know what is coming."

Micah watched the ships fire at the ball, but all that happened was that it brightened and grew fractionally. Several ships rammed it, but were absorbed as if it was liquid. His resident – no doubt being controlled by Kalaran – told him that that was exactly what it was: fluid organic metal, but highly processed: intelligent; nascent; hungry. Micah shivered.

As the indigenous population realised they could not stop the ball and that it was on a collision course, massive transports lifted off from the planet's surface. But even those on the opposite side of the planet were caught in powerful gravimetric tides that either sent them plummeting back to the ground or tore them apart, spilling their occupants into space.

The ball broke into a shower of billions of droplets that rained down on the planet. The view zoomed in. The inhabitants ran, hid. But each time one was touched by a droplet, the poor wretch froze, transforming, silently screaming before their skin turned an ochre colour and their eyes turned blood red. It worked fast.

"They are Qorall's now," Zack said, head bowed.

Where the drops touched the ground, they dispersed into gas, spreading faster. Their former kinsmen hunted those Wagramanians who went into hiding, until the entire population was Qorall's. The floor resumed its cloudlike haze, and Micah was relieved.

"This is what is coming, Micah. It has taken Qorall this long to perfect the weapon, to adapt it to the template underpinning this galaxy's species. But from here on his progress will accelerate." Zack looked beyond Micah, behind him. "Micah, it is best if you don't turn around." The other voice sounded to Micah as if it was right behind him. The skin on the back of his neck crawled. He'd had a debriefing from Pierre, and guessed who or what was speaking; Hellera, the other Kalarash. "The Scintarelli are still ours. I will send a ship. I must attend others, try to protect them." There was a pause. "I am glad you came back, Kalaran."

There was a sudden stillness behind Micah, and he knew she was gone, if she'd ever really been there at all.

Zack's heavy eyes tracked back to Micah. "You will have your ship. But you will have an additional task, one that must take priority." Zack walked a few paces away and beckoned. Micah wasn't that surprised by what he saw walking towards him. The four-legged spider stood next to Zack/Kalaran, who stroked its black, furry top fondly. The spider's communication band soothed a tranquil turquoise, a colour Micah had never seen on any of them before.

Zack's gaze returned to Micah. "The one called Louise sent one of her crew to kidnap a spider and take it with her just before she left. Quite a smart move. It will be a strong bargaining chip with Qorall." Zack's eyes grew fiery. "You must bring it back, Micah, or it must be utterly destroyed, so that nothing remains. Not a single strand of its DNA can be allowed to fall into Qorall's hands."

Micah thought about Qorall's weapon, transforming races into his own. He imagined those ochre balls spreading across the galaxy like a virus. When he had talked to Pierre, Kat had been there, too, and said that Qorall favoured biological weaponry. Something clicked in Micah's head.

"An antibody. The spiders, they're like an antibody, aren't they? They can't be transformed by Qorall."

Zack's face did not react. "The ship you will have is far faster than the Q'Roth destroyer carrying your friends and this one's brother." Zack patted the spider. "You will arrive a few days after they reach Savange. Louise cannot contact Qorall while onboard the Q'Roth vessel." Zack approached Micah, within arm's reach. "You will have three days for your rescue attempt. If you have not succeeded by then, I will send another, and it will be best if you are no longer there."

Micah's mind raced. "How will you know if I've succeeded?"

"You will have a Hohash onboard. Besides, Hellera is giving you a sentient ship."

Micah sensed an opportunity. "If we do succeed..." Micah turned and paced. It had been on his mind the past few weeks; no, the past eighteen years. He faced Zack. "Will you overturn the Tla Beth ruling on us, that all our children, all future generations have to be upgraded?"

Zack smiled. "This is a first, I believe. You don't *want* elevation?" Micah held his course.

"We want the choice. Some – including me – now feel the price may be too high."

"It will be difficult for your people without such advantage."

"We'll manage."

"Very well – *if* you succeed, Micah. Now, is all that I have said to you clear?"

"Yes, and... thank you." Micah gave a small bow.

"Good, we are finished here. We will not meet again." He paused. "It is customary when we meet someone to offer a gift in these circumstances."

"You're giving me a ship," Micah said.

"Hellera is giving you a ship."

Zack's eyes closed, his face relaxing, and suddenly he looked so much like the real Zack again. He beamed at Micah and held out his hand. Micah took a cautious pace towards Zack, and shook the warm, fleshy palm. Zack pulled him into a bear hug, then let go. "Well, look at you, Micah, starting to go grey!"

All the things Micah wanted to say collided, and got stuck in his throat. Before, when they'd lost Zack to the trial, there were two words he'd not had time to say.

Zack grinned, laid his hands on Micah's shoulders. "Don't sweat it, Micah, it was for the best. Hey, make sure you toast that bitch Louise next time, okay?"

Micah found himself back in the Council Chamber, his lips apart as if about to speak. He closed his mouth. *Goodbye, Zack.* All eyes were on him, though it seemed barely a second had passed since he'd 'left' the Council chamber. He collected himself, and held up his hand until there was silence.

Jen gave him a knowing look – she'd obviously had similar encounters with Kalaran, and had presumably been forewarned of the result of this one. She spoke. "You will have your ship in three weeks, Micah. Pick five crew."

She left, followed by a bored-looking Ukrull. In the ensuing noise Micah found Kat and Ramires next to him. "Of course," he said, "with pleasure."

"Good," Kat said, "as otherwise that ship would be looking for a new captain."

He smiled, glanced over to Petra, but she looked away; he'd have to talk to her later. Micah moved over instead to consult Blake and the others. By the time he'd finished, Petra was gone.

Micah found her at the top of Hazzards' Ridge. She sat on the coarse grass, her legs stretched out in front of her, propped up on straightened arms.

"I'd have signed you up if you'd have asked," Micah offered.

"Liar," she said. "Anyway, I have other plans."

He squatted next to her. This was the only vantage point from which to take in both Esperantia and Shimsha. He thought of the spiders, all this time Kalaran's secret weapon.

"So, who's your crew, besides my mother and Ramires?" Her voice had an edge.

"Well, not Kilaney, he plans to work with Xenic to bring the Mannekhi over to the Kalarash side."

She idly plucked at the ground, uprooting tufts of grass.

Micah studied her. "Blake wants to stay here, to work with the spiders, he says he owes it to Glenda."

She stared straight ahead.

"Vasquez will lead the militia here, and run things – "

"With me," she said flatly.

Micah cocked his head. "Excuse me?"

She got up, dusted herself off, and gazed towards Silent Hill on the other side of the valley. "We Genners have been pretty stupid, considering how intelligent we are. I'm going to act as Genner liaison on the Council. It's what Gabriel and Virginia would have wanted." She turned to him, eyes fiery and misty at the same time. "I felt so useless on that ship. Louise killed Chahat-Me right in front of my eyes..."

Micah stood. "Petra, there was nothing – "

"I'm no warrior, I know that now. But here... people listen to me." Her voice quietened. "Maybe I can make a difference. I've studied you over the years, how you ran the place."

"So, you can avoid all my mistakes." He smiled, and her strained look eased off, but only a little. She said no more. Micah decided on the direct approach. "Why are you angry with me, Petra?"

"Tell me your crew, Uncle, and stop saying who *isn't* going or we'll be here all night. I'm presuming your selection technique was not entirely a process of elimination?"

That was better, a return to form. "As well as Kat and Ramires, I've invited an Ossyrian, Vashta, especially as we learned the Alicians are planning to use Ossyrian genetic techniques on the captives. One of Xenic's people, a woman named Aramisk, whom Kat trusts. She'll prove useful as there are Mannekhi outposts between here and Savange." He paused. She was looking away from him, trying to mask the tension inside.

"That leaves one," she said.

He realised the source of her angst. "Rashid," he said. "He's been with Kalaran for a year – "

Petra turned her head, her face a mixture of confusion and relief. "What?"

He stood, walked up to her, and placed his hands on her shoulders. "I would not have chosen Pierre."

She tried to brush his hands away. "You should have, he's the obvious choice: Level Ten, hangs out with Rangers and Tla Beth. Christ, Micah, you're a bloody fool." She said it with tenderness.

He pulled her towards him. "I don't know how long Pierre will stay with you, Petra, before the Kalarash call on him again, but I hope to bring both your mothers back before then."

Micah had been something of a father toward her, but Pierre was back, and Micah wanted Petra to experience the real thing. "He's been looking for you, Petra, and you still have a few weeks before Kat leaves with me."

She nodded. "First, I have to ask you something."

Micah had the feeling it wasn't going to be an easy question. "What are your real plans when you get to Savange?" She stared straight into his eyes.

Micah checked himself. He'd been worried that Kalaran, Jen or Blake might ask him; he'd not expected it from Petra. In the past few weeks he'd done a lot of thinking, and had come to an unassailable conclusion. He had faced Louise and Sister Esma before, and had learned enough about them to know how Alicians were wired. Kilaney and Ukrull had confirmed it when they questioned the two Alician prisoners. Kilaney hadn't gotten much information out of them, whereas Ukrull had, though they hadn't survived his interrogation. Micah now had detailed schematics of Savange and intel on where the captives were to be held, as well as the planet's defences. But both Kilaney and Ukrull had confirmed the innate Alician hatred for humanity, the desire to erase mankind at any cost. The galaxy might be a big place, and it was tempting to think that there was room for everyone, but...

Before he could answer, she continued.

"I mean after you've rescued Antonia and the others. And don't say 'come home', because I know you, Uncle. You're hiding something."

In some ways he was relieved; he *had* hidden it, and it would be good to tell somebody. He took a breath. "I'm going to neutralise the Alician threat for good. Take revenge for the billions they helped slaughter. I'm... going to destroy Savange." He felt pressure in his chest and throat, and raised his voice. "They're a perennial danger, Petra, and not just Louise. Their whole existence is predicated on exterminating us."

Petra shook her head. "You're talking genocide."

"I'm talking about protecting our people, taking away the Alician threat for good."

"It's still genocide. The old, the young, children, mothers. It's a very ugly word, don't you think?"

"But –"

"Blake's a soldier through and through. Even he wouldn't go that far. Why don't you go and ask him? In fact, why haven't you discussed it with anyone else?"

Micah stared at her, then the ground. Why hadn't he? He'd wanted to assume responsibility for this himself, not implicate anyone else.

"Look, Uncle, right now you're hurting, in every way. But if you do this, you bring shame on all of us. Ask the dead. Ask –" Her voice cracked. "Ask Gabriel and Virginia if that's what they really want." She stood up, dusted off her pants. "Go ahead and kill Louise, Micah. You have my and the dead's blessing, because she's one sick bitch that needs to be put down. Bring back our people and send the Alicians a message they'll never forget, so they'll leave us alone for good. But no more than that, Micah. If you wipe them all out, there's no place for you here. And I for one will never want to see you again. Am I being clear?"

He stared at her, a young girl no more, then nodded.

"You know, us Genners know all about survivor guilt; it's practically hard-wired into us. So I recognise the symptoms. I think you came up here for a reason, and not just to find me. Sometimes you need to speak the words; thinking them isn't the same thing." She chewed her lip a moment. "And try to come back, Uncle. I don't want to lose anyone else. As Pierre... as my *father* would say, keep your *sang froid*, and keep your head." She turned and started her descent.

Micah watched her for a long time, mulling over her words. He'd felt his convictions had been made unassailable, but all his arguments just collapsed, undermined by that single ugly word. He would have to find another way. Walking over to Gabriel's headstone, he knelt beside his and Virginia's grave. "Petra just did you both proud; all of us."

Micah's anger had evaporated, but there was nothing to replace it, except a sucking, hollow feeling; grief began flooding in. In the past few weeks he'd not truly grieved for those lost during the battle, not shed a single tear. *Speak the words*, she'd said. His breathing became heavy, but this time he didn't fight it, didn't run from it or mask it with anger. He sat down, and leant back against Virginia's tombstone, his fingers resting on the soil covering her grave, and hung his head. "I'm so sorry."

It began to rain.

Blake and Micah gazed at the Scintarelli Scythe-ship hovering silently a foot off the ground like a massive, dark crescent, while they waited for Jen to arrive. There were no windows, protuberances or even ridges or exhaust holes anywhere on the smooth, matt black exterior. Where they stood, near one of the two 'blunt ends' as Blake had put it, the ship stretched upwards about four decks in human terms. Earlier, they had walked to the middle of the curved vessel, to the 'sharp end' that was about one deck high, where Micah presumed the bridge to be. The ship's entire leading edge tapered to a razor's width that he didn't want to put to the test with his finger. The vessel looked powerful enough to slice through another ship and remain intact. Jen had told him that the Scintarelli, legendary master ship-builders, hated all other ship designs so much they ensured their own could reap them like wheat. Evidently the Scintarelli wanted their ships to live up to their names.

Blake patted him on the shoulder, and almost grinned. "Looks mean, Micah."

Standing at the rear end of the ship, Micah wanted to touch its dark hull, but Ukrull had been very clear on that matter, and so he and the gathered crowd stood away from the ship. There were no visible signs of thrusters, engines, or gun ports, though he knew it had formidable weapons. When asked, Jen had confirmed that it had no teleportation – only Kalarash ships and Ukrull's Ice Pick had such capability, as well as Ngank surgeons whose physiology was extraordinary even by galactic standards. But there were two heavily- armed Rapier shuttle-craft in the aft sections, which they could use   to descend to Savange. Also, the Scythe's shields were coated with a specific form of strange matter, impervious to anti-matter and most other weapons; something Hellera had added, apparently.

Jen carved her way through the throng, making a bee-line towards him. "Touch the craft, Micah," she said in a business-like fashion. He stared at her a moment then walked toward the closest rear-end of the ship, the crowd stilling as he raised his hand and then pressed his right palm to the metal. It was cool, but quickly warmed to his body temperature. He felt something, almost heard something calling as if from far away, like the distant shriek of an eagle. His resident blurred into action, numbers and strange alphabets whirring through his mind's eye. Images from the recent past flashed by in subliminal fashion for several minutes, before settling on Louise's face when he'd last seen her, Antonia and Sandy, and the location of Savange on the holomap Jen had shown them three weeks earlier. He withdrew his hand, understanding – it was an intelligent ship, now attuned to his way of thinking, his goals, even his values and ethics. It would anticipate his needs, and never disappoint.

Micah stepped back and saw that the ship had changed colour to a deep blood red, with blue and violet serifs from an alien language. A name flushed onto its body in numerous human alphabets. *Shiva*, the Hindu god, the destroyer, but also the transformer, Micah recalled. Somehow, the ship conveyed the impression of being eager, ready for battle. He looked for Jen but she had moved off to join her partner

Dimitri, and merely nodded back to him that her part in this was over for now. He had no doubt that she and Dimitri would have some mission from Kalaran, as would Ukrull and Pierre sooner or later. They were all being enlisted, he realised, as his vision swept in Blake, Kilaney and Xenic, Pierre, Petra and Vasquez, all caught up in their own war with the Alicians, within a far larger war with Qorall.

His crew – Ramires, Kat, Aramisk, the Ossyrian Vashta, and Rashid joined him, all wearing the cobalt flight suits of the same design as Blake's original mission to Eden, the golden crest of Daedalus on the left chest pocket.

Micah raised his voice, addressing the crowd. "We haven't had an easy time of it." He looked around at the sea of faces, happy to see the Genners, normally in a separate group, standing with their parents. "We lost Earth and Eden, were nearly extinguished as a race. But we have prevailed, and fought off yet another attack. They've done their best to destroy us, and we're still here. Our worst enemies have always been the Alicians, who originally betrayed us to the Q'Roth, and now they have stolen our loved ones." Micah felt his own emotion stoking inside him again. "Well, no more. Now we take the fight to them, and when we return, there will be blood on our hands."

Cheers and foot stomping erupted from the crowd. His gaze shifted to Petra, Pierre behind her, holding her. He raised his hand, and the noise died down. "We hope to be back soon, with those dear to us, dear to you. In the meantime, take care of each other." His gaze fell upon Blake.

Micah cleared his throat, addressing everyone but also speaking directly to Blake. "Eighteen years ago I forced a decision on us, to save us, resulting in all children being Genned. I know many disagreed with this, and still do."

Blake's eyes narrowed.

"I have agreed with Kalaran that if we succeed in our mission, they will release us from this condition. We will have free choice again. Our children can be Genned, or not." Everyone stared, silent. "Think about it while we're gone."

As people started murmuring, Petra dashed up to him. "Bravo, Uncle. I'll keep that Council seat warm for you."

He kissed her once on the cheek, then turned back towards Blake, Kilaney and Vasquez, all three of whom were standing to attention, saluting. The crowd hushed, and Micah and his crew saluted back, then he strode towards the ship, his crew following.

Out of the nearest blunt end of the ship an arched doorway opened, a ramp extending to the ground. As they marched up into the vein-like corridor, the hatch sealing silently behind them, enclosing them in its innards, Micah's resolve solidified. He had three goals. Get the prisoners back, rescue or destroy the spider captive, and contain the Alician threat, gaining their respect in the only way they would learn – albeit without committing genocide. The ship had sensed it in him, too, and of the two meanings of the god Shiva, Micah knew which one applied.

Shiva had many weapons, but it had shown him one in particular, a Level Twelve device that would do the job. But it had to be deployed manually by someone on the ground. He fully intended to be standing with the weapon, right in front of Louise on Savange, when he activated it. The others would return to Esperia, and humanity would become the masters of their own destiny again. But Micah already knew that for him, this was going to be a one-way trip.

The Eden Paradox Novels

The Eden Paradox

A murder... a new planet mankind desperately needs... a thousand-year old conspiracy... What really awaits us on Eden? In a world beset by political turmoil, environmental collapse, and a predatory new religion, a recently discovered planet, Eden, is our last hope. But two missions have already failed to return. Blake and his crew lead the final attempt to bring back good news. Meanwhile back on Earth, Eden Mission analyst Micah Sanderson evades assassins, and tries to work out who he can trust, as he struggles in a race against time to unravel the Eden Paradox.

From the first paragraph, Barry Kirwan takes the reader on a journey spanning space and time in a fluid, action-packed flow of images, thoughts and words...The reader is pulled into an all too real future with memorable and thought-provoking men and women leading the way. Lydia Manx - The Piker Press

With the art of a master swordsman, Mr. Kirwan carves out a tale of diabolical intent and our desperate struggle against both ourselves and an implacable, superior enemy. His characters are instantly involving. Each has a unique history and cultural background that is made clear through clever use of exposition and offhand remarks that really convince the reader that these are real people involved in a visceral struggle for survival. - Mike Formichelli, SF author of the Blood Siren series

This is Orson Scott Card quality material at half the price! Jacob Millican, NJ

This is the best work of science fiction that I've read all year. This would be a five-star book anywhere. It's probably closer to six stars. Everything is top-notch. The writing, the editing, the characterization, the setting, all outstanding. S. Roiet, USA

I found myself cheering for humanity with each chapter's passing. Scott Welliver, Swartz Creek

Rejoice SF lovers and savour this, the first in a series. The Eden Paradox does not disappoint on any level. Peter Eerden, Melbourne, Australia

Well written, different ideas that I have never heard or read of for the last 55 years of reading Scifi! Jamey, USA

Eden's Trial

First contact did not go well. Survivors are fleeing Earth, into a hostile galaxy where alien intelligence and weaponry rule. Can a deserted planet offer refuge? Or will the genetically engineered Alicians finish the job started on Eden? While Blake fends off attacks, Micah seeks allies, but his plan backfires, and humanity finds itself on trial for its very right to exist. This stunning sequel to The Eden Paradox launches us into political intrigue and an intergalactic war of survival...

Lightning fast. New worlds and new enemies entwined with the main characters nearly as closely as their lovers - Lydia Manx, *Piker Press*

A great sequel to the first book, greatly expanding on the stage already set in the Eden Paradox. The story builds pace throughout to the point where you just don't want to put it down. Now waiting for the release of the next in the series! Jason Rickman, Manchester, UK

When humanity's survivors escape earth's devastation, it's out of the frying pan and into the solar flare... What I love about the second part of this trilogy is that whereas The Eden Paradox focuses on Earth and a quest to 'nearby' Eden, in this book the scale explodes to include - in a way that Iain Banks also does very well - multifareous alien races and civilisations with ancient scores to settle, making humanity appear very small and frail indeed. Favourite moment: an ancient, and supposedly dormant, enemy starfleet bursting through the skin of the galaxy to unleash hell... Gideon Roberton, London..

The second book is even better than the first. You are completely immersed in another world. Can't believe he is a new SF writer. Gerald Meehan, Blackpool, UK.

Eden's Trial is an extraordinary, fantastic, erudite, captivating, epical sci/fi action/adventure story par excellence. Filled with incredible alien races, inter galactic travel, genocide, war, intense pacing, nano technology, friendship, miracle cures, cruelty, love found, love lost, advanced civilizations, arachnids, annihilation, evacuation, richly developed characters, and exquisite backdrops. Buckle-up for the ride of your life! Dave H, Oregon

I thought it would be impossible to exceed how much I enjoyed the first installment of the Eden Trilogy. I was wrong! This is my favorite read in years. Dave Brueck, Reading, PA

Wonderful story with excellent plot and character development. Author clearly up there with Clarke and Asimov. I can't wait for the third book on the series! Anthony Price, USA

Eden's Endgame

Eden's Endgame is the stunning climax to the Eden Paradox series, bringing to a close the galaxy-shaking events of The Eden Paradox, Eden's Trial and Eden's Revenge. Humanity is depleted and marginalised, and its principal allies, the Kalarash, are losing the Galactic war. In an effort to hold back the enemy Qorall's relentless armies, a formerly vanquished and deadly machine race is unleashed, but can the machines be turned off once they have served their purpose? On the human scale, humanity's refugees take their fight to the Alician home planet, Savange, but Sister Esma left a nasty surprise for them: the original Gabriel – the deadliest ever Sentinel – is back, but he has been turned... Who will win the war, and at what cost? How will the Alician-human conflict be resolved? And who will be left standing at the end of this ground-breaking series?

Eden's Endgame is a terrific read! Kirwan takes us on a wild ride that ties together earlier storylines yet reads well as a stand-alone. From spiders to Hohash, I loved it! Emmie, USA

Plotlines from the earlier books re-emerge in a way that shows the books were intensely planned by the author. This is now my favourite book in the series! TFL reader, Florida

No stone is left unturned as all the plotlines draw towards a satisfying climax. Would another series like this be too much to ask for? Lynne, USA

What started off as a blog tour has turned into an emotional rollercoaster across four books. Characters have come and gone, grown and regressed. Humanity faced more perils than they could ever imagine and prevailed. The characters really shone in the previous book. But in this one, they were given the chance for one final fight to protect humanity and this time, the stakes, and outcome, were higher than ever. Without naming names, quite a few of the characters from book one don't make it through. Part of me expected this – there has been loss along the way already. But oh my word, I think my heart broke numerous times, which was awkward considering I was on a train. What made every sacrifice so moving, however, was knowing they all went out the way they would have wanted to: exploring new worlds; in a blaze of glory; the ultimate scientific experiment; fighting to protect those they love. Lindsey, UK

www.barrykirwan.com

Acknowledgements

A special thanks to Dimitri Keramitas and Chris Vanier for in-depth reviewing at all stages of this novel, and other members of our Parisian writing group (MWP), Mary Ellen Gallagher, Gwyneth Hughes, Vivienne Vermes, and Marie Houzelle. Thanks to my 'touchstone' pre-readers Andy Kilner and Jacob Bergsteiger, SF writer Mike Formicelli for some great suggestions on scientific aspects, Gideon Roberton for some 'scene direction' hints, and of course my publisher at Summertime. Thanks also to SF writer Sophia MacDougall for some excellent structural suggestions, and SF writer Gary Gibson. And last but by no means least, a special thanks to all those readers who kept asking me where on Earth (or elsewhere in the galaxy) they could get their hands on Book Three.

About the Author

Author of The Eden Paradox series, Barry Kirwan was born in Farnborough, England, home to the fast-jet Red Arrows. He did a doctorate in Human Reliability Assessment, which concerns predicting future behavior using psychological techniques and data. He has worked on the safety of nuclear power plants, offshore oil and gas platforms, and more recently air traffic, and publishes in the safety arena. He now lives just outside Paris in France, and writes Science Fiction short stories and novels. The psychological angle influences all his work, exploring where humanity is headed, but also just how different aliens could be, not only in looks, but in their values, thoughts and styles of communication. This is explored in all four books of the Eden Paradox series, but also in short stories, especially those associated with his 'Hell' and 'Sphericon' universes, available free on his website (www.barrykirwan.com).

Made in the USA
Middletown, DE
21 March 2022